Firstborn of the Sun

'Absolutely radiant. Anson has created a captivating,
intricate world with characters who will stay with me for a long
time. A perfect balance of political machinations and aching romance,
wrapped up in a fast-paced, action-packed adventure. I loved it!'
Bea Fitzgerald, author of *Girl, Goddess, Queen*

'Rich worldbuilding inspired by Yoruba mythology and a
strong cast of characters. This debut fantasy shines as bright as
the sun' L. R. LAM, author of *Dragonfall*

'A searing tale of ambition, love and survival . . . This is a
wildly imaginative debut which begins an epic story. Our characters
are thrown from disaster to disaster until an ending with a twist and a
schism that connects the dots all the way back to the beginning.
The imagery is exciting, cinematic and gorgeous'
Hannah Kaner, author of *Godkiller*

'A dazzling debut, with characters that leap off the page and
burrow into your heart. Filled with love, betrayal and questions of
loyalty, the twists and turns this story takes will keep you reading late
into the night' Andrea Stewart, author of *The Gods Below*

'Fierce, exciting and utterly original, *Firstborn of the Sun* is an
enthralling and epic fantasy, with a beautiful and tender romance
at its centre' Anna Day, author of *The Girl Who Grew Wings*

'Epic and gorgeous, *Firstborn of the Sun* enraptures readers in
the rich, complex Kingdom of Oru with intricate magic, fascinating
politics, swoony romance and gasp-worthy twists. A radiant debut,
not to miss!' Dhonielle Clayton, author of The Conjurverse series

Firstborn of the Sun

MARVELLOUS
MICHAEL ANSON

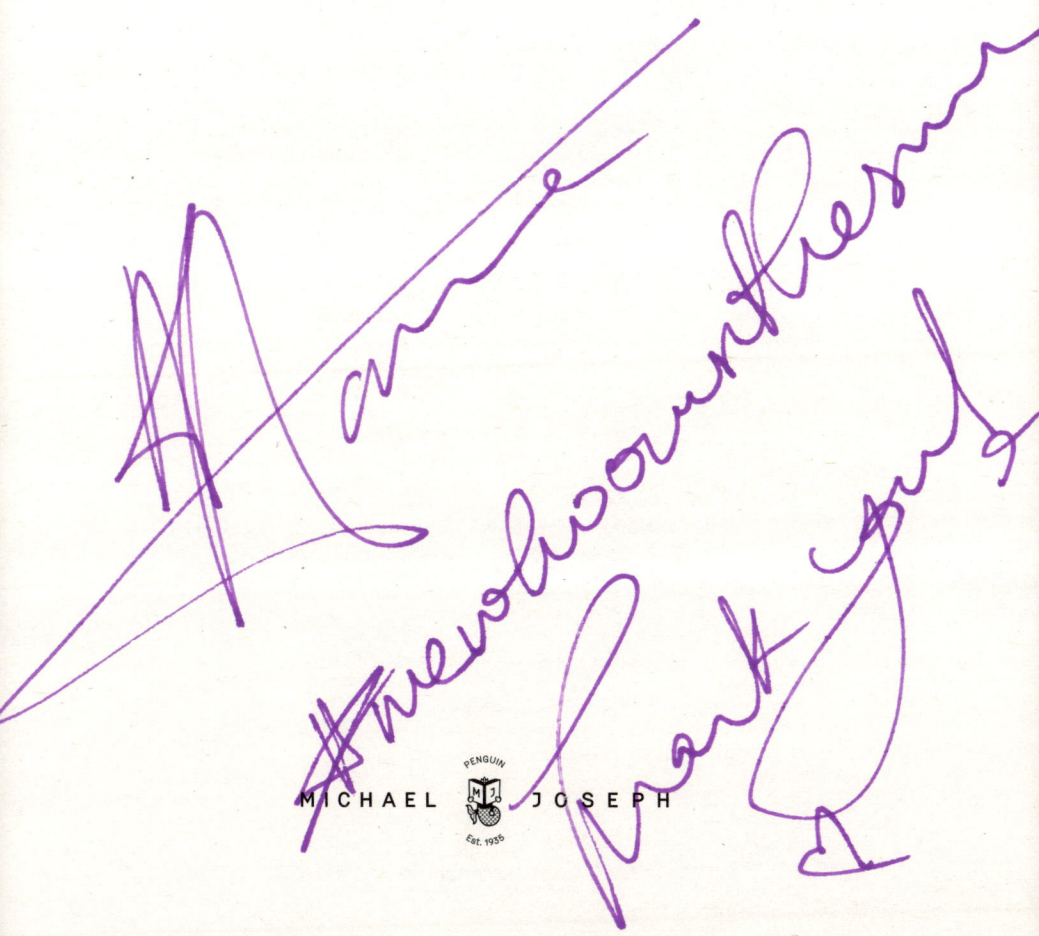

MICHAEL [PENGUIN Est. 1935] JOSEPH

PENGUIN MICHAEL JOSEPH

UK | USA | Canada | Ireland | Australia
India | New Zealand | South Africa

Penguin Michael Joseph is part of the Penguin Random House group of companies
whose addresses can be found at global.penguinrandomhouse.com

Penguin Random House UK,
One Embassy Gardens, 8 Viaduct Gardens, London SW11 7BW

penguin.co.uk

Penguin
Random House
UK

First published 2025

001

Set in 13.5/16pt Garamond MT Std
Typeset by Jouve (UK), Milton Keynes
Printed and bound in Great Britain by Clays Ltd, Elcograf S.p.A.

The authorized representative in the EEA is Penguin Random House Ireland,
Morrison Chambers, 32 Nassau Street, Dublin D02 YH68

A CIP catalogue record for this book is available from the British Library

HARDBACK ISBN: 978–0–241–70505–6
TRADE PAPERBACK ISBN: 978–0–241–70506–3

Penguin Random House is committed to a sustainable future
for our business, our readers and our planet. This book is made from
Forest Stewardship Council® certified paper.

To my mother, who made my dreams her own.

To my husband, who held close the midnight candle that burned while this book morphed into existence.

To you, dear reader, Ẹ káàbọ̀.

Foreword

Firstborn of the Sun is a revelation of the powers that existed in Yorubaland and the accompanying rivalry and power struggles throughout the ages. Moremi's odyssey, Alawani and L'ọrẹ's bond and blood oath, and the warrior maidens' ferocious nature all bring this novel to life. *Firstborn of the Sun* explores different ancient powers and reveals the effects of those powers on their possessors. Through this novel, you will realize that Ẹni t'o ṣe fún Iná kọ́ ló ṣe fún Oòrùn (*The person who gave the fire its powers is not comparable to the person who did for the sun*).

And in the end, Ikú ogun ní n pa Akínkanjú (*He who lives by the sword usually dies by it*). Ikú odò ní n pa Omùwẹ̀ (*Death by drowning is typically the fate of he who swims in water*).

Ayọ̀délé Ọmọbámitalẹ́ Adéwálé
(Marve's Grandma)

Author's Note

Dear Reader,

There is no Yoruba culture, tradition or tribe without the stories we tell, the songs we sing, and the tales of legends long gone. Our history remains alive on our tongues for as long as we have breath, and even when we leave this world, our story never ends. For who are you without the knowledge of those who came before you? How will you fight the uncertainty of the future if you do not know how those who came before you earned their victories?

With this book, I hope to introduce you to a world that feels so different from your own, yet so familiar, like a dream you've had once before. Either in this life or the one before. I hope that as you take in these words, the sands of Oru sing to you in whispers that resonate with your heart.

I hope that the characters in this folklore feel as real to you as the strangers that pass by your window, and when the time comes to reach in for the agbára within you, may you find the strength to do what you know to be right and true. May your courage be sung in songs that outlive you, and may your strength never fade when the shadows come dancing.

May your heart burn like the sun, bright, hot, and undying.

– Marvellous.

The Rings of Oru

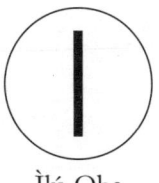

Ìlú-Ọba

Ìlú-Ìmọ̀

Ìlú-Ọpọ

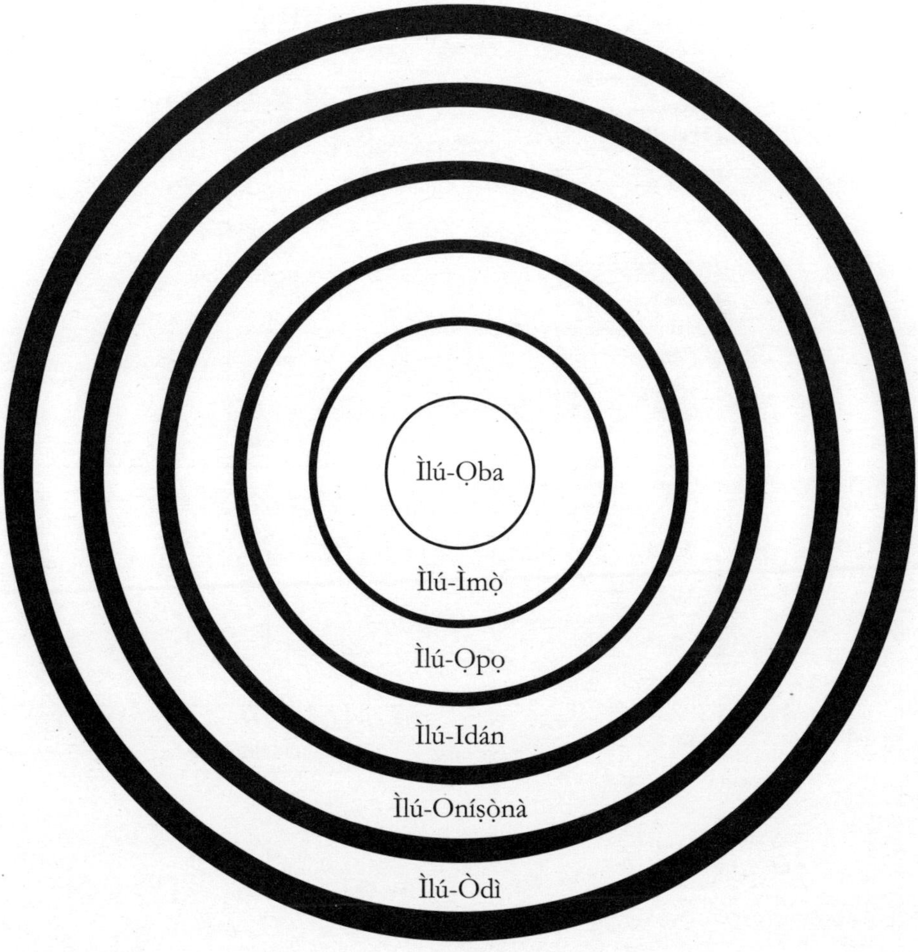

Ìlú-Ọba

Ìlú-Ìmọ̀

Ìlú-Ọpọ

Ìlú-Idán

Ìlú-Oníṣọ̀nà

Ìlú-Òdì

Ìlú-Idán

Ìlú-Oníṣọ̀nà

Ìlú-Òdì

Timeline of Oru

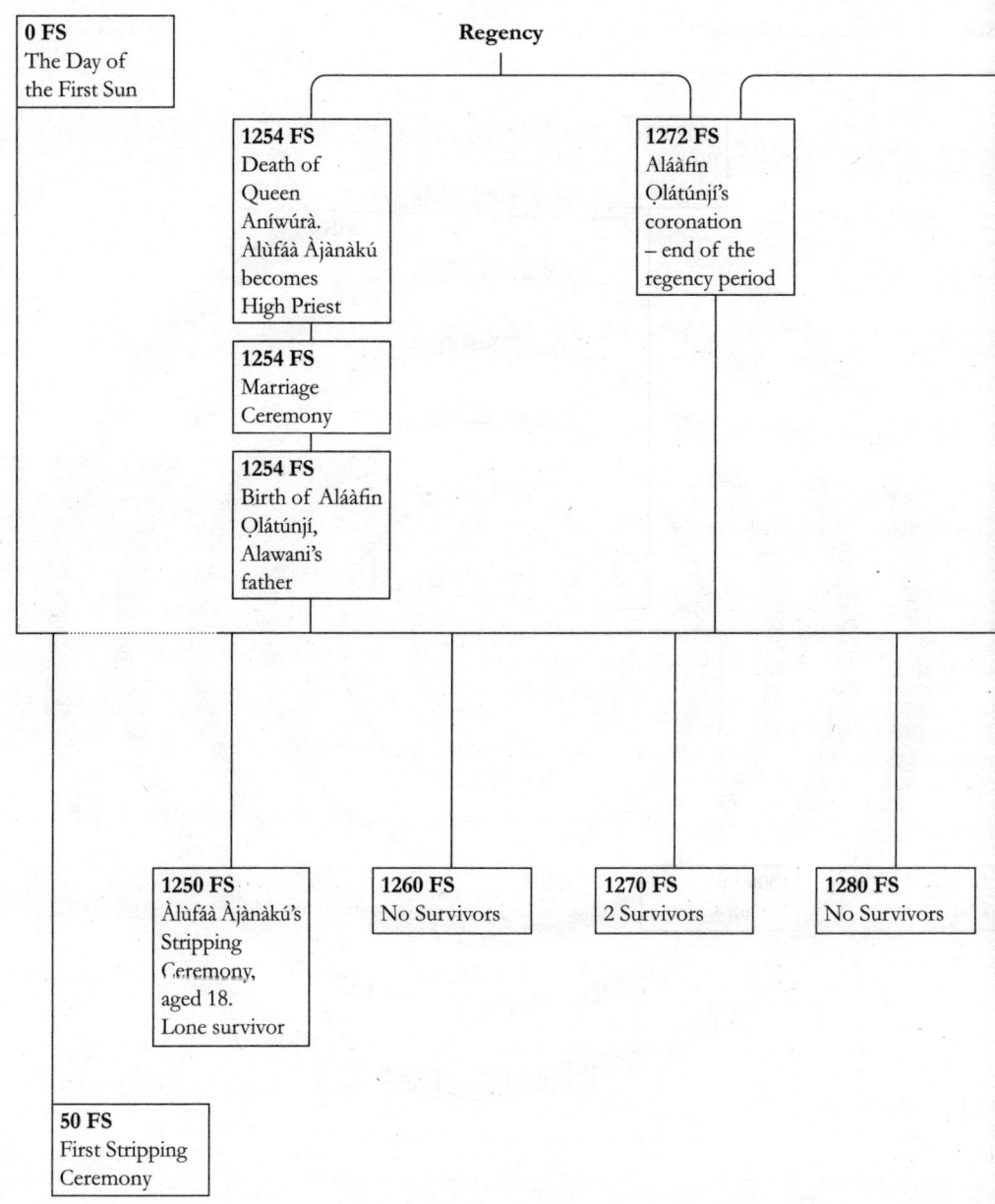

Regency

0 FS
The Day of
the First Sun

1254 FS
Death of
Queen
Aníwúrà.
Àlùfáà Àjànàkú
becomes
High Priest

1254 FS
Marriage
Ceremony

1254 FS
Birth of Aláàfin
Ọlátúnjí,
Alawani's
father

1272 FS
Aláàfin
Ọlátúnjí's
coronation
– end of the
regency period

1250 FS
Àlùfáà Àjànàkú's
Stripping
Ceremony,
aged 18.
Lone survivor

1260 FS
No Survivors

1270 FS
2 Survivors

1280 FS
No Survivors

50 FS
First Stripping
Ceremony

Timeline of Stripping Ceremonies

Timeline of Oru

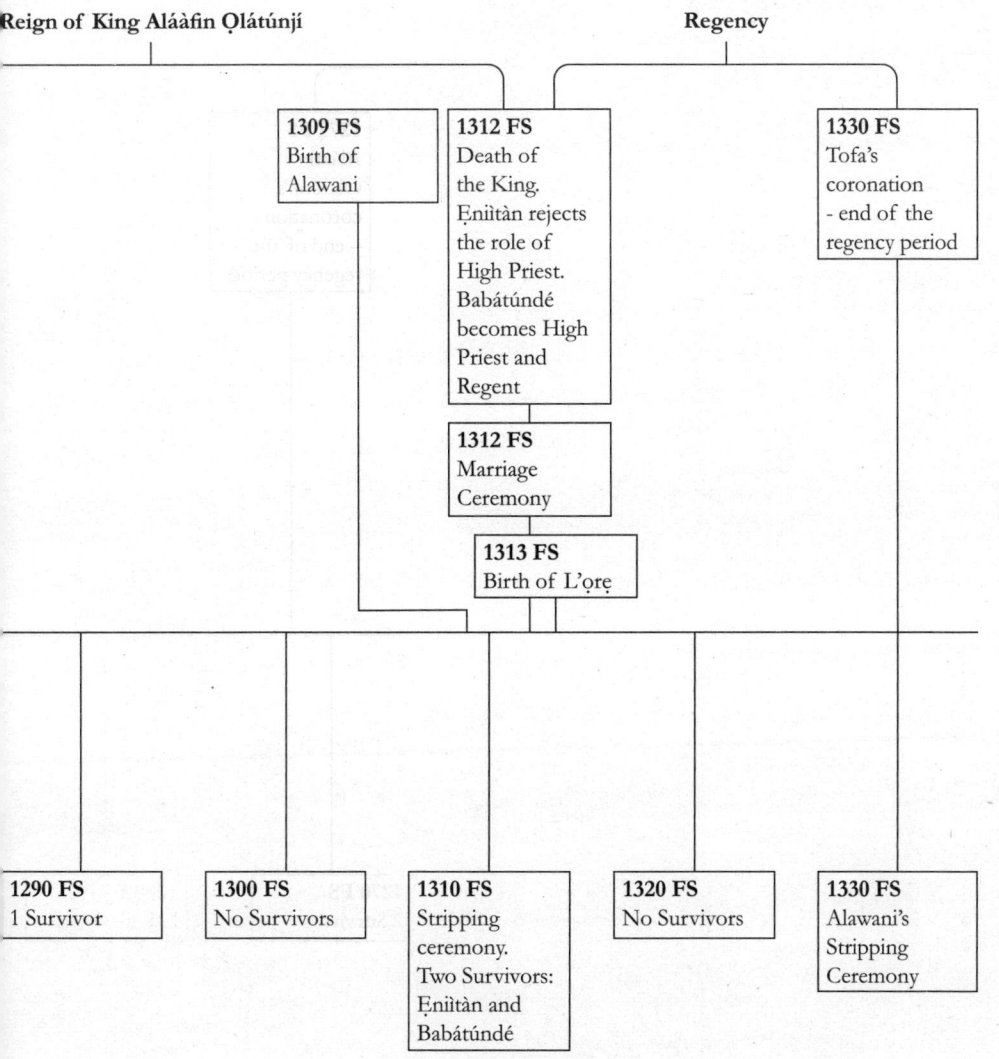

Reign of King Aláàfin Ọlátúnjí

Regency

1309 FS
Birth of
Alawani

1312 FS
Death of
the King.
Ẹniìtàn rejects
the role of
High Priest.
Babátúndé
becomes High
Priest and
Regent

1330 FS
Tofa's
coronation
- end of the
regency period

1312 FS
Marriage
Ceremony

1313 FS
Birth of L'ọrẹ

1290 FS
1 Survivor

1300 FS
No Survivors

1310 FS
Stripping
ceremony.
Two Survivors:
Ẹniìtàn and
Babátúndé

1320 FS
No Survivors

1330 FS
Alawani's
Stripping
Ceremony

Timeline of Stripping Ceremonies

Pronunciation Guide

Characters

* Àbèní	*Ah-Beh-Nee*	* Káyòdé	*Kah-Yoh-Day*
* Adékòyà (Kòyà)	*Ah-Day-Koh-Yah*	* Kéhìndé	*Keh-Yin-Day*
		* Keni	*Keh-Nee*
* Adémilúà (Milúà)	*Ah-Day-Mee-Loo-Ah*	* L'orè	*Law-Reh*
		* Márùn	*Mah-Roon*
* Àdùké	*Ah-Doo-Keh*	* Máyòwá	*Mah-Yoh-wah*
* Àdùnni	*Ah-Doon-Nee*	* Méfa	*Meh-Fah*
* Àjàgbé	*Ah-Jah-Gbay*	* Méje	*Meh-Jay*
* Àkanní	*Ah-Kan-Nee*	* Méjìlá	*Meh-Jee-Lah*
* Alawani	*Ah-Lah-Wah-Nee*	* Méjo	*Meh-Joh*
		* Mésàn	*Meh-San*
* Àníké	*Ah-Nee-Keh*	* Mókànla	*Maw-Kan-Lah*
* Aníwúrà	*Ah-Nee-Woo-Rah*	* Móremí	*Moh-Reh-Mee*
		* Olátúnjí	*Oh-Lah-Toon-Jee*
* Àríké	*Ah-Ree-Keh*	* Omo'ge	*Oh-Moh-Gay*
* Àsá	*Ah-Sha*	* Omótádé	*Oh-Moh-Tah-Day*
* Babátúndé	*Bah-Bah-Toon-Day*	* Onílè	*Oh-Nee-Leh*
		* Oyíndà	*Oh-Yin-Dah*
* Bánkólé	*Bah-N-Koh-Lay*	* Rèmí	*Reh-Mee*
* Bíódún	*Bee-Oh-Doon*	* Sège	*Sheh-Geh*
* Bùnmi	*Boo-N-Mee*	* Táíwo	*Tay-ee-Who*
* Eniìtàn	*Eh-Nee-I-Tan*	* Tèmi	*Teh-Mee*
* Èyítáyò	*Eh-Yee-Tah-Yoh*	* Tofa (Tofaratì)	*Toh-Fah-(Rah-Tee)*
* Gbéké	*Gbe-Keh*		

xv

Gods

* Aganjù   *Ah-Gan-Ju*
* Erinlẹ̀   *Eh-Reen-Leh*
* Irúnmọlẹ̀   *I-Run-Moh-Leh*
* Ọbàtálá   *Oh-Bah-Tah-Lah*

* Odùduwà   *Oh-Du-Du-Wah*
* Ògún   *Oh-Goon*
* Ọya   *Aw-Yah*
* Ṣàngó   *Sha-N-Goh*

Places

* Gbàgede   *Gba-Geh-Deh*
* Ìlú-Idán   *I-Loo-I-Dan*
* Ìlú-Ìmọ̀   *I-Loo-I-Moh*
* Ìlú-Ọba   *I-Loo-Uh-Bah*
* Ìlú-Òdì   *I-Loo-Oh-Dee*

* Ìlú-Oníṣọ̀nà   *I-Loo-Oh-*
         Nee-Shaw-Nu
* Ìlú-Ọpọ   *I-Loo-Uh-Pur*
* Oru   *Oh-Roo*
* Òtútù   *Oh-Too-Too*

Titles

* Ab'Ọ́bakú   *Ah-Boh-Bah-Koo*
* Aláàfin   *Ah-Lah-*
         Ah-Feen
* Àlùfáà-Àgba   *Ah-Loo-Fah-*
         A-A-Gbah
* Aya'ba   *Ah-Yah-Bah*
* Baálẹ̀-Iku   *Bah-Ah-Leh-*
         ee-Koo

* Baba-Ìtàn   *Bah-Bah-ee-Tan*
* Ìyá-Aye   *I-Yah-A-Yay*
* Ìyá-Idán   *I-Yah-ee-Dan*
* Ọmọ'ba   *Oh-Moh-Bah*
* Ọmọ Ìlú mi   *Oh-Moh*
         I-Lu-Mi
* Ọmọ ìyá mí   *Oh-Moh*
         I-Yah-Mi

Mọ́remí, Àjáṣòro o
Mọ́remí, Àjáṣòro
Ọmọ t'o fúnmi, má mà gbá o
Mọ́remí, Àjáṣòro
Ọmọ t'o fúnmi, má mà gbá o
Mọ́remí, Àjáṣòro
Mọ́remí, Àjáṣòro the child you've given me,
please don't take it away from me

Prologue

The Sun Temple, Royal Island, Kingdom of Oru

1313 FS

MỌREMÍ

Nine blood moons and one day.

That was how long Mọremí hung in the balance between life and death.

The cool evening breeze sent shivers down her spine. This was the night she had feared and with every passing moment she realized how wildly unprepared she was for it. Searing pain washed over her; she shut her eyes, forcing herself to breathe through it until the intense sharp pain dulled into an ache. Thoughts of her mother raced through her mind as she lay on the floor over layers of mats and wrappers. She wished more than anything that she wasn't miles away from home, scared and alone with only the older woman by her feet shouting at her.

Mọremí glanced around the empty room. No matter how beautiful, it was no place to be born. Her child ought to be born into the ocean like she was – like her mother was, and her mother before her. At home, she'd be kneeling in the wet sands at the edge of the sea, feeling the saltwater rush in and out of her, stinging and cleansing, preparing to greet the child whose first cry would be from the cold; born of water, born of Òtútù. When she closed her eyes, she heard the rush of the wind and the crash of the waves on the rocks that her home was built upon. She wouldn't have been pushing alone. She'd have had the force of the mighty ocean urging her child into the world. She could see her sisters standing barefoot in the sinking sand at the shoreline, singing to her, and she could feel the rhythmic strokes of her aunt's heavy hand drumming against her back.

Most of all, Mọremí could hear her mother's voice pouring strength into her. She needed that voice, but with every wave of contraction, it seemed farther and farther away, and a surge of heat consumed her. She felt a sudden tightness in her chest. Panic overwhelmed her. Her lips trembled as she cried for the mother she feared she'd never see again. The other wives of the High Priest had their mothers with them in the days following their wedding. They followed them everywhere, washing their feet and braiding their hair. But here she was, a stranger in a new world. Wishing that at any time in her twenty first suns, her mother had told her how much bringing forth life would feel like death.

'Calm down, Mọremí! I can't hear your child's heartbeat if you keep screaming down the temple,' the midwife's shrill voice cut through her thoughts.

'Oh gods, help me, please?' Mọremí prayed and lifted her gaze to the reddish-brown walls that seemed to close in on her. On them were sand portraits of women – wives of past High Priests. Their dark eyes peered into her soul. Hundreds of them. Had they been as terrified as she was? Had they left this room alive?

A few moments later, the midwife's eyes locked with Mọremí's; her shoulders dropped, and she shrunk back. 'I hear nothing.'

'Ah! Gods forbid! Ọmọ mi ò lè kú – my child can't die!'

'There is nothing to be done,' the midwife's voice shattered through her mind, and her ears rang. 'You've lost too much blood, Mọ́remí. Let the child come out.'

Mọ́remí groaned, her chest heaving as she struggled to control her breathing. Unable to move the bottom half of her body, she did the only thing she could think of – the one thing her husband would kill her for. She called upon her gods in the north.

The bargain was simple. Her life for her child's. She was nothing without her child, so she drew a deep breath and began to chant, 'Child of my womb, take from my blood, child of my womb, take from my life, come back to me.' She pitched forward and cried hysterically, 'Ọmọ̀ọ̀ mi, gba agbára à mi – my child, take my strength!' She'd journeyed south through the sands and storms. She'd lied, stolen, and done everything to carry the High Priest's heir. The child who would save her people. It couldn't die.

'Stop that nonsense,' the midwife shouted and pried herself out of Mọ́remí's grip. 'The gods can't help you. The sun has long set, and they are asleep. It's you holding this child back.' She lifted Mọ́remí to her knees and placed her on all fours. 'Your child will rot inside of you – it must be born, or it'll be the death of you.'

Mọ́remí ignored the midwife. Her gods didn't sleep at night. Her gods didn't rise with the dawn. She reached for the darkness enclosing the room and allowed the void to fill her mind. Hands and knees on the ground, she cried out to the gods of her people, 'Ẹ̀yin Òrìṣà àwọn bàbá babá nlá mi, ẹ má k'ẹ̀hìn sí mi – gods of my ancestors, please don't turn your back on me.'

Mọ́remí didn't know if her gods would answer, but she was prepared to die trying. There was no going back.

Mọ́remí's agbára ignited inside of her. The familiar warmth

3

of her magic rose to the surface of her skin. Her pupils turned an unnatural shade of blue, and wisps of mist seeped from her hands onto the mat. *No – not yet.* She needed her agbára flowing into her child, not bursting out of her. She shut her eyes firmly until she felt her agbára recede. In the years she'd spent in the kingdom of Oru, she'd never exposed her powers, and she couldn't afford to now.

A loud voice pulled her out of her thoughts. A hand-maiden had rushed into the room. 'It's Aya'ba Oyíndà,' she called out from the doorway. 'Her child is nearly here!'

Mọremí screamed, 'No!' She turned to the midwife. 'I'm ready! I'm ready! Get it out, get it out now!' her words tumbling over each other. If her child was not born first, it would all have been for nothing.

Mọremí summoned all her strength; the powers of the gods, new and old, north and south. She pushed from her shoulders, from the soles of her feet, from the core deep within her, and her agbára ignited like a raging fire flooding her mind and body. This time, she didn't stop it.

'I have the head. Push again!' the midwife yelled.

With a loud cry, Mọremí pushed the baby out, wet and wormlike, into the hands of the midwife crouched at her feet. She crashed to the floor and lay on her side. As soon as she caught her breath, she asked with a shaking voice, 'Is it alive?'

The midwife was busy with the baby, wiping off the fluid and blood that had accompanied it into the world. She care-fully removed the liquid from its nose and mouth, then cut off the rope that connected the baby to its mother. 'It's so cold,' the old midwife said, swaddling the child in a cloth and shaking her head. 'It's a girl.'

She placed the limp child in the basket next to her, and without raising her head, she said, 'You need to push out the afterbirth too.'

Mọremí followed the midwife's instructions as the woman skilfully kneaded the afterbirth out of her. Mọremí could feel that the midwife was intentionally avoiding her gaze. She watched eagerly as the woman mopped the blood of the baby with a wet cloth. After a few moments of eerie silence, the midwife picked up the baby and stood with her back to Mọremí.

'She's not crying,' Mọremí said, her voice breaking.

The midwife turned to speak but froze. 'Yo— you . . . your eyes!' she stammered and stepped back. 'You're not from here. You're not of the sands!'

'Give me my daughter!' Mọremí winced as she yelled, stretching her arms towards the woman. The people of Oru were utterly ignorant of powers that weren't of their gods and were taught to fear everything not of the sands and sun, but she wasn't going to let that keep her from her daughter.

The midwife took another step back and glanced at the door, her hand outstretched. Her palm started to glow a deep orange as she drew on her agbára. 'The child is gone, and a mother can't set eyes on her dead child – our gods forbid it. Don't come any closer.'

Mọremí struggled off the floor, and every move hurt more than the last. When she tried to walk, she fell to her knees. She rose again and was nearly blinded by the light emanating from the midwife's palm. Even from where she stood, Mọremí could feel the heat quickly filling the room.

'Not a step closer!' the midwife warned. A moment later, the smell of smoke caught her attention: a spark of flame had blossomed from the heat in her palms and spread to the outer layers of the cloth. She cried out and shoved the child into Mọremí's arms, staggering to the corner of the room to dunk her hands into one of the clay pots filled with water. A white mist rose from it, and she exhaled slowly.

A faint cry.

Mọrẹmí locked eyes with the midwife.

The baby cried again.

'Gods of sun and sands!' the midwife cried. 'What sorcery is this? The child was dead. What have you done to her?'

Mọrẹmí felt her heart tense. Hope blossomed in her chest as she realized what had happened. 'I didn't do this. You did. You warmed her with your agbára. My child lives. Your queen is alive.'

'There was no heartbeat,' the midwife said, her face full of horror. 'Who . . . What . . . Who are you? Where do you come from?'

Mọrẹmí held her child closer to her chest.

'Answer me! Who gives you life?' the midwife said, her voice warbling.

'Go and tell your High Priest that his daughter lives. Tell him that his firstborn is alive. Tell my husband that the queen is born!'

The midwife grew hysterical, 'Irọ! You lie! This thing will never be our queen. The Holy Order will hear of the evil that runs in your blood.'

Mọrẹmí noticed the midwife glance towards the doorway and a sudden dread overcame her. The woman would report her and ruin everything. Mọrẹmí had seen people burnt alive for merely saying the names of the old gods, let alone possessing the blue, glowing eyes of her agbára – and as a wife of the High Priest, too. Holding her baby tight to her chest, she launched herself at the midwife, grabbing her by the arm. Her agbára burst out of her, the warm, prickly sensation flowing through her hands. It happened so quickly that the midwife didn't realize what was happening to her until the sharp pain of frost bit into her skin, turning it dark and cold. She screamed and fell, hitting her head against the wall on the way down.

6

Mọremí stared at the woman sprawled on the ground, and could only think one thing: run. She moved quickly, pulling off her blood-soaked nightgown and finding a new ankara dress from her clothes. The large búbù gown gave her room to breathe. She tied a wrapper across her waist and tucked loose pieces of fabric firmly between her thighs to stop the fluid from dripping down her legs. She wrapped her daughter in another warm cloth and limped out of the room.

Mọremí stopped at the doorway, pausing to breathe. The birthing chamber was in the east wing of the temple – the birthplace of kings and queens. She closed her eyes, and tears formed in them again. Her daughter deserved to claim her birthright.

The open courtyard before her welcomed in the blood moon's red light, and she looked up to the sky and wondered if her mother was seeing the same moon this night. If her mother knew that despite her doubts, her daughter had birthed the next queen of Oru.

She raised her baby to her face, feeling the warmth of her breath, and sighed. Mọremí used the wrapper to strap the child to her back, tying a firm knot across her tummy to hold her in place. She peeped into the next room, checking that the coast was clear. All attention was on the woman at the room's heart, suffering through her own birth. Relieved, Mọremí made to run, but a loud cry stopped her short. 'It's a boy.'

Mọremí watched the other woman cradle her son, a thought crossing her mind. Only the midwife had witnessed her powers; if she killed her, she wouldn't have to run. No life was worth risking her people's survival. The midwife had to die.

The faint beat of her daughter's heart and the warmth of her skin gave Mọremí more courage than she could have imagined, more will than she thought herself capable of. She turned back towards her birthing chamber, but footsteps approached from behind – Àlùfáà-Àgbà's robes dragged along the ground, creating an eerie, sweeping effect as he walked. His figure moved like a ghost across the courtyard, his eyes fixed on the armed temple maidens before him.

Blood rushed to her head, and the sound of her own heartbeat made her choke with fear. Her fingers tightened against her daughter and she wrapped her agbára around herself like a cloak, hiding her from view. As his lanky frame loomed nearer, Mọ́remí saw the deep wrinkles etched into his skin as the torch flames flickered against his glowing white robes. She glanced towards her birthing chamber, the distance now too far to cover without drawing attention. Her chance was gone – the midwife would live to tell everyone what she'd seen.

Àlùfáà-Àgbà walked the length and breadth of the birthing square, coming to a stop just before the chamber of the woman whose son was still wailing from the terrors of being born. Mọ́remí drew carefully on her agbára, concealing herself again as he drew nearer. The only thing between them was the door to the other woman's birth chamber. Mọ́remí stood still as ice, praying for him to walk through the doors so that she could run, but instead, he stopped in his tracks, his deep-set eyes peering into the shadows. Although no more than ten steps apart, Mọ́remí knew that the Elder Priest couldn't see her, not with her agbára shielding her. But she also knew that he was perhaps the most powerful priest in the kingdom, and he could probably sense her magic. As she fought the pain still coursing through her body, she heard her mother's voice. *Don't move an inch. You're invisible, not untouchable. You can't be seen, but you can be struck down. Slow down your heart but don't faint, or you will fall, and the illusion will shatter.*

Her energy was slipping away. She was succumbing to the

pain from childbirth, her stomach still cramped, pulling in on itself, her muscles sore and fatigued, and she felt her heart slow dangerously. At any moment, she'd fall.

Àlùfáà-Àgbà swiped slowly, grabbing at the empty space a hair's breadth from her face. He knew something was there, and just as his hand was about to strike her illusion, the new mother called out to him from within her chamber, 'Àlùfáà-Àgbà, come and meet your king.' Choosing the boy over his curiosity, the Elder Priest walked into the room and his maidens followed behind him.

Mọ́remí would later think back to this moment so often that it would drive her to the edge of madness. She'd wonder if she should've revealed her child as the true firstborn, if her husband's love would've saved her from the Elder Priest's wrath. But at that moment, Mọ́remí broke the illusion and emerged from the cocoon of ice she'd hidden herself in.

And ran as fast as she could, leaving behind a crash like that of falling mirrors.

So it is you the gods sent to take my àṣírí.
Sit if you must, I've got a lot to say and so little
time. You see the sands of that hourglass dripping
slowly next to you? That's how long I've got to tell
you the story that keeps me bound in this oblivion.
So sit, please. Listen and release me,
for my soul lingers only until the last
of my àṣírí is given to you.
I am sorry for this burden that you will bear.
Whatever you do, remember to tell another
before death comes for you. Eternity is unkind
to those who go down to the grave with secrets
meant for the living.

So here's the truth:

Agbára oru is a curse that blinded our
kind to what the gods truly were.
Cursed are those born of the sun and sands. Cursed
are we all who wield the power of the sun. Cursed
are the sands that bury our bones. Cursed are the
gods that made us so.

I

Ìlú-Ọba – The Capital City
First Ring, Kingdom of Oru

1330 FS

L'ỌRẸ

L'ọrẹ's first sin was to be born in the dark of night when the gods were asleep. She often wondered if her mother, a maiden of the Sun Temple, knew when she birthed her that she'd wronged the gods. If she hadn't known the moment L'ọrẹ was born, surely she knew the moment the Holy Order's axe severed her head from her neck.

L'ọrẹ peeled off the hood of her cloak and inhaled deeply, taking in the cold desert air. The night was clear, the moon shone like a pearl in the sky, and the icy winds howled as they hovered over the tall buildings that formed the capital city of Ìlú-Ọba. The city was built with the whitest of limestone, bleached bright enough that the sun made the high points sparkle, and at night, the moon's light gave the city an other-worldly glow. In the distance, she could see the twin pillars that marked the entrance to Gbàgede, the arena, and she quickened her pace. The man trailing behind her moved faster.

L'ọrẹ had known he was following her from the moment she locked eyes with him while crossing the city gates. If she'd listened to her father and kept her gaze glued to the ground when venturing outside of her home ring, the man wouldn't have recognized her. It didn't matter that she'd never seen him before. He knew her. He knew her father. They all did. Everyone in Oru could spot them from a distance so they could either avoid, mock or spit on them. But L'ọrẹ couldn't back down from a fight – especially not when anyone called her a coward.

So, when the man now raging towards her awakened his powers – his agbára, turning his palms golden in the sun's light – she took a deep breath and whispered the words that even the wind must never hear. The words that made it possible to fool everyone into thinking she was like them; that she had agbára oru. *Dìde. Fún mi ní agbára rẹ.* Her crescent blades came alive with the same yellow glow that filled the man's hands, creating a mirage of the magic that refused to light up her skin. A spell her father had taught her to mimic agbára oru. A gift from the old gods.

The man lifted his chin and met her eyes. 'You're a disgrace, and a coward,' he spat. 'Just like your father.'

She knew what her father would have done, what he begged her to do every time something like this happened. Yet, the word rang in her ears like the echoes of a gong. *Coward.* The word that hung close to her like a shadow. Impossible to leave behind no matter how fast she ran.

She felt the heat of her blades sting against her skin as she roared towards the outraged man and leapt off the ground. L'ọrẹ kicked at his face, and a trail of sand followed and stung his eyes. Her assailant screamed and dropped to his knees, rubbing his eyes. If the agbára glowing in his palms could have burnt him the way it would another, he'd have blinded himself.

L'ọrẹ dropped to the ground and rolled onto her knees. Taking advantage of the man's frenzy, with a single swipe, her blades burned deep into his forearms. The glow in his palms faded as quickly as it had come on.

The man let out an anguished howl. 'I'll kill you!' he screamed, pressing his hands to his forearms, trying to hold back the blood that poured out of them.

People crowded the street quicker than L'orẹ thought possible at this time of night. Whispers became shouts, and finally, the words that threw her into a rage hummed in the air around her. Ọmọbìnrin Olójo yẹn mà ni – it's the coward's child. She raised her hood, planning to slip into the shadows, but three men emerged from the crowd. Their palms were bright and aglow with agbára as they leered at her. She was in for it now. The odds, as always, were against her. Where the hell was Alawani? L'orẹ turned and looked for her best friend, peering into alleyways and behind the shadows of palm trees, but he was nowhere to be seen. She turned on her heels and ran towards the arena, seeking refuge in the pit of death.

Gbàgede was as mysterious as it was frightening to most people in Oru. They only visited when the gods called for Ogun: a battle where the strongest warriors not born of royal blood came together to fight and show off their strength, celebrating the powers granted to them by the gods. The victor of Ogun – the battle of honour – would have the privilege of joining the royal guard. And the loser would grieve their loss from their grave. Some people claimed that even when Ogun was over, they could still hear the screams of the fallen being burned alive and the victorious cries of the winners. Being in the sunken pit that was the arena felt like you were descending into the underworld. The stench of burnt flesh filled the air, but L'orẹ had become used to everything the arena offered.

Step by step, L'orẹ ran further down, her lungs burning for air as she skipped through the white stones that led to

13

the training grounds far beneath ground level. The hexagon-shaped pit was surrounded by rows of stairs on all sides, with dark covers at each edge, held up by large pillars with intricate carvings and stained with the blood of the fallen. Rows of torches lit the lowest level, and the moon's light dimly illuminated the rest of the arena.

At first, L'orẹ hoped they'd be too afraid to wander into the pit of death with her, but a few heartbeats later, she heard a voice.

'What have you done?'

It came from the shadows, and L'orẹ swung around. She knew that voice, but that didn't make her any less afraid. Command stepped out of the shadows, and her six-foot frame made L'orẹ feel small in her presence as she knelt to greet the woman.

Command's steel armour glistened from beneath her cloak and the cowries in her thick locs danced with each step she took from behind the pillars. The cowries signified the number of people she'd killed. It was custom in Oru to wear the souls of those who died by your hands in cowries so that whenever the wind blew, you'd hear their voices and remember them. Most people hid theirs; they were sometimes even sewn into clothes – obeying the customs but keeping their secrets hidden – but not her. Command wore hundreds of cowries in her hair, and L'orẹ wasn't sure, but it seemed like they grew in number by the year.

The men chasing L'orẹ finally reached the top of the arena and began their descent down the hundreds of stairs leading to the pit.

L'orẹ cast a fearful gaze at Command, who looked at the raging men and frowned. 'What happened?' she asked, her voice a low husk that made every word she spoke reverberate.

'They started it,' L'orẹ said quickly.

Command cast her a sidelong look. 'Who threw the first strike?'

L'ọrẹ lowered her gaze like a child being scolded. 'He called me a –'

'I don't want to hear it. Finish this. Get rid of them,' Command said and slid back into the shadows.

L'ọrẹ steadied herself, grounding her feet into the loose sand beneath her, preparing for her attackers and calculating who'd be the easiest to strike first. It had to be the thin one with the scarf tied too firmly to his face. No way he could breathe easily under that mask. Knowing Command would never engage in a street fight, she prayed Alawani would join her before she had to attack the slowest but heaviest one. His yam-like muscles contoured in the moon's light, and she didn't want to know what it'd feel like to be on the receiving end of that fist.

By the time the advancing men were close enough, she'd chosen a different fighting stance, trying to determine her best move.

'Make up your mind!' came the order from the shadows. Her commander had obviously decided that this would be her training for the night.

L'ọrẹ held on tight to her blades and struck at the man who reached her first. This one flashed his yellowing teeth with pride as he ran towards her, jumping the stairs in twos.

Yellow Teeth evaded her blades faster than she'd expected, ducking and sidestepping her blows.

'Focus! Watch his feet,' Command said.

L'ọrẹ could smell the strong stench of days-old palm wine on his breath. Behind him, the dim light caused his comrades to trip and fall as they attempted to skip down the flight of stairs. L'ọrẹ returned her focus to the one before her.

'Try again, Ọmọ'ge,' Yellow Teeth winked and laughed, moving so quickly it looked like he was gliding over the sand.

L'ọrẹ's frown deepened. He was toying with her. She lunged at him and tripped onto the sand.

'Get up! Use your head, L'ọrẹ. End this,' Command said.

L'ọrẹ didn't allow his quick steps to distract her from the real danger – his hands. While his glowing palms wouldn't burn him – as agbára was an extension of oneself – it'd burn anything and anyone it touched. But her hands were wrapped in the heat-resistant fabric her father had sourced for her after one too many burns. Now, she never left home without them. It wasn't enough to cover her full arms, but she'd make do.

L'ọrẹ heard the bald man, the second of the trio, finally jump into the pit, a gash on his forehead from the fall earlier. She drew back from the pair, trying to take them on one on one, but as soon as she got close enough to the bald man, he grabbed a fist full of her hair and dragged her across the sand. Her blades dropped instinctively as she reached for his hand, scratching at his grip. She ground her teeth, preparing for the pain, and yanked her head in the opposite direction. Her roots burned from the pull, and she drew a dagger from its sheath and sliced at his calf. He went down quickly, screaming as his blood pooled around him.

Enough of this. L'ọrẹ ran towards Yellow Teeth and threw her dagger to the ground in a wide arc. He glanced at it, falling for the distraction. She jumped and pulled him by the neck, and did not let go until his head crashed against the sand. A jolt of pain shot through her elbows, but she rolled away before he could burn her. Whatever pain she felt, she hoped his head felt much worse.

It didn't seem to.

His lips curved into a wide grin. 'Notin do me! I resemble who dey fear blood? Na iron dey my head o!' he said, twisting and turning his head as if to check that it was still attached properly.

He lunged at her, and she ducked, but not before his hot palms grabbed the part of her arm that wasn't protected. She screamed. It felt like someone had poured boiling water on her. She pulled him in closer and knocked her head into his. He yelled and staggered, releasing his grip on her as she stumbled backwards, but didn't fall.

'You should've seen that coming,' Command said.

Or you could help me, L'ọrẹ thought but didn't dare say out loud. She glanced at the blades she'd thrown to the ground. They were too far out of reach. L'ọrẹ surveyed her burnt arm. Curse the sun! She wouldn't be able to hide this from her father. The wound had already formed blisters. She didn't initially notice when the masked man joined the fight and turned in time to see his fist inches away from her face.

'Too slow!' Command shouted. L'ọrẹ's knuckles cracked as her fist crashed into the masked man's hardened core. He grunted but didn't move an inch. She squared up to him again. But he was too fast. She couldn't land a single strike. Her sore arm stung with each blow as salty sweat pricked at the raw wound. A howling laugh erupted from him, vibrating his entire being. At that moment, L'ọrẹ knew she wouldn't win the fight. Not if she kept fighting without a plan. How would she explain to Command that she lost a fight to drunken street thugs?

'Strategy, not rage,' Command said, as though her commander could read her mind.

L'ọrẹ nodded firmly, her eyes fixed on all three men. Somehow, she felt like even if Command wasn't there ordering her steps, she'd still hear the woman's deep voice echoing in her mind.

'Keep your feet light on the ground,' Command's voice boomed.

'Who dey talk for there?' Yellow Teeth shouted, glaring at the shadows before lunging at L'ọrẹ, a deep grunt rumbling in his throat.

L'ọrẹ waited for him to get close enough before throwing a punch with her left hand, and he caught it. A wry smile crept up her face – the charred cloth was better than charred skin. The man pulled her close, and as he swung his head to slam it into hers, the stiff edge of her fingers met his throat. A long dry heave erupted from him, followed by short, ragged gasps. L'ọrẹ went after him, pulled him forward and kneed him in the face, breaking his nose and tossing him to the ground.

'Keep moving,' Command said.

Yellow Teeth was on his feet again. He cackled, revealing his now crimson-stained mouth. What were these guys made of?

Exhausted, L'ọrẹ lunged forward, landing on a single leg. She'd miscalculated. With only one foot on the ground, he took advantage of her mistake and swiped at her leg, sending her face-first into the sand.

'Recover,' Command said briskly.

Blood and sand clung to her lips, filling her mouth with the sour tang of metal and clay. She groaned as the heavy weight of his boot dug her face into the ground. Command's voice echoed like a distant bell in her mind.

Struggling beneath his weight, L'ọrẹ used her hands to twist at his ankle when suddenly, his foot was off her head. She looked up to see Yellow Teeth on the floor next to her, blood pouring from his mouth. Someone pulled her off the ground, and she knew by the feel of his hands that it was Alawani.

'Right on time,' she said, smiling and spitting out the blood in her mouth.

'What's going on? Why are we fighting? Who are these guys?' he asked, his naturally curved brows furrowing together in disapproval.

'I'll explain later!' She crashed her blades against each other, spilling sparks of light in the direction of the remaining duo, who were still raging for a fight.

'This is no be your fight, Ọmọ'ba. Commot make I no wound you,' the masked man said to Alawani as he pulled down the scarf that concealed his lower face, revealing a skull tattoo across his cheek.

The bald man looked to his comrade and then to Alawani, 'Ọmọ'ba or not, the girl cut Shaki hand. If we no do our own back, make thunder strike us.'

Of course, they didn't care that Alawani was the Ọmọ'ba. Long ago, the gods had declared that no child of a sovereign could inherit the throne, an unyielding part of the deal the first High Priest made with the gods in exchange for agbára, so the Holy Order found other ways to secure an heir. So it didn't matter whether the people called him a prince or not: with no inheritance, authority or claim, his title meant nothing and he was fair game.

'If you want her, you'll have to go through me,' Alawani growled.

The men sneered sinisterly.

Alawani looked at L'ọrẹ. She gave him a wicked grin, knowing what he was asking her to do. Muscles tensing, she set her stance to fight.

Alawani drew his sword and awakened his agbára, turning the cool steel from dull grey to gold. L'ọrẹ placed her back against his, and they stood firm, protecting each other as they fought the men. She faced the masked one. Was she suffering from a concussion that made her slower, or was he faster than Yellow Teeth? Whatever it was, she kept going.

Her strength renewed every time her back slammed into Alawani's, reminding her that she wasn't alone. They were in sync – this was their battle dance. When she threw one of her blades into the air so she could use her free hand to throw punches, he caught it before it reached the ground – using it seamlessly as a second weapon. When she needed it again, he found her hand without looking back. They'd practised every step for years. Behind her, L'ọrẹ heard the man Alawani fought scream. Then came the familiar smell of metal burning flesh.

The men went down, and just before they could exhale in relief, half a dozen thugs stormed into the arena. One glance at each other was all L'ọrẹ needed to know Alawani's next move. She took a step back. He clapped his palms together and took in a deep breath. As he separated them, his agbára's light intensified. His palms glowed so brightly that L'ọrẹ had to look away. She took another few steps back as he rapidly heated the air around them and held the form for a moment, radiating heat energy until his hands shimmered and the air began to boil. Through squinted eyes, she saw threads of light tracing the edge of the glowing orb vibrating in his hands. He threw it at the wall, and the rush of hot air hit the men descending into the pit and sent them flying against the stone stairs.

L'ọrẹ smiled. Prince or not, he was pretty impressive.

Now wasn't the time to be jealous, but she couldn't help it. In all her life, with all her tricks, she'd never been – and would never be – able to form an energy blast like that. Alawani was more powerful than ordinary people in Oru because he'd inherited the agbára of his father, the king. She couldn't stop her heart from squeezing tight against her chest every time she witnessed his powers. She even tried whispering the same words that awakened her blades.

Nothing. Her pale hands remained the way they'd always been. Ordinary. She closed her eyes and formed fists around her blade handles.

She was lost in her thoughts, and between the loud blasts and the crash of debris, she didn't hear the man creep up behind her. Not until a sweaty palm slammed against her face. She raised her blades to strike but could not move her arms as two men from the group restrained her, one on each side, and knocked them from her hands. She tried to scream, but her voice was muffled. Alawani spun, shocked to see the bulky man holding her hostage. He, too, had let his guard down.

Even in her panic, L'ọrẹ knew better than to look to Command for help. She couldn't let anyone know that the commander was there at all.

'Let her go, and no one will get hurt,' Alawani said, trying to keep an even tone, one glowing hand in front of him and another on his sword.

The man holding her face laughed. 'Why you go dey protect this coward pikin. You no hear wetin she do? If e be like say we rate you now dat one go be different matter but as e be like this, if you no commot for road we go clear you too abi you no see as we many? You wey suppose beg as we corner you so. Ṣẹgẹ, handle this boy, abeg.'

From the corner of her eyes, L'ọrẹ saw another thug rise from the debris and smash a glass bottle against his head. He used the glass-sharp edge of the remnant to cut an incision on his hand. He ignited his agbára and yelled out a battle cry, showing them both that he was ready to die there and then. There was nothing worse than fighting someone who wasn't afraid to die.

Even though everyone in the kingdom had agbára oru, every fight started with fists and weapons. Only fools used their powers when fighting an unknown opponent. The gods were cunning in how they distributed agbára, and you couldn't know how powerful your enemy's was until you gave them a reason to show you. Agbára changed the game. While it was hereditary, the intensity and strength with which it manifested was not. Those odds turned every fight into one against the whims of the gods.

L'ore was still trying to figure out a way out of the mess she'd found herself in when the ground beneath her feet started burning. Curse the sun. Alawani was going to burn them all.

She threw her head back, hitting her captor's nose. He cried out but didn't release his grip. His large sweaty hand held on tighter. She twisted and turned, but there was no way out.

'I won't say it again. Let her go!' Alawani growled, holding his glowing hand in the air.

One of the men stepped forward and tried to form an energy blast. Alawani didn't even move. They all watched as the other man's hands vibrated vigorously as he tried to form and hold the energy ball. It expanded too quickly and blew up in his face. He went down just as fast – a victim of his own weakness.

They should've backed down, but L'ore knew they wouldn't. If the man holding her didn't have his dirty hand so firmly against her mouth, she would've warned him to run for his life. But it was too late.

Alawani stretched out his glowing hands, and in mere moments, from behind them, the ground began to burn, and magma burst out of it. The brownish sand gave way to the hot orange liquid that spread, inching closer to the men with every moment. L'ore could tell that it had stung someone from the cries of one of the men.

They hadn't seen anything yet.

Alawani clapped his hands together, and when he separated

them, the magma followed his command. His hands moved in the air like a puppeteer manoeuvring his strings, and the burning substance floated inches above the ground. The air around them grew so thick with heat that L'ọrẹ felt her head spinning and her vision blurring as she grew faint.

'I'll bury you all in this if you don't release her right now.'

The men relinquished their grips so quickly that even L'ọrẹ was shocked. She ran to Alawani's side, and he shielded her with his body.

'I'm going to close my eyes. When I open them, be gone!'

And just like that, the horde of terrifying men turned into a pack of headless chickens, scurrying away.

L'ọrẹ couldn't take her eyes off Alawani as he returned the magma to the earth. He waved his hands over the ground and cast the red substance back into moulds of black rocks.

He turned and held her in his arms. 'Are you okay?'

She nodded. 'Yes, I just need air.'

In the blink of an eye, he awakened his agbára again and waved his hand around, removing some of the heat from the air that surrounded them. His eyes were still fixed on her, and the heat she felt this time was not from the air but within her. Her eyes fell away from his. She wanted more than what they were but she'd never dare say anything. She was, after all . . . just a coward.

Báabá sọnù, k'a ri'ra wa he, ni Yorùbá fí n kọ'là
*To be able to find ourselves if we get lost, is the
reason Yoruba people give tribal marks*

2

Ìlú-Ọba – The Capital City
First Ring, Kingdom of Oru

L'ỌRẸ

L'ọrẹ had seen ten first suns when she first walked into Command's arena. It had taken many blood moons for Command to agree to train her, and even then, only in secret under cover of night. Being the daughter of an exiled man, L'ọrẹ shared in his penance – serving time for a crime he'd committed long before she was born. A crime she'd have committed herself if she'd been in his position. So while L'ọrẹ loved her father, she hated the name she was forced to carry like a target on her back.

Winning Ogun and joining the royal guard was her only way out.

Upon seeing Command's figure emerge from the darkness, L'ọrẹ fell to her knees, awaiting her commander's next words.

'You disgrace me,' Command said finally, walking out slowly from behind the pillar.

Alawani prostrated low before her and stepped back. No doubt still very confused about everything but knowing better than to get in between her and Command when the woman was this angry.

L'ọrẹ rose to her feet. 'I'm sorry, Command, but –'

'I don't know what excuse you can give to justify this,' Command said in a cool even tone that scared L'ọrẹ more than when the woman shouted. 'You bring thugs to my arena, and you still can't win a fight against drunkards? Have I been wasting my time? Is this how you think you'll win when you get called for Ogun? You think this is what royal guards are made of?'

'Command, I was outnumbered,' L'ọrẹ said softly.

'I trained you to defeat two dozen men,' Command shouted, then glared at Alawani. 'He won't always be there to save you.'

L'ọrẹ lowered her gaze, knowing that nothing she could say would help. Command was right. That should've been an easy fight.

Command took a step closer, and L'ọrẹ flinched. She stilled then sighed, raising L'ọrẹ's burnt arm to observe. 'Turn around. Let me look at you. Are you hurt?'

L'ọrẹ shook her head, knowing that with Command, anything short of bleeding out her guts was not hurt enough to mention.

Command pulled out a small container and rubbed a sticky substance over the burn on her arm.

L'ọrẹ felt the ache dull immediately and let out a deep breath. 'Thank you.' She smiled, hoping the woman would return the sentiment, but Command only sighed again, brushing L'ọrẹ's hair with her fingers as if checking that the roots were still in place.

'You should never allow your opponent to get close enough to touch you,' Command said, pulling out blades from beneath her cloak. 'And for the sake of all that burns, don't ever run out of blades in a fight.' The woman tossed half a dozen blades of different sizes and lengths to L'ọrẹ – two of which she'd pulled out of her greying hair. 'Wear this.'

L'ọrẹ picked them up and hid them along the belt strapped to her thighs and in her hair.

'You have nothing to prove to anyone outside these walls. If you want to prove you're not a coward, do it here during Ogun; do it beneath the sun where even the gods won't be able to change your name from Victor,' Command said, her face still stern but her voice a soft whisper.

L'ọrẹ felt a lump form in her throat, and she had to swallow hard to keep from bursting into tears. In the absence of her mother, Command, in her own very unusual way, had kept L'ọrẹ safe and given her refuge within these walls, even when doing so meant risking her life. L'ọrẹ blinked the tears away. The only thing worse than losing that fight, worse than even disappointing her commander, would be crying in the arena. Only blood and sweat were acceptable in the pit of death – never tears.

Command leaned in closer to her. 'If I didn't think you could do this, I wouldn't be wasting my time training you or risking the wrath of the Regent by doing so. I told your father I could make a warrior out of you. Don't make me a liar.

'You,' Command said, pointing to Alawani. 'My arena is not your playground. You're paying for this damage.'

'Yes, Command,' Alawani said standing to attention.

Command glared at him, then said, 'If you have to pull the earth apart to win a fight with street thugs then you're not worthy of being in this space.'

Alawani gave a firm nod, his eyes fixed on the ground.

'Have I taught you both nothing?'

As L'ọrẹ moved to speak, Command raised her hand, silencing her. 'Go home, L'ọrẹ. Tomorrow I intend to see the warrior I've trained, not this silly dance you did today.' And with that, Command slid into the shadows.

L'ọrẹ slumped to the ground and buried her face in her hands. She wasn't ready. Alawani sat beside her on the warm sandy ground and placed his arm over her shoulders, drawing her close.

'She loves you, you know?' he said softly, tilting his head in the direction Command had disappeared in.

L'ọrẹ nodded slowly. 'I know. I just – I just want to be better. Stronger. She's right, I should've won that fight without you.'

'Tell me what happened.'

'You saw what happened.'

'No, tell me from the beginning, Tèmi.'

That name was like a trigger, making her heart skip a beat and filling her with a mixture of emotions. Only he called her that. Tèmi – my own. Her gaze roamed the arena, avoiding his eyes. 'One of them said it.'

'Said what?'

She allowed her eyes to rest on him until he understood.

'You're the bravest person I know.' The words left a smile on his face, and she wanted to believe him. But he only said so because he didn't know her secret. She *was* a coward. She just didn't like hearing it.

She shoved his shoulder. 'Yeah, yeah, I've heard. Thanks for helping anyway.'

Alawani laughed so loud his voice echoed through the arena.

'Why are you laughing?' L'ọrẹ said, frowning.

'This is exactly how we met.'

L'ọrẹ looked around the empty arena and the dwindling torches and smiled. 'I think you're right.'

'I am,' Alawani said, still laughing. 'You'd just finished training with Command. I was on my way home and heard someone screaming, and you were in here with two boys twice your size fighting like a tiny little soldier.'

'And winning too,' L'ọrẹ said, the corner of her lips lifted in a smile.

'Is that what you call winning? You're lucky I was here.'

'I guess,' L'ọrẹ said. 'Why did you help though? I mean, it's not every day the Prince of Oru gets into street fights.'

'Isn't it?' Alawani said, his brows raised.

L'ọrẹ smiled. 'You know what I mean.'

Alawani shrugged. 'It wasn't a fair fight.' He rose off the ground and stretched his hand to her, 'And no one deserves to carry the weight of their parent's crimes.'

'I guess,' she said again, taking his hand. They were both branded by the actions of their parents, and while Alawani would never talk about his father's reign, he knew exactly how she felt. The only difference was that his name protected him from being randomly attacked on the streets while she spent every day trying to survive the hostile place she called home.

'You didn't have to move all the way from the sixth ring just for me though,' L'ọrẹ added.

'I'd have done anything to get away from the Lord General,' Alawani said. 'I'm just glad Command allowed me to join in on this secret little thing you both have going on here.'

'Thanks anyway,' L'ọrẹ said with a smile. 'For showing up . . . and sticking around.'

'Always,' he said, his breath visible in the chilly air. 'You know that.'

She noticed the single bead of sweat that trailed from his neatly carved hairline past his bushy eyebrows to his prominent cheekbones.

'What?' He chuckled after a moment of silence. 'Is there something on my face?'

Only then did she realize she'd been staring at him, watching the sweat bead get lost in his trimmed dark beard.

His smile widened, and she saw a glimpse of the dimple on his left cheek. She blinked to pull her mind back to the present.

She shook her head gently, her braids swaying softly.

His eyes crinkled at the edges, and the corners of his lips turned upwards. She loved – no, not loved: liked. She liked his smile. She was staring again. This time, she noticed the full shape of his lips, the soft pink shades that coloured where his lips parted, the –

'Ouch!' she cried out, rubbing her arm where he'd playfully punched her.

His charming smile broadened, and a deep laugh erupted from him. His brown eyes sparkled, and she almost got lost in them again.

She turned her smile into a deep frown and moved closer to him, her hands tensed in tight fists. As expected, his voice deepened with concern, thinking she was upset – perfect. He carefully reached for her face, and she punched him in the stomach, laughing hysterically. He bent over, half-laughing and choking.

'Too slow!' she said, catching her breath.

When he didn't stop coughing, she bent low to lift his face, and he lunged at her. He wrapped his hands firmly around her waist and lifted her off the ground.

'Say sorry!' he said, grunting under her weight as she wiggled her legs in the air, struggling to get free.

'Never!' she laughed.

'Then you're never getting down!'

'I will bite you!'

'You can try!'

They roared with laughter as she squirmed around in his arms, trying to pry them open. The more she moved, the tighter his grip was. His brawny arms were locked tight, and she could feel his muscles flex as she rubbed against them, trying to get free.

But they were just friends. The best of friends. She always had to remind herself of this every time she caught her thoughts wandering too far. Recently, she'd needed the reminder more often than not. Maybe five or six times a day, but who was counting?

Finally, Alawani dropped her slowly. Her body pressed against his as he eased her feet to the ground. The moonlight shone above them like a spotlight, dimming everything around them, and for a moment, his face was the only thing she saw. Her chest moved with his as they both strained for air. The feel of the ground beneath her snapped her back, and she pulled out of his embrace, pursing her lips together and looking anywhere but at him. When she dared to glance at him, his eyes shot away from hers, and he cleared his throat. Her cheeks flushed, and she could feel her heart race much faster than she could breathe.

She looked away again. 'I've got to get home,' she said, heading for the stairs.

Every step away from him hurt more than every blow she'd endured tonight. She wanted to stay, to get lost in his arms, in his eyes, under the dark of night. With him, she was safe. With him, she wasn't L'ọrẹ the coward's daughter or L'ọrẹ the exiled one. But if she tried to break that unspoken rule between them and he didn't feel the same way, she'd never recover from it. She just wouldn't. She glanced back to see him climbing up the stairs after her. She broke into a run, removing herself from him and the thoughts that lingered, hoping that by the time he caught up with her, she'd have recovered from whatever spell he'd cast on her. They were nothing more than friends. That was already more than she could have hoped for.

The crown is immortal.
It is the head that wears it that rots.
The crown of Oru sits and shines
atop the head of the sovereign
its cone-shaped top rimmed with
strings of golden cowries
like a curtain that shields its wearer
from the common eye.
The one who wears the crown fuels
its eternal essence with their own soul.
Still, the question that keeps the kingdom awake
in the dead of night remains . . .
WHO WILL SEAT THE GILDED THRONE?

3

Ìlú-Ọba – The Capital City
First Ring, Kingdom of Oru

ALAWANI

Alawani's title as the prince of Oru meant nothing, and his people never let him forget it. His sisters bore the same burden, but they seemed to carry it much better than he did. The problem was that Alawani was always made to feel special. His father had married eight wives in search of a son, only for Alawani to be born by the late king's first wife a few years before his death. His three half-sisters might as well be strangers to him, with how adamantly his mother kept him away from them. For he was different, she'd often reminded him. He was a gift from the gods, destined for greatness, a sun among a sea of stars.

Many first suns ago, the title had meant something; he'd have inherited the crown upon his father's death. But since the time of the first High Priest, everything had changed. Passing the crown from father to son was too dangerous, creating power struggles within families and hoarding precious agbára within one bloodline. Now, the gods chose. When the king died, a High Priest was chosen to take his throne as Lord Regent. The next king would be the firstborn child of that regent, whose wives were selected from each ring of the kingdom.

For Alawani, this meant any respect he was shown was either to honour his father, the late king, or to acknowledge his wealth. But wealth didn't mean much in the capital city of Oru, which was full of royals from many bloodlines and merchants with more gold than they knew what to do with. So Alawani often had to resort to the only thing he truly inherited from his father – his agbára.

Only a handful of people in the kingdom were more powerful than he was when wielding agbára: the Lord Regent's children. And he'd grown up with all of them; one in particular he'd called a friend, brother even. But that was a very long time ago. Now, he had only one friend worthy of the title, and there she was, sneaking into her father's house, hoping to avoid the confrontation that she'd have to deal with the moment he realized she'd been out of the house and fighting with thugs. Again. He smiled as she waved at him, and he waited until her shadow disappeared from the window, then turned back towards the capital in search of the man who could put a stop to the attacks.

It wasn't often that he had to wield the power the gods gave him in a way that terrified people, but with a name that meant nothing, a title with no authority, and the life of a commoner, the fear that gripped those who crossed him when he wielded his agbára as the gods intended was enough to give him a sliver of respect. That was how he came to an agreement with the Underlord of the capital city. As he approached Baálè-Ikú's den, swarms of thugs hovered around the entrance, the air filled with the stench of palm wine fermented past the stage where it was sweet.

'Ahan, Ọmọ'ba, na you be dat? Wetin bring you come this side?' a voice called out above the drumming and singing.

Alawani ignored the man but lit his agbára, allowing his power to flow into his hands, getting brighter with each step until he reached the door. The man before him was a mountain of muscle, and he let out a low rumble in his throat as he spotted the prince's glowing hands.

Alawani spoke first. 'I'm here to see Baálè-Ikú. He is expecting me.'

'Liar,' the mountain said in a voice so low Alawani thought he felt the earth tremble.

'Let me in,' he said again, allowing his agbára's heat to flow out of him, warming the air around them.

The mountain did the same, then spat at him, 'You have no power here. Not here or anywhere else in this kingdom. Go back to playing pretend in your borrowed palace.'

Alawani hadn't wanted another fight. No. But he did need to confront the man responsible for those who attacked his L'ọrẹ. It had been many first suns since he first met the coward's daughter. Even back then, he quickly realized the horrors she endured at the hands of anyone who was itching for a fight, courtesy of her association to the man who raised her. Since Baba-Ìtàn stopped leaving their home altogether, she was the next best target. And so Alawani made a deal with Baálè-Ikú. Knowing he couldn't always be there to protect her, he paid the Underlord and his men a hefty fee every blood moon to protect her. So imagine his surprise on seeing the skull tattoo of death that marked the Baálè's men as they burned and fought his L'ọrẹ.

Alawani felt his blood boil as the memory of her injuries flashed in his mind. 'I'll show you power,' Alawani said as he slammed his glowing palm into the mountain's chest, burning through the layers of metal and cloth.

The man screamed as his flesh simmered and shoved Alawani off with his entire body. Alawani flung out a few feet into the sand. The music stopped, and the compound stilled.

The men around him responded quickly, pushing off

the women that danced on their laps and picking up their weapons.

Alawani rose to his feet, quickly regaining composure. 'Baálè-Ikú, come outside now!' he shouted at the top of his lungs.

The Baálè did not show, so Alawani boiled the sand beneath their feet. As the heat from his agbára flowed out of him and pulled on the molten fire beneath the ground, everyone began to scream.

Some managed to stand their ground, forming energy-ignited blasts to launch at him with their agbára.

He raised an eyebrow. 'Do you want to bet that you can launch those attacks before I sink you into the fire beneath your feet?'

'Stop this nonsense right now,' came a call from the doorway. There stood a man much slimmer and shorter than Alawani, and around him were women who wore bronze armours moulded to their bodies and short leather skirts adorned with cowries around their waists.

Alawani watched as the man they called Baálè-Ikú, the Lord of Death, cooled a patch of ground, using his agbára to draw the heat into himself, and walked the straight line that led right to Alawani. 'You should have knocked,' Baálè-Ikú said, chuckling as sparks of light crackled around his glowing arms, 'I would have welcomed you with open arms. Why do you bring a fight to my doorstep, Prince of Oru?'

Alawani had not even broken a sweat, and he could see from the beads soaking the man's forehead that his little act of confidence in the face of Alawani's agbára was taking a toll on him.

'Your men broke our agreement. They attacked L'orẹ.' Alawani could feel the steam rising from his hands as his blood boiled over. 'You promised you would keep her safe.'

Baálè-Ikú took a step back, and the women around him ignited their agbára.

'I'll handle it. You know me,' he said, dragging his words. 'There are many men under my command; maybe if you doubled the payment, we could both avoid this kind of unpleasantness.'

'You did this to bargain with me? They could've killed her,' Alawani shouted, then turned around, eyeing the men still standing. 'Where are the ones who did this?'

'As I have said, the boys are mine to command, Ọmọ'ba. Leave now, and we can still do business together, albeit at a newly negotiated price that works for us both.'

Alawani could see the fear he'd predicted in all their eyes. All except Baálè-Ikú stood with breaths held. Even with their glowing hands and weapons poised to fight, if they thought they could win, they'd have attacked already. He inhaled a deep breath and lunged at the women on both sides of the Baálè, sending them flying against the house with energy blasts. As Baálè-Ikú raised his hands, lightning sparked in the sky above; he pulled on the energy and shot a bolt at the prince. Alawani crashed to the ground in agony as the energy raged through his body. He remained crouched as Baálè-Ikú laughed over him, welcoming the cheers from his men. As the Baálè glanced away, Alawani jumped up and grabbed his wrists where his signature skull tattoo was inked into his skin and burned until his flesh began to char. As the man screamed, Alawani shouted so all the men could hear him, 'The deal was money for protection. Now it's your life for her protection. Touch her again and die.'

He turned to face the scattering crowd. Now this was fear. This he could work with. He wiped the sweat from his brow and walked out of the compound.

*

Alawani had just stepped off the bridge connecting the capital city to the royal island when a figure approached him. He couldn't be certain, but he thought he felt the weight of their eyes upon him. He looked at his time beads. Three past midnight. Nothing good happened this late at night, so he ducked into an alleyway, quiet and empty, lit only by the moon, hoping the figure hadn't noticed him disappearing. The footsteps got quicker, and he snaked through the alley until he reached a dead end. Trapped by high walls, he ignited his agbára and waited until the person walked into the light from his glowing palms. A maiden. A temple maiden. His heart stopped.

Before him was a young woman as beautiful as the night itself. When she looked at him, it felt like he was looking into the depth of the river he had just crossed. She wore the familiar blood-red ensemble, a fitted embroidered bodice that revealed her curves, while a flowing skirt of iridescent silk trailed behind her. Her hair was so dark that only the threads of gold in each braid allowed him to see where they started and stopped. And when she spoke, chills ran down his spine, and he could feel his heart failing.

'Prince Alawani, son of our late king Aláàfin Ọlátúnjí.'

Together, Alawani and the maiden echoed, 'May his soul find the city of light,' as was customary to proclaim after the name of the dead was mentioned. The words had poured out of him without a second thought.

The maiden continued, not acknowledging his participation, 'And son of our Royal Mother, Ìyáàfin Olorì Atinúkẹ́. The gods of the sun and sands call you to fulfil your destiny. They have spoken, and the High Priest of the Holy Order of the Sun Temple has confirmed the call. You are to be chosen from among many, blessed to be one of the Called, a priest of the Order.'

The maiden pulled out a string of white coral beads and stepped closer to him. Alawani backed away from her.

'No,' he burst out.

She tilted her head, and somehow, the deep frown lines creased across her face did not make her any less beautiful. She exhaled slowly, as though running out of patience with him, and repeated her words again.

'No,' Alawani said, interrupting her.

She snapped, 'The gods do not ask your permission. They command, and you obey. You have been called,' she said, holding up the beads. 'Come here and take this. This is your fate.'

'No one of royal blood has ever been called to be a priest of the Holy Order. Not since the day of the First Sun. It is forbidden.'

'Who are you to tell the gods what is forbidden?'

'Does your Order not claim that the gods forbid the crown to pass down from generation to generation within the same family lines? Is cutting off all connection to past royals not the reason why the Holy Order picks a new High Priest to sire a new heir every time a sovereign dies? I may not know much about what goes on within that temple, but I know that this should not be possible. A prince in the Holy Order? It has never been done.'

'The gods decide what is forbidden, and they have called you.'

'I said no,' Alawani said, moving further away from her. 'Tell the gods, the High Priest, and my grandfather.' Alawani's grandfather no longer held the titles of High Priest and Lord Regent – which he gained after the gods called him nearly seventy-six first suns ago – but remained a force to be reckoned with in the temple. 'Tell them you asked, and I said no.'

'Lord Regent Babátúndé confirmed your call, Prince of Oru. Your grandfather had nothing to do with it.'

Alawani scoffed, 'You want me to believe that the former High Priest of the Sun Temple had no influence over those called to join his Order?'

The maiden sighed again, and this time, when she spoke, she did so in a low, even tone as those recalling the words of another. 'Every decade since the day of the First Sun, many like you have been called to the Red Stone to return their agbára to the gods so that they might have a greater purpose. Today, you have been called to become a conduit for the gods of the sun and sands.'

'I will not die for your gods.'

The maiden tossed the beads at his chest. 'Do you know how many boys would give their lives for the honour of being called? How many will drop everything they have ever known or loved to even be considered worthy of the Order? You're right. No one as ungrateful and ignorant as you are deserves to be an Àlùfáà of the Holy Order, yet here we are.'

'If you don't think I should do this, then why are you here?' Alawani said, watching as the poise and grace with which the maiden had walked up to him faded with every word she spoke in anger.

'It is not my place to question the will of the gods, nor is it yours, no matter how unprecedented their decisions may seem.'

'Who are you?' Alawani asked cautiously.

'I am Milúà, daughter of Ìyá-Ayé, sword of the Sun Temple and spear of the crown. And I am your maiden.' Then she added quietly, 'Unfortunately.'

'Unfortunately?' he said, closing the gap between them.

She reached out in a quick move and cut him with a sharp blade. He didn't see where she pulled the blade from or where she returned it to, but a thin line of blood blossomed on his arms, and he flinched away from her.

'Curse the sun, what have you done?'

She stood silent before him, and within a few heartbeats, he could no longer feel his body, and the world swayed as he fell. He braced for impact, but it never came. Instead, Milúà caught him, put him to rest against a wall, and knelt before him.

'You poisoned me,' he managed to say as she blurred in and out of his vision. His body was still stiff and out of his control.

'Listen to me,' she said as she knelt before him. 'Earlier tonight, the priests of the Holy Order gathered to witness the names of the people who were called by the gods for the trials. Six blood moons ago, the High Priest sent out his Àlùfáà in pairs to live among the six rings of Oru, collecting the names of those they believed the gods wanted in the trials. Tonight, six gourds were placed before the Lord Regent, containing stones with those names inscribed upon them. A stone was pulled from the darkness of each gourd, and the one representing the capital city had your name on it. Prince Alawani.'

At that point, his eyes widened, but everything still blurred. Whatever she had given him paralysed him and dulled every sense except his hearing. Every word she said echoed as though the world had gone silent, and only her voice remained.

'At first, the priests grumbled as expected. We were all shocked. The priest who put your name in the gourd swore that the gods whispered your name to him on his travels. The other priests even cast the sacred stones, consulting the gods to confirm the choice. Your grandfather, Àlùfáà-Àgbà, spoke on your behalf, saying that there are two reasons we have the stripping ceremonies every ten first suns. One is to choose the next High Priest who will sire the next ruler after the death of the crown heir, and the other, which he says is just as important, is to fulfil the oath we made with the gods to repay them for the powers they blessed us with. The Red Stone will strip the chosen of their agbára, and without this sacrifice, and the sacrifice of all the chosen that have come before you and will come after you, the entire kingdom will lose the powers of the sun. He reminded the Order that never has a name been returned to the gourd once chosen. And he managed to convince them that your trial at the Red Stone will not break the rules the gods set for us about keeping royal blood from returning to the throne since we are still so many first suns and stripping ceremonies from the next High Priest choosing that you will be ineligible for the position.

'The Lord Regent was not happy, I can tell you that. But he could not deny that the gods made it so that your stone was picked. In the end, he confirmed your call, saying that if the priest who put your name into the gourd was not speaking the truth, then you would not survive the Red Stone, and your grandfather was only sending you to your death. And only if you survive will he decide and declare a verdict on your position in the Order. So all you have to do, Alawani, Prince of Oru, is say yes.'

As her image blurred in and out of focus, the strong smell of the temple incense lingering around her sent his mind back to when he was a boy, and he heard his father's voice reminding him of a promise he had made a long time ago. The collision of Milúà's hand across his cheek jarred him back to reality.

'Are you listening?' she said, peering into his face. 'The Order has decided that you will join them and journey to the sun. And I am your maiden, which means my life is now in your hands, so I need you to say yes to this. Say yes, and I'll give you the antidote for the poison.'

Alawani's eyes rolled back, and he heard his father's voice as clearly as though he were standing right next to him.

My son, you are Àlùfáà. The old laws no longer serve this kingdom. The gods have confirmed this to me. Death may come for us, but our line will never end. These were his father's dying words. *When the call comes, promise you will accept it.* He was as confused now as he had been when he made this oath. He did not know why his father had forced him to swear those words, and even now, many first suns later, he didn't feel like he could outrun them.

He opened his eyes and found himself staring into Milúà's dark gaze as she held his chin, turning his head back and forth. His body was still out of his control, and his heart beat so slowly that he struggled to stay awake, but he would not yield. He heard Milúà's quiet grumbles as she pulled out a vial from her skirt and poured it down his throat. He breathed slowly, inhaling the scent of her mixed with the cold night air. The bitter liquid worked quickly, flowing through his body and releasing him from his prison. He shoved her off and sprung up. She was on her feet as quickly as he was.

'You could have killed me!' he said with a strained voice.

'You are chosen now. No mortal can kill you without the wrath of the Holy Order and the gods. I just needed you to listen and see reason.'

'Oh gods, why is this happening to me?' Alawani said, leaning against the wall.

Milúà didn't respond.

'You say I can't walk away from this. But someone already did.'

Milúà cut him off, 'You want to live the life of a coward? In this kingdom? Your grandfather would see you dead before he'd let you dishonour his family name. Moreover, that man survived the Red Stone and then turned his back on the Order. He did not deny the call of the gods to return his agbára to them. If you turn away from this, be ready for what comes next.'

43

Alawani opened his mouth to say no again, and a gust of wind blew against him. The chill matched the shiver in his spine. And his father's voice repeated the words he'd once sworn to. Alawani let the tears building in his eyes fall as he said, 'I will go with you.'

Milúà straightened. 'Lead the way,' she said, pointing towards the temple.

Alawani shook his head, 'Not now.'

'What?' she said, igniting her agbára, her eyes sparking with shades of gold. 'You already said –'

'I'll come,' Alawani said, cutting her off, 'but not tonight. I need to do something. Speak to someone.'

Milúà frowned. 'Who is this someone?'

'She –' Alawani started to say, but Milúà interrupted him.

'You delay your destiny for a girl? Who is she? Tell me, and I'll slit her throat and end this.'

'I said I'll come,' Alawani growled.

Milúà let her powers fade into the night. 'The other maidens are informing their chosen from all six rings as we speak. It'll take two days for the last of them to arrive. Then, the Holy Order will officially announce the names. Be here, or I'll kill you long before the Red Stone can.' She moved so close to him that he could feel her warm breath on his skin. Another spark of gold flashed in her eyes. He was so lost in the darkness of her gaze that it was as though she had imprinted on him. 'There's nowhere in this kingdom or this continent you can go that I will not find you, Prince of Oru,' she said in a smooth, silky voice, then turned on her heel and walked back into the dark of night, leaving Alawani terribly afraid that death had found him, and he had no way of escaping it.

Alawani's mind and vision cleared as he stumbled back towards the bridge. He'd have thought the last few moments were a dream but for the string of white beads firmly tied to his wrist. He hadn't even noticed the maiden slip it on. He let out a deep frustrated sigh. His life as he knew it was over, and he could not help the tears that flowed from his eyes as he turned towards the bridge that led to L'ọrẹ. His Tèmi.

She would never understand why he'd say yes to a fate that could only lead to his destruction. He ran through a series of explanations in his mind but even he couldn't explain this bond, this connection he had to a father he hardly even knew. Alawani did not have it in him to say no to the gods or his dead father. And so he had to find a way to explain to the one he loved with all his heart that his heart was not his to give.

He shouted and slammed his fists into the ground with his agbára. His breaths came short and quick. He'd chosen today to tell L'ọrẹ that he loved her. But then the thugs had attacked, and then the gods had called him to a fate he did not know how to escape. L'ọrẹ hated the Holy Order, and she always had a visceral reaction just at the mention of them. They had killed her mother. But it was only when he followed her home for the first time that her father told him it was Alawani's own grandfather who had killed her, and that he must never speak to L'ọrẹ again.

Although Baba-Ìtàn was not L'ọrẹ's birth father, their bond was stronger than any father and child Alawani had ever known. Alawani knew he had to respect Baba-Ìtàn's wishes even though it broke his heart. He hated his own grandfather from that moment on. Many blood moons later, L'ọrẹ found him again, and this time, she didn't let him cower and hide. She chose him, and then even her father couldn't keep them apart, and he loved her with every breath.

This news would break her.

He glanced at the darkness Milúà had walked into, and for the first time in a very long time, he felt like the boy he was when his father died — alone, scared, and in need of someone who'd understand his situation. He would talk to L'ọrẹ tomorrow. Today, he needed someone who might ease his fears. Today, he needed his old friend Tofa, the crown heir of Oru.

As he walked the sun path leading to the palace, he snuck past his home and the royal guards and crept into the crown heir's room on the west side of the island. Avoiding the guards stationed at the main entrance, he walked through the false wall they'd both found when they were boys. One foot in, and there was a knife at his neck.

'Kẹni, it's me. It's Alawani,' he said with his hands up. He didn't have to see her face to know the knife belonged to Tofa's twin sister and personal guard.

Kẹni pulled him into the room and shut the wall as quietly as she could. 'Let this be the last time you crawl through these walls,' she said, turning to face him.

Alawani couldn't help the smile that crept onto his face. She did not acknowledge it. She stared blankly at him. Alawani had known Kẹni as long as he'd known Tofa, and while she was nothing like the girl who'd chased him around the palace grounds playing games, that was exactly how Alawani saw her every time she looked at him with those large brown eyes. He felt the urge to hug her, to remind her that – She walked away, breaking his line of thought.

The birth of twins was a special blessing for every family in Oru – all except the family who had to bear an heir. Where there ought to be one, there were two. Tradition demanded the death of the spare heir at birth, but their father had fought for Kẹni to live under certain conditions. One of which was never leaving her brother's side.

'What do you want?' she said as she walked towards the window, checking for movement. Always on guard.

The large, gilded hall was twice the size of Alawani's, and he eyed the closed doors in the middle of the reception that led to Tofa's room. Alawani ran for the doors, and Kẹni lunged after him, reaching him just as he cracked open the doors. She raised a blade to strike him, and he caught her hand midair and laughed. 'I taught you that move.'

She stilled. She dropped the knife, waiting for his gaze to follow the drop to strike him with her other hand. He dodged it. 'And that one too.' He smiled and raised his hand when she awakened her agbára. He was no longer surrounded by people less powerful than he was. Under the right circumstances, Kẹni and her brother could burn him to ash.

'I just want to talk. Come on, let me in,' he said with a wink and her stoic expression cracked.

'What's going on here?' Tofa said, walking out of the inner room, his royal robes glistening in the candlelight. Then he noticed Alawani and paused.

This time, Alawani gave in to the urge to hug his friend and rushed towards Tofa, who welcomed him with open arms. 'It's been too long!' Tofa said, as he held Alawani close.

You know why, Alawani thought as he remembered Tofa's mother's threats, promising to send his family out of the palace if their friendship continued. Since the king's death, Alawani's family had kept their home on the royal island and an allowance only at the pleasure of Lord Regent Babátúndé, and as the Regent's Aya'ba, the crown heir's mother had all the influence to destroy Alawani's family's life in a heartbeat. Although, it dawned on Alawani that without that separation, he may never have wandered outside the royal island and never have met L'ọrẹ.

Kẹni scoffed at them and rolled her eyes. 'Close the doors behind you,' she said, pointing towards the inner room. Then said to Alawani, forcing down a smile, 'You have until the sun is up.'

Alawani watched as Tofa prepared a space for them at the foot of his bed, laying mats and wrappers and gourds of wine. He was treating him like a guest. They were brothers once, and the formal gesture stung more than Alawani was willing to admit.

His gaze roamed round the gilded room, intricately decorated with the best of everything their kingdom had to offer. Alawani had never been jealous of the crown heir. He'd always known that Tofa would inherit his father's throne. Even though that was what the council had used to forbid their friendship, they'd have a few stolen moments together before reality caught up with them. Tofa was born heir to the throne of Oru, and his father, who had been the High Priest at the time of Alawani's father's death, rose to the station of Lord Regent, holding the crown for his son until he was old enough to rule. Tofa was now a few blood moons from his coronation, and Alawani could see in the way his old friend moved that he was, in his mind, already a king.

They both settled into the space, and Alawani waited until Tofa had drunk a cup of wine before saying, 'I'm in trouble.'

'I figured,' Tofa said, smiling. 'We haven't seen you in more first suns than I can count, and then you come sneaking into my room. So who died?'

'No, it's nothing like that,' Alawani said, trying to form the words in his mind and struggling to start the conversation. 'I've been compelled into a decision I cannot escape, and I'm scared.'

'You? Scared? You great prince of Oru,' Tofa said, smiling. 'What's happened? Tell me, and I'll fix it. Is it the Lord General? I heard he was forcing you to go back to the sixth ring. I know that royals are meant to train under him, but he doesn't care about anyone but himself. After my time there, and Kẹni's too, I wouldn't send anyone I love into that man's den. I'll gladly redeploy you to the capital. Do you need me to intervene?' And without waiting for a response, he continued, 'I will speak to Command in the morning to keep your training in the capital. And once you win your final battle in the arena, I will declare you as the new Lord General. I promised you this a long time ago, and I haven't forgotten. I know it's been a long time, and much has happened, but I can still do this for you.'

Alawani squeezed his friend's hand. 'Thank you. But I don't think even the word of a king can save me from the gods.'

'The gods? Alawani, what have you done?'

Alawani opened his mouth to speak. Looking at his friend's concerned face, he wondered what Tofa's reaction would be if he were to tell him what he had come to say, and began to think better of it. His fingers rolled over the string of beads Milúà had attached to his wrist. And suddenly, his mouth went dry. He was so foolish to come here seeking restitution when this might be the thing to break their already strained friendship.

Alawani shook his head. 'It's nothing. I'm sure it'll pass with the night. I might be overreacting,' he said, rubbing his neck. 'I should have asked, how do you feel just a few blood moons before your coronation?'

Tofa leaned close, 'There is nothing you cannot tell me, Alawani. We grew up together within these walls. Your secrets are my secrets. Tell me what bothers you, brother.'

'Ah, it's nothing, I promise. It's like you said – as Lord General, nothing should scare me,' he said, patting Tofa on the shoulder.

'I can command you to tell me the truth,' Tofa said, smiling. 'I just want to help.'

Alawani smiled back, but the reminder that his friend was really going to be his king and the realization that he could have put himself in serious danger by coming here alone on the night of his call made his heart beat faster in his chest. What if Tofa already knew and was playing along?

'I should go,' Alawani said, dropping his gourd, 'before Kẹni cuts my head off.'

'Wait,' Tofa said, rising to meet him. 'It was good to see you, old friend. Come again.'

Alawani nodded, 'Maybe.'

As he turned, Tofa said, 'I heard you have a girl in the second ring. Is she the reason for all this?'

'No,' Alawani said quietly, smiling. 'She's perfect.'

'Ahan Alawani, is that love I see on your face? Come, sit, tell me about her,' Tofa said, handing him another cup of wine and pointing back to the mats.

Alawani wanted to leave. He also did not want to be alone with his thoughts tonight and could think of worse ways than spending the early hours of the morning talking about the love of his life, so he accepted the gourd and smiled. 'Her name is L'ọrẹ. Tèmil'ọrẹ.'

Ẹni bá ṣetán à ti ta iyì àti ẹ̀yẹ tó ní,
á rí ẹni ràá láì san'wó
Whoever is willing to sell their honour and
prestige will find someone who is ready to
buy it without paying.

4

Ìlú-Ìmọ̀ – The Home of Knowledge
Second Ring, Kingdom of Oru

L'ỌRẸ

The following evening in the arena had been exactly as Command promised. She had worked L'ọrẹ so hard that every muscle in her body burned and it took every bit of strength to walk the miles back home that night. L'ọrẹ groaned and raised the hood of her cloak firmly over her head as she and Alawani walked past the city gates into the second ring. He had skipped training and only arrived a couple of beads after Command retired for the night. He walked quietly beside her, and L'ọrẹ wanted to ask why he'd been so late and why he was so moody but was distracted by thoughts of how she'd explain coming home past midnight to her father again.

She hid in the shadows as they approached her house, hoping to sneak in again, but it was no use. Baba-Ìtàn saw her and Alawani the moment they were close enough to be seen. *When the nights are long, the gods sleep, and so should we.* Those were the words her father used to keep her within reach when she was younger, but she was older and wiser now, and she knew that there was nothing roaming at night but the cold winds and loose sand.

Baba-Ìtàn sat under the tree in front of their house, holding his nightly meeting with the children who snuck out of their homes and came to hear the tales by moonlight told by the kingdom's coward. Coward. The name for the one who turned his back on the gods. L'ọrẹ didn't know the details of what he'd done, and neither did most of the kingdom. All they knew was that one day he was a priest of the Order, and the next day, the Holy Order declared him excommunicated. His punishment was swift and without mercy.

Baba-Ìtàn's hunched frame was lit by the flames into which he spoke his tales. The flickering light made the tight curls of grey in his hair sparkle like silver threads in the night. His faded homemade tie-and-dye shirt, which he and L'ọrẹ had managed to piece together, hung loosely like an oversized bag across his shoulders. From where she stood, L'ọrẹ could see that the seams in the matching calf-length shorts were coming loose and made a mental note to fix them later that night. L'ọrẹ wasn't alive when he had been a part of the Order, but she imagined that the figure before her was a far cry from the wealthy priestly presence the man who answered the call of the gods would have exuded. Now, he was cast out and exiled yet trapped. No one was allowed to leave the kingdom of Oru and venture into the rest of the continent, so she and her father lived here in this dejected compound with a leaking roof, broken walls and this tree as old as time.

Children, however, did not care about who was good or bad; they just wanted an exciting story. And so around Baba-Ìtàn tonight were thirteen little ones. Fewer than yesterday but more than the day before. They'd surely be beaten if their parents ever caught them, but her father's stories were worth the risk. A fire pit separated them, and L'ọrẹ saw the children's large brown eyes widen in amusement as the story reached its climax. Baba-Ìtàn had them in a trance, smiles plastered on their faces as they waited to hear if Queen Aníwúrà won the war against the sand raiders.

'And so, when they reached our gates, the people were terrified,' Baba-Ìtàn's voice boomed across them. 'The enemy in the east was threatening the peace of Oru, nearly breaking down the walls of the sixth ring.'

'Oh no, what happened? Did they get in?' one boy asked, concern etched on his face.

'Don't be silly. There's never been a war in Oru,' the oldest boy among the lot replied.

The children began murmuring, most agreeing with the boy who spoke last.

'Shh . . .' Baba-Ìtàn placed a finger on his lips. 'The story says that when our great Queen Aníwúrà awakened her agbára, channelling the power of the sun into her weapons, she was so powerful that her agbára filled every part of her body. Those who saw her said she became the sun itself.'

The children gasped. L'ọrẹ smiled. She'd heard the tale many times before. It was impossible for anyone's agbára to fill all of their body. Agbára oru lit up everyone's palms, sometimes forearms. Very occasionally, and only for people with royal blood, their entire arms would light up with the energy of the gods. But that was as far as it got.

L'ọrẹ glanced at Alawani. She didn't like to think of agbára at all. Not when she couldn't even fill her little finger with the magic from the sun. Without the spells Baba-Ìtàn had taught her, which made her blades turn fiery, she'd be even stranger than she was now. Everyone here had agbára, proving they were of the sun and sands. But not her. A secret she kept deep in her heart from everyone, especially Alawani. Only the gods knew what would happen to her if anyone realized she didn't have agbára oru. She felt a low rumble in her chest and shuddered at the thought.

Baba-Ìtàn's voice filled the air as he continued his story, 'When the enemy saw the power of our great queen, they surrendered, but it was too late. However, instead of killing them, she sent them back to their land to tell their people what they had seen in Oru.'

'Will they come back?' a boy said.

'If you can show your enemy the might of your strength before you strike a blow, their imagination alone will be the thing that keeps them away. The sand raiders haven't returned since and never will.'

Baba-Ìtàn groaned as he rose from his stool. 'I'll be back in a moment.'

L'orẹ knew what he'd say before he reached her. She tried to hold on to the ends of Alawani's shirt, but he stepped out of her reach, leaving her to face her father's wrath alone. As Baba-Ìtàn approached them, L'orẹ knelt to the ground and greeted him. Alawani greeted him by bending low to touch the man's feet with his fingers – the same way he would greet any other elder in the village even though no one else thought her father worthy of such respect. L'orẹ often thought her father was too young to be tagged with the name Baba-Ìtàn, having only seen about forty first suns and six blood moons. But once the children started calling him the father of stories, the name stuck. *Better than his other name, coward*, L'orẹ thought grimly.

'You're late. Again. You think I didn't hear you sneak in last night? I've told you several times that you must be home before –' He paused and leaned in closer. A deep frown formed on his brow. 'Is that a wound on your face?' He didn't wait for her to reply. He grabbed her arm and moved her closer to the light. She yelled, and he released her immediately. Her burnt arm stung, and the pain which had only just dulled sprang back to life.

'What happened?' His face was contorted with frustration. Alawani quickly walked away from them and towards the children by the fireplace. L'ọrẹ lowered her eyes and grinned bashfully, trying to ease the tension.

Baba-Ìtàn wasn't amused. 'Open your mouth and talk before I get angry.'

'It's nothing, really. Some agberos in the market running their mouths again yesterday. I had to put them in their place.'

'And is that what I taught you to do? To be a thug?'

L'ọrẹ frowned. What kind of question was that?

'They called you a –' She paused, refusing to say the word.

'How many times will I tell you that I don't need you to fight for me or for my name? There's nothing to fight for!' He shouted so loudly that all the children and Alawani turned at the same time.

L'ọrẹ kept her eyes low to the ground. Staring at his feet, she counted his toes like she often did to distract herself when he was scolding her.

'Look at me!'

Her head sprang up to meet his gaze.

He held her chin and let out a deep sigh. This time, more quietly, he said, 'I don't need you to fight for me, L'ọrẹ.'

She slowly moved her face out of his hand. 'I'm fighting for us. Your name is my name, and I don't know about you, but I'm tired of it. It's a curse!'

Baba-Ìtàn let out a heavy sigh. He looked at her the way he often did, with a stony expression on his face and a sad look in his eyes. There were no tears. Baba-Ìtàn would never cry. She'd never even seen the shadow of a mist in his eyes. What she did recognize, though, was disappointment. Disappointment and fear. Fear that she might one day do something really stupid. But he was wrong. She was too smart for anyone to catch her.

'I'm sorry,' she said under her breath.

She didn't mean it, and so she didn't meet his eyes. He

knew her too well to think she'd ever apologize for fighting for a better life than the one she was trapped in. She was sorry, however, for always falling short of the high standards he'd set for her.

His chest deflated and a pained sigh escaped his lips. He turned to the children, 'That's all for tonight. Go home.'

The children moaned, but he'd made up his mind.

'Make sure no one is left, and clean up when they're gone,' he said to L'ọrẹ before walking towards the entrance of their home. The old library-turned-house was a three-storey relic of the life Baba-Ìtàn had lived long before L'ọrẹ was born. When his family name held weight throughout the kingdom of Oru. Now, its high walls made of brilliant clay stones crumbled in parts where the mould and rot ate them away. Against the dark of night, it looked like something haunted, with all the boarded-up windows and patch work her father had done in an attempt to save their home from crumbling to dust.

Alawani waited for Baba-Ìtàn to be out of sight before returning to L'ọrẹ's side.

'Why'd you tell him? I've never heard him so angry.'

'What should I have done, lied?'

'Yes!'

'I'm not going to lie to my father. Anyway, it's good for him to know,' L'ọrẹ said, glancing at the house.

The children scattered off, clashing their wooden swords and laughing as they ran away. It was too late to play 'soldier and thief', but who was going to stop them?

L'ọrẹ and Alawani sat across from each other by the fire, delaying the inevitable. He had to go. Baba-Ìtàn would never allow him to stay over in their home.

'Come here,' L'ọrẹ said, shifting to make space for him on her mat, hoping to get out of him whatever had fixed worry lines across his face.

Alawani snuggled next to her, and they put their hands towards the fire to warm up.

He smelled like earth, and she couldn't stop herself from inhaling, pretending to be taking in the heat. His face was angular, with high, strong cheekbones that made him appear chiselled from stone. His arms rubbed against hers, and she glanced at the tattoos that decorated them. A pair of black bands against his reddish-brown skin and an intricately designed image of the sun between both bands. A sign that he was of royal blood. She couldn't see the other arm, but she knew it had the design of flames, like a fire starting from his wrist and growing towards his shoulders. And, of course, the single lines on either temple told the world he was born of Oru. His marks represented Ìlú-Ọba – the capital city and first ring that shielded his birth place, the Royal Island of Oru.

She raised her hand to her own temple, feeling the three lines inscribed with a hot blade when she was a child, which told the world she was born of Oru and was from Ìlú-Ìmọ̀ – the home of knowledge and second ring of Oru.

L'ọrẹ stared at the sands beneath their feet to avoid gazing into his eyes. The cowries around his ankles came into view – two rows of them. Nearly two dozen kills. L'ọrẹ never asked whose souls they belonged to. Especially as a couple of those shells would have been hers if he hadn't stepped in to protect her. He was the reason L'ọrẹ didn't have a single cowrie anywhere on her person. She'd often done a lot of damage but had never taken a life, and for that she was grateful. She was so lost in thought that when he touched her fingers, she flinched.

'You're freezing,' he said. Without waiting for her response, he cupped her palms in his and blew warm air into them.

Her face grew hot, and her heart raced. She shoved him off and pulled her hands to her side.

'I was only trying to help,' he said, laughing.

'You can do that without eating my fingers.'

'Okay, fine, come here.' He took her hands again and wrapped them in his. He awakened his agbára, and a soft glow flowed through his palms, warming her to her core. Even the harsh breeze that had threatened to freeze her nose off now felt like the heat of a midday sun.

She quickly removed her hands again. It felt good. Too good. She couldn't trust herself not to do something stupid with the way his beautiful brown eyes peered into hers.

They were just friends. Nothing more and thank the sun nothing less.

'That's new,' she said, pointing to the string of white coral beads on his wrist.

His eyes shot to them, and he placed a hand over them. By the next moment, he'd slipped the bracelet off and tucked it away. 'It's nothing,' he said. 'I was trying something new but it doesn't fit.'

L'ọrẹ wanted to pry further, as she was prone to do, but he spoke first.

'I want to tell you something,' Alawani said, slowly reaching for her hand and locking his with hers.

'About why you skipped training and have been moody all evening?' L'ọrẹ said, keenly aware of how perfectly their hands fit together like missing pieces of a puzzle.

L'ọrẹ moved to stand and Alawani blurted out, 'I heard something today. Apparently, someone from Ìlú-Ọ̀pọ arrived at the capital gates.' He paused and swallowed. 'It was a boy who said he'd been called. He said he was Àlùfáà – one of the chosen.'

L'ọrẹ bent low, closer to the fire and held the crescent pendant that drooped from her neck. It was a gift from Baba-Ìtàn when she was younger, although she didn't remember receiving it. It had always just been a part of her.

'What does that mean?' L'ọrẹ asked.

'Didn't your father explain how all this works?'

'You think my father, who turned his back on the Holy Order and their gods and is still living out his punishment for leaving, will sit under this tree and tell me how the stupid hierarchy of the Order works?' she scoffed. 'I've had to pick up all I know by myself.'

'I guess not,' Alawani sighed. 'Well, the call is about appointing new priests to the Order and continuing the royal line.' He paused. 'To explain this, I need to talk about my grandfather, and I know you don't like any mention of him or what the Order did to . . . It's important, I promise.'

L'ọrẹ nodded, eyeing him cautiously as he went on.

'My grandfather was no one before his call,' Alawani said, avoiding her gaze. 'But then the gods called him and changed his life. And as the lone survivor of the stripping ceremony right before the queen's death nearly eighty first suns ago now, he was chosen to be the next High Priest. His firstborn son, my father, became the new crown heir and in the eighteen first suns before my father's coronation, my grandfather ruled as Lord Regent of Oru. The day my father died, the cycle continued, and your father left the Order, so Babátúndé was chosen as the new High Priest and Lord Regent for his firstborn son, crown heir Tofa.'

L'ọrẹ shrugged. 'So, it's that time again. When the Holy Order leads boys to their death. Why do you care?'

'I. I just –' Alawani sighed. 'I don't remember much about my father. I'd only seen four first suns and a few blood moons by the time he died. It's been so long now that without his statue in the palace to remind me of his face, I might have forgotten what he looked like. What I do remember are his last words to me.'

'What did he say?' L'ọrẹ said, closing the gap between them and wiping off the single tear that rolled down his face.

'He – he –' Alawani tried speaking, but his voice broke. He cleared his throat and tried again. 'I think he wanted me to join the Order.'

'Gods forbid,' L'ọrẹ said as quickly as the words could get out of her. 'It's against the law. No one's going to make a prince an Àlùfáà.'

'They shouldn't,' Alawani said, his face grim with fear. 'I've been thinking about that. Tofa's coronation is in a few blood moons, and because he is so young, whoever survives the trials now is unlikely to ever become High Priest. So if there is little risk my bloodline could return to the throne, maybe I could be called up?'

'Why would you even consider this?'

'The trials aren't all about priests and heirs. Without the Red Stone, the people of this kingdom will lose their agbára. What kind of a life would that be? Children of Oru would be born without the blessing of the gods. That's a fate worse than death. I don't want to be responsible for such a curse on our land.'

'Even for the sake of preserving the agbára of future generations, you cannot truly think any of this is worth your life.' L'ọrẹ's heart tightened as she spoke. What she wanted to say was, *I have no agbára and I can confirm that it is in fact a curse.* But that would mean telling him her secret and even after many first suns together, she wasn't ready for that just yet. So instead, she said, 'Your father couldn't have wanted this. What exactly did he say to you?'

Alawani shook his head, the tremor in his voice returning. 'He scared me. He said the gods would change the rules and I had to yield to their will. It shouldn't happen, but I've just begun to fear that it might. I am so scared, Tèmi. I don't want to die. I don't want the life of a priest.'

L'ọrẹ's heart skipped a beat every time he called her Tèmi and it hurt now to see him so terrified. 'Listen to me,' she said, moving to kneel before him and placing herself between his legs. She held his face in her palms. 'Your father, may his soul find the city of light, is dead, and the dead cannot decree. He cannot condemn you to a fate worse than death. Forget the sound of his voice, Alawani, and listen to mine,' she said with a shaky smile, and wiped at his tears. 'They haven't called you, have they?'

Alawani stared at her blankly, his eyes glassy with tears.

'Have they?' L'ọrẹ asked, panicked. In her mind's eye, she saw herself standing on a platform alone in a desert of black sands and stones, surrounded by two pillars that held a shade over her head – shielding her from the blistering heat. At that moment, one of those pillars cracked at its base, the split running all the way up to its top, shaking the platform she stood upon. Her world was crumbling. He could be taken from her.

No. She shook away the thought. 'Have they?' she shouted.

'You're right, they won't,' Alawani said, shaking his head.

L'ọrẹ let out a deep shaky breath and pulled him into an embrace. 'Damn these trials and rituals, damn the Holy Order and their murderous ways.' She pulled away and wiped the tear that hung on his eyelids. 'This is what you'll do. You'll go about your life like normal. Like you were born to. A prince with no claim, no title, no responsibilities. And if for some senseless reason the gods call you their own, you tell them no.'

'Your father left the priesthood and look at his life. He's an outcast. He's been branded a –' Alawani didn't complete his sentence.

Her eyes widened, and she could feel her fists clenching with rage. The only thing that kept her from punching him was the crestfallen look on his face. He knew he'd gone too far.

'I'm sorry,' he said quietly.

L'orẹ leaned in closer to him. 'There's no way your father wanted death for you.'

'I don't think he thought the trials would kill me.'

'But he's not here to keep you alive, is he?'

His eyes fell, and with those words she'd tipped the scales. It was her turn to be sorry.

'It's you and me against the world, Alawani. Against it all. Don't let the gods ruin your life and take everything from you. Please, I'm begging you.

'Promise me,' she said, her voice, soft with the night's breeze. 'If the Order calls for you, you'll choose us. Choose me. Choose this life with me.'

A light-hearted smile tugged at the edges of his mouth. His gaze turned towards the flames, fixed as though the dancing sparks spoke to him.

The pillar cracked again. The deep split branched off in all directions. The lonely life she had lived before he came into her world threatened to return.

L'orẹ brought out a knife from her pocket, drew a cut across her palm and handed the blade to him. He looked at her, his jaw dropping in surprise. He hadn't seen her do it, so the blood startled him. But he knew what she meant.

'Nothing in this world binds stronger than the words of oath spoken in blood. Even the gods won't dare break it,' she said, her voice cracking. 'If one breaks it they will go mad; this is your way out of whatever oaths they want to bind you to.'

He stared at her bleeding hand for so many heartbeats that she worried he might not agree to the oath. But finally, he took the knife from her and made a similar cut on his palm.

L'ọrẹ placed her bleeding palm in his and said, 'Us against the world. Till the sun falls from the sky.'

Alawani's face softened into a smile, and he nodded in agreement. He intertwined his fingers with hers and squeezed, then lifted the bond to his chest. 'Us against the world. Till the sun falls from the sky. This is our vow.'

To seal the oath, he turned on his agbára and waited for her to awaken hers.

'Close your eyes,' she whispered.

His forehead creased in a frown as he contemplated her request.

'Do you trust me?' L'ọrẹ prompted.

He sighed heavily, his shoulders sagging in resignation before he obeyed. Gently, she led both their hands into the flames. One heartbeat. Two heartbeats. Three heartbeats. His powers would protect him from the heat, but she had nothing to protect her. Only the will to keep her secret hidden. So even as the flames burned her skin, she said in unison with him, 'Hand to flame, we burn the same.'

The moment lasted only a few heartbeats, but she felt every sting of the fire. She clenched her jaw to keep from screaming and allowed him to pull her into an embrace, and it was all she could do not to cry in his arms.

Her hand hadn't burned but the pain was so agonizing she felt dizzy and allowed her body to rest on his, placing her head in the crook of his neck.

'Tomorrow,' L'ọrẹ said abruptly. 'Tomorrow we'll get tattoos.'

Alawani cocked his head. 'Tattoos? You literally have no tolerance for pain.'

L'ọrẹ smiled and glanced at the flames, then hid her bloody palm. 'You'd be surprised.'

'Are you sure?' Alawani said.

L'ọrẹ nodded furiously. 'You can draw the design.'

'You really don't have to,' Alawani said, smiling softly. 'But if you're sure,' he added when she raised an eyebrow, 'I know a place.'

'Perfect, I'll get paper and you can sketch something for us,' she said as she walked towards her house.

She'd heard once that tattoos were a constant reminder of an oath. So even when she wasn't with him, he'd see it and remember. At least this way, she'd keep him in her life. A blood oath was sacred and couldn't be broken. Not even by the gods of the sun and sands.

In her mind, the crack in the pillar remained, but now it was sealed and held in place by blood.

Ẹni ejò bá ti bùjẹ rí, bó bá rí ekòló, yóò họ
Whoever had once been bitten by a snake,
would flee at the sight of an earthworm

5

Ìlú-Ìmọ̀ – The Home of Knowledge
Second Ring, Kingdom of Oru

L'ỌRẸ

The next morning L'ọrẹ's muscles ached from the fight in the arena, and her palm stung every time she tried to make a fist. She quietly went about her work as her father's apprentice, waiting for the perfect time to sneak out of the house. She hid the tattoo sketch that Alawani had drawn the night before inside her boot, and waited for the perfect opportunity to return to Ìlú-Ọba.

The room her father worked in was both a library and a workshop – the largest room in their house. For making books while surrounded by books. The thought excited her when she was younger, but she was grown now, and she knew the truth. Bookbinding was a boring business. It was just the two of them, alone on the far edge of Ìlú-Ìmọ̀, living as outcasts.

Baba-Ìtàn called out instructions from his work table without raising his head, as he often did. 'Wash your hands before touching the papers.'

L'ọrẹ looked at the clean bowl of water he'd left and sighed. Her hands were already clean. But she didn't say that. She quietly obeyed, turning her back to him so he didn't see that she'd washed only one hand, keeping the bandaged hand dry.

Making and binding a book took forever, and the endless paper cuts only made her more irritable.

'Make sure you measure correctly. We can't afford to waste anything.'

She bit back her words and squinted to find the right point to mark the paper.

Measure, cut, fold and repeat.

'Did you clean that bone folder before using it?'

Her back was turned to him, so he didn't see her roll her eyes. She knew he wasn't really expecting an answer. He just liked to go on and on about her work. It wasn't like she made mistakes every day. In fact, she hadn't ruined anything in two days. She was doing well.

L'ọrẹ removed the papers she'd placed in the cast-iron press and placed a new set between boards before tightening the clamp.

'Why are you grunting so much? Did you remember to put oil in that press?'

No. She'd forgotten. She brushed some used cooking oil on the joints and rubbed her hands on her apron before returning to her work table.

'Wash those hands again.'

Curse the sun. He was insufferable sometimes. She'd already wiped them. There was no need to do it again. She peeked at him. He was working quickly and precisely, loop-ing the needle and threading through the holes in the spine of the papers held firmly in the sewing frame. His head was still down. She was sure he hadn't looked up even once.

'It's not like the people of this town care how the books turn out,' L'ọrẹ said.

'If it's worth doing, it's worth doing well,' Baba-Ìtàn said.

'For what they pay us, it's not worth doing at all. Some books take days, and we get what? Two sun coins for a whole book?'

'It's enough not to starve, and that's all that matters.'

'Barely,' L'ọrẹ said.

'These people don't have to bring us any business at all. Yet they do.'

'You're the best bookbinder in the kingdom. They've got no choice but to come. And even then, they don't come when the sun is in the sky. They come like thieves in the night, too ashamed to let their neighbours know they need you yet not proud enough to pay a decent fee. Other bookbinders charge twenty suns, sometimes thirty! While we starve.'

'That's enough, L'ọrẹ,' Baba-Ìtàn said sternly.

'Neither does it stop them from trying to burn our house every other blood moon!'

'I said that's enough!'

L'ọrẹ ground her teeth to keep herself from talking back. It wasn't the right time to remind him that their lives would be much easier if they moved to another city. Maybe the third or fourth ring. Somewhere deep in the kingdom where no one would recognize them. But of course, she couldn't say that. Last time, he made her promise never to ask again.

L'ọrẹ sighed, returned to her papers, and as soon as she lifted them, she saw the black oil marks smeared on them. Curse the sun. She quickly folded the incriminating evidence, tucked it between two books on the shelf, and quietly washed her hands again.

'You've stained the paper, haven't you?'

She tensed up and her breath caught in her throat.

'Just don't throw it away. We'll use it for something else.' There was a lightness in his voice, and she thought she heard a chuckle, but still, she didn't dare look back just in case she was wrong. When he didn't say anything more, she turned to peep. She was right, there was a smile stretched across his face.

L'ọrẹ smiled and continued the rest of her work in silence. After binding the blank pages from the night before, she still had a tower of papers to stack and bind, but she was running out of time. If she wanted to make it to the capital before sundown to meet Alawani for their tattoos as they'd agreed the night before, she'd need to leave soon. She looked at the time beads on her wrists. Eleven red beads and one gold one – the gold represented the sun and the moon. At noon, the gold bead shone like the sun, and at midnight it turned white. This, of course, worked only for those who had agbára oru, which was everyone except her and Baba-Ìtàn. Bodies without warmth, souls without agbára. Though unlike Baba-Ìtàn, she was born this way; he had traded his agbára for a different kind of power and ultimately lost everything. So though her father could live openly as an outcast, L'ọrẹ – a well-trained fraud – had to use old magic he secretly taught her to create an illusion of the powers that eluded her.

'Come here,' Baba-Ìtàn said, startling her out of her thoughts.

L'ọrẹ jumped to her feet, wondering if her father knew what she was planning.

'Come,' he repeated, dragging the word. 'I need some wax; light up the lantern and get the candles.'

L'ọrẹ sighed in relief and walked over to the chest by his desk. She pulled out a heavy lantern made of glass and iron, and a couple of candlesticks. When she was younger, Baba-Ìtàn had taught her the names of all the old gods, and when she called only one answered. Ṣàngó – the god of fire and thunder.

She took a deep breath and whispered the words that sparked flame when spoken, 'Mù'ná jáde.' The lantern blazed with fire, and she lit the candles and handed them over to her father. He nodded in approval at her precision with the spell. She didn't *have* to whisper when she was home – after all, Baba-Ìtàn had been the one to teach her the words she needed to fool everyone. But she'd gotten used to keeping this secret; whispering was now second nature.

Most importantly, she couldn't risk using spells in outright visible ways. Even when L'ọrẹ used her blades, her hands remained wrapped to hide the fact that they did not glow golden as her steel did. Power without hands that glowed meant old magic, and old magic meant death.

No one could know her secret – not even Alawani – or she'd probably be killed for being the weak link in the kingdom. If one person could be without agbára, then maybe they were at risk of losing their gods' given gift as well. The only thing L'ọrẹ was sure of was that, if discovered, her father would die with her for concealing the truth.

She spoke to her time beads and the eleventh one lit up. One to noon. Her father was lost in his work with the wax so she quietly walked out of the room and snuck out of the house before he could notice her absence.

As soon as L'ọrẹ crossed into the centre of the capital a few light beads later, heading towards the tattoo salon, a soldier grabbed her arm and shoved her into the growing crowd.

'Move! Move! You there, olóshì, don't let me come there! You, move! Move your feet!' The orders came from a soldier who was using his heated sword to herd people together.

L'ọrẹ pulled the hood of her cloak firmly over her head, still trying to figure out what was happening when her eyes fell on the raised platform in the distance. She'd come to the capital on the worst of days. The crowd turned into a frenzy as more soldiers appeared. A few people carried their children and ran as fast as their legs could go. Some tried hiding, but the soldiers had come in squads, and there was nowhere to hide. Others walked on, allowing the soldiers to lead them towards the raised platform. L'ọrẹ found herself stuck in a sea of heads, suffocated by rancid body odour.

A darkened chopping block sat in the middle of the platform, and on the ground in front of it was a large fire pit already ablaze and roaring. Time passed slowly, and when the people quietened down into low murmurs, two priests of the Holy Order climbed onto the platform, their maidens at their side.

'The time for judgement is now!' the first priest shouted to the crowd. He wore white robes with red sashes across the waist and a white Abetí-Ajá – a cap with two flaps on both sides of his head like dog ears.

As the priest began speaking, temple maidens climbed onto the platform wearing long gowns with sleeves reaching their feet, the same shade as the priest's coral beads. L'ọrẹ wasn't fooled by how delicate the dresses made them look. The low-cut plunge that showed their bronzed glowing skin and the high slits were a distraction for anyone who didn't know that beneath all that was a deadly assassin with knives in places they shouldn't be.

Soldiers led a weeping trio bound in chains onto the platform. L'ọrẹ recognized the black bonds immediately and knew the crime they'd committed. She tried to squeeze out of the packed crowd, but every move seemed to pull the crowd tighter against her body.

'These people have shamed themselves,' the priest continued. 'They claim that because they are from Ìlú-Idán they have the right to use the magic of their ancestors. But I say who are they to use what the gods have claimed as theirs? Do we all not exist to serve the gods? How then can we permit such disregard for their laws? They've shamed us all and threatened to bring down the wrath of the gods on our kingdom.'

The low murmurs grew louder as people's curiosity started to rise above their fears.

L'ọrẹ tried to move even further away from the front, but she was stuck. She was just three lines from the fire pit, and the wind brought the smoke into her eyes. She closed them, partly because of the burn and partly because she remembered the last time she watched the priest give a speech like this. She knew what was going to happen next. The urge to be sick hit her suddenly, overwhelming and intense.

The priest spat in the direction of the bound three. 'Old magic is forbidden in this kingdom for a reason! The gods of the sun and sands have blessed us all with their agbára. No child of Oru is born without the magic of the sun. Yet, these people mock our gods and their blessings.' He spun towards the crowd. 'We priests of the Holy Order are permitted to use old magic as compensation for the sacrifice of giving up our agbára in service of this kingdom. If not for greed, why would you want even more power? When you take from that which is not yours, you mock our sacrifice! When you call upon the old gods for magic and spells, you defy the gods of the sun and sands that have blessed you with agbára.'

L'ọrẹ eyed the three in chains. The man looked lost, a pained stare on his face. The young girl next to him was shivering right under the desert sun; she couldn't have been any more than fifteen first suns. As for the older woman next to her, if she was as afraid as the others, she didn't show it. Her face was like carved stone. She didn't blink or move an inch the entire time L'ọrẹ had her eyes on her.

L'ọrẹ winced as the second priest slammed the staff in his hand on the platform to quiet the crowd. Her hands moved to her crescent necklace, something she always did instinctively when panicked, and she rubbed against its smooth blue surface. Were they really so cruel as to kill a young girl? In truth, she didn't expect anything less from the priests who'd ruined her father's life. She glared at them with disdain, and tears stung her eyes as the man in chains walked forward.

'Àwọn t'egún n bẹ l'orí wọn – these ones are cursed! They are a stain on our kingdom, weeds that need uprooting. We do this to cleanse our land and temper the anger of the gods, lest we all burn for their sin.'

The people murmured in agreement. They were the real cowards, not her or her father. Was no one even going to beg for them or try to help? They all swallowed the priest's words like poison-laced wine. Their fear was replaced by apathy, and an uproar filled the air. Soon, the crowd shouted curses. They wanted the land cleansed and their families safe. They wanted the prisoners – the users of old magic – dead.

L'ọrẹ had learned to use old magic since the moment she realized she had no agbára. Her father had taught her just enough to create the illusions she needed for her blades and time beads. And so, every time she spoke those words, she knew she risked being put on a platform like this, but she had no other choice. After many first suns of practice, L'ọrẹ had realized that the old god she called upon needed only the smallest of whispers to awaken her blades. Ṣàngó's fury was always on the tip of her tongue, needing no coaxing to come alive. But these people on trial weren't like her. They didn't need tricks to survive. They had agbára-ignited cores, yet they sought more power from the old gods. Was that not greed? She couldn't help but wonder how easy it was for them to have avoided this fate.

She looked up at the sound of heavy boots climbing the platform. The masked executioner was nearly seven feet tall, his body at least twice the size of anyone else's. He dragged his heavy axe across the wooden platform, and the clawing sound made L'ọrẹ realize just how real it all was. She should've never left home today. Behind him was a young girl who wore a white wrapper tied firmly to her chest. She had a clean-shaven head and white dots all over her skin, and in her hand was a brown calabash.

The events that followed happened so quickly that all L'ọrẹ could do was stand with her hand over her mouth, eyes unable to move from the horror playing out before her. The man in chains walked up to the young girl in white and whispered into her ear. The girl, in turn, whispered into the calabash gourd and nodded, confirming his àṣírí – his secrets would outlive him.

The man knew where to kneel. The axe knew where to fall. His head dropped like an orange from a tree and rolled to the feet of one of the maidens, who picked it up by his thick hair and tossed it into the fire pit.

Were they cheering? L'ọrẹ looked around in disgust. They were. Of course they were. Most people in Ìlú-Ọba didn't know how to use old magic, so they never had to worry that it could be their sons or daughters up there on the platform.

The other young girl's scream was cut short with the swift axe. L'ọrẹ closed her eyes and placed a firm grip on her throat as if holding her neck in place. That could be her. One whisper too loud, one random stranger with a wolf's hearing and that would be her up there. Her breaths came in short uneven bursts, and her sight blurred. Her fingers trembled as she lifted them to cover her mouth. Every part of her burned with hatred for the Holy Order. For their vile acts and for herding all who were out and about into the town square to witness their atrocities. If she'd known that there would be a reckoning today, she'd never have left her house. Why had she?

Alawani. She'd completely forgotten about him between

the chaos and the bloodshed. She looked around, stretching and standing on her toes. Was he here? She hoped he wasn't caught somewhere in the crowd. After leaving hers the night before, they'd planned to meet at the tattoo salon not far from where she was now, but even as she stretched, there was no sign of the prince.

The last woman still stood defiantly, refusing to move from her spot. One of the maidens moved closer, shouting at her, but the woman didn't budge. The young girl dotted in white walked over to the older woman, offering her a chance to say her àṣírí, but she refused. A silent plea for her to offer up her secrets, but the woman was unyielding. The maiden got impatient and put her hand firmly against the woman's neck and squeezed. Still, the woman didn't move, clearly choking but refusing to speak.

'If she wants to forsake the afterlife as she's forsaken her gods, so be it,' the maiden said.

L'ọrẹ thought she saw the hint of a smile right before the maiden awakened her agbára. They all heard the scream before they saw the glow in her palm. The scream didn't last long as the maiden burned her way through the woman's throat, sending her into a world of pain and keeping her secrets lost forever.

The smell of burnt flesh filled the air.

The maiden took the axe from the executioner, grunting under its weight. She chopped off the woman's burnt head and tossed it into the fire.

The priest gave a slow, approving nod. 'I don't need to remind you all of the laws of the land, yet I will so no one can say they didn't know. Only those called by the gods, those who've sacrificed their agbára to the gods, may use the old magic. I hope that this here today burns into your minds the laws you must live by. I hope this is the last day of judgement we'll ever see. As you return to your homes, remember that our eyes are everywhere. The gods' eyes are in the sands. They see everything. If we discover that you are hiding anyone using old magic, you'll burn together with them. May the gods bless the sands beneath your feet.'

'And the sun above!' replied the crowd in unison.

All but L'ọrẹ, who was too stunned to speak. This wasn't the first day of judgement she'd been forced to watch, but she'd never seen anything like what the maiden just did – the pure cruelty of burning that woman's throat. She felt a chill as the warm breeze blew across her sweat-drenched skin.

Her mother had been a maiden. Did she also send people to their death with a smile on her face? L'ọrẹ imagined herself lying headless on the platform. And as the maiden yelled out the sacred prayers, L'ọrẹ imagined her mother standing there, holding her own severed head, leading the crowd to chant, 'Abomination,' before tossing it into the fire.

L'ọrẹ shut her eyes and covered her ears from the noise of the crowd. No way her mother was anything like these maidens. If she had been, the Order wouldn't have killed her for breaking their laws by birthing a child. A maiden with a child was a dead maiden, Baba-Ìtàn often said when he recalled the story of her mother's end. Without him protecting and hiding her from the Order, L'ọrẹ would have met the same fate her mother did. Was this how they killed her? Did her mother die refusing to bow to their will or did she crumble and fall, headless, into a fiery pit?

L'ọrẹ fought her way out of the crowd, forcing the hot desert air into her lungs. No longer able to fight the urge to throw up, she bent over and lurched onto the ground. She eyed a woman who acted like that was the worst thing she'd seen today while standing mere yards from the headless bodies still on the platform. Her throat burned, and the sour taste in her mouth only made her feel even sicker. She wanted to go home. Baba-Ìtàn was right, she shouldn't have gotten so used to going to the capital. If she was ever caught, it'd no doubt be here.

Alawani. She had to find him. She had to remind him of their oath. The Holy Order took her mother from her and ruined her father's life; she wouldn't let them take Alawani's life too. If she told him what she'd seen today, there was no way he'd ever want to be a priest for the gods of the sun and sands. Not while she lived.

*Behind closed doors and in the whispers of night
the gods gaze down upon the kingdom through the
warm gaze of the blood moon.
The gods make their choice from within
the six rings of Oru.
A boy is culled from each ring surrounding
the Sun Temple.
These chosen ones are called Àlùfáà – priests.
Those who survive the journey to the sun
will be called to be priests of the Holy Order.*

6

Ìlú-Ọba – The Capital City
First Ring, Kingdom of Oru

L'ỌRẸ

L'ọrẹ kept still as the older man dug his hot-inked needle into her back. As it pierced her skin, she distracted herself from the pain by keeping her eyes fixed on the row of ants making away with clumps of chewed sugar cane scattered across the sandy wooden floor. Alawani hadn't been at the shop when she arrived from the Holy Order's vile demonstrations, and while she could've gone back home, she needed to prove to Alawani how committed she was to their pact. If she were being honest, she needed him to show how committed he was too, and yet he wasn't here.

She tensed her body against the table. Her fingers firmly gripped its frayed edges, digging splinters into her skin. She squeezed her eyes, trying to keep the tears from falling every time the needle tore through her. Like a hammer to a nail, the short rhythmic taps of the stick sent spikes throughout her body. She repeatedly took deep breaths and forced air out of her lungs to keep herself from fainting.

The old man muttered, 'Even person wey get belle no do reach this one, Wetin do you? Abeg dey one place make this circle no turn square.'

L'ọrẹ stilled for a moment then peeped at the entrance

to the shop. No sign of Alawani. Hoping he was fine and just late as usual, her attention returned to the needle point going in and out of her back. Why did she ever think it was a good idea to get a tattoo from a man whose shop ceiling was a thin sheet of metal rusting in more places than she could count? She sighed. She'd been the one to ask for it. Insist on it even. She could already see her father's face scrunched with tight, angry lines when he saw what she'd done. But getting the double rings of fire inked into their skin was the perfect reminder of her and Alawani's bond. She could've waited for him, but if her gut was right and he was having doubts, she hoped seeing her inked skin would remind him of their sacred pact.

The man placed the needle down and picked up another. From the cracked mirror, L'ọrẹ could see him channel his agbára to his hands and use his fingers to burn and steril-ize the sharp end of the new tool. The next puncture sent pain throughout her body. That definitely hit bone. L'ọrẹ clenched her jaw and forced herself to swallow the scream that rose from her guts.

'E jọ́ọ́, sir, are you sure no one came here earlier today asking for the same tattoo?' she asked, still looking back. The artist was, no doubt, ready to pin her down if she kept dis-turbing his work.

'I told you before. You are my first customer for today.'

She peered at him when he said nothing more, then quietly lay back down on the table. It wasn't lost to her that every strike of the needle felt harder and deeper, but she didn't care anymore. Something was wrong.

'Oga Busco! Oga Busco!' a young man came shouting into the shop. 'Dem say the prince na Àlùfáà. All of Ìlú-Ọba wan craze,' he said, practically bouncing. 'I never hear this kain thing before for my whole life, abi you don hear am before?'

L'ọrẹ sprang up from the table. 'What did you just say?'

'Ọmọ'ba Alawani, the one and only son of our late king, e don accept the call to be Àlùfáà just today! Them say hc go enter the trials for priesthood,' the man said enthusiastically.

'Liar!' L'ọrẹ barked at him. 'Who told you that?'

'Everybody don hear am. You no hear as kasala don burst for outside?' the man replied, a deep frown etched on his face.

L'ọrẹ's head spun, and it wasn't the pain from her sore skin. Her sight blurred, and she groaned as she climbed off the table. The tattoo was just below her left shoulder, and she flexed her arm to bring it back to life. She could hardly steady herself.

'Sit down, jọ̀ọ́. I never finish,' Oga Busco said. 'The gods no fit allow royalty become Àlùfáà. Abi the law don change?'

The man who brought the news shook his head. 'E be like everything don scatter because na the High Priest been call the prince, na e the prince follow am go temple.'

'The prince go die for that temple,' Oga Busco said plainly. 'If hin try enter that trial, na death go meet am for there.'

L'ọrẹ jumped off the table and grabbed her cloak. Blood rushed into her head, and everything around her seemed to buzz.

She kept walking, one shaky step after the other. Crimson trickled down her back like rain. Through the haze, she could hear the same words – *The gods have spoken. The prince is Àlùfáà* – over and over again as she walked through the stream of people heading towards the palace.

Rage blinded her as she stomped through the cobbled streets that led to the palace. The gods had started looking for her trouble again. Ordinarily, nothing they did or said interested her. Now they'd crossed the line.

As she crossed the bridge that separated the royal island

from the rest of Ìlú-Ọba, the river reflected the sun's waning light. Crushed on every side, pain surged through her like lightning, and she yelled so loudly that the people around her stopped and moved out of her way. She marched through, holding her blood-stained arm, her anger growing with each passing moment. So this was why Alawani hadn't come with her? Why would anyone choose near-certain death over life? His life was something she could only dream about having. He was the prince. He had everything he'd ever want and yet no obligation to his people. Most of all, he had her.

What else did he want?

Did Alawani really want to be a priest of the Holy Order? To spend the rest of his life as a shadow of his former self, a slave to the Order, and executioner of all whom they deemed worthy of death? He was risking everything – his life, his family, and any chance of having a family of his own. Even as an outcast, if she was offered life in the sanctuary of their order, she'd never take it. So how could he?

The sound of the dùndún welcomed L'ọrẹ onto the island, playing a tune she couldn't get out of her head. The talking drum didn't care how you felt; when it spoke, you listened. The drummers held the hourglass-shaped drums firmly under their arms and beat the flat animal-hide surfaces with curved sticks. The tone made the crowd grow wild. L'ọrẹ wearily eyed the masquerades that danced in the circle made for them by the crowd. She watched their tall figures dance, their feet barely touching the floor. The fringes of their colourful fabrics swayed with the wind, their faces well hidden beneath masks of straw. Nothing good could come from this.

The sun had nearly set when L'ọrẹ reached the first of the palace gates. It never ceased to amaze her how different the oasis that was the royal island was from the dusty haze that was the rest of the kingdom. The clear waters that sprang into the air from the fountains and the deep green plants that decorated the surroundings always drew her attention. Hardly a speck of sand could be found through its cobbled streets. If not for the sun that shone down on the rich and poor alike, the royals of Oru would not have noticed that their kingdom was a desert.

As she walked in with the others who had come to witness this unprecedented event, she noticed the long shadows cast by the row of ten-foot-tall golden statues of the former kings and queens of Oru. Opposite them, on her left, were the bronze statues of their regents wearing their priestly robes. For every king or queen that died, there was a regent who held the throne after them until the firstborn son and heir had seen eighteen suns. During that time the regent's role in the kingdom was one of dual authority. They also held the position of High Priest of the Holy Order. The rulers of Oru had lived and ruled as the gods demanded. And there she was in the middle, forcing her way through, trying to change the will of the gods.

As she stormed through their path, she felt the heat of their judgment on her sore skin. She didn't dare look up at them until she reached the end of the walkway. The soaring towers of the enormous buildings in front of her still felt as intimidating as the first time she had seen them. The palace grounds were the most magnificent thing L'ọrẹ had set eyes on in her life. The vast dome-shaped building that housed the Lord Regent was surrounded in a half circle by five large mansions, one for each of his councils. And behind those were smaller manors that housed the rest of the royal court.

L'ọrẹ raced towards the south side of the palace, away from the group that had crossed onto the royal island with her. Her face contorted in rage when she reached the door-step of Alawani's quarters and saw that some of the crowd had gotten there before her. They'd grown louder and had already planted the vase of sinking sand next to his door. A ritualistic sign that the gods had spoken, and the people accepted his calling despite his position as prince. Anger flared in her chest, and the sting of the needle still burned in her back – a reminder of what she'd begun and what she had to lose.

Ìbẹ̀rẹ̀ ogun là ń mọ̀; Ẹni kan kì í mọ ìparí i rẹ̀
The beginning of war is what anyone knows;
no one knows how it will end

7

The Royal Palace, Royal Island, Kingdom of Oru

L'ỌRẸ

L'ọrẹ ran between the palace walls just like Alawani had shown her when they were younger and passed through a hidden door into a large, gilded room. And there he was. Robed in white and knelt before the fireplace, his hand aglow with agbára, touching and whispering into the flames that held the essence of the gods. His voice was a soft echo that filled the room. He turned and looked at her with his eyes the colour of flame. Her heart sank, and her vision blurred as hot tears stung her eyes. He had accepted the call.

'What in the godsforsaken names are you doing?' she screamed at him.

She ran towards him and knelt next to the fire he prayed to. 'Get up.'

He ignored her.

She shoved him. 'The things you'd have to do, Alawani. With the Order, you either survive their trials or you succumb to death. There's no way out,' her voice trembled. 'To fail is to die.' She hugged him. 'Please don't go. Just say no. Just say no, please.'

She held his face with both palms as tears rolled down her cheeks. His watery eyes looked everywhere but hers, though prayers stopped spilling from his lips. His head fell. She moved in closer and lifted his face again, forcing him to look at her. 'Stay.'

'My father –' he started to say.

It had been many first suns since the late king died and Lord Regent Babátúndé took over control of the kingdom. And while the kingdom mourned the loss of their king for many blood moons, Alawani remained beholden to his father's legacy – and in the shadow of the king's last words.

'You don't have to do what he would have wanted,' she said. 'He's got no control over you. You're his son, not his heir. He can't give orders from the grave! He can't command you to join the Holy Order. They are murderers and you are not. You are not an Àlùfáà!'

She followed Alawani's gaze to the portraits of the king and the Lord Regent hanging next to each other on the wall. Their dark eyes looked right into her soul. She saw the unmistakable resemblance between the king and Alawani. The law was the law, and the law demanded that the spawn of a king must never inherit the throne or be called Àlùfáà. Their system depended on it; the king or queen was always gods-chosen. No one, no matter how powerful, could choose when a child was born or in what order the High Priest's children would be born, so they entered this world as the gods willed, selected neither by man nor blood. In that way, the gods had already chosen their firstborn and heir long before they arrived at birth. Alawani was a prince in name alone, just like every prince or princess before him. He didn't rule or govern. He had the freedom he needed to live his life as he pleased, without duty, pain or sacrifice.

But on his deathbed, Alawani's father had decided otherwise for reasons L'ọrẹ could not quite understand, and from her last conversation with him, neither did Alawani.

'I have to honour my father's dying wish,' Alawani replied quietly.

She peeled her bandage and raised her hand to his face. 'Does this mean nothing to you?' She turned to show the tattoo on her back. 'And this? Does our oath mean nothing?'

Alawani looked up at the sand portraits. 'The Holy Order has announced my name. I guess they used that loophole, after all. The Regent's council agreed to support them because, as I told you, no one from this trial will ever be High Priest or Lord Regent, so there's no chance of me getting anywhere near the throne. So, technically, they aren't breaking the law. Even the people agree. They have placed the sinking sand at my doorstep. It's already begun.'

She stared at him as he spoke. Looking into his eyes, she saw the truth. He'd accept this calling, and he would die for it. 'You swore an oath to me! A blood oath!'

Before Alawani could speak, a temple maiden burst through the doors with guards on her heels. She stormed in wearing a blood-red dress that plunged deep and swayed with the breeze that followed her into the room. Her figure reminded L'ọrẹ of Baba-Ìtàn's hourglass. Her smouldering dark eyes pierced through L'ọrẹ as her black braids swung in thick waves behind her. The maiden's every step rang with the sound of her numerous pieces of jewellery clanging together, from the drooping rings on her ears to the anklets that graced her legs. She moved with purpose towards Alawani as though he was the only one in the room and pulled him to his feet. 'The Order is waiting for you.' She cupped his face in her hand. 'Your journey to the sun begins now.'

Her voice was soft but stern, and L'ọrẹ couldn't help but notice how her hand lingered in his. She immediately knew who this temple maiden was and what she'd be to Alawani. The image left a sour taste in her mouth as she imagined the man she thought would always be in her life, binding himself to another in an oath much like the one he'd made with her. Maidens and their priests – everyone knew what happened between maidens and their priests. The bond that surpassed even marriage. She'd often wondered if her parents had that bond, if she'd been born out of love or duty to the Order. L'ọrẹ cringed at the thought.

The maiden must have noticed L'ọrẹ's red eyes and dripping nose because she said to Alawani, 'It's a privilege to be chosen to journey to the sun and an even greater honour to return to the world of men to guide us. Your glory days are ahead of you.'

'If he survives,' L'ọrẹ seethed.

An irritated look crossed the maiden's face, like L'ọrẹ's voice was a fly buzzing in her ear.

'And who are you?'

L'ọrẹ stepped to her, 'I'm his family.'

The temple maiden gripped Alawani's hand tighter. 'The Prince Àlùfáà has a new family. Where he is going, his past cannot follow.' She scowled. 'He can't be associated with cowards.'

'Say that again!' L'ọrẹ shouted.

'L'ọrẹ, please,' Alawani said.

'Guards, get her out of here!' the temple maiden shouted.

In moments, the guards had drawn their swords and stepped towards her. Alawani's agbára shone through his raised palms, ready to protect L'ọrẹ. 'No!' his voice echoed. He turned to the temple maiden, 'I want her here.'

The temple maiden glared at L'ọrẹ, and L'ọrẹ glared right back.

The room stilled.

'Please give us a moment, Milúà. I'll come out soon,' Alawani finally said to the temple maiden.

Milúà turned on Alawani. 'Whatever this is. End it. Now!'

she ordered and stormed out with the guards, leaving L'ọrẹ and Alawani alone in the prayer room.

Alawani rushed towards L'ọrẹ. He tried to hold her, but she stepped out of his reach. 'I'm sorry, Tèmi. I'm so sorry.'

Tèmi – my own. Her heart skipped in her chest despite her anger. How dare he call her that now? He no longer had the right to.

'I'll come back. I'll survive this,' he continued. The corners of his lips curved upward, hinting at a smile. 'I have to, or I imagine you would wage a war with the gods so great, the sun will hide from you.'

She turned towards the door, 'You have a new family now. I'm the past you mustn't look back on, isn't that it?'

He moved closer to her again and, this time, caught her in his arms.

She turned her face away from him. 'You can say no. I don't know how many times I need to say this for you to hear me. You don't have to do what he wants,' she said, pointing her chin to the king's portrait.

'The gods have chosen,' he said. Before she could speak again, he added, 'They chose me.'

'Oh! Alawani! You know they didn't choose you – the Holy Order did! Your grandfather is pulling your strings. Never, not once since the day of the First Sun, has a prince been chosen as Àlùfáà. Why don't you ask yourself why? Why now?'

'I don't know … I just – please, let me do this.' Alawani released her from his arms, holding on to her with only his eyes.

'Last night, you swore by blood. My blood. You promised me –' Her eyes caught the string of white beads on his wrist. The same ones she'd asked about and he'd slipped off the night before. She looked up at him. 'When did you get the call?'

'What?'

'Don't play dumb with me, Alawani. When you swore to me, did you already know?'

He silently pulled his hand away. She could read him like a book. So when his gaze fell, and he pursed his lips and pulled his brows together, begging with his face, she knew.

Blood rushed to her head, and she kept blinking to remove the black spots that filled her vision. A quivering rage consumed her, and her voice broke, 'You – you lied to me.'

He tried to speak, but no words came out of his mouth. It just hung open like a waste basket waiting for flies.

Finally, as the tears poured from his eyes, he said, 'I knew what was coming, but I wanted you to know – I want you to know that you – you. You are everything to me.'

She reached for the beads and pulled until they snapped and danced across the floor, bouncing like rain around them.

Alawani shut his eyes and inhaled and she thought he'd shout at her but instead, he held her face and wiped her tears. 'If death threatens, it's your face that I'll cling on to. It is for you that I'll survive this. For you, Tèmi.' He leaned in so close that his nose slowly moved to touch hers. He breathed in deeply as though inhaling all of her and exhaled in short ragged breaths. The space between them was so insignificant that even though his lips were not touching hers, she could feel them vibrating between soft silent sobs. The tension crackled, a charged silence enveloping them.

The world seemed to still, time slowing as they hovered, breaths mingling, on the cusp of a moment that held the promise of everything they'd dared not speak of. She hated him for what he was doing, for shaking her world so violently, destroying the pillars that kept her hidden and safe. Yet, she couldn't pull away. But she couldn't move any closer either. Even without hearing the words, she knew he was asking, *Can I kiss you?* And she desperately wanted to say yes, to do what she'd only done before in her dreams. But no. Her first kiss with him wouldn't also be her last. She wouldn't have him, only to lose him.

Time stood still, and she felt her heart pounding against his chest. Or was it his pounding against her? She held on to him so tightly she forgot to breathe, desperate to freeze time and keep him in her arms forever. Hating herself for not giving in. Hating him for waiting so long to hold her the way he did now. When he finally pulled away, their breaths came in short heavy gasps. She couldn't describe how she felt even if she tried. Fear, anger, longing – everything.

Her lips trembled, and tears rolled down her face as he placed a warm kiss on her forehead. That was what broke her. She couldn't fight it any longer. She raised her eyes to his, and the corner of his lips twitched. He rubbed her tears away with his thumb and lifted her chin.

'The Order is waiting. It's time to go.' Milúà's voice froze them in place.

L'ọrẹ shut her eyes and frowned. How could she hate someone she'd just met so much?

Alawani let out a deep sigh and lowered his head to rest on the nape of her neck. 'I'm so sorry, Tèmi.' Then he turned to follow the maiden out of the room. Those were his last words to her.

L'ọrẹ trailed behind them through the hallway to the main doors, where the royal guards kept the crowd at the bottom of the stairs from breaking the barrier.

Milúà glared at her as she led Alawani to the balcony over-looking the cheering crowd. 'We're witnessing history today!' she began, and the crowd quietened to hear her speak. 'Our gods cannot lie. They see everything and have called our prince as one of the six who will go through the trials to become Àlùfáà. Today, our Ọmọ'ba begins his journey to the sun!'

Loud cries filled the surrounding air.

L'ọrẹ stood behind them, watching from the shadows. She didn't want the world to see her break, but the tears didn't stop falling, and her lungs burned for air. She placed her hand over her mouth to muffle the sound of her sobs.

The crowd roared, and Milúà raised Alawani's hand above their heads. 'Send forth your prayers!'

'May your heart burn like the sun, bright, hot, and undying!' the crowd yelled back.

Milúà smiled at him and led him down to the heap of weapons, trinkets and jewellery that the people had brought to be blessed. 'Your people have brought these that you might bless them with the last of your strength.'

L'ọrẹ could feel her heart breaking inside her chest. Poking her with its sharp broken pieces, taking her breath away.

Alawani looked back to find her, but even though she could see him, she'd hidden herself too well for him to see her.

The people took hands full of sand and tossed them into the air, spraying it over themselves and everyone who stood around them. Alawani picked up a sword and held it over his head, releasing his agbára into the weapon. It turned fiery red. He raised the sword higher and yelled as it got hotter and brighter until it looked like it was in a blacksmith's fire. The people cheered as the blade grew hot and glowed but did not melt. Then, he fell to his knees, panting and sweating intensely.

In her mind, the bloody pillar cracked at its side as though someone had taken an axe to it, chopping it down like a tree, and she flinched as the phantom pieces flew at her. L'ọrẹ felt the urge to run to him and hold him up. But when she saw Milúà do precisely that, she remembered the temple maiden's words.

Where he is going, his past cannot follow.

And here are the rules that bind the kingdom:
Any priest can become a High Priest
Every High Priest must become the Lord Regent
Every firstborn of a Lord Regent must be Sovereign
Every child of a Sovereign must be no one
The call for Àlùfáà is the highest honour of a man's life
and the gods' decision is final.

8

The Sun Temple, Royal Island, Kingdom of Oru

ALAWANI

Later that night, Alawani stood quietly in a straight line with the other boys chosen to represent each ring of Oru in the stripping ceremonies. His terror rose with every breath, and he kept his eyes fixed on his feet as the temple maidens' eerie songs filled the room. The stripping chamber was deeper within the temple's gilded halls than Alawani had ever dared venture before.

The cold air filled his nostrils with the smell of rain, and he inhaled deeply. It didn't rain very often, so he knew the sky wouldn't weep that night, but still, he looked up. The hole in the dome-shaped chamber let in the moon's warm red light. Every thirty days, the moon shed its silver glow for this reddish tinge, the same colour as the sand beneath his feet.

A few paces from him were members of the Holy Order. Each priest of the Order stood alongside his assigned maiden. The maidens wore blood-red garments similar to Milúà's, with sheer veils covering them from head to waist like brides. He looked at Milúà and noticed hers was different. Her gown had gold-tipped sleeves that reached her heels, and she wore a gold belt across her waist – these signified she had not yet been bound to a priest. She was to be bound to him if he survived his journey – and she'd made it clear how she felt about that.

Earlier that evening, Milúà had prepared him for the ceremony.

'I didn't know the first stripping was tonight. I thought I'd have more time to prepare,' he said when she broke the news.

She looked him dead in the eye. 'You can never be pre-pared for a stripping ceremony. Keep your head down when you get in there, and for the love of all that burns, do not speak until spoken to.' She fussed over him, making sure his robe was white, spotless, and perfectly arranged across his bare chest.

When he tried to ask her more about what to expect from the ceremony, she glared at him and said, 'You have one job. Survive. That's all you have to do. When you feel like giving up, and death feels like a way out of your suffering, remem-ber the sound of my voice and know that if you die, I'll find whomever you care about most in this world, and I'll send them to you in the life beyond.'

Alawani didn't doubt that she meant every word, but still, he had to ask, 'Why do you care? Don't you just get assigned to another chosen one if I die?'

She shot him a dirty look. 'Let me make this clear. I do not want you, I do not want to be bound to you and you have no right to be here. When you climb that Red Stone and the gods see their mistake, they will burn out your core and leave you for dead. And I will be . . .' She sighed. 'Do you know what happens to a maiden whose Àlùfáà dies? I curse the day the Order asked me to be your maiden but that does nothing to change my fate now. We may not yet be bound in flesh but our lives are linked forever now. So don't die!'

'It's that easy, is it?' he said, raising an eyebrow.

She placed a cup in his hands. 'Here, drink this.'

He smelled it and squeezed his face. 'Is this bitter leaf water?'

'I don't know, just drink it.' When he didn't move, she added, 'Àlùfáà-Àgbà commands it. There's no scenario in which you don't and survive. Obey or die. Your choice.'

Alawani waited for more information, but Milúà remained still as a statue, eyes peering into him until he drank every last drop. When he was done, she took the cup and stormed out of the dressing room, leaving him with even more questions than he had had coming into the temple.

Now, in the stripping chamber, here she was, at his side, holding his hand.

'Stop shaking. They can smell your fear,' she whispered to him.

Bells rang in rhythmic sequences. Alawani tried not to jump as a ring of fire shot to life around them, and more temple maidens walked in and stood around the altar in a circle, dressed in white, holding fire lanterns and incense plates. Then, his grandfather walked in slowly, wearing a white crown with strings of cowries like a curtain obstructing his face from view. The old priest's floor-length agbádá was made of white and gold aṣọ-òkè with delicate embroideries around its edges. Àlùfáà-Àgbà leaned on his golden staff, which stood taller than himself. The top of it was shaped like a flame and adorned with gold and rubies. When the priest reached the Red Stone, all the other priests and maidens fell to their knees.

Milúà yanked Alawani down to his knees. 'Kneel.'

The High Priestess walked in next, dressed and veiled in gold garments similar to the other maidens' but covered in stones and sparkle, and also wearing a golden crown designed with tongues of flames. On the other side of the Elder Priest was his maiden and the former High Priestess of Oru. She was much older than the priestess and wore a gilded gele that reached for the sky instead of a crown. Alawani's first guess was that this was the mother of maidens.

The hall was silent for a moment and as side looks and whispers filled the room, Alawani noticed what everyone was likely talking about. The Lord Regent who was meant to take this ceremony was missing. His absence was intentional and Alawani couldn't shake the feeling that it had something to do with his presence there.

'Rise,' Àlùfáà-Àgbà finally said, taking over the ceremony. He lifted both arms into the air as if controlling them with strings. 'The gods of the sun and sands have chosen from among us the ones who are pure of heart,' he pointed at Alawani and the other boys who were now lined up before the Red Stone. 'Each one of you represents the best of your state, the best of our good kingdom. And here on this stone carved by the gods, you will fulfil your destiny.'

'Àṣẹ!' the priests and maidens replied in unison.

Àlùfáà-Àgbà's voice seemed to fade, and all Alawani heard was the sound of his own heartbeat. For the first time, he considered what would have happened to him if the gods truly hadn't called him. What if the Holy Order had made a mistake? To be chosen, to be Àlùfáà, meant the gods had searched your heart and found it pure – and this stripping ceremony was the true test. Alawani played back memories of his life in the blink of an eye. He wouldn't call himself a saint by any standard.

'Every decade since the day of the First Sun, many like you have come to the Red Stone,' Àlùfáà-Àgbà's voice rose louder than Alawani's thoughts and shocked him back to the present. 'They return their agbára to the gods who bless them with great power and pure hearts so that they might

99

have a greater purpose. Today you also become a conduit for the gods of the sun and sands, or you die a worthy death. Either way, the gods will decide.'

The priests started chanting in a low baritone. The temple maidens joined in a harmonious tune. And if he wasn't terrified out of his mind, he might have enjoyed the melody, but at that moment, it felt more like a siren's song that led only to death.

The first boy climbed the altar, led by his maiden. 'I bring before you Èyítáyò of Ìlú-Òdì, chosen by the gods, a saint among many,' the temple maiden called out as the boy climbed on the stone.

'May the gods bless his journey to the sun,' the room echoed.

Àlùfáà-Àgbà hovered his hands over the boy. 'Àlùfáà,' he said, nodding to the priests.

All the priests nodded in agreement, 'Àṣẹ.'

Then came the scream. The guttural sound that erupted from the boy's mouth was like nothing Alawani had ever heard before.

'Don't look,' Milúà said, squeezing his hand.

Alawani's gaze fell to the ground at her command. He clenched his teeth and shut his eyes. None of that blocked out the boy's screams. Panic flooded his senses, and he tried to force back his agbára, but when he looked at his hands, a dull glow shone through. He shook his trembling fingers and took in deep breaths. Somehow his agbára knew he was about to destroy it. He stared at his palms and forced the light to dim. Soon his hands would never glow again, his eyes would never turn gold, and his core would burn to ash. His royal blood made his agbára one of the most powerful in the kingdom. How would he live without it? His powers were an extension of himself; his essence, his soul.

Alawani's head shot up when the screams finally died out, and on the Red Stone was the limp body of the boy from Ìlú-Òdì. The gods had decided he wasn't Àlùfáà. Èyítáyọ̀ of Ìlú-Òdì was dead and the cries of his maiden filled the air. Alawani's body went cold with dread, and he wanted to run.

The next boy climbed the Red Stone, and the scream-ing began again. His maiden announced him as Bánkólé of Ìlú-Oníṣọ̀nà, chosen by the gods, a saint among many. Ala-wani dared to watch this time, and his mouth fell open as flame-coloured smoke rose from the boy, and the screams of agony filled the night air. The louder his voice, the louder the priests chanted until his voice was gone. All that echoed were the whimpers and sobs of a broken boy.

The next boy climbed the altar – Káyọ̀dé of Ìlú-Idán, chosen by the gods, a saint among many. Alawani's legs felt like they would give way. He couldn't do it. His time would come, and he wouldn't be able to move. He knew it. This must be why the priests never explained the details about what was done to strip them of their powers. This was a gruesome death. And while Alawani had always known the chance of survival was small, seeing it was something else. He wasn't confident he'd survive it. Not anymore. How in the name of all that burns were they supposed to survive all three stripping ceremonies?

The last boy before Alawani climbed the stone, and Ala-wani returned his gaze to the sand beneath his feet. He slowed his breathing and counted the number of steps he would need to cut through the circle of fire and out of the chamber. Then he heard his father's voice, as clear as though he was standing right next to him.

You are Àlùfáà. The gods have confirmed this to me. Death may come for us, but our line will never end.

He'd been so young when his father died that the memory

felt more like a dream to him. He remembered sitting still, filled with grief, not truly understanding what his father said yet holding on to his hand, praying that his king wouldn't die – praying to the gods of the sun and sands that death wouldn't find his father. He'd heard that kings never died and believed it with all his heart, so when his father first fell ill, he paid no attention to it. Until his grandfather came to him that evening telling him to sit by his father, for he may not make it to dawn – he didn't.

'Death may come for us, but our line will never end,' Alawani's voice trembled as he repeated the words now, a whisper under the screams of the boy on the stone.

Back then, Alawani didn't know the implications of what his father demanded of him. His father had looked at him sternly with weak eyes. Alawani had trembled under the weight of his father's words.

'Say it with me, boy!' his father had commanded.

Alawani had responded, tears in his eyes and fear in his voice – as was the case now, as Àlùfáà-Àgbà called his name from the altar.

Out of the corner of his eye, Alawani spotted a figure that hadn't been there when the rituals began. As the shadows cleared, he recognized his oldest friend, the crown heir.

He found himself unable to move from his spot, his eyes fixed on Tofa. His familiar face felt like a sign that his old life was pulling him back from the one he was about to walk into. The hall fell quiet, and looking around him, Alawani realized he was the last of the chosen ones to be called to the Red Stone. Milúà pulled him by his arm and led him to the altar when the Àlùfáà called his name for the second time. Alawani Ọmọtádé Àkanní of Ìlú-Ọba, chosen by the gods, a saint among many. Ọmọtádé – the child equal to the crown. That was what the name his father gave him meant, and as he lay on the altar, he felt the loss of giving up his connection to the crown forever.

His stomach clenched as Àlùfáà-Àgbà's hands moved over his body slowly. The stone was burning hot, and it took everything he had not to scream as his bare back sank into it. He wriggled until Àlùfáà-Àgbà pinned him down, with words that summoned the powers of the old gods. Àlùfáà-Àgbà's hands didn't glow and burn like everyone else's in the kingdom. Like all other priests, he'd given up his powers and this ritual would make Alawani like him. The journey to the sun started with returning the heat energy – the agbára oru that the gods of the sun and sands had given them at birth. This was his destiny. Afterwards, he would learn the old tongue and the magic of the gods long forgotten by many. It was an honour and privilege, or at least that's what he told himself, as fear threatened to consume him.

Somehow, Alawani found himself exactly where his father had promised he'd be. He was here now, and he was determined to survive. For what was destiny, if not the call of the gods?

The Elder Priest finally stopped, and nodded. 'Àlùfáà.'

One of the priests whispered to another, 'It's a shame that the Lord Regent allowed this to happen. The gods can't permit what they forbid. This is not right. A prince on the Red Stone. Abomination.'

'Mhnnn,' the priest next to him hummed in agreement.

Alawani didn't see the man who spoke but heard every word. And if he did, his grandfather would have done too. The Elder Priest froze, and Alawani's body tensed. Alawani realized what he'd been feeling in the moments before was not fear. *This* was fear. Àlùfáà-Àgbà's position and authority over all the priests in the Sun Temple was well known. A long time ago he had ruled over the entire kingdom. Now, the

Elder Priest ruled over nothing at all, officially. But within the Sun Temple, for as long as the reigning High Priest ruled from the palace as Lord Regent, the old man laid claim and exercised authority over everyone in the temple.

The room fell silent, and although Alawani couldn't see the priest who had spoken out of turn, he saw the anger on Àlùfáà-Àgbà's face.

'Bíọ́dún, do you question the choice of our gods?' Àlùfáà-Àgbà growled, calling the priest by his first name, stripping him of his official title of Àlùfáà. The words were a clear threat. 'Now we all know that none chosen here will ever be a High Priest or be burdened to sire an heir, not while the crown heir lives. So unless Bíọ́dún knows a reason why our future king won't live till old age, surviving many first suns and many stripping ceremonies, I can't imagine why the prince cannot be here. Should his survival not be decided by the gods?'

Àlùfáà Bíọ́dún spat to the ground, 'We cannot accept the son of an oath-breaker. Unlike those before him, the king did not fulfil a single promise he'd made to the rings of this kingdom. Even if he were to abandon the outer rings, how about we in the capital who support the stability of this kingdom? We can only thank the gods that, in his incompetence, he didn't oblige the requests of the outer rings. Imagine if he had lifted the ban on old magic as he had foolishly promised, or reduced the food tax on the third ring. How long before we'd have starved to death? Every priest in this temple knows what we lost when the king broke his promise to give us official positions outside this temple and governing authority in our respective rings. Should we now reward such abhorrent behaviour by defiling our Order with a family that has no integrity? I say to you, my brothers, Prince Alawani is not an Àlùfáà.'

The uncomfortable silence that filled the room extended awkwardly as the Elder Priest walked off the altar to where the other priests were gathered. The quiet was finally broken by the sound of the slap that fell upon the priest's face and rang through the air. 'How dare you sully my son's name in my presence?' Àlùfáà-Àgbà roared. 'Even in death, he is your king! Is your lust for power so great that you forget the low-born ill-bred pit the gods pulled you out from?'

Alawani was used to being called the oath-breaker's son. He'd never had anyone defend him before. Most of what he knew about his father was from the whispers of the towns-people. That tainted legacy alone made him unable to break the vows he made both to his father and the Order long before L'orẹ found a place in his heart.

All Alawani heard was the sound of his grandfather's heavy breathing, and he guessed that terror gripped the younger priest's voice. Only when Àlùfáà Bíọdún fell to the floor before Àlùfáà-Àgbà did Alawani see his face. The priest's eyes darted from left to right, and as panic seemed to overwhelm him, he tugged at Àlùfáà-Àgbà's garments, grunting. Àlùfáà Bíọdún opened his mouth, but no words came out. His fingers interlocked and folded inwards, touching his chest – the sign of deep regret and begging forgiveness.

Alawani's eyes widened. Oh, gods, Àlùfáà-Àgbà had seized the priest's voice with his magic – old magic.

Àlùfáà-Àgbà was unmoved. The old man looked silently at the others who stood around him as if passing on a warning. They all bowed their heads deeply, avoiding his gaze, pretending they did not even know the man who begged on the floor. Àlùfáà-Àgbà then placed his hands on the flailing priest, who begged at his feet, whispering words that Alawani couldn't understand.

Tension filled the air, and Alawani wanted it all to be over.

'Speak the truth and the gods will loosen your tongue,' Àlùfáà-Àgbà said finally to the priest.

Àlùfáà Bíọ́dún nodded and rose to his feet, still trembling. He coughed then tried speaking. Panic filled his eyes when no sound came out. Finally, Àlùfáà-Àgbà whispered a spell and nodded slowly, giving him permission to speak. Standing over Alawani, the priest declared with a trembling voice, 'The prince is Àlùfáà.' The priest's voice had returned in a whisper, and Àlùfáà Bíọ́dún must have known it was not nearly loud enough to please Àlùfáà-Àgbà, so he spoke louder, 'The prince is Àlùfáà.'

The room replied in unison, 'Àṣẹ,' agreeing with the priest's declarations.

Àlùfáà-Àgbà led the group in the ceremonial chant. The older man's bold features were wrinkled, and his voice sounded like an echo from a gong. His stern look convinced Alawani that if he were to hit Àlùfáà-Àgbà across the face with a rock, the rock would crack and crumble, leaving the old man's face unscathed. He felt like he was looking at himself through time. Was this what he would become? An old priest, staring down at another young boy who had been called and wondering how a lifetime had passed in what felt like the blink of an eye. Would he become just another priest beheading people for using magic meant only for the few? Would he lose himself to this dream he'd been pulled into? Or would he die today?

But when he looked into Àlùfáà-Àgbà's eyes, what he saw wasn't his future but his past. He saw himself and his father in him. He knew the voice and the face of the man who wore the cowrie crown because, since the day of his father's death, he'd feared that Àlùfáà-Àgbà, his grandfather, would one day bring him to this altar as Àlùfáà. Now, for the first time in over ten first suns, he was looking into those eyes, scared that the gods would reject him as they had so many before him.

The chanting stopped, and Alawani didn't recognize the

sound of his own screams. Pain surged through him, and he clenched his jaw so hard he thought his teeth might shatter in his mouth. He felt like he was engulfed in flames; blisters blossomed over his hands and his muscles felt like strings in a tight rope snapping off as the fire within consumed every inch of his body and mind. At that moment, he held on to a single thought. He'd promised her that he'd survive. His Tèmi. This was the time to hold on to that promise. Of all the vows he'd made, this was one he knew he couldn't break. So, he fought desperately to keep his essence in as his agbára was ripped out of him.

But in the end, he lost the fight.

Tí iná bá ń jó l'óko, màjàlá á ṣe òfófó
When a farm goes aflame,
the flakes fly home to bear the tale.

9

Gbàgede – The Arena, The Capital City, First Ring, Kingdom of Oru

L'ọRẸ

The next morning, L'ọrẹ was off to Gbàgede – the arena in the capital city. Her commander had only one rule: never visit the arena when the sun is in the sky. Due to the terms of her father's punishment, she wasn't supposed to be in the capital at all – and everything looked different in the sunlight. She remembered the first time she'd come to Gbàgede with her father in the dead of night, begging Command to train her, to give her a chance at rising above her bond to a traitor.

L'ọrẹ had only seen twelve first suns when Command made her swear her first vow. Promising that as long as she lived she wouldn't tell a soul about her training, and that she'd only train at night and only on nights when Command had sent for her. Back then, L'ọrẹ was as sure as the breath she swore upon that she'd never break that vow. She almost thanked the gods as she walked closer to the arena that it hadn't been a blood oath. For when blood oaths are broken so are the minds that swore them, and now was really not the time to lose her mind.

At the entrance to the arena were twin arching pillars connected at a midpoint where the sun's image sank deep into the stone. The sunken pit of the arena was home for her in many ways. It had broken and rebuilt her more times than she could count. She rubbed her fingers against one of the pillars, brushing off the dust to reveal the initials she and Alawani had etched into its side. In that pit, L'ọrẹ had found the two things she'd desperately needed: friendship and strength.

L'ọrẹ scanned the group training in the pit. She was looking for . . . there he was. 'Kòyà,' she called from behind a wall, keeping her face hidden inside her hood. Four first suns ago, Alawani had introduced her to Kòyà. Adékòyà – the one whom the crown saved from suffering. A name that portrayed his family's debt to the royal family, although L'ọrẹ never knew what that debt was. Kòyà never spoke about it and she had too many secrets of her own to go prying into others'.

Two kinds of people came to the arena. Royal guards, and those aspiring to be royal guards – hoping to be chosen to join the elite force one day, just like she'd hoped before her world began to crumble. They had a plan, she and Alawani – a good plan. She was to join the royal guard, and he was to take command as a captain in the royal army. But then the gods came calling.

Kòyà towered over the girl he trained with, but she seemed fast enough to evade the strike of his long limbs. He was shirtless, wearing only the clay-brown trousers assigned for training, and the girl he fought wore a matching ensemble that exposed her torso and legs, allowing for the high kicks she sent his way. Kòyà dodged her strike and his cloud of hair bobbed with every move; his bare chest was drenched in sweat, and his brown skin glistened in the light that illuminated the pit.

'Kòyà!' she tried to keep her voice low but also loud enough for him to hear. He didn't, but another trainee did. They turned, and she quickly hid behind the wall, hoping they wouldn't be curious enough to come looking for her.

She wasn't supposed to be in the arena, but she desperately needed to speak with Kòyà. Command's words echoed in her mind, reminding her of their deal: 'Not while the sun is in the sky.' If she were caught, she and her father would be punished – and if anyone suspected Command of training her, they would both be executed without trial. Showing favour to those the Holy Order had deemed unworthy was always going to end with their heads rolling into a firepit.

L'ọrẹ didn't hear Kòyà's footsteps, so when she turned to peek again, there he was, staring at her. She pulled him behind the wall.

'What are you doing here?' Kòyà asked, looking around. No doubt searching for the same person she'd been avoiding. 'If she sees you here, it's over,' he whispered, still looking over his shoulder.

'I had to see you. I need your help,' L'ọrẹ replied.

And as if seeing her for the first time, he stood and looked into her eyes, then pulled her into an embrace. 'I'm so sorry. I heard what happened.'

Curse the sun. He was making her cry again. She untangled herself from him. 'I need you to speak to your brother.'

'What do you need my brother for?'

'He's a royal guard, is he not? I need to know where Alawani is being held in the Sun Temple. Like a map or directions. Something. Anything. Your brother's girl is a maiden, isn't she?'

'Shh . . .' Kòyà covered her mouth with his palm. 'Curse the sun, L'ọrẹ, keep your voice down! Are you trying to get my brother killed?'

'I'm not asking for anything dangerous – just information. You don't have to get involved. I need to know –'

'You're asking me to commit treason! And you're asking my brother to do the same.'

'He doesn't need to know why you're asking.'

'No, L'ọrẹ. The answer is no. How can you ask me to do this? I don't know what you have planned, but Alawani accepted that call because he wanted to. You can't change his fate.'

'I'll ask someone else then,' she turned to walk away from him.

He pulled her arm, and her back pressed against the wall, his tall figure towering over her. He leaned down to her face. 'Please don't do this, L'ọrẹ. Don't go looking for trouble. The priests have killed for less. I'm begging you.'

'I have to,' she said, freeing herself from his grip. 'If I die, I die.'

He gestured with his hands, 'Why? Why can't you just let him go? He made his choice.'

Why couldn't she let him go? To the Order who destroyed her father's life, murdered her mother, and would gladly sever her own head. She lived in a constant state of fear and desperation, trying to claw her way out of the grip the Order had on her life. She wasn't just going to let them have her best friend and take everything from her. How much more would she lose to the gods of the sun and sands? No. They couldn't have him. Not while she lived.

'So you'll just let them torture him to death?' she spat back. 'I shouldn't have to beg for this. Help me. He's your friend too! And you'd be dead without him, and you know it. You owe him.'

'You don't know that he'll die. Many people survive the stripping. Your father did!'

'Alawani isn't my father, and this is different,' she said through gritted teeth. 'And even if he survives, what will he be without his agbára?'

'You mean what would he be without you?'

The question shocked her into silence. This wasn't about her. Why did no one else see what she did? Why was everyone just okay thinking that because Alawani had accepted the call, that was what he truly wanted? She couldn't believe that. No one wanted to die.

'He'd do this for you. He'd never give up on you. He never did,' she scowled.

Kòyà's eyes narrowed. She'd hurt his feelings, but she was right. The arena would have chewed up and spat out the lanky boy with lofty dreams of being a royal guard like his brother if Alawani hadn't protected him when he needed it most.

Finally, Kòyà let out a deep breath. 'I don't know that I can help you with this, knowing if you get caught, they'll burn you alive.'

'They won't catch me. Will you help me or not?'

Kòyà's eyes reddened, and he held her hand in his, quiet for a moment, then closed his eyes and nodded. 'I'll get my bags.'

L'ọrẹ watched as he walked back to the others and felt a pang of guilt in her stomach. She'd never felt anything for Kòyà in the way he wanted her to. Even when she could feel his breath on her, though she felt something within her flutter in her stomach, it never quite reached her heart. She'd decided a long time ago that she'd never ask anything of him. But now she needed him to help save the one she truly loved.

'Ahem, hhem.'

It was only the briefest rasp, but L'ọrẹ's heart sank like a stone dropped in water. She turned to find herself looking into the eyes of her commander. L'ọrẹ eyed Command's intimidating military uniform and the golden collar around her neck which bore the insignia of the royal house of Oru. The dust-coloured loose-fitting ensemble was firmly secure beneath the hard curves of the chest plate which covered her chest and torso like an armour made of tortoise shells. A glance at the strategically placed weapons, from the spiked gauntlets to the gold rings on each finger, made L'ọrẹ regret every step that had brought her to the arena today. She tried to explain herself, but the woman's raised eyebrows made the words choke in her throat. Just by being there, she'd broken her trust.

Command's gaze often made L'ọrẹ want to shrink, and after many years of seeing the tall and imposing frame of the woman behind the dead-eyed stare that her commander was famous for, L'ọrẹ had learned to stand up tall in her presence. But at that moment, she could hardly meet her eyes.

'Look at me,' Command said softly, her narrow dark eyes piercing into L'ọrẹ's.

L'ọrẹ saw the vein in Command's temples bulge, and she took a slow step back. Command closed the space between them, and the cowries in her hair smashed against each other, reminding L'ọrẹ of the dozens of people that had fallen to her commander's fury. Before L'ọrẹ was a woman who'd seen many battles and spent many years fighting the sand raiders that threatened the outer walls of Oru and returned whole without a single scar. Nothing on Command's body told of her fighting days other than the cowries that clung tight to her long greying locs. A woman of honour. A woman who was now likely to die at the hand of the Order for helping the coward's daughter, all because L'ọrẹ couldn't keep her promise of staying away when the sun was in the sky.

Command eyed the sunlight streaming into the pit and when her eyes landed back on L'ọrẹ again, they were red and full of fury. 'Why are you here?' she said, her voice a low husk that carried the tone of threat with every word.

L'ọrẹ didn't know what to say. She bent her knees to curtsy but didn't realize how fast she'd fallen until her knees crashed to the ground. She clenched her teeth to hide the pain and kept her gaze fixed on the stones.

'Look at me when I'm talking to you!'

L'ọrẹ's head shot up, and she slowly rose to her feet, her shoulders still hunched before the terrifying image of her furious commander. 'I came to see –'

'Are those tears?' Command seethed, and L'ọrẹ begged the ground to swallow her whole. 'In my arena? L'ọrẹ? So, this is about the prince, then. You came here to mourn?' Her face twisted as though the words left a bitter taste in her mouth.

'He's not dead yet,' L'ọrẹ retorted, more loudly than she would have liked, which made Command raise her eyebrows even higher.

'I warned you when you joined yourself to his hip like a twin that your paths were not to be merged. You did not listen. He has chosen his path, and the gods will decide his fate,' Command said. After a brief pause, watching L'ọrẹ struggle to find her next words, she continued, 'But I trained that boy. I know his strength. He's nothing without his agbára. He won't survive the journey to the sun. So, I ask again, why are *you* sneaking around my arena in the middle of the godsdamned day?'

L'ọrẹ stared at her, matching her stern glance but remaining silent.

Command scoffed, 'You come in here with red eyes and puffy cheeks like a widow in mourning. Crying for a boy and risking everything we've worked to achieve? You mock your training and insult me with this nonsense. You break your word. I trained you to be a warrior – a champion. When the gods call for Ogun, and you enter this arena to claim victory, will you cry for your opponent then, or will you burn them to ash?'

Tension filled the air, and the faces watching from the

edge of the ring seemed to know what she was thinking. She found Kòyà's face, and he slowly shook his head, telling her no. She's baiting for a fight. Don't fall for it.

'I raised you, L'orẹ. Here. In these very pits,' Command said quietly so only she could hear. 'I risked everything for you. Your father begged, cried, blackmailed – everything he could think of. His desperation was pitiful. Yet I agreed. I risked my life for you. Every time you came here in the dark of night was another night I could've been hanged for helping the coward and his daughter.' She looked around the arena, surveying the clusters of trainees already throwing glances and whispering. No doubt wondering why Command hadn't thrown L'orẹ out of her arena at first sight, as was the law. Her eyes returned to L'orẹ, cold and piercing; she leaned in even closer and whispered in a gritty tone, 'What do you think they'll tell their parents when they get home today? How long before the Lord Regent hears that I trained you to join his guard?'

Her words cut deep, and L'orẹ felt tears sting the back of her eyes, but she dared not let them fall. She'd broken her word and put her commander's life in danger. The law forbade people in the kingdom from helping her family. No aid, no food, no mercy. Nothing. And not even Command's station as part of the royal court or a commander in the royal army could keep her from death if the Order found out.

Every few blood moons, the trainees in the kingdom fought for a spot on the royal guard – a status envied by all not of royal blood. And if L'orẹ won, she would force the kingdom to recognize her as the winner of Ogun and elevate her to the prestigious position of royal guard, even though she was the daughter of a coward. Helping her to achieve this, Command had become the closest thing to a mother

L'ọrẹ ever had. Over the years, she'd cleaned up every wound, bandaged every cut, set every broken bone – even the ones she'd broken herself as they trained together. Most of all, she'd given L'ọrẹ hope when she needed it the most.

'I'm sorry,' L'ọrẹ whispered, unable to keep the tears in. Her hands crept to her chest, and she rubbed against the pendant on her necklace, trying to keep her heart from bursting out of her.

'Don't come back here. Ever again.'

L'ọrẹ's lips trembled as she shook her head. She tried to reach out to her, but Command slapped her hand off. 'I never want to see you again, L'ọrẹ.'

L'ọrẹ's vision grew hazy with tears. All she heard was the sound of Command's cowries knocking against each other as she stormed out of the arena. With every step, she took all hope of L'ọrẹ ever shedding the name coward. And once again, in her mind's eye, L'ọrẹ stood between her cracked pillars, as a storm raged on around her. She looked up at the ceiling, and it cracked and burst, raining down sharp shards of stone and sand.

Kòyà rushed to her side. 'I'll take you home.'

'Will you help me save him?' she asked, forcing herself to remember the reason she'd come to the arena in the first place. The whispers around her grew louder, but there was nothing she could do about the danger she'd put Command in now. She hoped that her commander's position and life-long allegiance to the crown would keep her safe from any real consequences. She couldn't be sure, but first, she had to save Alawani.

He nodded. 'I'll ask my brother tomorrow.'

'No,' she said, pulling away. 'We need to get to him before the first stripping.'

He frowned. 'L'ọrẹ, the first stripping was last night.'

'What?' L'ọrẹ gasped. Those words somehow felt worse than every strike she'd taken in the pit. 'How do you know?'

'The Order doesn't announce when they do the stripping ceremony, but they likely decided to do it yesterday because of the blood moon. I'm sure even Alawani didn't know when the first stripping would be.'

'So he could be dead?'

'Maybe. But if he's alive, he won't be able to scale walls or run. Look, I want to help you, I'll even go with you into the damn temple, but it can't be tonight. We need a plan. You might be quick on your feet, but not when carrying a whole body on your back. Or are you ready to die for his freedom?'

He was right. She conceded. 'Fine, tomorrow.'

'Also, check your house, or ask Baba-Ìtàn. If anyone knows where the chosen ones are kept, it'll be him.'

L'ọrẹ rolled her eyes. 'He won't help me, and no way I'm going to tell him either. He'll only try to stop me.'

They reached the top of the stairs, and just as she turned towards her home, Kọ̀yà called her back, 'Wait.'

'What is it?'

'We can't go tomorrow.'

'Curse the sun, Kọ̀yà! I can't keep doing this. Are you in or out?'

'No, that's not it. Tomorrow is Ogun. My Ogun.'

She stopped. He'd been waiting for his chance to fight for nearly twenty-six blood moons. He'd been passed over every time since he qualified to fight for a position. As he approached his twentieth first sun, he was getting nervous, and she'd completely forgotten that his turn had finally come around. It meant everything to him and his family, especially since they lost his younger brother to the burn – the disease that consumed people who burned out their energy cores by overexerting their agbára beyond the point their bodies would cope. If Kọyà and his older brother were paid a royal guard's wage, his family could move into the capital. It'd change their lives.

She drew a deep breath. 'You can try again in a few blood moons. But Alawani won't make it that long.'

'What?'

'Please, I'm begging you.'

'L'ọrẹ, *no*. We can just go the day after.'

'No! We don't know when the next stripping will be. We need to get him out now.'

He frowned, and she looked away.

He clenched his teeth, 'If I die as a victor of Ogun, my parents get more money than they would ever need. The third ring is not like here; they are just farmers, and they are struggling. When I become a royal guard, my brother and I will be able to relocate them to the inner rings. Maybe even here to the capital. But if I die before then, they get nothing. You know that, don't you?'

'You won't die, Kọyà, I will protect you. I promise.' The corner of his lips lifted, but she couldn't call it a smile. 'I promise after we do this, I will train with you every day if I must until you are called again. I want this for you. I want you to win.'

Kọyà stood still. His eyes grew glassy, and she cupped his face in her palms. 'Please, Kọyà.' She hugged him so tight, the bruises on her body stung, but she didn't let go. 'Please help me, and I'll owe you. Forever.'

He eventually peeled her hands off and said, 'Yes, you will,' and turned away from her, returning into the sunken pit of death.

*On the continent that harbours the kingdom of
Oru, there are two eras to remember:
The days before the day of the First Sun and the
days after the day of the First Sun.
All of Oru lives to remember the day the gods
placed a drop of sun in our cores.
Every child born of the sun and sands inherits
agbára oru.
Agbára oru – the magic of the sun.*

10

Ìlú-Ìmọ̀, Second Ring, Kingdom of Oru

L'ỌRẸ

L'ọrẹ's favourite place in the entire kingdom was under the tree in the middle of her compound. Her fondest memories were of her and her father staying out late beneath the moonlight, listening to the songs of winds and night creatures. There he had told her stories that made her laugh, cry and scream in fright.

Today, she wished none of the children had come, and they'd have the tree to themselves. *Would it make any difference?* She eyed the gathering – she hadn't spoken to him since Alawani took the call.

Baba-Ìtàn wrapped up a story about how the masquerades – ritual dancers with masked faces – came to be a part of the kingdom, and were the reason no one was allowed to be out in the streets on the night of blood moons. The story warned that whoever left their homes on those twelve special nights in a year would be flogged with seven-mouthed horse whips by the faceless Egungun, who roamed the streets looking for anyone foolish enough to be outside on their night.

'Is uncle prince Alawani going to die?' said the boy seated opposite Baba-Ìtàn, his voice soft, and the group fell silent instantly.

Baba-Ìtàn's eyes widened. He wasn't expecting that question.

The boy continued, 'My father said he thinks I am an Àlùfáà, but I don't want to die.'

'No one has to die,' Baba-Ìtàn said. His voice was so loud and firm that the boy shrank back.

L'ọrẹ scoffed under her breath. That was a lie. There'd never been more than two survivors in any given calling since the day of the First Sun. Yet, every decade the boys still gladly accepted the call.

'The call for Àlùfáà is – it's complicated and nothing for you to worry about,' Baba-Ìtàn said to the boy. 'Your father shouldn't have told you that. Only the gods can call an Àlùfáà, and if they do, then you have nothing to worry about.'

'Can I say no,' the boy asked softly, 'if I don't want it?'

Baba-Ìtàn said nothing. He only stared at the boy's teary brown eyes. The boy was too young; they all were too young to truly understand why their parents forbade them from entering L'ọrẹ's home. Why everyone in the kingdom was free to raise up arms against her and her father at the mere sight of them. But the children would soon grow up. L'ọrẹ knew from experience that they would grow up to hold the same prejudices. Guilt squeezed at her heart, and she turned away. She knew very well the life she would have condemned Alawani to by asking him to reject the call. She was living that life of exile and rejection, and it was hard – but still better than death.

'Were you afraid to die when they called you?' the boy asked Baba-Ìtàn.

L'ọrẹ returned her gaze to her father. She wanted to hear this. Baba-Ìtàn never talked about his time in the temple or as a priest of the Holy Order.

'No,' Baba-Ìtàn said, 'not at first. Not until I discovered –'

His head shot up as though he'd remembered something. He bent low and scooped a handful of sand in both palms and poured it into the firepit. The night was over. 'That's enough for tonight. It's time to go home,' Baba-Ìtàn said.

Another boy from the group spoke softly, his voice choked with tears. 'My brother was chosen to represent this ring a few days ago. My father said we shouldn't expect him to come home. I want him to come home. He's my best friend.'

L'orẹ felt a pang in her heart, and for the first time, Baba-Ìtàn looked up in her direction, and she walked out of the darkness. His eyes fixed on her.

'Bàbá?' the boy's voice broke their gaze.

L'orẹ sat on the floor next to the boy with tears pouring down his face.

Baba-Ìtàn looked around at the wide-eyed children whose laughter had turned to sadness and fear in mere moments. L'orẹ saw her father's resolve weaken, and after a few silent moments Baba-Ìtàn said to the girl next to him, 'Bring back the fire. I think we have time for one more story.'

A few smiled but most of them still looked haunted by the questions Baba-Ìtàn clearly didn't know how to answer. The girl next to him leaned forward and summoned her agbára. She placed her glowing palm into the flames, and they blossomed back to life, bright and roaring.

'Who here knows the story of the first Àlùfáà?'

The children all shook their heads.

He took in a deep breath, 'Okay, then I'll tell you, but then you all go straight home. Yes?'

The children nodded in unison, and Baba-Ìtàn leaned back and nodded, 'Story story.'

'Story,' the children replied in a single voice.

'Once upon a time?' Baba-Ìtàn asked.

'Time, time,' the children answered. Completing the series of phrases that started every story told under the moon's light.

L'ọrẹ looked at the boy beside her. His tears had stopped flowing. His wide brown eyes now fixed on her father as he spoke from the other side of the fire pit.

'A long time ago, the people of the continent were scattered across the desert; small tribes formed in settlements and villages, constantly at war with each other. One day, the king of one of those tribes asked his High Priest for a weapon to defeat his enemies and unite the continent. The High Priest discovered a way to summon the magic in the sun. The king convinced all the tribes of the continent to join his new kingdom, promising them the power of the sun. The tribes agreed, and on the day of the First Sun, gathered right in the middle of this kingdom ready for the coronation of the king, who was blessed with agbára oru – the power of the sun. And every generation since the day of the First Sun has been blessed with agbára – the gift from the gods of the sun and sands, as was promised in the days of old.'

L'ọrẹ held her hands in a fist and tucked them around her sides. Being reminded of how she was the first person in centuries to be born without agbára oru was not how she'd wanted to spend her night. Her father's brown eyes glistened in the flames as his words fell upon them like a song. As he leaned forward to speak closer to them, the streaks of grey in his short black curls sparkled in the light. When he told stories, it was as though he came alive in a way he wasn't at other times. By the end of this story of bravery and loyalty, none of them would remember the tears they had shed moments before.

'Years later, when it was nearly time for the High Priest to ascend into the city of light, the king asked who would succeed him after he was gone. The High Priest told the king that only someone like himself – someone empty of agbára – would be suitable to take his place.

124

'You see?' Baba-Ìtàn said, slowing his words. 'Whoever the new High Priest was, it was his job to be a conduit between the gods and the people of Oru. And so only one without agbára could do that. Since that moment, every ten first suns, chosen ones have accepted the call of the gods living as priests of the Holy Order. They are our kingmakers, keepers of history, and through their sacrifice the gods keep agbára flowing in our blood from generation to generation.'

L'ọrẹ felt her heart start to hurt again and grabbed at her pendant, rubbing its smooth cold surface to calm herself. It didn't work. What Baba-Ìtàn didn't say was the stripping ceremony before his yielded no survivors, and the one after his only ten first suns ago, also yielded no survivors. It was by sheer luck or the cruelty of the gods as far as L'ọrẹ was concerned that both he and the Lord Regent, who now ruled the kingdom, survived.

Baba-Ìtàn's eyes fixed on the children. 'The child of a man with powerful agbára may inherit only half his agbára, but the child of a High Priest – an Àlùfáà, one touched by the gods – will always be the most powerful person in that generation. So, in addition to the Àlùfáà's duties as High Priest, he'd also sire the next sovereign who'd rule after the king left the land of the living. To select the mother of the next sovereign, the High Priest told the kingdom to bring five brides, one from each ring, excluding his own – the capital.'

'How were kings and queens chosen before?' interrupted one boy, blinking.

'Before that, the king's eldest child was always the next monarch, so the crown stayed within the royal family. But this king was willing to sacrifice the continuity of his line for the sake of the kingdom, so that there'd always be agbára in Oru. The king knew that without the stripping ceremonies, our agbára would begin to fade. Without the sacrifice of the

125

brave men called to the Red Stone, the gods would take from us the powers they gifted us. Even more, their sacrifice was rewarded, and the children of those who survived the stripping had the greatest agbára in the kingdom. Knowing this, the new High Priest, a survivor himself, wed all five wives, and the firstborn of those unions was our next sovercign, and the siblings born to each of the other wives formed his sacred council. The call of the Àlùfáà keeps our connection to the gods and our agbára alive through time, from generation to generation, until the sun no longer burns in the sky.'

'But the son of the new High Priest, he was just a baby. How could he be king?'

'Yes, his father, the High Priest, ruled as Lord Regent until he was old enough to rule on his own, just as our Lord Regent Babátúndé took over the throne on the day our late king died and has held it for eighteen first suns. He will continue to do so until the crown heir's coronation in just a few blood moons.'

L'ọrẹ wrapped her arms tighter around her body. Alawani was now bound to the gods, the Holy Order and his maiden. Bound to everyone and everything that took him farther away from L'ọrẹ. She remembered the warmth of his breath as his lips touched hers, and she shivered in her seat. The tears she tried to push back filled her eyes, and she felt herself on the brink of falling apart. Again.

'Baba-Ìtàn, so why did you leave? Didn't you like the palace?' the girl who'd lit the fire asked. 'Are you still Àlùfáà? My father said you are and that even if you left the Order, you're still part of them. Is it true? And will our agbára go away because you left?'

L'ọrẹ didn't need to see her father's face to know how he felt about questions like that. Even though his story was a cautionary tale taught to every child in their kingdom, still it must have felt like a wound being reopened every time he had to talk about it. Even she'd never had the guts to ask why he left the life of an Àlùfáà. Still, on days like today she did wonder why, after all her father had been through to survive the stripping ceremony, he'd chosen not to live in wealth and comfort within the walls of the Sun Temple. The people called him a coward, but even though she didn't know his reasons, she knew her father was braver than any of them could imagine. There had been no precedent for what happened to an Àlùfáà who left the Order, because it had simply never happened. No one dared, no one questioned, they all complied. Until him. The first of his kind. That had to count for something. Now she just had to get Alawani to do the same.

'My mother said it was because –' The voice belonging to another young girl broke off. As though whatever her mother had told her was too much to say out loud.

L'orẹ raised her gaze to meet her father's.

She sat quietly with the rest of the children, waiting for the answer she'd wanted to know her whole life.

L'orẹ had known from a very young age that Baba-Ìtàn was not her birth father. Beyond knowing that ordinary priests could bear no children, he had told her many times about her mother the temple maiden, who had fallen in love with a palace guard, and how they both paid for it with their lives. Still, L'orẹ occasionally wondered what her life would have been like if she'd been born of an Àlùfáà, with fire in her blood and the power of the sun in her hands. She looked at her hands and wished with all of her might that they would glow. Nothing happened. Nothing ever did, and now only the shadows of the night danced across her palms.

Baba-Ìtàn rose from his seat and said, 'I think that's enough for tonight. Go home.'

The children moaned as they left the compound.

When silence fell, Baba-Ìtàn turned to her. 'All who go into the Order come out broken. Alawani should never have accepted that call.' He added quickly, 'But he did, and we must accept that. Don't visit him, don't beg for him, don't write to him, don't appeal to the Holy Order. Do nothing.'

'Is that an option? An appeal? Will they –'

'L'ọrẹ! This is serious,' Baba-Ìtàn said sternly. 'If you get caught going near that temple you'll be dead before dawn, and then they'll come for me too.'

L'ọrẹ felt her resolve melting away in her father's teary eyes, and she crumbled into his arms and wept.

Bí a bá sọ òkò s'ọ́jà, ará-ilé eni ní n bá
He who throws a stone in the market
will hit his relative

11

The Sun Temple, Royal Island, Kingdom of Oru

ALAWANI

Alawani had held on with all his will to the only two things he inherited from his father – his name and agbára. Now, in one move of surrender, he'd given to the Red Stone all he had. He felt weak and untethered and terrified of the future he'd committed his life to.

He gazed over the balcony overlooking the maze that surrounded the Sun Temple and scanned the courtyard for his maiden. The sun was already high in the sky and . . . was it always this hot? The scorching heat made him sway on his feet, gasping for breath. Like everyone in the kingdom, his core had been constantly working to cool the effects of Oru's fiery sun on their skin. Taking out the heat from the air around him was one of the first things he had learned to do as a child. It was a basic survival skill. He wasn't sure whether it was fear, panic or pain, but one of these kept him from trying to use his agbára after this near-death experience on the Red Stone the night before.

Milúà's face had been the first thing he saw as he pulled himself out of oblivion that morning. He thought he must be dead, but the warmth of her hands and the strong scent of jasmine lingering around her convinced him that he hadn't gone to meet his father. She'd given him more of that bitter liquid he'd drunk before the stripping ceremony. It was the worst thing he'd ever tasted in his life. And he'd eaten everything from sand to chalk. Yet somehow, that horrible liquid had cleared his vision and given him enough strength to walk. Now, he needed more. He needed sleep. He needed L'ọrẹ.

He'd done his best not to think about his best friend. She'd never forgive him, and she'd be right not to. He shook his head as if to shake thoughts of her, but it was too late; he'd cracked open the door, and his mind was flooded. He slammed his palm against his forehead. *Oh gods, she actually got the tattoo.* He'd so wanted to be there with her, to hold her hand as she flinched from every needle strike as he knew she would, and to watch as she flinched on his behalf while he got his. But the Order came for him sooner than he'd expected. He remembered designing the tattoo. Two suns intertwining with each other, beautiful on the paper when he'd sketched it out for her. Bloody and smeared when he saw it across her back.

Alawani didn't know when he would next see L'ọrẹ again, but still, he practised what he might say to her; how he'd start his apology, begging her forgiveness. *I'm sorry for leaving you. I'm sorry for accepting the call.* Nothing was good enough. Words wouldn't fix this. He hated himself for so many things he'd done in the past couple of days, but most of all, the blood oath. As they swore loyalty to each other he'd already gotten his call and had known that he'd accept. He'd always known that he'd accept it, which was why he'd prayed that the call would never come. But it did, and he had no choice. He hoped she'd understand. She might. She had to. She wouldn't. His fingers moved to his lips, and he closed his eyes and inhaled deeply.

Now he had Milúà . . . and his grandfather, Àlùfáà-Àgbà, the once great regent of the kingdom. A man whom Alawani had spent most of his life avoiding, hoping that he'd forget about him. The old man had not. Alawani remembered the look on his face as he'd chased Milúà away that morning and sat next to his bed, and he knew his grandfather had been waiting for him from the moment he left the Red Stone. He shook his head, forcing out the thoughts, the words, anything and everything the man had whispered into his mind.

'What are you doing here?' a voice cut through his thoughts, and Alawani turned to find Milúà standing behind him.

He leaned over the balcony again, forcing air into his lungs. 'Waiting for more of that horrible drink.'

Milúà sighed as she pulled out the gourd, offered him the drink and returned it to its hiding place beneath her dress. 'If you must die, at least do it on the Red Stone. Not here. I don't need any more damage to my reputation.'

She adjusted her skirt angrily and a long metal key fell to the ground. She quickly picked it up and tucked it inside her cleavage.

The look on her face told Alawani that he'd better pretend nothing had happened and not question her about it. She didn't seem moved by the frown on his face either. 'You should be in the lecture hall, or is it over?' she said, changing the subject.

Alawani sighed. 'You don't know how it feels to have the very core of your soul, the thing that burns in your heart dulled into a coldness that leaves your bones aching. It's ridiculous to ask us to sit in a hall and listen to lectures. They're lucky any of us are alive.'

Milúà turned on him. 'Everyone in this temple knows exactly what it feels like to have the life sucked out of them.

Everyone from the priests to the maidens to the servants and scholars. Even those apprentices from Ìlú-Idán waiting in that hall are not just teaching you the old tongue; they've given their blood to the temple, bleeding just so that you can have the privilege of learning the tongue and the magic of the old gods. Besides, when you give up your agbára to the Red Stone, should you survive, how will you protect yourself without learning the old tongue?'

'I know it's important, I'm just – this isn't the time to learn anything. I can't think. I can hardly stand,' he said. 'Anyway, isn't that what you're here for? To protect your Àlùfáà?'

'Within these walls, you're not the Ọmọ'ba. There are no princes or princesses in this temple. So whatever privilege you had in your palace doesn't extend to these grounds,' Milúà seethed.

'Maybe not, but you're still mine to command?' Alawani said before realizing he'd said the wrong thing. Her face contorted the same way a cat's face would when its tail had been stepped on.

She moved in closer to him, her eyes filled with rage. 'You can go back to the training on your own, or I can drag you by your hair. Your choice.'

'I'd like to see you try,' he said. He should've known better than to taunt a temple maiden. On his best day, even with all of his agbára flowing through his veins, he was unlikely to win a fight with her. Unlike the selection of the Àlùfáà, decided by the gods through the priests, no one knew how or why a maiden was chosen – but he'd yet to meet one without incredible agbára.

Milúà's lips curled into a snarl, and Alawani glanced at the faint glow in her hands, which had formed fists by her side. He took a step back and raised his palms in the air to show surrender. 'I don't want to fight you. I just don't want to go back there. Every single part of my body feels like it's breaking and tearing away from the inside.'

She looked at him for a moment, then said, 'You really don't understand, do you? Do you think this is about you? This is how it has always been done. This is the path to proving that you're not here because your grandfather wills it but because you are Àlùfáà!' She smacked his shoulder, and he did his best to hide the pain that still jolted inside him like a spark every time he breathed.

'You have no idea what I've given up to be here. I know how important it is, and I promise you nothing the priest is saying in there about the old gods is going to help me survive the final two stripping rituals on the Red Stone.'

Milúà went quiet and Alawani turned back to watch the horizon, feeling her glare on him. Even though she wasn't yet officially bound to him and hadn't said her vows of allegiance, she was still expected to be as close to him as his own shadow. He glanced at her tribal marks – one dash on each side of her temple. She was born in the Ìlú-Ọba – the capital city. Her name was interesting. Adémilúà, the one whose birth shook the kingdom. Names were promises or prophecies, and unless the earth tore in half the day she was born, whoever named her had given her a tough one to live up to.

Like everyone else, he'd also heard rumours about the mysterious temple maidens. Her parents had probably offered her as a gift to the gods, or maybe she was an orphan that, by the stroke of luck or ill fate, wandered into the wrong house and got churned out as a maiden of the Sun Temple. Maidens who could never bear children. A law that, if broken, meant death for mother and child, but there had been no need for that since the Order found a way to make them barren.

From the end of the hallway, they both turned at the sound of footsteps approaching them. Milúà leaned into him, pulled out the key from her cleavage and tucked it firmly into the back pocket of his trousers. 'Hide this,' she whispered, looking into his eyes, and for the first time, Alawani didn't see the fierce maiden whose words were always laced with anger. He saw a young girl, her black eyes wide with fear.

He held one hand behind his back, holding the key in place, and waited patiently until the High Priestess stopped before them.

Milúà fell to her knees quicker than he had seen anyone kneel before. 'High Priestess Àṣá.'

High Priestess Àṣá's gaze moved slowly to Alawani. Her eyebrows shot up in a wide arch, and even though she didn't speak, he felt the force of her presence. Her dark eyes sent shivers down Alawani's spine, and for some reason, he was sure she saw right through him to the key behind his back. Alawani noticed that the High Priestess had an intricate tattoo around her temples, obscuring her tribal marks – instead, black flames stretched from her eyes to her hairline. Alawani couldn't tell where she'd been born. People only covered their tribal marks when they wanted to sever the connection they had with their hometown.

The High Priestess was the temple maiden bound to the Lord Regent and ruled alongside him. Everything about her presence displayed her position and authority, not just in the temple but in the kingdom. She wore a gold lace gown with a crown at least three inches high, a delicate design of suns and stars shooting for the skies. Thick layers of gold necklaces set with rubies adorned her neck, and huge gold bracelets covered her forearms. Her hair was pulled back in a tight beaded bun that lifted the corners of her oval face, accentuating her high cheekbones. Her skin glistened in the sun, shimmering as though she bathed in gold dust. One thing stood out among these details: a string of cowries snaked along her legs from her ankles all the way up, peeking through the high slit in her gown, displaying the souls that had died by her hand. Behind her were six maidens of the Order dressed in blood-red attires identical to her. They looked right through him as though he wasn't there.

Alawani bowed as low as his body would allow, which wasn't very low at all. 'Forgive me, High Priestess, my body is –'

'Tales of your incompetence don't interest me, boy,' she said in a voice so stern even the temple maidens behind her flinched.

High Priestess Àṣá turned to Milúà. She turned on her agbára, and a warm dull light flowed through her palms. She placed her hands on the maiden's face and lifted her off the floor. Milúà didn't flinch, but Alawani saw how her nails dug into her palms behind her. The High Priestess's nails traced the edges of Milúà's face, and still, she didn't flinch. High Priestess Àṣá was careful not to burn her skin, but Alawani knew from experience the pain that would be simmering inside Milúà. But he dared not speak. Whatever this was, it was maiden politics, and he'd only make it worse for her.

'Where is it?' High Priestess Àṣá finally asked, dragging her words.

'Where is what, High Priestess?' Milúà asked, her voice as soft as the early morning breeze.

High Priestess Àṣá smiled and nodded. Then took a step back. The maidens searched Milúà thoroughly. From inside her thick hair to beneath the soles of her feet, touching everything and everywhere. Alawani looked away, understanding why Milúà's fierce resolve seemed to melt away at the sight of the High Priestess.

The maidens found nothing. High Priestess Àṣá stepped forward one more time and slid her hand into Milúà's cleavage. The whole time Milúà did not shift from her spot on the ground. After what felt like too long a moment, her hand came out empty. She raised her eyebrow as if impressed. She knew Milúà was hiding something.

'Follow me,' High Priestess Àṣá commanded as she walked away from them, a trail of gold lace and temple maidens behind her.

Milúà started to follow but slumped into Alawani as though she missed her step. He quickly caught her with both hands. She straightened and followed behind the High Priestess and her entourage, not once looking back at him. When he checked his trouser pocket, the key was gone.

The sound of the temple bells startled him, and he had a choice to make. He could go to his room, or he could join the rest of his group in the prayer chamber. He turned to look at the wall Milúà disappeared behind towards the Àlùfáà tower. Then sighed and started walking in the opposite direction.

He'd reached the top of the stairs when he met Máyọ̀wá, one of the remaining chosen. He was from Ìlú-Ọ̀pọ – the food basket of the kingdom. Máyọ̀wá was tall – taller than Alawani – and the six short horizontal dashes on his cheeks revealed his home state even before he spoke. And the boy had a lot to say.

'I was looking for you. Where did you go? Are you okay?' Máyọ̀wá said with a deep bass that made his words echo off the high ceilings in the stairway.

Alawani smiled and nodded slowly. They both limped down the stairs towards the prayer chamber. He didn't mind that Máyọ̀wá talked like he had hot yams in his mouth, words pouring and tumbling over themselves. Máyọ̀wá's was the only friendly face. It wasn't often that people lived up to their names, but Máyọ̀wá definitely did. In the mere hours that Alawani had shared with him, he could tell that the boy truly was a bringer of joy. No matter how fleeting.

As they walked through the hallways, Máyọ̀wá briefed him on all he could remember from the lessons earlier in the day. He then started telling Alawani about his plans to move his family from their village farm to the Ìlú-Ọba – capital city.

He lifted his calloused hands to Alawani's face. 'See these hands, they've worked hard, but they'd never have earned even half of what we will get once we get inducted as priests. If you'd seen how my mother danced when I got the call. The whole state heard before my father got home that night,' he chuckled.

Alawani forced a smile. His call to the Order had ruined the life he'd hoped to have. When it came, no one danced. They knew better.

Máyọ̀wá went on. He wanted it all. The riches and glory but none of the killing. It shocked Alawani to know that the boy had built his dreams on such fickle grounds. There was no planning or dictating how their lives would turn out. There was only the will of the Holy Order. It seemed reckless, stupid even, to plan for such an uncertain future. Despite that, Alawani listened as Máyọ̀wá spoke of the world he was sure he'd live long enough to see.

'Did you know our first stripping would be last night?' Alawani asked when Máyọ̀wá finally stopped talking.

Máyọ̀wá paused, then shook his head. 'I thought it wouldn't be for a few weeks. Only the priests know the timeline and days for all three ceremonies and I think they intentionally keep it secret too. However, I suppose it makes sense that they'd use the blood moon.'

'But why this one? Why not the next one? Why the rush?'

Máyọ̀wá shrugged. 'I suppose it makes no difference.'

'But it does. If we don't know what's coming and when, then we'll never be prepared.'

Máyọ̀wá laughed, 'I don't think we could ever be prepared.'

Alawani sighed. 'Aren't you scared?'

Máyòwá shrugged again. 'I was. Before. But my mother said the gods don't lie. If they say I am Àlùfáà, then I am, and the Red Stone will prove that. I'm still here, so I suppose there must be some truth in it.'

Alawani didn't want to burst his friend's bubble but surviving the first stripping meant nothing when they had two more to go. Each one worse than the one before.

The temple bells rang again, and Alawani watched Máyòwá head towards the prayer chambers but didn't follow. The sun had set, and the dark skies revealed the stars that hid behind them. He walked further along the corridors, and the heavy perfume of prayer incense filled the open air. The maidens' voices echoed as they sang in an ancient dialect. He turned the corner and made his way to the back of the temple, towards the old ruins. The pain had only intensified in the time he'd spent on his feet. A sharp, nauseating ache pierced through his stomach and his arms wrapped tightly around it. It was all he could do not to collapse and wither in misery on the floor. Every part of his being ached for an end to the agony, but this was only the beginning.

Agbára oru is a curse that blinded our kind to the
truth of what the gods truly were.
Cursed are those born of the sun and sands.
Cursed are we all who wield the power of the sun.
Cursed are the sands that bury our bones.
Cursed are the gods that made us so.

12

Ìlú-Ìmọ̀, Second Ring,
Kingdom of Oru

L'ỌRẸ

L'ọrẹ had always known when she was in a dream because she only ever had one dream. When she drifted to sleep, she always found herself alone in the middle of the desert, the sky as red as the sand. She stood on a raised platform, with two pillars either side of her. Although the pillars weren't holding anything up, she somehow knew they were keeping her safe from the elements. Sometimes in the dreams she was exhausted and dehydrated – other times, she pressed herself up against one or other of the pillars and felt safe. In her nearly eighteen first suns, that image never changed. Not when it popped up in her mind's eye during the day nor when she was fast asleep at night.

The sands were always as slow-moving as a lazy river, the sun was so hot that she could see the heat simmering in the air, and there was nothing and no one as far as her eyes could see. And even if there was, she'd never know since she couldn't move from the platform of pillars that protected her. Her father was the pillar to her right, the one she always leaned on. And Alawani was the pillar to her left, the one that shielded her from the glare of the sun. This was her life. And then the gods called her best friend to his death, and her pillars started to crack and bleed, and the winds picked up and every time she closed her eyes, the nightmare flooded her mind.

L'ọrẹ forced open her eyes and sprang up from her bed, breathing heavily and drenched in a pool of sweat. She took a few deep breaths and surveyed her hands for any of the blood that had sullied them in her dream. She sighed deeply, relieved that nothing from her dream world had made its way to reality. She'd fallen asleep waiting for the sun to set. Waiting for the dark of night to hide her as she stole a prince from the temple of the gods. Her heart raced at the thought of that and hoped that Kọ̀yà would hold up his side of their bargain. Outside her window, the sun was still high in the sky and she slumped back to her bed. She still had a few more light beads to wait so she walked out of her room and roamed the dark halls of the house. Her fingers gathered dust as she traced her own jagged writings on the wall from when she was much younger. On those walls, she had learned to map out the stars she saw from her window in the years before her father let her out of the house for the first time.

Their home was big enough to fit at least a dozen rooms, but Baba-Ìtàn's thousands of books occupied more space with every passing day. His great-grandfather had built the house as a lab on the edge of town for his family's research, exploring books, stars, hills and dunes – everywhere, secrets and treasures were hidden from plain sight. Once upon a time, Baba-Ìtàn's family of scholars and inventors had wealth and status. They'd been the pride of Ìlú-Ìmọ̀ – the land of know-ledge. Then the gods called their youngest son, and oaths were broken, so their heads were severed, and Baba-Ìtàn became the last of his family line. A reminder to the kingdom of what happened when anyone dared to turn their backs on the gods or the Holy Order. This building had become his refuge as

well as their home, and so he hoarded and preserved everything that the house held. Holding on tightly to the remnants
of what once was.

L'ọrẹ crept into the dark hall turned library. The chandeliers hanging from the ceiling had layers of cobwebs swinging
through them. Bookshelves stretched up the walls and a
ladder on each side reached the top layers. She imagined it
might have once been a dance hall or used for something
fancy, but to her, it was the room she'd spent most of her
life in. Reading and reading and reading. She hadn't gone
to school like the other children, so this was where she had
learned all she knew. Well, all Baba-Ìtàn knew – which was
mostly history. In that way, she was like the elites of the
state. Only the poor sent their children to school. The richer
families, usually descendants of monarchs who had rebuilt
their lives outside the royal island, had enough collections of
libraries and tutors within the family to teach generations of
children at home without doing something as disreputable as
stepping foot in a school.

She curtsied low to her father and as usual he nodded without looking up. They worked in silence a few feet from each
other, binding and sewing books and fixing spines. Finally,
the sun began to set. L'ọrẹ avoided speaking with her father
because she knew he'd bring up Alawani, reminding her that
he had made his choice. She didn't need to hear any of that.
Especially not today. As convincing as her father had been
the last time they spoke about the prince, she'd woken up
this morning with a fury that gave her more courage than
she'd ever had before. The gods of the sun and sands simply
could not have her best friend.

'What's the time?' Baba-Ìtàn said quietly.

L'ọrẹ looked out the window and then to her time beads.
She paused. He had taught her everything she knew about

old magic as he'd learned from his days as a priest in the Sun Temple. Yet, in all her life, she'd never seen him use it. He claimed that none of the old gods answered him when he called but L'ọrẹ found that especially hard to believe. But much like everything that pertained to his time in the temple, it was off-limits for discussion.

'What's the time, L'ọrẹ?' Baba-Ìtàn asked again, this time looking at her.

She took a deep breath and whispered, 'Ago.' Calling forth the time.

Nothing happened. She repeated the words a little louder, and the beads remained as they were. Dull and without light.

She looked at Baba-Ìtàn, whose eyes were now fixed on hers.

'You're saying it wrong,' he said, his voice etched with concern. 'Try again.'

She did.

Nothing.

Baba-Ìtàn rose from his desk in haste and ran to hold her wrist. He inspected the beads. 'Have you been practising your spells?' he said, tugging at the band.

'Yes,' L'ọrẹ said, pulling her hand away. 'Every morning, like you said.'

Baba-Ìtàn's eyes widened. 'You didn't call upon any other Òrìṣà, did you? I told you, choose an old god and never stray –'

'I didn't,' L'ọrẹ said, cutting him off. Frustrated, she shouted, 'Ago.'

The sixth bead lit up. Six past noon. She let out a breath and a nervous chuckle. 'It's nothing, I told you. Just the gods being fickle as usual.'

'Don't say that.' Baba-Ìtàn exhaled, holding his chest as if he'd been holding his breath too. 'Old magic is the only reason no one has discovered your secret. If the Òrìṣà of fire and thunder turns his ears from you, what then?'

L'ọrẹ shrugged off his words. 'He won't. Ṣàngó and I have an understanding of sorts. He keeps me from getting my head chopped off, and I keep his name alive. With the Holy Order's murderous rules, people are too scared even to remember the names of the old gods.'

Baba-Ìtàn shook his head. 'What will I do with you, child?'

L'ọrẹ plastered on a fake smile as he walked out of the room, still complaining about how she hadn't learned the old tongue as well as he'd taught her. Her sweat-soaked shirt made every move uncomfortable and she moved to open one of the windows – the only one her father permitted them to open on smouldering days like this one. She almost wished Ọya, the goddess of winds and storms, had been the one to answer her when she called the old gods by name. Sure, Ṣàngó was keeping her alive but the heat might get her before the Holy Order did.

Once Baba-Ìtàn was out of sight, and his grumbles were a distant sound, she rushed to his worktable. He was hardly ever away from this room, and she couldn't miss the chance to search places she hadn't dared before. Her mission was clear in her mind. Search and run. She'd always known about the hidden space beneath her father's table, she'd just never opened it before, but if he had anything regarding the Sun Temple, that was where he'd hide it.

She pushed the heavy desk, cringing as it scratched against the floor. She paused, waiting to hear his voice or footsteps. Nothing. Beneath the rug was a wooden patch on the concrete floor. Using a small knife, she lifted the wooden slab and inside were dusty old scrolls; lots of them, from his time in the temple. L'ọrẹ didn't know why he still kept all this information about an Order that had ruined him, but at that moment, she couldn't be more grateful for his tight grip on the life he lost. She quickly scanned the scrolls one by one. Some were texts she couldn't read; some were maps. Careful not to tear the fragile papers, she hurried through each one until she found it: a map of the Sun Temple. She held it to her chest and let out a deep breath. She looked at it more closely. It showed the number of entrances in the temple. It wasn't as detailed as she'd have liked, but it would have to do.

Footsteps. L'ọrẹ heard the sound of her father's slippers hitting the ground and froze. She jolted to her feet, hiding the map in her top, closed the wooden slab and returned everything to how it was. She quickly picked up one of the books on the shelves and hid the map in it, and held it firmly to her chest as Baba-Ìtàn walked into the room.

Worry still deepened the lines on his face, making him look older than mere moments ago, and she ached as she watched him move, wishing she didn't have to do what she'd planned. She hoped nothing was out of place as his foot dragged along the floor. Her heart thumped hard in her chest. She had never lied to her father, much less stolen from him.

'Come over here,' Baba-Ìtàn said as he slumped onto his chair.

The silence in the room unnerved her, and she was moments from telling him what she had done when he said, 'I'm sorry about last night. I didn't mean to be so angry. I just –'

Something caught his eye; a lone scroll lay on the floor at the edge of the desk. He picked it up and put it to the side. L'ọrẹ could feel herself growing faint with worry. Any moment now, he'd hear her heart beating like a drum.

'It's okay, Bàbá. I know I upset you and –'

'It's no excuse,' he said, rising from his chair to meet her. 'I love you, L'ọrẹ, and I want you to be safe, and if keeping you in this house is what keeps you safe,' he looked around at the dusty dark hall, 'then I'll take every scorn, every insult, every stone thrown.'

L'ọrẹ didn't notice the tears rolling down her face until his fingers went to wipe them.

'I love you too, Bàbá. I promise I do,' she said and hugged him tightly.

This time, he noticed the book between them and pulled her back. 'What is this?'

'A book,' she choked and chuckled as she cleaned her face, hoping he wouldn't ask much more, and she could leave before she crumbled before him.

'I know it's a book,' he said, a hint of a smile on his face. 'What are you reading today?'

'Same as always,' she smiled and stepped back from his desk.

As she turned, he said, 'The children aren't coming today. We could sit out when the moon is high in the sky, just the two of us.' He smiled. 'Go and rest. I think we still have ẹ̀kọ; I'll make some móín-móín and call you when it's ready.'

She nodded and bit her lip, trying to hold back her tears.

'Or would you prefer àkàrà, although it's a bit late in the day for that. The bread is a bit stale so maybe –'

'Móín-móín is fine, Baba,' she replied. It broke her heart to keep secrets from him. But she would just do it this once, never again.

He wiped her tears and nodded firmly, turning to leave the room.

L'ọrẹ quickly hid the book behind the desk, and softly called out, 'Baba.'

Her father turned, and she knelt before him, leaning forward until her forehead touched his feet.

'Ahan, my girl,' Baba-Ìtàn said, lifting her to her feet. 'Wipe your tears, no more crying.'

L'ọrẹ nodded. 'Thank you,' she said, then sobbed again. 'Thank you for —' her voice croaked. She wasn't sure what to say or where to start.

He embraced her and held on tight as he stroked her hair. 'You are my daughter. Everything I am and everything I have is for you. You never need to thank me.'

Before she could speak again, he headed for the door. 'I'll get some food, and then we can talk some more.'

She wanted to call him back, but her words would not come. One more moment in his presence, and she'd lose her resolve.

The sun was but a sliver of orange across the horizon by the time she returned to her room to prepare for her mission. She detangled her messy afro and plaited it down in cornrows, leaving a big puff at the base of her head. She hid every blade Command had given her on her person, wondering what she'd say the next time she saw her. L'ọrẹ hadn't meant to break her rules or the bond they shared. It was Command who had taught her what to do when she saw her first blood, it was she who had taught her how to go through crowds unnoticed, it was she who had taught her everything she would need today to save her best friend. Would Command really never forgive this one thing? The thoughts started making her anxious, and her hands started to shake. Her fingers moved to her necklace, and she rubbed against it and shook her head. No, once this was over, she would beg her forgiveness. But for now, she had an axe to grind with the gods who had stolen her friend.

As soon as it was dark enough, L'ọrẹ put on her cloak, placed the hood over her head, grabbed her bags and jumped out of her window. She knew her father would look for her when she didn't show up at dinner, but she forced her mind to ignore the guilt that ate at her as she raced towards the arena where Kòyà waited for her.

The kingdom of Oru was made up of seven concentric rings. Settlements wrapped around each other, divided in half by a single road: the sun path that cut through from north to south. Each ring was a different state, with the royal island floating on the golden river in the middle of the kingdom. All the rings of Oru served as layers of protection for this one island that was home to royalty and priests alike. L'ọrẹ lived in the second ring and the journey to Gbàgede, the arena in the city capital, was a treacherous one she made often. She'd gotten used to hiding in the shadows, keeping her face hidden and sneaking in through the city gates, snaking among the crowd always bustling in and out of the capital. But the road was long, and by the time she reached Kòyà, two light beads later, she was already tired.

'Where did you get these?' L'ọrẹ asked, running her fingers over the leather guard uniforms Kòyà gave her.

She and Kòyà were standing inside the arena. It was the day of Ogun, the single-combat battle which determined the members of the royal guard, and the city was bustling with spectators. They hid in a quiet spot to change their clothes, avoiding the eyes of the wandering crowd and most of all, Command. 'Did your brother give them to you?'

'Please don't ask,' Kòyà said.

L'ọrẹ did want to ask, she wanted to say much more than she'd done last time they'd met, but now wasn't the time. And she could tell from the look on his face he wasn't interested in talking.

The uniforms were a fine match of brick-red and black. L'ọrẹ put on the black trousers first, then matching long black boots. The uniform's red top was a bit too small, so it cropped just above her layers of waist beads. She put on the well-fitted black armour which felt more like an extra layer of clothing than metal, and on it was a carved image of the golden sun signifying the royal house the guards swore to protect. A well-placed arrow would go through in a single shot. However, Command had once told her that the priests enchanted the armours with magic from Ìlú-Idán, the home state of all old magic. The truth of that would be tested soon, she thought to herself as she slid her blades into the sheath at her side.

Kọ̀yà stared down at his uniform. 'I always wanted to wear these. I just thought I'd earn them, not steal them,' he added bitterly as he glanced towards the pit.

L'ọrẹ opened her mouth to speak but he cut her off. 'Did you find anything helpful in Baba-Ìtàn's library?'

L'ọrẹ nodded and pulled out the map from her boot. She unfolded it, her finger tracing over the paper to a spot that said *Àlùfáà*. 'See this tower here? They could be in there.'

Kọ̀yà glanced towards the arena's entrance at the sound of voices. 'It's getting too crowded in here.'

'Let's find somewhere to wait until the fight starts,' L'ọrẹ said, nodding. 'It'll be the perfect distraction.'

He paused. 'We'll get him out . . . but what happens when we do?'

'I don't know,' she replied. All she did know was that Ala-wani was in danger every day he spent within those walls.

'What? You don't have a plan?'

'We'll figure it out.'

Kọ̀yà stared at her in disbelief. 'You think the Holy Order won't burn down the whole of Oru looking for the Prince Àlùfáà?'

She shook her head. 'We'll figure it out,' she said again, tucking the map back into her boots. 'Let's just go.'

How could she tell him that her plan was to run – as far as

her legs would take her? She could barely even admit it to herself. Ìlú-Ìmọ̀ had never been the kind of home she wanted, yet the thought of never again seeing the dusty brown walls of her father's house made her heart ache, longing for something she didn't understand or recognize.

L'ọrẹ picked up her bags and walked through the crowds out of the arena, Kọ̀yà following closely. But she stopped abruptly when she saw a figure approaching her. The man stormed towards her, and though the scarf he wore hid his face from view, L'ọrẹ knew those steps, that walk, that cane.

'B . . . ba . . . Bàbá?' L'ọrẹ said, stuttering in shock. 'Why are you here?'

Baba-Ìtàn was furious. He pulled her aside, into the quieter shadows at the side of the arena. His brows furrowed, and his lips quivered when he tried to speak. When he was reasonably upset, he shouted the skies down. When he was angry beyond reason, he found it hard to even speak, and all that L'ọrẹ could see was how his eyes twitched as he struggled to find words terrible enough to show his rage.

'Bàbá,' L'ọrẹ said again, her voice a soft whisper, too scared to speak any louder.

Baba-Ìtàn was quiet. His red eyes brimming with tears.

'I'm sorry,' she said.

He said nothing.

'I need to do this. I need to save him, please,' L'ọrẹ begged, unsure what precisely she was begging for. There was a lot to beg for.

'And who will save you?' he finally said, his voice breaking.

'We have a plan,' she said hurriedly, bringing the map out of her boot. 'We'll be safe and careful, and –'

'Where did you get that?' Baba-Ìtàn's voice now boomed in her ears. Her heart stopped. She'd forgotten she wasn't supposed to show him the thing she'd stolen from him.

151

Baba-Ìtàn looked at the paper in her hands and back at her. His voice dropped low, 'You stole from me.'

L'ọrẹ couldn't meet his eyes. She looked at the sand and rubbed her hand against the back of her neck.

'Look at me,' he demanded.

She forced her gaze to meet his, and her formidable will unravelled. Her eyes stung with tears, but she didn't let them fall.

'I can't force you to see the value of your life. Do what you must,' Baba-Ìtàn said coldly and turned away.

'Tell me where he is. Tell me how to get into the temple and how to save him.'

He turned and raised his eyebrows at her. She wanted to recoil from him, but she stood upright. 'He's my friend, Bàbá, my best friend. I'm only doing what you taught me to do. To not be afraid to fight.'

'To fight for what is right, not this. This is suicide!'

'Not if you help. You know the temple. You know how we can get in and out without being caught. We'll be even better prepared with your directions.'

Defeated, Baba-Ìtàn took the paper from her. And with his hands, he traced out a path for them. He told them what to expect at each entrance, where Alawani would most likely be, and how to avoid the temple maidens. They'd be the most dangerous people to encounter on this mission.

L'ọrẹ thought she had finally won him over, and she formed a weak smile. He glared at her with eyes filled with both anger and emptiness before handing the paper over to her. 'Your life is in your hands now.'

She knelt on the ground and placed her head on his feet. 'Ẹ ṣé, Baba.'

He removed his feet from her and turned to walk away,

then stopped. Reluctantly, he asked, 'Where will you go when it's done?'

L'ọrẹ looked away.

'You don't have a plan? Did I raise you to be so foolish?' He looked to Kọ̀yà and back to L'ọrẹ, his hands clenching and unclenching, unable to stay still.

L'ọrẹ rose to her feet. 'I thought we could leave,' she said, tears streaming down her face. 'We could all find somewhere quiet, hidden, far from here.'

'Eh?' Kọ̀yà shouted.

L'ọrẹ looked at Kọ̀yà, her eyes pleading with him, saying *not now*, and hoping he'd understand.

Baba-Ìtàn glared at them, then ran his hand through his hair. 'I told you! There's nowhere to go. Nowhere in Oru is safe!' Spittle built up in the corners of his mouth as he raged on, 'Why are you doing this to me?'

L'ọrẹ sobbed and reached for her father, but he slapped her hands off.

'So when you stole from me and left the house today, it was to leave and never return?'

'Ah, Bàbá, no. I'd have come back for you. I'd always come back for you.'

'Don't bother,' Baba-Ìtàn said quietly and walked away from them, this time without turning back.

L'ọrẹ didn't know what to say. All she could do was weep as her father walked away from her with a broken heart.

Ohun tí Àgbàlagbà rí ní'jókò,
Ọmọdé ò lè ríi ní'dúró
What an elder sees while sitting down, a child can
never see while standing up

13

The Sun Temple, Royal Island, Kingdom of Oru

L'ỌRẸ

The night was dark, and the moon cast shadows over the temple, which loomed over L'ọrẹ like a monster with tendrils reaching for whoever dared to enter. It had six narrow, square towers scattered in a seemingly random pattern, but L'ọrẹ knew better than to think the Holy Order did anything by mistake. The towers were connected by strengthened, thick walls made of bronze stone, and the entire collection of buildings was decorated with stylish windows displaying different sizes and designs of the sun's image. There were only so many ways to depict the sun, and the temple seemed to have used all possible variations when carving the stones that held up its towers.

The Sun Temple grounds were eerily quiet, and the breeze seemed colder as they stepped through the vast golden gates and into the open courtyards. They passed by a few servants but no maidens. Not yet. L'ọrẹ sighed in relief, every step a small victory. The temple had a few people roaming about, but no one paid them any attention. They kept their hoods up and heads down and approached the maze leading to the inner temple grounds.

'Stop,' a voice called out, and L'ọrẹ felt every part of her body clench.

Beside her, she could feel Kòyà slowly move a hand to his sword. This was it. They hadn't even taken one step into the temple, and someone had caught them. L'orẹ wrapped her hand around the handle of her blade and turned to see who the voice belonged to.

'Why are you outside at this time?' A few feet from them, a maiden wearing a dark red dress scolded a young girl dressed in white, carrying a massive gourd on her head. The girl curtsied and started explaining in a hushed tone. The colours of a maiden's apparel announced her status within the temple. Red meant she'd completed that training; white that she was a maiden in training; and gold that she was more than a temple maiden: she had become a weapon, the sharp end of the temple's spear. The maidens reminded L'orẹ of the song she'd grown up hearing. *When you see white, hide. When you see red, run. When you see gold, pray to the gods, new and old. Either way, you're going to die.*

L'orẹ was still watching when Kòyà grabbed her hand and whispered, 'Step back slowly.'

'You there!'

L'orẹ froze again. The pointing finger and the maiden's glare made it clear she was talking to them this time.

'What are you doing here?'

It wasn't unusual to see royal guards in the temple during the day, but they weren't stationed at the temple, especially not at night, so they needed to come up with a story. Fast.

Kòyà spoke first, 'We came for prayers.'

'It's late. Get out,' the temple maiden said, and turned but stopped when L'orẹ and Kòyà didn't move.

L'orẹ remained still. A lump caught in her throat as the maiden eyed them from head to toe, surveying their uniforms. That was probably the only reason she hadn't slit their necks yet.

Kòyà answered again, 'This is my sister. Our brother is fighting Ogun tonight, and we came to pray for his victory.'

It was a good story. Quick and plausible, but the maiden's frown only deepened. She wasn't buying it, or she didn't care. 'If your brother needs your prayers, then he's dead already. Out!'

L'ọrẹ squeezed her fingers tighter against her blades, ready to unleash them if needed. Just then, they heard a loud crash. The young girl in white had dropped the gourd on her head and spilt its contents. The temple maiden looked like she would burst, and when she scolded the girl, even L'ọrẹ trembled.

L'ọrẹ looked at Kòyà, and they dashed into the maze that circled the inner temple. It was both a refuge and a trap. The five-metre clay walls shielded them, but if they missed a single turn, they'd be lost for hours and would definitely get caught. Baba-Ìtàn had told them that temple maidens were stationed at each tower, looking at people as they navigated the maze. Those who wandered or lost their way got spotted and plucked out quickly.

She'd learned a few things after spending her entire life reading and studying maps and stars. And one of them was to remember. She never forgot a single line of text or image committed to memory. So, as she led the way through the maze – turning left, right, right, left, right, left, left – she saw in her mind the exact path Baba-Ìtàn had traced out for them.

'The entrance to the inner temple is here. There should be a false stone,' she said, rubbing her fingers over the stone wall on the east side of the temple.

'How will we find it? Everything looks and feels the same,' Kòyà asked, then turned on his agbára.

L'ọrẹ quickly folded his palm into a fist. 'No, put that away.

The priests don't have agbára oru, remember? They won't make a secret passage that needs powers they don't possess.'

Kòyà nodded. 'Okay, you search low, and I'll check high. We'll have to do this quickly. Anyone can come by here.'

They both started working the stone wall, tapping and checking for something that felt different in the darkness. They went back and forth the length of the side of the building twice before Kòyà finally found the right spot. The wall sunk into itself, letting out a soft groan, and he used his full weight to push it open, revealing the tunnel they needed to get to the south tower unseen. Baba-Ìtàn had said that it was an old passageway with a secret entrance that the priests used to leave the temple or sneak in their mistresses when they got bored with their maiden and the routine life of priesthood.

L'orẹ let him lead the way, one hand lighting up the tunnel and the other holding on to her. They hadn't walked far when they found a door set into the tunnel's right wall, light glowing from the other side.

Kòyà walked through the door first. L'orẹ gasped when she entered the room. She stepped onto a wet mush of something dark and sticky. The stench of stale blood was so strong it wiped out the heavy incense that filled the rest of the temple. The once white limestone walls of this hidden sanctum were streaked with blood splashes. All around them were displays of knives and blades, different shapes and sizes, and in the middle of the room was a large wooden table with four metal cuffs at each edge and a pile of rumpled, bloody sheets. It looked as though someone had been wiping off and soaking up the blood that pooled around the table and left in a hurry.

An uncomfortable shudder passed through L'orẹ, and she tensed. 'What in the world is happening here?'

'I don't want to find out,' Kòyà said, heading back into the tunnel.

'Hold on. We can still check where that other door leads to. We could be close.'

'Any moment now, someone is going to open that door,' Kòyà said. 'I don't want to be here when that happens. Besides, your father said we'd have to go to the end of the tunnel.'

L'ọrẹ looked around again and pursed her lips. 'Fine,' she said, following him back into the tunnel. She took in a deep breath and plunged back into the darkness.

After what felt like forever, creeping through the under-belly of the temple, they came out into a passageway full of lanterns hanging on the walls. They followed the trail of lights and ended up in a courtyard with a large willow tree in its centre.

'That's the tree Baba-Ìtàn told us about,' L'ọrẹ said. 'We are going in the right direction. We need to get to the other side, and the tunnel beneath it will be a straight line to the south tower.' She pressed forward, but then her eyes caught on something that made her stop in her tracks.

'What are you doing?' Kòyà asked, a tone of panic in his voice as she headed off in another direction, through a part-open door in the wall of the courtyard.

L'ọrẹ ignored him and walked into the room in front of her. It was empty but for the sand portraits on the wall, all of women. The floor looked like it had been scrubbed, but when she squinted, she could see traces of dark spots on it. Something tugged at her mind, a strange yet familiar feeling.

'Who are these women?' she asked, looking around the room.

'This must be the birthing square. Those must be all the wives of High Priests who gave birth here.'

'Hmnnn . . .' L'ọrẹ said, her eyes fixed on the portraits. 'So every king and queen of Oru has been born here?' L'ọrẹ felt a connection to these women that she couldn't understand. One frame, in particular, called out to her. Unlike the others, it didn't have the image of a woman. It was just filled with black sand.

L'ọrẹ's fingers moved to touch it, and Kọ̀yà grabbed her. They heard footsteps approaching down a nearby corridor. Even with only six surviving priests of the Order itself, the temple was still full of hundreds of apprentices, scholars, servants and of course, maidens. 'Don't touch anything. Let's go!'

L'ọrẹ allowed him to pull her out of the room, but the image of the black portrait remained in her mind.

They returned to the tunnels and snuck into the south tower – the Àlùfáà tower. The first room they came to was much bigger, and L'ọrẹ led the way this time. Decorated pillars held up the roof on both sides. Everything in the room seemed placed to lead the eyes towards the carved image of the sun at the front of the hall. In its middle was a large red flame that cast flickering light across the walls. 'I think we're here.'

'They're definitely in this tower,' Kọ̀yà said, moving around the large dining table in the middle of the hall.

'At least they feed them,' L'ọrẹ said, picking up one plate. A cold shudder ran down her spine as she noticed the number of places set on the table. Three.

She couldn't let herself believe that Alawani wasn't alive, so she turned to Kọ̀yà as she held the handle of the door that led out of the dining hall. 'Quick and quiet. In and out.'

'In and out,' Kọ̀yà gave her a firm nod.

The door opened and shut behind them soundlessly. L'ọrẹ and Kọ̀yà stood with their backs glued to the door, which had opened straight into the tower – its huge circular walls stretching above and below. L'ọrẹ walked forward to the railings that went around in a circle, shielding her from the large hole in the middle of the floor that sunk deep into depths she could not see. The inside of the tower was much larger than L'ọrẹ had thought it would be. Darker too. On each side were winding stairs leading to the level below. L'ọrẹ leaned further over the railings, peering into the shadows cast by the moonlight seeping through the circular skylight at the tower's ceiling. She could feel herself falling from a great distance and crashing into the unknown. She stepped back.

'How do we know what door is his?' she said, spinning round and looking at the four doors around them. Two on their side and two on the other side of the railings. 'Baba-Ìtàn said we'd know by the markings on the door, but these are all plain.'

A door slammed shut from below, and L'ọrẹ instinctively brought out her blades.

Opposite her, Kòyà already had two knives in his hands, ready to attack. Guards weren't allowed this far into the temple – there was no talking their way out if they got caught. L'ọrẹ raised a finger to her lips and pointed to the stairs on the other side. Kòyà nodded slowly and crept down, one step after the other, in sync with her.

As L'ọrẹ walked down the stairs, she hoped with all her heart that Alawani was still alive. Even now, as the drumming in her heart threatened to expose her, she had one thought that echoed in her mind. *He'd better be alive.* She'd burnt too many bridges and broken too many hearts. There was no going back. He had to be alive.

They reached the next landing, and L'ọrẹ hid in a tight corner where the moon's light did not reach. She peered out to see Kòyà hiding in a similar spot on the other side, his knives still in his hand. The floor was quiet and empty. *Thank the sun*, L'ọrẹ thought, scanning the area. This floor had four

161

doors too, but unlike the ones on the level above, two of them had markings. Even better, she recognized them. One door had three horizontal lines etched into its centre, and the other had three lines that met at a single point, like cat whiskers. Baba-Ìtàn was right. L'ọrẹ found Kọ̀yà's eyes, and she could see his hand move to touch his temple. He knew what she was thinking. The marks on the door were identical to the tribal marks for people from Ìlú-Òdì and Ìlú-Onísọ̀nà. They only had to find the door with a single dash – the tribal mark representing the capital city. That's where the Prince Àlùfáà would be.

Another door slammed.

Without thinking or turning, she moved back into the dark corner. So fast that she hit her elbow. The collision with the sharp edge of the tower's old, rugged stones sent jolts of pain throughout her body. She crouched and forced down the pain in silent gulps, hoping no one would have heard. She clenched her teeth and hoped the voices they heard were descending the stairs and not ascending towards her. Not daring to peek again, she pushed her back further into the wall, digging its jagged surface into her skin, trying to disappear.

L'ọrẹ held her breath until the voices died out. Whoever had opened any doors on the lower levels was gone. She peeked out again, and it was all clear. She used one of her blades to reflect the moonlight into Kọ̀yà's corner, and he put his head out, looked around, and then pointed down. They had to keep going.

The next floor was identical, with two of the rooms marked for Ìlú-Ọpọ and Ìlú-Idán. The floor directly below had to be the rooms for Ìlú-Ìmọ̀ and Ìlú-Ọba – Alawani should be there.

Halfway down the stairs, a door opened on the level below,

and L'ọrẹ's heart stopped. In the blink of an eye, she saw Kòyà's long legs carry him in a single jump to the downstairs landing, and he disappeared into the corner. But L'ọrẹ didn't have time. A maiden turned and spoke to someone on the other side of the door that L'ọrẹ couldn't see – she glanced around for a hiding place. If she ran upstairs, her footsteps would surely attract their attention – but maybe she could still slide down the last few steps and into the shadows, as Kòyà had done, if she was quick. But just when L'ọrẹ thought she had found a chance to run, Milúà walked out of the door.

L'ọrẹ knew what it was to be afraid. She'd felt it when she walked alone at night. When her home was burnt by the villagers. She'd felt it earlier tonight when she thought Baba-Ìtàn might never forgive her. This was different. Her head throbbed. She could hear her heartbeat as if she was holding her own heart in her hand. Her entire body froze as she stood mid-step on the stairs. She was unable to command her body to move.

She tried to move her fingers. Her toes. Anything. Nothing happened.

All she could do was pray as hard as she could in her mind, *Please don't let her see me. Please don't let her see me.*

And then the pain hit from deep within her. It was so intense that L'ọrẹ could feel her eyes burn and tear up. It felt as though she was being burnt alive from the inside. Knowing that the slightest whimper would mean instant death, she did not scream. She could feel herself trembling, but her hands were still as stone. The hairs on her body rose to attention. It felt like tiny needles digging into her skin, twisting deeper whenever she tried to move. Somehow she remained still, one hand on the stair railing, her other hand clenched by her side, hoping the shadows would hide her as the two maidens approached.

'I don't know why she'd think I'd ever steal from her,' Milúà said to the maiden next to her.

'You mean, you don't know why she ever thought you'd allow yourself to get caught,' the other maiden said.

Milúà smiled and shrugged.

'You need to be careful if she reports to Mother –'

'Ha! And admit that she's too incompetent to run her temple? She'd rather die than give Mother any reason to return here.'

'I guess so,' the other maiden said. 'Why did you even take it?'

'Take what?' Milúà said. They were so close to L'ọrẹ now that they could touch her, but somehow their eyes slid past. How was this possible?

The other maiden laughed, 'You like trouble.'

They both walked right by L'ọrẹ and down the other stairs where Kòyà had hidden in the corner. He was well hidden so they could not see him. But she was right there, and they didn't even look at her once.

L'ọrẹ let out the groan she'd been biting down. Her body felt heavy as stone, and every breath stung. When she tried to call out for Kòyà, a white mist came out of her mouth. Her eyes darted back and forth, the only part of her body that was still under her control.

'L'ọrẹ, where are you?' Kòyà whispered, peeking out of his corner. 'L'ọrẹ.'

'I'm here,' she breathed, but he didn't hear her. She said it louder, but he kept searching for her, looking right through her. Only then did she realize her lips hadn't moved, and she didn't appear to be breathing. She tried to force air out of her nostrils, but it was like her entire body was covered in a thick layer of something, leaving her unable to move, breathe, or speak. An icy shiver went right through her. Her frazzled mind struggled to regain control of her body. Terrified that she'd walked into a cursed trap set by the priests, she fought with everything in her, trying to move every part of her body until, finally, a crack. Like a hammer to a slab of ice, her hands looked broken. Lines like veins trailed around her body like a cracked clay pot about to burst. She didn't have time to think about it. The moment her finger could move, a crack ran through the length of her and as she inhaled her first breath, freeing herself from the mould, she jumped into Kòyà's arms. A loud sound like that of crashing mirrors echoed through the tower.

Kòyà recoiled and shoved her off. He looked like he'd seen a ghost.

L'orẹ forced down a scream as her head slammed against the wall. She flexed every part of her body to break off the ice shards that clung to her skin. The world blurred, and the ringing in her ears was loud enough to drive her mad. All she could think about at that moment was that she must have touched or triggered an old magic spell or trap within the tower. With her shaky breaths, she cursed the priests who had built the Àlùfáà tower.

Kòyà took a step closer, squinting as if checking it really was her and then rushed to her side, scooping her into his arms. 'Oh, gods, L'orẹ, I'm so sorry, you scared me, you came out of nowhere, I thought –' He paused and looked back at the stairs, then back to her. 'Where were you?'

'What was that?' Milúà's loud voice boomed from the level below.

Kòyà pulled L'orẹ into a corner just before the staircase, and they both squeezed in. It was almost too small to fit two people, so their chests pressed against each other, and they held their breaths.

L'orẹ struggled to breathe. She wasn't crying, but tears

poured out in streams from her eyes and dripped from her nose, and she was sweating by the bucket. The next few agonizing moments seemed to drag on until finally, she couldn't hear the maiden's voice, footsteps, or even the sound of the wind. Then she shuffled out of the corner, shivering, sweating and soaking wet.

'Are you okay? How are you so drenched?' Kọ̀yà asked, looking at his own soaked clothes.

'I – uh –' Panic cut her words off.

'How did you do that?' Kọ̀yà asked, still bewildered. 'I swear, I was looking right at those stairs. One moment, there was nothing, and the next, you were falling into me.'

'I . . . I don't know,' L'ọrẹ said, still looking at her trembling hands. 'I don't know what just happened. I felt like I was suffocating, dying. I couldn't move.'

'You were invisible! Those maidens walked right past you. If they'd seen you, you wouldn't be alive. How did you do that? What did you do?' he asked, pointing at the ice that now melted away on the floor.

'I don't know! This place is cursed,' L'ọrẹ replied, still shaking and shivering. She wanted to tell him that whatever had happened could not have been from her since she had no agbára, but this was not the place to reveal such secrets. Her heart raced in her chest, and she felt the burning within her. She was terrified and hoped that whatever curse the temple had placed on her, Baba-Ìtàn could remove it the moment she got home. 'Let's find Alawani and get out of this place.'

L'ọrẹ reached to touch her necklace, and this time, rather than the usual comfort, she felt a surge of energy flow through her. On instinct she snapped the necklace from her neck. Kọ̀yà put his hands around her to hold her. She groaned as she fought the pain, but it felt like something had exploded in her core. Sweat continued to pour out of her, and for a moment, she didn't think the pain would ever pass, but after what felt like a thousand heartbeats, it dulled into an ache.

She forced her head down to see the spot where the necklace had been, and she could see a blistered black scar. 'Is there something on my chest?' she whispered to Kọ̀yà.

Kọ̀yà narrowed his eyes, focusing on the spot, then shot them back at her. 'You're burning up,' he said, touching her skin. 'I'm not sure what's happening but I don't think you should wear that anymore.' He tried to touch it, and she flinched back. 'It's left a mark the shape of the pendant's crescent moon,' he added.

She could feel herself unravelling as her body continued to surge with heat and the pain seemed to build with her panic. Of all the things Baba-Ìtàn had taught her, she didn't know what to do when attacked with old magic. She was wildly unprepared for this. She needed to get out of this damned temple. She shoved the necklace into her pocket, seized with panic, and all she could think was, *Why in the world did Alawani say yes to this?*

In the days before the day of the First Sun
the lands across the continent were green with life.
Rivers streamed from one end to another
and people did not know what it meant to thirst.
Then the Sun turned dark in the sky
and the waters turned to sand
and the gift of Agbára was given
for a price still being paid to this day.

14

The Sun Temple, Royal Island, Kingdom of Oru

L'ỌRẸ

L'ọrẹ opened the door representing Ìlú-Ọba, which was marked with a single line. The mark reminded her of a cat's eye; sharp at the tips and wide at the middle. She stepped into the warmth of the room to find an empty bed, the largest piece of furniture in what felt more like a confinement than a room. The room was warmer than she'd expected, and she was grateful for the heat since every breath still brought out mist from her mouth and nostrils. She let out a frustrated sigh. *Where in the world is he?*

Her heart sank like a heavy stone dropped into water. 'You don't think he's –' She couldn't bring herself to say the word.

But Kòyà knew what she meant. 'We'll keep looking,' he said.

L'ọrẹ threw her head back, forcing back the rise of panic and nausea that threatened to overwhelm her. 'We can't be here when the sun comes up. This was our only plan. He should be here!'

The door handle turned, and L'ọrẹ ran behind the door faster than she thought possible. She wouldn't allow whatever had happened before to take over her again. Kòyà ran underneath the bed and pulled the sheets down to cover the gap. L'ọrẹ put her hand on her blades, ready to wake them at a moment's notice. The door opened, and an older boy walked in. L'ọrẹ waited for him to close the door before kicking the back of his knee, sending him to the floor. She pounced on him, sat on his back, and covered his mouth with her hand. He wriggled beneath her, and she pressed her blade against his neck.

'Pleeease,' he muffled out, kicking the air.

'L'ọrẹ, wait! I think – Máyọ̀wá, is that you?' Kọ̀yà asked, slipping out from under the bed.

The boy nodded vigorously.

L'ọrẹ leaned in closer to him. 'I will take my hand off. You scream, and it'll be the last thing you ever do.'

The boy nodded again.

L'ọrẹ got off him, and the boy scrambled to his feet, and ran to embrace Kọ̀yà.

Kọ̀yà welcomed him with open arms, and they held on to each other for a moment before letting go. 'He's the chosen one called to represent Ìlú-Ọ̀pọ, the third ring. His parents' farm is close to mine back home,' Kọ̀yà said, stepping between L'ọrẹ and Máyọ̀wá. 'I can't let you hurt him.'

'Thank you. Ọmọ Ìlú mi – son of my homeland,' Máyọ̀wá's voice came as a soft whisper. The six horizontal dashes that they bore connected them to each other. Tribal marks signified the long-standing generational vow to protect all from one's home state, no matter where in the world they found themselves.

'What are you doing in this room?' L'ọrẹ asked.

'I came to check on –' Máyọ̀wá stopped, and for a moment, he looked like he was trying to remember something. He rubbed his hand over his head. 'Wait, did he call you L'ọrẹ? Are you Alawani's L'ọrẹ?'

L'ọrẹ's eyes darted to the floor, and she took a step back

from him. Máyọ̀wá clearly took that to mean yes because he went on, 'He told me about you.' Máyọ̀wá smiled. 'You're exactly as he described.'

L'ọrẹ frowned, fighting back the smile that wanted to creep onto her face at the thought that Alawani hadn't lost his entire mind and still knew who she was.

'Where is he?' Kọ̀yà said.

Máyọ̀wá shrugged, 'I don't know. I came to check if he's here, but I haven't seen him since before evening prayers.'

'Where could he be?' L'ọrẹ said.

He paused, thinking. 'Perhaps the old ruins?'

'Take us there,' L'ọrẹ said.

'What? No. You can't be here. The maidens will kill you. You need to leave now.'

L'ọrẹ's blade was back at Máyọ̀wá's neck before he could move out of her way.

Kọ̀yà was beside her in a flash, a firm grip on her hand. L'ọrẹ kept her eyes on Máyọ̀wá. Did Kọ̀yà really think she'd hurt an innocent person?

Máyọ̀wá held his hands up, a quivering smile on his face. 'He did say you liked to fight.'

'So you know I'm not afraid to use this if you don't help us,' L'ọrẹ said. 'I need to find him, and I've come too far to give up now. Take us to the ruins.'

'Just tell us where the ruins are. We'll find them ourselves,' Kọ̀yà added.

Máyọ̀wá shook his head. 'You'll never make it out of this tower.'

'He's right – we need him to show us,' L'ọrẹ said. 'We can't trust his directions anyway. At least if he's with us, we can kill him if he leads us astray.'

'L'ọrẹ!' Kọ̀yà hissed.

L'ọrẹ noticed that Máyọ̀wá was no longer afraid. He

looked at her like he knew her well enough to know when her threats were empty, and it unnerved her.

'Alawani told me how you feel about the call and how you tried to stop him,' Máyọ̀wá said. 'You can't save him or anyone from the call of the gods. We've all accepted our fate. If he leaves, they'll kill him. You know that. If he stays, he stands a chance to be a priest of the Order, to be a vessel for our gods. How can you deny him such honour?'

'I'm not leaving this temple without Alawani. So help us find him or feel the burn of my blade!' L'ọrẹ slid the knife slowly across his neck, showing him that her threat was real.

Now he looked afraid again. 'Please. It's too dangerous – you should leave. My maiden will know I'm missing. They check on us every light bead,' Máyọ̀wá choked.

Kọ̀yà pulled her hands off Máyọ̀wá. 'Stop. We're wasting time. He's right: we have to leave now. We tried our best, L'ọrẹ. I don't want to die at the hands of the priests!'

L'ọrẹ ignored him and leaned in closer to Máyọ̀wá, standing on the tip of her toes to reach his height. She wasn't giving up. 'If you don't show us the way, I'll kill you. I've got nothing to lose. So, what's it going to be?' She wanted him to know just how desperate she was and what that meant for him.

Máyọ̀wá didn't struggle or fight. He just stared at her, searching her eyes with a long calculating look. After a few moments he said, 'I'll take you to the prince.'

He led L'ọrẹ and Kọ̀yà out of Alawani's room, up the stairs and back to the hole in the wall of the dining hall that led to the tunnels beneath the tower. They crawled out the same way they'd come in. Máyọ̀wá led the way to the ruins behind the temple. The only way L'ọrẹ knew to describe what she was seeing was as if someone had split the building in half, raised it to the sky and crashed it into itself. Around the ruins were giant blocks of what were once beautifully decorated stones spread in all directions, some covered in creeping thorns, others piled in a way that suggested that the slightest breeze would send them crashing to the ground.

There wasn't a soul in sight. Despite that, L'ọrẹ moved quietly through the cracked blocks, stopping every time something crunched beneath her feet. The unique smell of chalky dust and ewé-efinrin – the local scent leaves – filled the air. L'ọrẹ had read about the temple that housed the old gods in her history books. They said that one day the earth trembled, thundered and fractured, leaving cracks in the ground. The chaos brought down the mighty temple. But now, seeing the evidence before her eyes, the sculpted archways stained by mould, the blast marks on the weather-worn stone pillars, and the deformed statues all told a different story. It looked like there had been a war. But that wasn't possible. There had never been a war in all of Oru's history. Not since long before the day of the First Sun.

Máyọ̀wá and Kọ̀yà went off in opposite directions around the corners of the fallen temple, quietly calling for Alawani. L'ọrẹ had been too stunned to speak, entranced by the destruction before her, wondering how anyone had survived such carnage. Finally, she inhaled and spoke Alawani's name. As her voice filled the night air, the temple bells rang in a loud clash, sending shock waves through her body. The long, deep sound of metal hitting metal vibrated the ground she stood upon. The temple was awake, and this had officially become a suicide mission.

L'ọrẹ could no longer count how many times tonight her heart had stopped in her chest. Her fingers raced to her neck, searching for her pendant, and she only remembered that she had tucked it away when her fingers roamed over bare, sore skin. In the distance, she could see someone running towards her. At first, she thought it was Kòyà or Máyòwá. But then Kòyà was next to her – he followed L'orẹ's line of sight and saw the figure too. Impatient, he awakened his agbára, and a beam of light shone from his palm. The darkness gave way, and there in the distance was the man she'd defied everyone and everything for. Like a shadow running out of darkness and towards her light, he appeared in full view. Alawani. He stopped and even with the hundreds of yards between them, she could feel his gaze on her like a fire that set her skin ablaze. He moved. Quickly. Jumping over broken walls, bending under cracked arches, and running towards them.

Alawani stopped in his tracks when he got to them. His eyes were fixed on L'orẹ and hers on him. He had lost weight since she last saw him. He had dark shadows beneath his eyes, and his once brilliantly bright eyes were bloodshot as though he hadn't slept at all, his cheekbones sunken. He looked dehydrated, sucked dry – like he was withering away. How could this happen in just two days?

Lost in his gaze, she hadn't considered what she'd do or say when she saw the boy who'd turned her life upside down. The boy she'd bled for, the one she'd bound herself to in a sacred oath that was now a shadow of himself. The boy who'd taken her fragile heart and, intentionally or not, shattered it into a thousand pieces. She wanted to take one of the sharp edges of her broken heart and cut him with it. She wanted to hug and kiss him. Most of all, she wanted him to be alive. And he was. So she took one step towards him, then another, and another.

The temple bells' deafening sound matched the beat of her own trembling heart. Once she was close enough to see his eyebrows raised in shock and feel the warm air coming out of his mouth in short bursts, she raised her hand to slap him. Then paused. Instead, she moved her hand to cup his face. He hadn't even tried to stop her. She hoped that meant he knew how much he deserved her wrath. Still, she couldn't figure out what to say, and obviously, neither could he because he simply stood staring at her, his brows tilted up in a pathetic appeal.

'We don't have time for this. We have to go,' Kòyà said, his voice edged with tension.

L'orẹ stepped back from Alawani but couldn't take her eyes off him.

Alawani's mouth hung open, unable to form words, stunned by her presence in the temple. Ignoring Kòyà's urging, he finally said to L'orẹ, 'You can't be here.' His gaze fixed on her.

Máyòwá cut in, 'Okay, okay, we need to move now!'

'I can't believe you did this,' Alawani said. 'We talked about this.' The ringing of bells sank into silence, replaced by the sound of shouts.

L'orẹ pulled the bandage off her palm and revealed the healing scab where she had cut her palm. 'Yes, we did. And still, you left!'

Kòyà grabbed L'orẹ's arm, 'I'm leaving with or without you. Those bells didn't stop ringing because they changed their mind.'

L'orẹ allowed him to pull her towards the main temple building. Máyòwá ran fastest, his long legs allowing him to lead the way, and Alawani trailed behind.

L'orẹ fell back to run next to Alawani. 'Are you okay?' she asked as they ran through the side of the building, sticking close to the walls.

Alawani nodded, forcing air into his lungs with every step. When she'd first seen him moments ago, she thought it was confusion or surprise she'd read in his features. But now she realized he was terrified.

Máyọ̀wá stopped in his tracks when they reached an old wooden door on the side of the building. 'I'm taking this way back to the tower.'

'No, you need to stick with us,' L'ọrẹ said.

'I'm not going with you,' Máyọ̀wá said calmly. 'This is my destiny. Long before the gods called, I knew this was my fate. I am Àlùfáà. And everyone knew – my family, my people, my friends. I'm not turning my back on my gods. I don't want to find out what will happen if I dare do such a thing.'

L'ọrẹ couldn't find the right words to speak. What spell were these boys under? Not boys, men. Alawani had seen twenty-four first suns and five blood moons, and Máyọ̀wá, if she was right, was maybe a first sun or two older than her. They weren't children. What magic held their minds so strongly that they could not see reason? Why did she have to beg them not to die? Was death suddenly something not to be feared? Or was she missing something?

Kọ̀yà's eyes flitted around anxiously, searching for any figures or shadows that might approach them. 'Leave him if he wants to stay, we need to go,' he said.

'I'm not leaving this temple,' Máyọ̀wá said, holding on to the door's handle.

'Neither am I,' Alawani added.

'What?' L'ọrẹ could not believe her ears. Was he joking? 'Do you know what I've risked, being here? Everything I've lost just to save you from this insanity? We are getting you out today.'

Alawani pulled her close to him, and she allowed him to pin her against the wall. 'L'ọrẹ, I'm begging you. I'm asking you to trust me. I can't leave.'

The eerily quiet temple grounds felt like a graveyard – and it would be, for them, if they didn't move fast. From the moment the temple maiden had taken him from her, L'ore had believed with all her heart that he'd been forced, maybe even manipulated to accept the call. So, hearing him say that he wanted to stay was just not something she could understand. She searched his eyes for signs of the boy she'd raced through the town with all those years ago. The one who was always by her side. He was grown now – different. A voice higher than hers had claimed him and called him Àlùfáà. And he'd said yes.

'Why am I the only one who cares about leaving this temple alive?' Kòyà hissed at them.

L'ore shoved Alawani off. 'I'm giving you a chance to keep your oath. And keep your life!' She turned on Máyòwá. 'Why would you want to die for these gods?'

'I'm not like him,' Máyòwá said, pointing to Alawani. 'He is the Omo'ba – the prince of Oru. He is untouchable. If he leaves, even if they catch him, the worst they will probably do is bring him back here in chains. If I defect, the priests will kill my family.'

She knew by the look on Alawani's face that Máyòwá's words had hurt him; even the friend he'd made here didn't truly accept him.

L'ore tugged at Alawani's shirt, 'Look at me. You leave with me, or I stay here and die with you.'

'L'ore, please,' his voice broke.

'Even he doesn't believe you ought to be here,' she said, glancing at Máyòwá. 'What use are you to an Order that doesn't want you?'

Alawani's eyes brimmed with tears and L'ore wasn't sure if it was her words or Máyòwá's, but she saw resignation etch soft lines on his face, and she knew her best friend was coming home with her.

Whatever he was trying to prove would mean nothing if

no one believed he'd earned it, even after surviving his first stripping ceremony.

The temple bells started ringing again, and the door Máyọ̀wá was leaning on cracked open.

Máyọ̀wá jumped back, and L'ọrẹ brought out her blades so quickly she didn't even remember saying the words to awaken them. They glowed red hot in her hands, ready to cut through whoever came through the door.

A young temple servant stood frozen at the door. There was no one behind her, but L'ọrẹ could hear voices and footsteps echoing through the inner halls. The temple buzzed with activity. L'ọrẹ considered tying the servant up and leaving her in the hallway. Before the thought fully formed in her mind, the girl had slumped to the floor. None of them had seen Kọ̀yà's strike coming. They all stared at him.

'Like I said. I'm leaving,' Kọ̀yà replied to their unspoken question. He shoved the girl back in and closed the door. Then used his agbára to melt off the metal handle.

L'ọrẹ reached for Máyọ̀wá, whose mouth was still open from shock. 'We need to split up.'

Máyọ̀wá looked at Alawani, who still avoided his gaze, then back at L'ọrẹ. He must have realized that they were his only way back to safety, whether or not he approved of their methods. He nodded slowly.

Still addressing Máyọ̀wá, she said, 'I'll take you to the east wall on the other side to reach the tunnels so you can get back inside. You'll never find the tunnel entrance on your own.' She turned to Kọ̀yà and Alawani. 'You two need to get horses. You know where the stables are?'

Alawani nodded.

'Good. I'll meet you at the maze. If we have a head start, we can be over the bridge before anyone reaches us.'

Alawani finally looked at Máyọ̀wá, and even though they

were silent, they seemed to communicate in a way L'ọrẹ couldn't understand. Máyọ̀wá moved in to embrace Ala-wani. And L'ọrẹ saw Máyọ̀wá's lips move, hearing the softest 'I'm sorry.' They held on tightly and whispered the words in unison, 'May your heart burn like the sun, bright, hot, and undying,' before pulling apart.

L'ọrẹ and Máyọ̀wá moved fast and low, close to the temple wall, taking advantage of the shadows cast along its breadth. The entrance to the tunnels where Máyọ̀wá would sneak back into the temple was on the other side of the building. Slowly, stepping as lightly as they could, they approached the main entrance to the temple. L'ọrẹ surveyed the area. Just around the corner were steps that led to large golden doors – the king's entrance, which Baba-Ìtàn had said was nearly always sealed shut. Each stair had fire lanterns on both ends, and two huge gold chalices had fire roaring out of them on both sides of the doors. The doors overlooked an open space with an archway that led to the maze. The tunnel was across the open ground in front of the maze. All they had to do was run across the courtyard and hope that the doors remained shut until they were safely on the other side. Then, she could send Máyọ̀wá into the tunnels, wait for the others in the maze and finally be out of the temple forever.

'Why don't we see anyone?' L'ọrẹ asked. 'There were at least a few maidens walking around when we came in.'

'I think that's intentional. They'll be watching – so they see us before we see them,' Máyọ̀wá said, glancing nervously up at the various sun-shaped windows scattered across the walls.

'Not if they can't see at all,' L'ọrẹ said, looking around her again. 'Take out those lanterns in front of the doors.'

Máyọ̀wá peered to see, then pulled back in. 'I don't know if I can. The stripping –'

'They didn't take it all, right? At least not yet. You should still have some of your agbára until the last stripping ceremony.'

'Yes,' he said reluctantly, 'but I haven't tried to use it since. I'm afraid it'll hurt. Why don't you do it?'

L'ọrẹ glanced at her hands. Why couldn't she do it? Because the gods he was so eager to die for had cursed her, that's why. 'My agbára is weak,' she lied, then held his hands and looked him in the eye. 'We can't get caught. That'll hurt much more, I promise you.'

Máyòwá nodded and stretched out his hands. He groaned quietly as light glowed through his palms. He held on tight to L'ọrẹ's hand, squeezing so hard she felt her bones rubbing against each other. She bit her tongue to keep from yelling out in pain. Using his agbára so soon after his stripping was clearly agony, and L'ọrẹ feared he wouldn't be able to do it. Finally, with a wave of his hand, he extinguished all the fire lanterns. Only the trail of smoke showed evidence of the fire that once lit the stairs.

'Now run – I'll keep watch. Go!' L'ọrẹ hissed, pushing Máyòwá to get through to the other side of the courtyard. She watched him speed across, impressed with how fast he moved. Two, four, six. She counted, waiting breathlessly for him to be out of sight. Once he was safe, she'd make the run, too. And that was it. The rest was easy.

Máyòwá had just gone past the main doors when they flew open, and two temple maidens burst out – dressed in red, weapons drawn, ready to kill.

Ẹní bá ṣe ǹkan t'ẹ̀nìkan ò ṣe rí,
yóó rìí ǹkan t'ẹ̀nìkan ò rí rí
*He who does what no one has done before
will see what no one has seen before*

15

The Sun Temple, Royal Island, Kingdom of Oru

L'ỌRẸ

L'ọrẹ's heart stopped and blood rushed into her head. The world around her grew darker in the light of the maidens' agbára. One maiden blasted a wave of agbára at Máyọ̀wá. A flare of energy like the sun sent his body a few feet into the air and crashed it to the ground with a loud thump. The other maiden waved a glowing hand over the lanterns, and all the fire Máyọ̀wá had taken out relit out of thin air.

L'ọrẹ crouched low, hiding from view. She couldn't fight two red maidens alone – and protect Máyọ̀wá. The maidens attacked and that meant they either didn't know or didn't care that he was an Àlùfáà. She took deep breaths to calm her trembling chest. At that moment, fear was a greater enemy than the maidens. She drew her blades and briefly closed her eyes. A voice echoed in her mind. Command had only one word for her. *Fight.*

L'ọrẹ ran to Máyọ̀wá, pulling a dagger from her side and throwing it at the maiden farther away, allowing her to focus on the one nearer to her. It caught her in the thigh, and she tripped to the ground. L'ọrẹ ran towards the other maiden, who reached her first and struck hard. The clash of her blades on the maiden's golden spear created sparks that tossed her back a few steps.

L'ọrẹ moved fast, her blades reaching for the head and stomach, taking away the maiden's room to dodge both. The maiden's spear moved in a blur, blocking every strike, and then she slid out of L'ọrẹ's reach and smiled, moving her spear from one hand to the other, spinning it, taunting her.

A glance sideways, and L'ọrẹ saw that the other maiden had pulled the knife out of her thigh and was fighting Máyọ̀wá, who she could hear trying and failing to negotiate. 'Stop! I'm Àlùfáà!'

'An Àlùfáà who runs is a coward,' the maiden growled. 'Any right you had to be chosen by the gods, you threw away the moment you walked out of those doors.'

'Please!' Máyọ̀wá held out his hands in supplication. L'ọrẹ could tell he was trying not to use his agbára.

Focus! Command's voice shouted in her mind.

L'ọrẹ turned back to face her maiden only to find the sharp end of a spear hurtling towards her face. She leaned back so low that her back nearly touched the ground. She plunged her second blade into the ground behind her to hold up her weight and propel her body back upright. She moved lightly on her feet, placing herself between the maiden and her spear.

Think! Your next strike must take her out. Watch her steps, watch how she swings, find an opening. Command's voice was so loud in her mind, L'ọrẹ could feel her presence. *Move back. Let her get her spear. If she feels trapped, she'll use her agbára and burn you to dust.*

L'ọrẹ offered the maiden time and space to run for her weapon. She could have struck then. But if she missed, and caused the maiden to panic, the red maiden would no doubt unleash her agbára. Agbára that L'ọrẹ did not have. L'ọrẹ was always forced to keep every fight on even ground where fists and kicks determined the winner, remembering to make her opponent feel like they were winning. Because while she had the firepower of Ṣàngó a mere whisper away, she'd rather lose the fight than lose her head for calling upon the old gods on holy ground.

L'ọrẹ lunged towards the maiden. A quick strike, but her timing was off. Distracted by Máyòwá's shouts and pleas, L'ọrẹ allowed the maiden to catch her blade with both palms.

Under her breath, L'ọrẹ summoned the old gods as she often did in soft whispers – her crescent blades did not glow. Her eyes widened in panic. *Not now, not now, please.* She called out louder, not caring that the maiden would hear her cry to the old gods, and her blades glowed with the light and heat of a furnace. With a shout, L'ọrẹ slid a blade through the maiden's palms. But the maiden didn't make even the slightest noise. No grunts, no whispers – just cold, dead eyes locked into L'ọrẹ's, ignoring the blood trailing down her hands. The maiden fired up her own agbára into the blade, extending the heat towards the hilt, forcing L'ọrẹ to drop it with a yelp. Then, she let go herself. Blood poured out of the maiden's hands, seeping into the cobbled stones on the ground. The maiden quickly recovered and struck L'ọrẹ square in the jaw. The sting of what felt like hot coals on her face hurt more than the blow itself. That would leave a scar.

L'ọrẹ staggered back, but the maiden didn't let her recover. She heated the air around them, forcing raging particles in the air into a single point. It was invisible, but L'ọrẹ could tell from the way the maiden's hands curled and the sudden heat that she was in trouble. This maiden's agbára was strong.

She's creating an air cannon. Get out of the way! Command's voice shouted in her mind.

The blast went off, and although she'd jumped out of the way, it still exploded near her and sent her flying head-first onto the ground.

L'ọrẹ blinked to clear the spots in her vision. Her head throbbed, and Máyọ̀wá's voice seemed too far away to make out his words. She noticed the scorch marks on her armour. That blast should have caused a lot more damage. Perhaps the uniforms were enchanted, after all. She hadn't seen how he did it, but Máyọ̀wá's maiden was flat on the ground, still as stone, smoke rising from her burnt clothes. It made L'ọrẹ wonder how powerful Máyọ̀wá would have been before the stripping and why he would ever give that up to be a priest. Next to her, Máyọ̀wá was throwing up his guts. His body wasn't ready to use his waning powers after all.

At that moment, she heard Command's voice again: *If the farm boy can take out a maiden, then what in the gods' names are you doing? Move!*

The voice didn't need to finish its taunt. L'ọrẹ was already wiping the blood trickling down her face. She spat on the ground, cracked her neck, and allowed the maiden to come to her.

Watch her. See how she leans to the left? She drags her left foot. Just a heartbeat slower. Go! Command's voice ordered.

The maiden's hands glowed with agbára, but no matter how powerful she was, it was unlikely she'd be able to form another air cannon that quickly. Also, L'ọrẹ was used to getting burnt. She remained still, eyeing the smug look of confidence on the maiden's face as she approached her. When the maiden was just a few feet away, L'ọrẹ jumped high, stepping first on the maiden's left knee, then on her torso, and finally, she slammed down with her elbow. L'ọrẹ fell as the maiden swung for a finishing blow. Before reaching the ground, L'ọrẹ stretched and pulled the maiden's long braids.

She went down, grunting for the first time since their fight began. The maiden had been so silent, L'ọrẹ had thought the girl had no voice. L'ọrẹ jumped on her, punching away at her face, not stopping even when she heard a bone crack. Even when the maiden let out a guttural scream that shocked L'ọrẹ to her core. The maiden blocked what she could with her elbows and forearms and finally stretched her hands to the sand beneath her, using her agbára to heat and transform the grains into shards of glass to throw at L'ọrẹ.

L'ọrẹ jumped off her, screaming and pulling out the glass that stuck to the side of her face. The maiden got to her feet, spat blood onto the sand and smiled as she poured sand from one glowing hand and watched it turn into glass shards before reaching the other.

L'ọrẹ's eyes narrowed. 'You're going to lose those hands.'

The maiden smiled, a knowing tilt to her lips. L'ọrẹ felt her stomach drop. The maiden had noticed how L'ọrẹ hadn't used her agbára without her blades. Or had she heard her shout earlier? The image of the executions days before flashed in L'ọrẹ's mind and her heart dropped.

I warned you! Command's voice echoed in her head.

The maiden's eyes glowed like the sun as she formed a glowing orb of energy so visibly chaotic that it looked like fireflies caught in a storm, and as L'ọrẹ watched it slowly grow wilder and bigger, a sense of dread overcame her. Her trembling fingers instinctively raced for her necklace, but they met bare skin. She checked for it in her pocket, just to feel its smooth, cool surface as she usually did, but it wasn't there. She could feel the panic rise in her, but this wasn't the time. She turned her focus to the only thing that could save her in this moment – agbára oru.

L'ọrẹ ran towards Máyọ̀wá, but as soon as she held him, he slumped into her arms. His breathing was shallow and weak. He couldn't help her. She scanned the ground for her blades. They were several feet away. She wished she could call out to them, and they'd find their way to her hands, but that was just desperation talking. The maiden's devouring gaze and wry smile made L'ọrẹ's heart beat even faster as she crossed the grounds in slow strides, as if knowing her prey had nowhere to run.

If ever there was a time for her agbára to show up, surely it would be now. It was as good a time as any for one last try.

Don't be foolish, Command's voice rang in her mind.

But she had no choice. She closed her eyes and imagined all the times she had seen Alawani or Kọ̀yà use their powers. She just needed to try.

L'ọrẹ tried to calm her heart and reach for something within her that she wouldn't recognize. Something boiled inside her. A mix of desperation and fury. She screamed to let it out. A wave of energy tossed her to the ground. L'ọrẹ groaned as she tried to lift herself, but her back spasmed and ached with every move. Just then, she felt someone's hands lift her, and she didn't have to look to know Alawani had returned and saved her yet again. In lieu of agbára, he had been her secret weapon, always showing up just when she needed him.

'You weren't supposed to come back,' she said, her voice weak and hoarse.

'Looked like you could use the help,' Alawani said, his face lit by the agbára in his hands.

L'ọrẹ turned to see the maiden that had been attacking her sprawled on the ground. She held on to Alawani and tried to balance on her own feet.

'That's what I planned to do,' she groaned, and smiled at Alawani.

'I know,' he said, and smiled back at her, panting.

L'ọrẹ was glad for Alawani's help, but the dread that had formed inside her only sank deeper into her bones. She used to tell herself that the reason her agbára had never materialized was that she hadn't pushed herself far enough or wanted it deeply enough. Now, as she felt the heat in the aftermath of Alawani's agbára, she knew that even when her life depended on it, the power wasn't in her. Never had been and never would be. And this was why, among many other reasons, she despised the gods of the sun and sands.

L'ọrẹ and Alawani both helped Máyọ̀wá to his feet. Unable to stand on his own, they hung his arms around their shoulders and dragged him through the grounds, heading for the maze.

Suddenly, there was a whistle and a thunk – then blood splattered to the ground in front of them. L'ọrẹ's eyes widened in horror and confusion, finding the sharp edge of the arrow stuck through Máyọ̀wá's stomach. Máyọ̀wá's hands went slack on her shoulders as he slumped.

'Máyọ̀wá!' Alawani shouted, holding on tightly to his friend.

L'ọrẹ spun towards the temple doors. On the stairs were half a dozen temple maidens in red on one side – and on the other side, half a dozen maidens in white, with arrows in bows, ready to release on command. In the middle was none other than Àlùfáà-Àgbà – Alawani's grandfather.

L'ọrẹ's wet eyes returned to Máyọ̀wá. She'd never seen fear more real than in the eyes of the boy whom she'd forced to join her mission that night. She looked back at what seemed like an army waiting for them at the temple stairs. Then back to Alawani, who was frantically trying to stop the blood from pouring out of his friend's stomach, using his waning agbára to cauterize the wound. The stench of blood and burning flesh ignited something deep in L'ọrẹ's body. As the world dimmed around her and her breaths grew shallow, something inside her snapped.

L'ọrẹ's hands trembled, and her fingers grew cold and numb. Her heart was beating loud but not fast, like a slow but mighty thump propelling her forward. The icy feeling in L'ọrẹ's veins cooled the boiling heat that roared in her core and sent shivers through her spine. Something was fighting inside her, clawing its way out, overcoming her. She coughed, and gulps of water poured out of her mouth. Her rage dulled out the pain that tore at her insides. Her eyes burned, her vision grew dimmer, and the world around her turned a dark shade of grey, yet she could see clearly. With every exhale, a burst of dark mist shot out of her nostrils and mouth.

L'ọrẹ felt like she was watching someone else control her body, and she was just there to see how much damage they could do. When she clenched her fist, she couldn't feel her hands. Yet she could feel the hairs on her body stand at attention. Feeling the slightest breeze brush against them, the chill energized her, making her feel more alive than she'd ever felt before. The world stopped. She could tell because even though the maidens moved, they moved so slowly, she could wait for a thousand heartbeats and they still wouldn't reach her. L'ọrẹ wanted them to reach her. She wanted nothing more than to burn the temple to the ground with all of them in it.

The archers released a volley of arrows, and L'ọrẹ stretched forth her hands and screamed with all her strength, until she could no more, and when she opened her eyes, she couldn't believe the sight before her.

There it was, standing between her and the entire force that had stood against them – a mountain of ice with black mist oozing from it. Enormous shards of ice had formed like crystals layered upon each other, their sharp edges pointing to the sky. The archers' arrows had got stuck in the middle of it. Through the clear ice, she could see their faces. They all looked at her like she had transformed into something otherworldly. But it was her. She had done that.

L'ọrẹ fell to the floor, too stunned to speak, just staring at her hands. What was happening to her? This wasn't agbára oru. This wasn't anything she knew or could recognize. Her hands trembled before her as streaks of black veins crawled up her arms. Why was this happening? From the other side of the ice barrier, she could see Àlùfáà-Àgbà's rage as he shouted at the maidens who were trapped near the entrance of the temple.

L'ọrẹ flinched when Alawani's fingers touched hers but she allowed him to pull her further back as Àlùfáà-Àgbà formed a fireball in his hands and threw it at the ice. They both cowered, expecting ice fragments to rain down on them, but the crystals remained unscathed. Àlùfáà-Àgbà's old magic did nothing to break the structure she'd created, but within its crystals, a black mist hovered like a wild, angry beast trying to escape its prison.

The ground shook, and the loose stones danced as the deafening cry of an animal filled the air. Behind them, L'ọrẹ turned to find Kọ̀yà mounted on a battle rhino racing towards them from the maze. Battle rhinos were like small mountains on the move, usually ridden only by warrior maidens. She'd never seen one before. Nearly three times her height and the size of two fat oxen, it had a giant horn sharpened to a point and adorned in gold to match its thick armour – which she was sure was impenetrable. This wasn't the horses she'd asked for. How in the world had Kọ̀yà got a battle rhino to let him ride it?

'We need to go now!' Kọ̀yà screamed from atop the mighty beast.

'We can't leave Máyòwá,' Alawani said, tears in his eyes.

Kòyà looked at Máyòwá. 'He is as good as dead. There is nothing more we can do for him.'

L'ọrẹ moved to hold Máyòwá. He flinched when she touched him as his skin pinched together, and blackened from her touch. Little pricks of ice grew on top of it. L'ọrẹ quickly removed her hands from him. The dread inside her grew with every passing moment. What was she turning into? What was happening to her?

On the other side of the ice, Àlùfáà-Àgbà was still throwing fireballs, screaming incantations and summoning the old gods. The ice crystals still weren't budging. The maidens started using agbára oru, and after a few tries, L'ọrẹ saw the faintest crack, and the black mist inside it spun like sand caught in a storm. On the ground, Máyòwá's mouth was still spouting blood. She knew Kòyà was right. He wouldn't make it. It was all her fault. He didn't deserve to be caught up in her mess. When he'd asked to leave, she should've let him go, and for that she would never forgive herself.

She turned to Alawani and shook her head. Never in their decade-long friendship had she ever seen him look so broken. His empty eyes stared at Máyòwá's body for a moment, then he turned away to climb the rhino's ladder to the top.

Hot tears filled L'ọrẹ's eyes and rolled down her cheeks. 'I'm so sorry, Máyòwá. You shouldn't have been a part of this. Forgive me.'

'L'ọrẹ! Climb now! Whatever that is, it looks like it's coming down soon!' Kòyà shouted.

Máyòwá's eyes closed and opened slowly.

'Kíni àṣíríi rẹ? Tell me your àṣírí – give me your secrets,' L'ọrẹ whispered. 'Let me do this for you, please.'

Another crack in the wall.

'L'ọrẹ, let's go!' Alawani shouted, 'It's breaking!'

'I'm coming!' L'ọrẹ screamed back. 'Máyọ̀wá, please!'

Máyọ̀wá smiled softly in L'ọrẹ's arms. 'I . . . I have none. Ju . . . just tell m . . . my parents I . . . I died on the Red Stone a . . . an . . . and not trying t . . . to escape.'

'Are you sure, Máyọ̀wá? Think about it. Take nothing of this world to the one beyond. Let me bear your burden.'

'I have no burden to give you,' and with his last breath, he whispered a few words into her ears.

L'ọrẹ closed Máyọ̀wá's eyes, whimpering, and rushed to climb the battle rhino, holding on tightly to Alawani as Kọ̀yà led the animal through the maze. It crashed through stone and cleared a path right across the rubble with its horn. She huddled behind Alawani, trying to avoid the debris that splattered around her as the beast raged through the temple gates, stomping over those who tried to stop them. They rode over the bridge, moving so fast that L'ọrẹ was sure the bridge would collapse and she'd find herself at the bottom of the golden river, but somehow the bridge held. Once off the island, they sped through Ìlú-Ọba as fast as the beast would go.

L'ọrẹ kept looking back at the temple, unable to take her mind off the young boy who lay dead on its grounds. Her eyes poured out hot tears, and she'd never wished for anything the way she wished she'd never laid eyes on Máyọ̀wá, the chosen Àlùfáà of Ìlú-Ọpọ. In the quiet of her heart, she said the words she'd thought she'd never say. 'May your heart burn like the sun, bright, hot, and undying.'

*In the days before the day of the First Sun, seven
tribes called the continent home.
In those days, the gods who ruled listened only to
those who spoke their tongue.
Only to the descendants and scions of their blood,
those who had àṣẹ in their veins.
And so the people of Ìlú-Al'àṣẹ were
a force to be reckoned with.
Manipulating the life force of everything around
them to their will.
With the gods on their side, they had no foe or enemy
for no one would touch those protected by Òrìṣà.*

16

The Sun Temple, Royal Island, Kingdom of Oru

MILÚÀ

Milúà stood before Àlùfáà-Àgbà as he rained curses on her and her entire lineage. It wasn't like she had any family anyway, she thought grimly as his voice reverberated through the room. She kept her eyes fixed on her feet. The Elder Priest's age and station meant he was so far above her in the pecking order that it was her duty to remain still as a statue until he was done berating her and probably even thank him for taking the time to do so.

'Your foolishness could cost us everything,' Àlùfáà-Àgbà barked.

Milúà bent her head even lower to hide her grimace as his spit landed on her forehead. She dared not wipe it. Instead, she allowed her mind to think of answers to the question she hoped he wouldn't ask. Where was she when her Àlùfáà ran away from the Sun Temple? Many thoughts crossed her mind, but the truth kept barging in. She couldn't well say she'd stolen the High Priestess's key to the secret library beneath the temple to search for records of her mother, could she? Maidens were supposed to be fully devoted to the mother who trained them. But Milúà had overheard one of her sisters of the Order talking about how her birth mother

194

was a maiden, and like an itch that drove one mad if not scratched, she had to know if it was true. And the records in that library, the record of all temple maidens since the day of the First Sun, would tell her the truth. She couldn't miss the chance to find out. She'd been deep beneath the ground, searching through rows of books, unaware of the chaos unfurling over her head. And the truth she'd found was too heavy to speak of.

'The kingdom our forefathers built is on the edge of ruin! For nothing,' Àlùfáà-Àgbà raged on. 'Because you couldn't keep hold of a boy! Never, never in our history has a chosen one run away or been killed on our very own land!' He was brimming over with so much fury, she thought he might pass out.

First, that was not true. Chosen ones died all the time. Sure, not by arrows, but death is death. She wondered if it was the fact that a chosen one was taken that enraged him so much or that it was his grandson. Whichever way, it was ridiculous that she was getting the brunt of his anger when the maidens at the entrance couldn't capture the boys. Although, losing the chance ever to be a high-ranking maiden was punishment enough. Maiden Bùnmi, whose Àlùfáà died, went mad with rage.

As soon as she had seen Máyòwá injured on the ground after the intruders had escaped, Bùnmi had run out of the temple, screaming at the top of her lungs, 'Máyòwá!' Her brown eyes had turned golden, her hands had shone the sun's light, and she'd run towards the maiden who'd shot the arrow. The maiden had held her hands up – it was an accident, Máyòwá hadn't been the intended target – but Bùnmi's rage couldn't be tempered. Milúà had watched as Bùnmi shot sparks of light that blasted on impact until the girl fell to her knees. The girl was only a white maiden, still in training, still learning. In the moments before she died, the girl begged her sister for mercy, begged to speak her àṣírí. Bùnmi's anger contorted her face into an ugly scowl. She inhaled a deep breath and screamed out a river of ash from her mouth into the girl's face – choking her to death.

The sight of the girl's dead body only seemed to agitate Bùnmi even more. She cried as she placed her hands on the lifeless body and burned it to ash, leaving charred bones where the girl once lay. No one had stopped Bùnmi as she raged on, screaming and throwing herself to the ground like an injured animal. Afterwards, Bùnmi had cried over Máyọ̀wá as though she was his mother, but Milúà knew she wept not for him, but for the life that she could now never attain.

Milúà knew she'd have done the same to anyone who killed her Àlùfáà. But she wasn't sure she'd have risked dying from the burn just for revenge as Bùnmi had now done. She'd grown up with her and knew the limits of her sister's agbára. Creating all that ash from within her core was bound to ignite the burn within her; the disease that would blacken the girl's insides until she was nothing but a charred corpse. Bùnmi simply wasn't powerful enough for the kind of power she'd channelled tonight. Milúà cringed at the thought – nothing was worth risking that kind of death. Not even vengeance.

Milúà fell to her knees and bowed before the old man. 'Forgive me, Àlùfáà-Àgbà, may the gods have mercy on me. May the sun burn away my sins. Give the word, and I'll chase after the prince and bring him to you before the next stripping ceremony.' There was nowhere in the kingdom Alawani could hide from her. Of this, she was certain.

Her words only seemed to enrage the old man. 'You'll do nothing until I tell you. Get out of my sight!'

Milúà gathered her skirt, hurried off the floor, and turned

to leave. 'Stop,' Àlùfáà-Àgbà said without looking back at her. 'Get rid of that thing in the courtyard.'

Milúà spun on her heel. 'Me? Àlùfáà-Àgbà, I've never seen such a thing in my life. How would I –'

'Figure it out! You have only a few hours until the first light. It mustn't remain when the sun rises. Let the eyes of our gods not look upon that abomination.' The light from the flickering flames cast shadows that made his heavily bearded face more threatening. 'It must be gone, or you will meet your gods today!' Àlùfáà-Àgbà said as he stormed out of the room.

The maidens in the maze courtyard stood back from the abomination, keeping their distance lest they offend their gods. The gods of the sun and sands favoured light; this thing seeped out a strange mist as dark as night. None of them could believe that this atrocity came out of a person, but it had; they'd all witnessed it. Milúà tried to understand what exactly it was she was looking at.

It couldn't have been formed with agbára oru because a dozen maidens had failed to destroy it when they shot at it with blasts of agbára. Nor could it have been formed with old magic because Àlùfáà-Àgbà couldn't destroy it either. What was this thing? Fear gripped her every step, and a chill seeped into her bones the closer she got to it, cold rolling off the wall in waves. Her chest grew so tight it was hard for her to breathe. All eyes were on her, and even though she could not see him, she knew Àlùfáà-Àgbà watched too from behind the temple walls.

When she finally got close enough to touch it, she poked it as though it were a wild animal that could turn on her and chase her through the courtyard. The previously clear crystals had turned so black that parts of it had merged with the night, turning it nearly invisible. Milúà tuned out the whispers around her and raised her hands, calling forth her agbára. Her palms got brighter and brighter, and when she thought it was just hot enough to melt even herself, she thrust them against its surface. The maidens gasped. At first, nothing happened, and then slowly, the ice beneath her palms turned to water dripping to her feet. Black and wet.

Emboldened, she let out a loud cry and pushed both palms deeper into the melting tower. A loud crack sliced through the air. Ice splinters rained down as the top half exploded in a loud bang. Her breath grew thin and ragged. Using all the agbára oru she could summon, her hands burned brighter than she'd ever seen before, her agbára now raging through the ice. Black liquid poured out, soaking the ground. By the time she was done, the liquid had drenched her clothes from head to toe.

Exhausted, Milúà turned back to the building behind her. She had no idea how she'd been able to do what her sisters and the other priests could not, but she didn't care to know how, as long as Àlùfáà-Àgbà saw her succeed where he'd failed. Her eyes were full of pride and defiance even as her knees weakened and the agbára slowly faded from her hands, allowing the darkness of night to hide her. She fell to the ground, and the light faded from her eyes, and she was sure the gods had decided that her punishment for losing her Àlùfáà was death.

Milúà woke to find Àlùfáà-Àgbà at the foot of her bed. She fell to her knees and bowed to him. The silence in the room was masked only by the crackling of the flames in the torch lamps that surrounded them.

'Do you know what this room is?' Àlùfáà-Àgbà asked.

'No, Àlùfáà,' Milúà replied, looking around the room. It wasn't too different from many other rooms in the temple. It had the same stone walls, designed with gold ornaments and curtains made of embroidered fabric.

'You wouldn't. This was where the Chosen of the Chosen were kept long before your time. This was where I received the gift of the gods to be the channel for agbára oru.' He paused. 'Tell me everything that happened yesterday from the moment you opened your eyes.'

Milúà lowered her gaze to the intricately designed marble floor and recalled everything she had done. The morning had been normal. Routine training of her maiden apprentice, Mojí, then temple duties in the prayer halls, and finally shadowing her Àlùfáà throughout the day as they learned their history and purpose. During the evening study for the Àlùfáà, she trained with her sisters on the grounds near the temple ruins as they often did. And by evening bell, she prayed with the entire Holy Order in the main temple halls, after which she did the rounds with Maiden Bùnmi to check that the chosen ones were where they were supposed to be and then she was off to bed.

She skipped the part about how she hadn't checked on the chosen ones but instead had crept through the walls to the hidden and restricted library beneath the Àlùfáà towers. She'd deny it till her dying breath, but she knew this attack, this failure, was hers and hers alone. From Àlùfáà-Àgbà's expression, Milúà could not tell if he believed her story or not.

'What happened when you separated from Bùnmi?' he asked, stepping closer to her. 'What did you see in the corridor? Was anyone there?'

Milúà paused. It was a strange question, like he already knew the answer.

'Àlùfáà, I saw nothing,' Milúà said, honestly. 'I swear on the agbára in my blood.'

'Stand,' Àlùfáà-Àgbà said, lifting his hand as though pulling her by strings. 'Close your eyes.'

Milúà froze where she stood. A tight knot lodged in her throat. Masking fear was a speciality of hers. Distracting herself with thoughts she'd never be able to say out loud comforted her and kept signs of panic off her face. So, while Àlùfáà-Àgbà couldn't see even a glimpse of her fear, her heart was ready to run out of her chest. It wasn't the man himself that Milúà feared. It was the power he had over her and every other maiden in the temple and all the stories of how he extracted information in his interrogations.

Àlùfáà-Àgbà moved closer to Milúà. 'Relax. This is the easy part.'

Milúà inhaled slowly, every part of her body tense as he moved closer. Then she exhaled, fortressing her mind, barricading the parts of herself that had to remain hers.

'Open your hands,' Àlùfáà-Àgbà said.

Milúà frowned. She peered at him. His dark skin creased with every word. His red eyes drilled holes into her.

Milúà did as he commanded.

'Bring forth your agbára.'

Now, this was strange. Priests hated reminders of their lost powers and always berated their maidens for using them in their presence, even though the entire point of having maidens was to be protected by the powers they gave up.

Milúà reached into her core and followed the thread that flowed through her veins and into her hands.

'Close your eyes. Focus on the power flowing through you. Focus on the heat in your palms and tell me again what happened.' Àlùfáà-Àgbà dragged that last word in a way that made her know. He didn't believe her story.

Milúà took in a shaky deep breath. Her thoughts raced through her mind. She looked around the room instinctively, looking for what she could use to protect herself if he attacked her. Agbára oru or not, Àlùfáà-Àgbà was still the most powerful man in the kingdom, emboldened by the old magic he claimed from the old gods. Magic that was forbidden to all but his kind in the Holy Order. Running was no use. She wouldn't get as far as the door. What stuck in her mind though was why she'd ever want to run. That wasn't how she'd been trained. She'd fallen short and deserved whatever came her way.

Milúà focused on the choice before her and chose to play Àlùfáà-Àgbà's game with him, knowing that at any moment, she could be fighting for her life. Slowly, she closed her eyes and said, 'We walked through the corridor to the stairs. The hallway was dark.' She remembered it as dark but as her agbára flowed within her, the light inside her lit up her memory of the space and she could see clearly. 'When I thought I heard something, I went back to check. But it was empty.'

'Okay, now focus. What did you hear?'

Milúà could feel his breath on her face. She remained quiet for a moment. In her mind, she saw a faint glow on the stairs she passed by. A faint yellow light in mid-air, floating and growing like a blossoming flower. Someone had been there. How could she see a person's agbára without seeing the person? She wanted to move and touch it and feel for herself whatever she'd missed.

'What did you hear?' Àlùfáà-Àgbà's voice boomed in her ear, forcing her back to reality.

Milúà flinched and stepped back from him. She didn't know exactly what she'd heard or how she'd describe it.

'I heard – I heard the sound of glass breaking.' She opened her eyes. 'What does it mean?'

Àlùfáà-Àgbà stood before her, looming like the monstrosity she'd had to destroy in the courtyard. And like it, she faced him with panic in her chest and fury in her eyes.

'Are you sure?' Àlùfáà-Àgbà asked, his gaze fixed on her.
'Yes, Àlùfáà, that's all I heard.'

The corner of his lips curved upward. 'Then, I know exactly who our intruder is,' he turned away from her, 'and exactly who has been hiding her from me.'

Milúà remained quiet as Àlùfáà-Àgbà contemplated. His eyes glanced back and forth, and he mumbled words she couldn't understand. The old man's face hardly ever gave away anything, and this was probably the first time she'd ever seen him smile. It was as sinister as she'd imagined.

'Ọmọ Òtútù ti dé,' he whispered into his clasped palms. 'Ọmọ Àjẹ́ yẹn l'áyà láti wá sí ilé mi.'

'Àlùfáà?' she said quietly to match his tone. What did he mean by 'the child of cold had come'? Or that 'the witch's child had dared enter his house'? Did he know the girl? Did he know the magic she'd used? If he did, how come his old magic had done nothing to destroy it?

In a sudden mood change, Àlùfáà-Àgbà barked, 'Get out.'

Milúà moved without thinking. 'Yes, Àlùfáà-Àgbà. I will join my sisters for prayers,' she breathed. Hoping not to agitate him any further.

'No,' he replied in a bitter voice, and Milúà halted. 'Go home. Return to Ìyá-Ayé. I don't want to see you in this temple again.'

Milúà fell to the floor so fast that pain jolted through her as her knees cracked against the marble. 'Àlùfáà-Àgbà, please have mercy.'

'Your mother will decide your fate,' Àlùfáà-Àgbà said coldly.

Milúà begged, pouring out words that stumbled over each other. Each plea was more desperate than the last. When she'd left home, she'd promised herself never to return. She folded her clasped hands inward and held them to her chest. No matter how full of danger the Sun Temple was, it was still a safer place for her than the home Ìyá-Ayé built for her maidens. To her mother, she couldn't lie, she couldn't hold back secrets, nor could she hide her fear. A familiar sense of terror gripped her like an old friend. The sound of her heartbeat thrashed in her ears like the pounding of a pestle in a mortar.

Still on her knees, she begged, 'Àlùfáà-Àgbà, if you would only permit me, I will find Alawani and bring him to you. I swear on my life, please, let me fix this.'

'Don't let dawn meet you within these walls,' he replied.

Milúà tried again, reaching for his feet. She reminded him of her skills, her powers, and how she had defeated the abomination that stood tall in the courtyard. She begged with everything she could. Tears filled her eyes and rolled down her face in narrow streams.

Àlùfáà-Àgbà stood before her, unshaken. 'As the words have left my lips.'

There was nothing more to be said. Àlùfáà-Àgbà had spoken the words that made his decision absolute. He used the spoken seal of power to send Milúà off to the devil herself.

'So let it be done.'

A fi Ọ́ j'ọba, ò ń ṣe àwúre; dákun,
ṣé o fẹ́ jẹ oyè Ọlọ́run ni?
*You have been crowned as a king,
and yet you're making spells and charms;
do you also want to be crowned God?*

17

Ìlú-Ìmọ̀, Second Ring, Kingdom of Oru

L'ỌRẸ

Two light beads later, as the first light of dawn streaked across the sky, L'ọrẹ, Alawani and Kòyà were still about a mile away from the gates that led out of Ìlú-Ọba, the capital city, and into Ìlú-Ìmọ̀, L'ọrẹ's home state, where Baba-Ìtàn was waiting for her. Kòyà held the reins, controlling the mighty beast, Alawani sat behind him, and L'ọrẹ held on to Alawani's clothes as tightly as she could. The cold numbness and the black veins that trailed her hands remained and she was grateful for the warmth from his body.

They had taken the King's Road, also called the Sun Path, a single paved road leading from the Palace, across the golden bridge and down to the last walls of Ìlú-Òdì.

The pit in L'ọrẹ's stomach sunk deeper – surely the Holy Order was on their tail, watching and waiting. The morning harmattan fog hadn't yet lifted and the city was largely asleep. But how long would their luck last? The battle rhino was hardly subtle. An icy shiver ran through her, and she held on tighter to Alawani's garments.

To her surprise, they had passed through the main gates of the capital city without incident, their hooded cloaks hiding their faces in the dim, foggy light. L'ọrẹ had only allowed herself to breathe when they'd crossed over and were on the other side of the capital's walls. Once they were out of sight of the guards, they had ridden as fast and as hard as they could.

L'ọrẹ found a gap in the rhino's armour and touched its skin as they galloped into her hometown. The beast was so warm that she took her other hand from Alawani too and placed them both on each of the beast's hind legs. The warmth from the beast flowed into her and thawed the shiver in her core. For the first time since they had left the temple, she felt like they might actually escape.

Now she only needed to get her father.

Suddenly, the rhino tripped and staggered. L'ọrẹ's life flashed before her eyes, and the cold in her core sprang back to life. If they fell and the rhino crushed them, they'd never survive it. Kọ̀yà jumped first, yelling for the others to follow.

At the speed they'd been moving, L'ọrẹ was sure she'd break her neck, but she flung herself off anyway and rolled to a stop on the ground. Stones scraped her elbows, a few sticking to her bruised flesh.

Alawani got to his feet and ran straight for L'ọrẹ, lifting her to her feet and checking for injuries. She held her head in her palms to stop it from spinning.

'Are you okay?' Alawani asked, holding her.

'I think so,' L'ọrẹ replied. 'What happened?'

Alawani looked at the rhino a few paces ahead, where it had finally fallen. It was lying still in the sand. He placed his hands on it then shrieked, leaping backwards as if burned. L'ọrẹ's eyes widened as she examined the rhino. Its eyes were surrounded by crystals, and the beautifully designed gold armour had darkened. Black mist oozed from its nostrils. Kọ̀yà and Alawani looked at her in shock.

The realization hit her, and everything she'd done that night came crashing into her mind like a whirlwind. She'd taken yet another life. How? All she'd done was . . . she'd touched it. She'd liked the heat coming off it and had – she'd killed it. L'ọrẹ walked closer to the rhino. Did she really bring down this mountain of a beast by simply touching it? Draining all the heat and life from it, leaving it overtaken with ice? She glared at her shivering hands. The black veins were gone. Bile rose to her mouth, and she hurled out her guts.

L'ọrẹ sobbed loudly. 'What am I turning into? What is happening to me?'

Alawani reached out for her but she avoided his hands, scared to touch him.

'People are coming,' Kọ̀yà said, his eyes darting between L'ọrẹ and the shapes of travellers approaching further down the road.

'Come on,' Alawani said, gently. 'We have to go.'

They'd been lucky to cross to the second ring before the guards got word of trouble, and behind them, although the sun was not yet in the sky, the city was buzzing. Awoken by the heavy patrol of guards, ordering people out of their homes and searching them. As they raced through the streets, they weaved through the deserted corners that L'ọrẹ was used to taking when she wanted to avoid the townspeople. Three light beads later, they finally reached her compound, exhausted from running the entire way home. L'ọrẹ's eyes were weak from crying, her body ached from the fight, her face stung from where she'd pulled out glass shards, her arms hurt from the fall, and her heart hurt from everything. As soon as Baba-Ìtàn opened the door, she crumbled into his arms, crying and sobbing and begging forgiveness.

After settling down, Baba-Ìtàn made L'ọrẹ some herbal tea to calm her nerves and listened quietly as Kọ̀yà explained all that had happened that night. There was a loud ringing in L'ọrẹ's head that made everything around her sound muffled.

The home she'd been running to felt strange now. Different. She'd changed, and this safe haven that had harboured her for her entire life seemed to know that too. She walked over silently to the edge of the room and sat in the corner, the tea cooling in her hands, her stare blank.

L'orẹ couldn't hear the exact words Kọ̀yà spoke, but as he did, the horrors of the night replayed in an endless loop in her mind as hot tears poured from her eyes. Kọ̀yà described how she'd disappeared and reappeared before his eyes. Pain still hummed in her hands and streaks of black veins had branched out and crawled over her skin. Each one burned like hot coals on her hand and she pulled her sleeves over them to hide them from her father. She hugged her legs, making herself as small as possible, pushing her back hard against the wall. Avoiding the glances that Alawani and Baba-Ìtàn sent her way.

Eventually, Alawani held her, wrapping his arms around her whole body. He rocked her and offered promises that she was glad not to hear so she couldn't hold him to them.

Finally, Kọ̀yà said, 'We didn't see anyone following us, but surely, they will come.'

Baba-Ìtàn sighed and groaned as he walked towards L'orẹ, and Alawani stepped aside to give him room. She didn't dare look up at her father as he bent down and lifted her chin. L'orẹ closed her eyes and wept. A low constant groan hummed in Baba-Ìtàn's throat as he wiped her tears and she flinched but allowed him to pull her into an embrace. His hands smoothed over her braids. 'My child,' he whispered. 'It's time to go home.'

L'orẹ pulled back from him and asked with a shaky voice, 'Home?'

Baba-Ìtàn opened his mouth to speak, then looked at her neck. His eyes widened so much she could see the whites of them. 'Where is your necklace?'

L'ọrẹ touched her neck instinctively. 'It burned me,' she said, her voice hoarse from crying. 'I put it in my pocket, but it must have fallen out. I lost it.'

Baba-Ìtàn ran his hand through his greying hair. 'That's why this happened. I put a protection spell on it. Your agbára forced itself out once the necklace was gone.'

'It felt like lava on my skin! I thought it was going to kill me.'

'It couldn't have killed you. The necklace was to protect you, L'ọrẹ!'

'She was still wearing the necklace when she became invisible. She took it off after she reappeared,' Kòyà said, his voice nearly a whisper as he stared at L'ọrẹ.

Baba-Ìtàn's eyes widened even further. 'You turned invisible *before* you took it off?'

'But whatever she did, it wasn't agbára,' Kòyà said. L'ọrẹ hated the note of fear in his voice.

'No, it wasn't agbára oru,' Baba-Ìtàn said, then turned to Kòyà and Alawani. 'Go to L'ọrẹ's room, pack what you can. Take only what can fit in a single bag. Do not return until I call for you.'

'What about the Order?' Kòyà said. 'There's a growing number of guards in the city. We barely escaped in time.'

Baba-Ìtàn shook his head. 'They won't risk a public chase and capture. They know better than to do anything to expose things they want to keep hidden. To do so is to risk the people of this kingdom learning about your powers or that their prince was taken from their temple. It's much harder to explain your kind of agbára to the people.' He sighed bitterly. 'They'll come quietly.'

Alawani shot one last glance at L'ọrẹ, a hand across his chest. Telling her that was where she was. In his heart, always. She gave a slight nod, and he walked out of the room. Until that night, she'd never had a reason to doubt this. But something had shifted. He'd left. He'd sworn to her, sealed his vow in blood and left. Even now, miles from the Sun Temple, it still loomed between them.

Baba-Ìtàn placed his palms in hers, and L'ọrẹ pulled her hands back to her sides. 'I don't want to hurt you.'

'You won't. Do you feel anything now?' Baba-Ìtàn asked.

L'ọrẹ shook her head.

He stretched out his hands to her. 'You can touch me, you won't hurt me.'

L'ọrẹ reached for his hands, and he flinched at how cold they were but held on and squeezed. She looked into her father's eyes, and tears welled up in hers.

'What am I, Bàbá?' L'ọrẹ asked with soft sobs.

'You're my child,' Baba-Ìtàn said, taking his hand from hers and wiping the tears from her face. 'A child of Oru,' he said, squeezing her hands tighter. 'This is a gift, not a curse. You don't need to be afraid.'

His words told her to be brave, but the way his deep voice gave way, exposing the well of pain he must be feeling, made L'ọrẹ's heart break. She'd completely ruined the life they had together. She might have resented their solitary life, being stuck in their house for days on end, hiding from the world that hated them. Now, all she wanted to do was shut the door and never leave. She'd do anything for the life she'd desperately tried to run from.

L'ọrẹ held her father's gaze. 'Bàbá, I *am* scared. What's happening to me?'

Baba-Ìtàn let out a deep sigh. His hundredth since she had walked in through the door that morning. His brows furrowed, and he whispered words in a dialect she didn't understand. Then he said, 'I will tell you the history you don't know. You got these powers from your mother.'

'My mother? But she was a maiden of the Sun Temple.

She was a child of the sun. How could she pass on powers she didn't have?'

'I need you to be quiet, L'orẹ, and listen to what I'm saying.' He paused and raised an eyebrow, waiting for her acknowledgement. She nodded, and he continued, 'You know the history of our kingdom as I've told you, the origin of our agbára, the first High Priest and the king who built this kingdom. But there are parts I've left out. The parts the storyteller oath binds us from speaking of, the part that demands to be forgotten. *Your* history. In the days of the First Sun all those years ago, after the High Priest Àlùfáà Àkanní, the first Àlùfáà, blessed the people with this agbára, something unexpected happened. The gods played a fickle game with us, and this was perhaps the cruellest of them all. While almost everyone in the kingdom could summon the powers of the sun – agbára oru – a few others had what we now know as agbára òtútù.'

'Agbára òtútù?' L'orẹ asked.

'These people were different,' Baba-Ìtàn continued. 'The story doesn't say why this happened or how, but these few couldn't summon the sun; instead, they could bring forth ice, and some could vanish into shadows like the sun in the night sky. The Holy Order grew afraid of them and made the choice to remove them from this earth, remove their stories from our history, and cleanse them from existence.'

'They killed them all?'

'Not all,' Baba-Ìtàn said. 'Your mother wasn't a temple maiden of Oru. She had served as a handmaiden in the Sun Temple for a while; that was where I met her. But no, she was not of this land at all. She was a descendant of those people, and through her, you got these powers.'

L'orẹ turned on him, 'You knew all this time who and what I was, and you let me grow up thinking something was wrong with me, feeling even more like an outcast everywhere I went? You used that necklace to trap my powers? How could you?'

Baba-Ìtàn struggled to his feet. In her anger, she still helped him to get off the floor. 'Listen to me, L'ọrẹ, there is no time to be angry – now is the time to listen. I wish I had more time to tell you everything about your people, your mother, your true home –'

'What home? My mother died because she was –' Realization hit her, and she stopped. 'The Holy Order didn't only kill her for having me, did they? They killed her because she had this agbára,' L'ọrẹ asked with her arms outstretched.

'I couldn't tell you the truth about her because it would have gotten you killed. Protecting you has been my life's mission. I failed to protect your mother and won't make the same mistake twice. You're my priority. You're more important than anything else. When your mother placed you in my hands, I swore to her to keep you safe. She didn't want you to use these powers. She put that necklace around your neck, keeping your agbára hidden and her child safe.'

Every word that he said drove a knife deeper into L'ọrẹ's heart. She could hear the words he spoke and understand them, but she couldn't believe them. They sounded like the stories told by the moonlight with the kids from the village. Like some far-away legend for them to gasp and laugh at but not to live, not reality.

Tears filled her eyes again and they stung. Every revelation filled her with rage. After staring at him blankly for what felt like forever, she said, 'You lied to me.'

Baba-Ìtàn moved closer to her, but she stepped out of his reach. He raised his sleeve to show a deep cut in his upper arm. 'I swore a blood oath to your mother. To keep you alive.

So no, I didn't tell you the truth about your mother or your agbára because I wanted to keep you safe.'

'I could have protected myself with the truth,' L'ọrẹ said, her eyes burning with tears.

'Your mother came to Oru to change the will of the gods. Defying everyone in her life who tried to convince her otherwise,' he smiled bitterly, 'much like you tried to last night. And like her, you found the enemy there much greater than you imagined. And I'm trying to keep you from meeting the same fate she did.'

'What did she want from the gods? How did she defy anyone?'

Baba-Ìtàn shook his head, 'That's not important now. What matters is what needs to happen next.'

L'ọrẹ looked at this man she'd known her whole life. He was different too. The pillar in her mind's eye that she saw whenever she thought of her father shook furiously, spitting out sand and dust. Not even the ground beneath her feet felt solid enough to stand on.

'Where did my mother come from?'

'The north. From the snow mountains deep in the north.'

L'ọrẹ pulled out a rolled piece of parchment from the wall of scrolls that surrounded them and spread out a map. 'Show me.'

The map of Oru was similar to the target board L'ọrẹ used when training to throw knives. Seven concentric circles from small to large, each ring a different state, with the royal island as the dot in the centre of the kingdom.

'The kingdom of Òtútù is far past the borders of Oru.' Baba-Ìtàn pulled out a smaller piece of parchment from a hidden corner. He put his map over hers and pointed to a cluster of mountains at the top side of the map. 'I drew this map myself; this is where your mother was from, where you're from.'

L'ọrẹ slammed her fists down on the table. 'I am a child of Oru. You've said this to me my entire life.'

'L'ọrẹ, if I sat here to tell you everything, it would take an entire lifetime.'

'You had an entire lifetime to tell me! That is exactly what I am saying.'

'Maybe. But teaching you anything about agbára was a risk I was not willing to take. I may not be an Àlùfáà of the Holy Order anymore but I know them, and to them, L'ọrẹ, you are a threat. A threat to our kingdom, our agbára and our lives. And there is nothing but death waiting for you now that they know of you.' Baba-Ìtàn straightened, confident he'd made the right decision. 'Time is running out. Those they will send after you won't hunt in the chaos of daylight. But I assure you, they're coming. You must leave, journey north and find your people. Only there will you be safe.'

'You are my people, Bàbá,' L'ọrẹ said. The reality of his words hit her like a rock to the head.

She looked into Baba-Ìtàn's glassy eyes, which had filled with tears, and all her anger seemed to melt away into a part of her she kept hidden. On the surface, all she wanted to do was hug the man she called father, so she did.

'Come with me,' L'ọrẹ said. He hadn't said that he wouldn't, but somehow, in her heart, she knew that her father would not leave his home.

Baba-Ìtàn held her tight in his arms, allowing the tears to roll down his face. 'Take Kọ̀yà.'

'And Alawani?' L'ọrẹ said. It was something between a question and a statement.

Baba-Ìtàn shook his head. 'His grandfather killed your mother. I can't entrust your life into his hands.'

The pit that now lived inside L'ọrẹ's stomach sunk even deeper. The truth about Àlùfáà-Àgbà giving the order that took her mother from her was something she'd done her best to keep far from her consciousness. If she allowed herself to fully understand what that meant, there would be no saving whatever she and Alawani had. There would be no saving her from the brink of madness that would no doubt consume her.

As though Baba-Ìtàn knew what she was thinking, he said, 'Àlùfáà-Àgbà didn't just give the order. He killed her himself! I watched it happen,' his voice broke. 'After hiding for three blood moons, we made it all the way to the fourth ring before the Order caught up with us. I watched him cut down the woman I loved, unable to do anything but hold you close as you cried in my arms.'

L'ọrẹ's fingers scraped at her bare chest, instinctively feeling for the necklace her mother had given her as panic flooded her mind and her heart began to ache. Images of Àlùfáà-Àgbà's raging face at the temple replayed in her mind, distorted through the dark ice of her creation. He threw those fireballs with such fervour, such anger. She still couldn't believe all his efforts had done nothing to break down her wall.

Her best friend's grandfather had killed her mother. L'ọrẹ shook her head, scrambling the next thoughts that formed. She couldn't dwell on that, or she'd never return from that dark place. She focused on the truth she knew, which was that Alawani wasn't his father or grandfather. He wasn't an oathbreaker. He was her friend, and he'd proven himself to her more times than she could count. But she couldn't help but ask herself, did Alawani know what his grandfather had done?

No, she shook her head. 'He's coming, Bàbá. All of this has been to save him. I won't leave him now.'

The door slammed open, and a young boy ran in, holding his chest and struggling to speak. L'ọrẹ recognized him as one of the children who came to listen to the stories Baba-Ìtàn told beneath the tree in their compound.

'What is the meaning of this?' Baba-Ìtàn asked, startled.

'Bàbá, they are – the royal guards are coming for you,' the boy said through shallow breaths.

Alawani and Kọ̀yà burst in from the bedroom. 'What's happening?' Alawani asked.

'There's no time for questions. You must all leave now.' Baba-Ìtàn brought out a red pouch of coins, and tossed it into the bag Kọ̀yà was carrying. L'ọrẹ recognized it as the pouch where he kept all their life savings. The pouch that had kept them alive, one coin at a time. She tried to object but he said, 'You'll need it more than I will.' She could've crumbled to the floor and wept – if she had the time. She managed to turn the corners of her mouth upward and give half a nod. Baba-Ìtàn reached for the maps and tucked them into her bag too. 'Go to Ìlú-Idán, avoid the King's Road. There's a letter here for a woman who will help you,' he said with reddened eyes and shaky hands. 'Her name is Àdùkẹ́, she's an old friend. Once you cross the borders into Ìlú-Idán, you need only say her name to the wind, and she will find you and help you out of Oru. Do you understand me?'

'You're not coming?' Alawani asked.

'No,' Baba-Ìtàn replied, and L'ọrẹ heard the coldness in his voice. Only then did she realize he'd always taken that tone with Alawani. She'd thought then that he was an over-protective father, but now, knowing what she knew . . . it all made sense.

'I can't go either. My family is here. My brother,' Kọ̀yà said to L'ọrẹ. 'The Holy Order don't know who I am. Between the hoods and the dark night, I don't think they could have recognized me. I'll be fine.'

L'ọrẹ selfishly longed for his steadfast company but she

couldn't imagine ever asking him for anything else. She'd disrupted his world far too much already. She only hoped that Kọ̀yà's face and name were as hidden as he assumed. She moved to hug him and placed a kiss on his cheek. 'Go. Thank you. I owe you, Kọ̀yà. I'll make it up to you. I swear it.' She hugged him again and smiled as his arms went around her. 'Thank you,' she whispered one last time, and pulled out of his embrace.

Kọ̀yà leaned into her ear, 'I don't know what your magic is, but remember, you were trained in the pits of Gbàgede. You're a warrior. Make them sorry they ever tried to hurt you.'

L'ọrẹ nodded, the lump in her throat heavy and tight. She didn't know what it was like to have a sibling but she loved Kọ̀yà so much in a way that was different from the way she loved Alawani – and different from the way Kọ̀yà loved her.

Kọ̀yà smiled at her and bowed to Baba-Ìtàn. He looked at Alawani, and L'ọrẹ could feel the tension between the boys, who'd been friends long before she came into their lives. They didn't touch or hug. Just a mutual firm nod of understanding and then Kọ̀yà quietly slid out of the library's door and disappeared around the corner.

'What about you?' L'ọrẹ said to Alawani. She wished she didn't have to ask, but she did.

Alawani raised his palm to show the mark of their oath, and her heart leapt in her chest. 'I'm with you,' he said, holding her gaze.

'Are you sure?' she asked, and again hated that she did.

Baba-Ìtàn interrupted, 'Don't make promises to my daughter that you cannot keep. I blame you for this. If you had left us alone when I told you to, none of this would have happened.'

'Baba?' L'ọrẹ called out, stepping between Alawani and

her father. 'Don't say that. Alawani would never do anything to hurt me.'

'That remains to be seen,' Baba-Ìtàn scoffed.

'I made my choice the moment I followed her out of the temple,' Alawani said to Baba-Ìtàn. 'As you know, there's no going back now.'

L'orẹ sighed in relief. She'd been holding her breath until his response. Then she returned to Baba-Ìtàn, whose lips quivered.

'But you won't come,' L'orẹ said.

Her father only shook his head. 'My place is here. Between you and the evil that comes.'

L'orẹ looked at her father, trying to commit his face to memory. Carving every line and curve, every shade and blemish into her mind.

'Tèmil'orẹ mí,' Baba-Ìtàn said with a sad smile on his face. He guided her hands into his, 'be careful with this power. It's not a curse but it can do a lot of harm.'

L'orẹ nodded, fighting back tears as her eyes caught the loose seams in his clothes that she never got around to fixing. There was so much she was leaving undone. So much she should have done.

Her father pulled out a single cowrie from his pocket and placed it firmly in her palm. 'In this land, this is a sign of one's kills, but in your mother's homeland, your homeland, this is a sign of those you loved and lost. I kept this when I lost your mother – take it with you, and may her spirit sing to you the way she did when she was alive.'

L'orẹ choked at his words, and it took all of her to not crumble as the pillars in her mind trembled as if shaken by the ground beneath them.

Baba-Ìtàn held her face in his palms, 'Remember the daughter of whom you are.'

While the rest of the continent fought with bows and
arrows, swords and spears
the scions of the old gods used àṣẹ to command
the elements.
They summoned the winds, moved the earth,
controlled water and breathed fire.
With all this power, they should have won the
fight to come
but a kingdom is only as great as its weakest link.
They did not win the war to come.

18

The Sun Temple, Royal Island, Kingdom of Oru

TOFA

As Tofa and his father walked through the gates of the Sun Temple, the Lord Regent's jaw clenched tight, and the veins in his temples bulged and throbbed beneath the scorching sun. Tofa felt exposed without his shadow. His sister hated when he called her that but she was always at his side. Except when he went into the Sun Temple. She'd made it clear that she'd rather face death than ever again walk into the building where they'd been born. So here he was without her, on edge, unable to stop checking to see if she'd appear.

'I can't imagine why Àjànàkú would keep something like this from me. I shouldn't have to rely on spies for information in my own kingdom.' When the Lord Regent was displeased, he didn't call Àlùfáà-Àgbà by his title, choosing the priest's first name instead. Àjànàkú – the name the Elder Priest bore before his position in the Order. Of all the people alive in Oru, only the Lord Regent had the authority and the guts to do such a thing.

Tofa didn't respond. He instead sped up to match his father's quick angry strides. Around them, the people walking the temple grounds noticed their presence and bowed.

Whispers of the Lord Regent's appearance in the temple spread like wildfire as a crowd blossomed out of thin air.

From the day Tofa knew what the word 'father' meant, he knew that the man called the Lord Regent was his. As he grew older, he realized he was born for a life more extraordinary than most. Tofa was the firstborn of an Àlùfáà and crown heir to the kingdom of Oru.

'That I should leave my palace and come here is an insult. That man thinks he can do as he pleases in my temple. Keeping secrets from me? Am I not still the High Priest of this temple or will Àjànàkú lay claim to that as well? It's my fault. I should have put him in his place a long time ago,' the Lord Regent said, shaking the horsetail in his hand angrily as he spoke.

Tofa knew he was walking into a fight he didn't want to be a part of. His father slowed his stride and sighed deeply as a group of children ran to prostrate themselves before him. The Lord Regent didn't smile, but he paused long enough to ease the tension in his temples. They took in the sight of him as though they were in the presence of a god. His father's full-length gold embroidered agbádá glistened in the sun, and the many layers of the ensemble made him look much larger than he really was. He wore layers of gold and red coral beads draped around his neck, wrists and ankles, signifying his royal position, and waved at the crowd before picking up his pace again.

Watching his father was often like watching two sides of a person fight for dominance. One side was the person his father wanted to be: kind and compassionate. And the other was the person the crown compelled him to be: ruthless and unyielding. As Tofa's coronation day drew nearer, he felt the pull of the throne, the heaviness of the crown and the call of duty that he had to yield to. His whole life, he'd seen how the weight of the kingdom turned his father from the man who taught him how to love into the man who taught him how to be broken.

'I thought they said the temple grounds were damaged?' the Lord Regent said.

Tofa scanned the grounds. The temple compound looked as it did on any day. There was no evidence of the incident his father's spies had revealed to them. The crunch of his father's heavy steps on the cobbled stones rang in Tofa's ears, and he quietly fell one step behind him as they walked on.

'If I wanted to talk to myself, I wouldn't have brought you along,' the Lord Regent said without looking back.

Tofa quickened his stride to match his father's. 'Ẹ má bí'nú, Bàbá.' He apologized for his quietness but didn't add anything; he was too worried about saying the wrong thing. His father was never more unlike himself than when he was in the Sun Temple. The Lord Regent despised the days he had spent locked up in the temple towers watching his fellow chosen ones die like flies one after the other, following each stripping ceremony. Tofa had snuck into the temple to see for himself the nightmare rituals that had haunted his father for many first suns. He'd watched his old friend climb the Red Stone, and he'd watched others like him die upon it. It was a sight he knew would forever be burnt into his memory. But for all its horrors, Tofa felt a new understanding for what and who his father had become.

'Surviving was a cruel joke that the gods played on me,' his father had always said.

The scowl on the Lord Regent's face deepened with each step as they walked through the maze. The man moved swiftly through the corners, avoiding every dead end as though he'd built it himself. Only then did Tofa notice the fading marks of old magic inscriptions on the walls of the maze. Spells written in the old tongue always gradually disappeared after they'd accomplished their goal. Since the temple looked untouched, and Tofa had heard that several walls across the maze had been crushed down in the escape, the restored walls were evidence that the Order had worked hard to hide the truth about the invasion before the sun reached the sky. He wondered what else the Elder Priest was trying to hide from his father with the fading spells he couldn't read from a distance.

Next to him, his father marched on, his gaze focused on the gilded doors that led into the temple. Tofa often questioned what would become of his father once he ascended the throne. Would he return to the Sun Temple and focus on leading the Holy Order as the High Priest, like Àlùfáà-Àgbà? In truth, the one thing his father wanted was the thing he couldn't have. To return to the life he lived before he was called Àlùfáà. Tofa glanced at his father and eyed the tribal marks etched into his temple. Three short vertical lines over three short horizontal lines. Ìlú-Idán. He wondered if there was anything left of that old life to return to.

They walked the length of the courtyard, approaching the main temple doors, as priests, servants and maidens alike gathered outside to sing his father's praises. Talking drums beat to the rhythm of his name – Babátúndé – and the women used his oríkì – his praise name, Àdìó, the righteous one – to sing blessings to him. A cloud of dust surrounded them as they moved to the beat of the drums. Their shoulders rolled effortlessly. The beads clinging to their waists danced like snakes swimming along their bodies. The men jumped high in the air and fell flat on the ground. It wasn't every day this High Priest of the Sun Temple visited his home. The people used their agbára to shine beams of light onto the path, creating a trail of gold across the ground leading to the temple doors. The Lord Regent held his head high as they parted the way before him and fell to their knees as he walked by. His agbádá crunched with every step. The glowing fabric was starched firm to avoid the risk of wrinkle, and glittering silver threads formed delicate embroideries that ran the full length of the outfit.

The temple doors swung open, and the Lord Regent stormed in through the gilded entrance. Tofa walked in after his father, surveying the carved walls, decorated pillars and painted ceilings that filled the temple hallway. 'Do you think they'll find the prince?'

The Lord Regent slowed his steps and Tofa matched his father's pace again. 'For his sake, I hope they find him,' the Lord Regent said. 'It's better to die on the Red Stone than be hunted down like an animal in the street. At least here, his death would mean something.'

Tofa considered the fate of his old friend. Truth be told, it had been many first suns since he deserved to describe Alawani as a friend. And until the day Alawani broke into his chambers, it had been even longer since he laid eyes on the boy who had played with him in the palace courtyards, teaching him the way of the sword. Perhaps more importantly, ways to talk to girls. Once, he'd have given anything to switch places with the prince. To have a life with no apparent responsibility and no expectations. How unfortunate his friend's life had turned out to be in the end. For who could say no to the call of the gods? He couldn't.

The hallway got brighter as they walked further in.

'There are others. Can't they just let him go? Can't *you* let him go?' Tofa asked, knowing his question was on the edge of what was appropriate. It made no difference that Tofa was heir to the throne until the crown was on his head. He was subject to the Lord Regent's authority just like the people outside the temple, still singing his father's praises.

'If running away was an option, don't you think we'd all

have run?' the Lord Regent said before turning a corner and walking into the first room on his right. 'Only cowards run.'

Àlùfáà-Àgbà was already inside, waiting for them. The older man bowed his head but not his knees. 'Lord Regent,' he said with an exaggerated groan as he shifted his body back upright. The law demanded that anyone who came before the crown had to lie flat on the ground with their foreheads touching the ground until they were permitted to stand. This half-hearted half-curtsy the old man had done was an insult and they all knew it. Àlùfáà-Àgbà had himself held the dual position of High Priest and Lord Regent before Lord Regent Babátúndé and it seemed as though the old man used every opportunity to remind everyone of this fact, especially in the way he spoke to the Lord Regent. Tofa wondered if his father noticed it as keenly as he did.

Lord Regent Babátúndé only nodded in Àlùfáà-Àgba's direction and walked towards the raised dais, and sat upon a replica of the palace throne. Tofa hated watching the power struggle between the two men who raised him – his father and the man he had turned to when his father's heart had hardened. For that reason alone, he couldn't wait to be king.

For a certain period in every cycle of life and death of sovereigns in Oru, the position of the High Priest of the Holy Order and Lord Regent was held by a single person. But sometimes, the new Regent ruled while the former was still alive and well. When that happened, conflict was unavoidable, Tofa thought.

'Tell me what happened,' the Lord Regent said in a single breath.

Tofa stayed a safe distance away, keeping quiet and hoping they wouldn't notice his presence. He could feel the fight brewing in the air.

'I don't like this, Kẹni,' Tofa said to his sister, then glanced back when she didn't respond. Of course she didn't respond. She wasn't there.

Àlùfáà-Àgbà looked at Tofa and then back to the Lord Regent. 'We should discuss these matters in private.'

'Speak,' the Lord Regent's voice boomed.

Àlùfáà-Àgbà clenched his fists. But the law was the law, and the current Lord Regent Babátúndé now had the power he'd once had, and Àlùfáà-Àgbà had to bend the knee.

Àlùfáà-Àgbà talked about the passageway that the intruders had come in through, the boys they had taken, and how they escaped using strange powers to shield themselves from the maidens' arrows.

'Agbára òtútù,' the Lord Regent said as Àlùfáà-Àgbà described the thing the intruder had created.

Tofa listened intently, even though he made sure his gaze avoided them both. He wondered how his father knew so quickly the magic that Àlùfáà-Àgbà was describing. There was a whole world of things his father and Àlùfáà-Àgbà, who had been his teacher and mentor from young, had kept from him, even as they claimed to prepare him for the throne. For starters, Tofa wondered what in the world agbára òtútù was. Never in the time he spent studying under Àlùfáà-Àgbà had he ever heard that term before.

'How is this possible?' the Lord Regent said. 'You told me they were all wiped out. When I took your place as High Priest, you were supposed to tell me all the secrets of the Order from before the days of the First Sun until now, and you said that the people of Òtútù and their cursed magic would never be a threat to this kingdom again.'

'I told you what I had to,' Àlùfáà-Àgbà replied with a straight face. From the look on his father's face, Tofa knew he was mere moments from calling his guards.

'Àjànàkú, I wear the crown. To lie to me is treason worthy of death. Tell me the truth. The whole truth.'

The older man shifted where he stood. Clearly uncomfortable and deeply insulted that the Lord Regent had called him by his first name and without his title, the law was the law, and so quietly, he began. 'The girl must be found. That's the truth. Our forefathers had the right mind to eliminate her kind. They're an abomination.'

The Lord Regent listened quietly, leaning forward on the edge of his seat.

'History says the cursed people of Òtútù were lost to the sands, and the gods claimed back their lives, but some still live. Somewhere deep in the north, beyond the sands, at the edge of the continent.'

The Lord Regent's frown deepened. 'I know my history, Àjànàkú. I don't need you to tell me what the people of Òtútù can do, I need you to tell me how they can still be alive and how long you've known about this threat to our kingdom. How could you keep something like this a secret? You've put us all at risk, and for what?'

What history was this? Who were the people of Òtútù and why had his ancestors tried to eliminate them? How could there be something other than agbára oru? And a kingdom outside of Oru that he hadn't heard of? As far as he and the rest of the kingdom were concerned there was no rival kingdom on the continent. Tofa only knew of the sand raiders that lurked around the outer walls, and they had no magic at all. They were barely surviving and could hardly be called a kingdom, least of all rivals. Was there really an enemy dangerous enough to rattle two of the most powerful men in Oru? Tofa's unease grew as he wondered what other secrets the Holy Order were hiding from everyone and from him.

'Did you know about this?' Tofa whispered and glanced

back to his sister, then sighed. He'd done it again. His shoulders slumped and he turned towards his father.

'Who else knows about this?' the Lord Regent asked after a few moments of silence from the Elder Priest.

'No one else,' Àlùfáà-Àgbà replied and turned back to face Tofa, 'other than you and the crown heir.'

Tofa adjusted his body, rising to his full height, preparing to step forward if he had to.

'How do you know where exactly the people of Òtútù are?' the Lord Regent asked.

Good question, Tofa thought, raising his gaze to Àlùfáà-Àgbà for the first time since he walked into the room.

'Eighteen first suns ago, there was a girl of Òtútù hiding in this kingdom. Luckily, we found her and interrogated her. We learned that the people of Òtútù settled north in the mountains.'

The Lord Regent stood from his throne, his voice was a low growl, 'Eighteen first suns ago I was Lord Regent. Why didn't I meet this girl?'

Àlùfáà-Àgbà tried unsuccessfully to hide the ugly scowl on his face. Eighteen first suns ago, the transfer of power would have still been fresh. No doubt Àlùfáà-Àgbà made that decision as though he was still in charge. Tofa was certain of one thing. When he was crowned as sovereign, for as long as he ruled, his word would be final above all.

'And where is this woman now?' the Lord Regent said.

Àlùfáà-Àgbà looked at Tofa and then to the Lord Regent knowingly.

'Oh, gods! Àjànàkú! What's this that you have brought to our doorstep? You killed her?'

'I did what was right for my kingdom and honoured the gods who blessed us with this gift to protect ourselves. We must protect ourselves from their rot, chaos and destruction! We can't leave them alive! This is war. You, of all people, should understand what's at stake.'

'How can I? I didn't see for myself what magic the girl left behind last night. And in the tradition of keeping your secrets, you have removed all evidence of it,' the Lord Regent said.

Àlùfáà-Àgbà had been many things to Tofa over the years they'd spent together. Years he remembered fondly. But Tofa knew Àlùfáà-Àgbà well enough to know that this wasn't the full story. It wasn't ever the full story. There were more secrets to be uncovered. Right there, Tofa decided he wanted to know more about these people and their power that threatened his kingdom.

'That abomination couldn't be left to mock our gods. The people mustn't see it. They mustn't know of the past our ancestors fought to erase.' He paused. 'Lord Regent, the war that Oru fights is behind closed doors, in whispers. Our real enemy, our only enemy, is the people of Òtútù. It is our solemn duty to finish what our forefathers started. You know what powers they hold; their core is blackened, turning everything and everyone they touch to rot. No one with the blessing of agbára oru is safe as long as people who can take away those abilities are out there planning our destruction.'

The Lord Regent sighed deeply. 'We must call a confidential council meeting to discuss this.'

Àlùfáà-Àgbà frowned. 'The existence of the people of Òtútù is a secret the Order has held for generations. To tell the council is to break that oath.'

'I swore no such oath,' Lord Regent Babátúndé said sharply. 'I will not let this secret fester until it is too late to save our kingdom. I will bring this to the council, they *must* know . . . But we must make sure that this doesn't leak out to the rest of the kingdom.'

Àlùfáà-Àgbà yielded, bowing his head slightly. 'As you wish, Lord Regent.' Then just as quickly, he said, 'One more thing. No one knew about the tunnels in the walls. Even the temple maidens don't know that they exist. Only someone who has been called and is now a priest could know about their existence.'

'So how did this girl of Òtútù know about these secret passageways?' the Lord Regent asked.

'You tell me, Lord Regent,' Àlùfáà-Àgbà replied. 'None of my priests would ever reveal such secrets.'

Tofa watched his father's face keenly as the realization hit him.

'Ẹniìtàn,' the Lord Regent said in shock.

Àlùfáà-Àgbà nodded slowly. 'I believe the coward goes by Baba-Ìtàn now.'

'It's not possible. Ẹniìtàn disavowed the Order years ago. He wouldn't dare.'

'Oh, but he would,' Àlùfáà-Àgbà replied.

The coward. The only person who'd ever left the Holy Order alive. The one marked as an outcast, condemned in this world and in the afterlife for rejecting the call of the gods. Knowing what he knew about the Order, it was a surprise that the coward had been allowed to leave where others had not – another mystery Tofa had to figure out when he was king.

The Lord Regent took a few moments to think, then said, 'Bring him to me.'

'I have already sent the royal guards to fetch him,' Àlùfáà-Àgbà replied.

'*Alive*,' the Lord Regent said sternly.

'How many times will Ẹniìtàn be allowed to mock this Order?' Àlùfáà-Àgbà asked.

'I want to look him in the eye when he confesses this crime,' the Lord Regent said.

'And the Òtútù girl? We already have orders out to the guard to search every home. Let them know we are looking for the coward's girl and give orders to kill on sight – we don't have time to wait for a council meeting.'

'I cannot believe that Ẹniìtàn would do something like this. He raised this girl?' the Lord Regent said, confused. 'Bring them both to me, I will decide their fate.'

'No,' Àlùfáà-Àgbà said, 'she must die now.'

Babátúndé raised an eyebrow and tilted his head as a deep frown formed across his face. 'Is it me you are speaking to like a child born of your lions? You speak so carelessly, like one who owns the sands beneath our feet. Do you also own the sun? The gods? Who is it that gives you the audacity to say no to me?'

Àlùfáà-Àgbà shifted uncomfortably, and Tofa had to stop himself from going to defend the Elder Priest as he usually would.

'You have no authority in my kingdom, Àjànàkú,' the Lord Regent said in an even tone that sent chills down Tofa's back. 'I shouldn't have to remind you that you serve at the pleasure of the crown. I know my son is fond of you and if he were not here in this room, this would have gone very differently. Do not force my hand, old man.'

'Even after all these years, you are still that scared young boy who walked into this temple hoping to die a coward's death,' Àlùfáà-Àgbà said.

Tofa shrank back in horror.

'And now, I am your king!' the Lord Regent said, rising from his chair.

'Regent,' Àlùfáà-Àgbà murmured.

'Guards!' the Lord Regent shouted at the door.

Immediately, the guards that had been dismissed earlier rushed into the room in pairs, awaiting orders.

Tofa stepped closer to his father, squaring his shoulders and placing a hand on his sword. It wasn't often that Tofa had to pick sides between the pair, and he'd never been sure where he'd land, so he was surprised to find himself instinctively at his father's side. A man he knew much less than he did Àlùfáà-Àgbà, who practically raised him.

'On your knees,' the Lord Regent said to Àlùfáà-Àgbà.

Tofa saw the look of defiance still etched on the Elder Priest's face, mixed with disbelief. When he didn't obey, the guards quickly held Àlùfáà-Àgbà and pushed him down to his knees. Tofa stretched out his hand to intervene, but his feet remained rooted.

Lord Regent Babátúndé walked closer to Àlùfáà-Àgbà, so close that he towered over the old man.

The Lord Regent's eyes sparked golden with agbára as he bent over Àlùfáà-Àgbà and said, 'Wherever the light of our gods shines, there I am king. And even here within these walls. I am your High Priest, chosen by the gods, so don't cross me, or you will force me to show you which one of us wields true power in this kingdom!' He paused, then said, 'You are not the High Priest. You are a priest in my temple, a shadow of what once was. Remember that in your old age.'

The Lord Regent glanced at Tofa, then back at Àlùfáà-Àgbà, then walked towards the door, leaving the old man still on the floor.

À á n pe ẹran t'ó ni'wo, ìgbín náà n yọ'jú
*When animals with horns were called,
the snail also showed up thinking it was worthy*

19

The Home of Maidens, The Capital City, First Ring, Kingdom of Oru

MILÚÀ

Milúà and Bùnmi woke before the first light, so they could leave before the priests awoke and the first bell rang. The walk was far, but neither complained nor suggested a faster means of travel. They weren't in a hurry to meet whatever awaited them at home. The home of the maidens that raised those discarded by fate, orphans and the poor alike. No one knew why the mother of maidens said yes to some and no to others but with every passing first sun, more and more orphans strolled in seeking refuge, more mothers brought their girls seeking favour from the gods. Milúà often wondered about those who gifted their children – did they know what it truly meant to join the Order?

When Milúà was younger, it had been easier to believe her birth mother was dead rather than somewhere in the kingdom living a life without her. She couldn't bear the thought of it. Perhaps Bùnmi was stronger than she gave her credit for. Bùnmi knew exactly where her mother was. She knew the face of the woman who abandoned her, and to Milúà's surprise, Bùnmi had let the woman live.

The kingdom discarded its unwanted girls in Milúà's home and while it nurtured, trained and turned them into the fiercest warriors in the kingdom, it also watched them cry, bleed and break. This was the house where their mother still lived and to which they now returned. Ìyá-Ayé was every maiden's worst nightmare. She may have been called 'the mother of life', but Ìyá-Ayé couldn't be further from it, Milúà thought to herself as they walked the open grounds that led out of the temple.

Two light beads later, the girls turned the corner onto the long road that led to their home. Milúà's shoulders drooped, and she walked even more slowly. Temple maidens, good maidens, maidens who didn't lose or get their priests killed, never returned home alive. They served the temple and died, and returned to their mother as ashes in urns. When Milúà left home a few blood moons ago, she'd sworn that only her charred bones would return to be consecrated with her sisters who'd passed on before her. Now, all that seemed like the dreams of a naïve young girl.

Milúà looked sideways at Bùnmi, who bit her lips to keep them from trembling. She was walking towards a life sentence, and Milúà admired the girl's courage, however much she quivered. In all her life, she hadn't heard, seen or read of any maidens who lost their priests to death at the hands of strangers. At least her chosen one was alive; poor Bùnmi's was dead. The horror of what awaited her sister made Milúà's blood run cold.

Milúà had seen only five first suns when she realized she had the true sight. She could see agbára oru within a person as tangibly as she could see the sun. It wasn't something she could explain, so she told no one about it, especially not Ìyá-Ayé. The first thing she learned with this ability was to know who was worth fighting and who wasn't. While other people blindly went to battle, not knowing how much agbára their opponent had been blessed with, she was never caught off guard. But it wasn't often that she met someone whose agbára threatened her.

When she looked at a person with her true sight, a blur of colours and webs of glowing threads filled her vision. Their agbára appeared to her in tendrils of gold, leading to the shining orb in their chests. It pained Milúà to know that she could have stopped the escape. If she had known the girl was in the temple, she'd have found her before she could reach the gates. If the girl really was on the stairs when Milúà passed by as the priests say, she saw nothing at the time that made her feel the need to use her powers to see. She saw nothing at all.

Back at the temple, as Milúà had watched Bùnmi scream ash from her insides, choking the maiden that killed Máyòwá, she had known her sister was not long for this world. And looking into her core now, Milúà confirmed that Bùnmi's act of rage had in fact ignited the burn within her. The first thing they learned from their mother was to never give in to rage. Rage meant carelessness, and carelessness with one's core could mean triggering the disease that consumed all who pushed their agbára past its limit. It would be many blood moons before Bùnmi would see the first patch of charred skin appear on her flesh, but by then, it'd be too late. Her core was already dimming, her light fading, and with it, her life.

'I should run away,' Bùnmi said in a flat tone.

'Don't be stupid,' Milúà said, meaning every word. 'She'll only send me to kill you, and I'm too tired to chase you.'

Bùnmi smiled bitterly. 'I'm faster than you.'

'Sure you are.' Milúà tried to return her smile, but it faltered, and the corners of her lips fell. 'Don't worry, she can't be angry forever.'

'Yes she can,' Bùnmi said. 'And it's not just that . . .' She paused, and her voice dropped. 'I've lost my chance to be High Priestess.'

Milúà didn't mean to laugh but the chuckle burst out of her. 'You were never going to be High Priestess.' Bùnmi scowled but Milúà continued before she could interject. 'I mean, none of us were ever going to be High Priestess. You know that. Even if Máyòwá hadn't died, no Àlùfáà from this set of chosen ones is going to be a High Priest. The king is young; in fact, the king hasn't even ascended the throne. There's no need for a new High Priest and so no need for a new High Priestess. Not for many first suns to come.'

'I suppose that's true,' Bùnmi said. 'But didn't you ever think about it? Having all that power?'

'No,' Milúà said plainly. 'Best to think of more important things, like surviving each day.'

Bùnmi rolled her eyes.

'Do you know how many people have to die before a new High Priest is chosen? Many people, including the crown heir and the Lord Regent. So no. I don't think about being bound to a High Priest who may not be chosen until we're both dead from old age. I want something more and I want it now.'

'So, it's true that Ìyá-Ayé is grooming you to replace her.'

Milúà knew that her sisters all thought this. And although she'd never dare bring it up with their mother, she'd once considered what life with all the power and authority of the name Ìyá-Ayé would mean for her. But that wasn't what she wanted. She hadn't decided yet how to get the power she needed but it definitely wasn't anything that would keep her stuck in that house.

'No, she's not,' Milúà said. 'At least I don't think so.'

'But you'll take it if she offers,' Bùnmi said.

Milúà thought back to the boys who gave up their agbára to join the Holy Order and wondered what she'd give up for power.

'I just wish she'd let me die,' Bùnmi said defeatedly.

'She won't,' Milúà said plainly. For reasons such as this, Milúà had found it difficult to extend pity to the boys who died on the Red Stone. They got to die. Dying was easy; living with their mother after such a blunder was a fate worse than death. Even as she watched the stripping ceremony, which filled her ears with shouts and cries, all she could think of was how it wasn't much different to the screams and cries she heard growing up. Sometimes, from her very own mouth. So even though Bùnmi hid her fear of their mother in an angry and stern face, Milúà knew that beneath the maiden's blood-red exterior was a young, terrified child.

She supposed Bùnmi had been fortunate to have known a mother other than Ìyá-Ayé. At least her birth mother had wanted her – if only for a little while. Milúà, meanwhile, had been born into Ìyá-Ayé's hands, that much the woman had told her. Milúà knew nothing about her parents, so she'd assumed she was an orphan, and no one ever told her otherwise. Until now, after the records she'd found in the library had given her the truth she'd searched for her whole life.

Her mother was a maiden.

Milúà hadn't seen a death record, or any order for execution, and she hated the hope that bloomed inside her. What if her mother was still alive?

Another light bead later, they arrived at the entrance to the House. The maidens' home was a collection of single-floored bungalows spread across the large compound.

Bùnmi's legs nearly buckled at the sight and Milúà moved to hold her up. 'Don't let her know your thoughts. Protect yourself. Protect your mind,' Milúà said in a low voice. 'Don't give her the satisfaction of breaking you, sister. Remember your training.' Bùnmi nodded briskly and blinked away her tears.

Inside, Milúà and Bùnmi fell to their knees in unison before their mother, who sat in the centre of the room, waiting. The room smelled of smoke and crushed herbs, which meant someone had been burned and healed and burned again. Milúà kept her head down, but every single corner of the room was a fixed image in her mind. She knew exactly how many paces their mother was from her seat on the elevated dais. And the feel of the carpet she knelt on. Many of her childhood tears had soaked deep into its depths. Milúà even knew how hard the granite walls were. Her fingers instinctively moved to the scar on her head, remembering where her mother had crashed her head into it. Ìyá-Ayé had said then that since Milúà was as stubborn as a rock, it was worth testing which would break first. Milúà dared a glance at the stone and was proud of its crack.

When Ìyá-Ayé didn't speak, they bowed deeper until their heads touched the floor and chorused, 'Ìyá-Ayé, mother of life, we greet you. May your reign be like the sun.'

'Now tell me, my children, why you've brought disgrace to this house that has never been seen or heard of since the birth of our beloved kingdom.'

Bùnmi jumped in first. 'Ìyá, it wasn't my fault. I wasn't even there. The boy in my charge, the foolish boy, tried to escape the temple and got himself killed.'

'Got himself killed?' Ìyá-Ayé tilted her head and asked, 'Where were you, his maiden, his shadow, when he was,' she chuckled, 'getting himself killed?'

'Ìyá, please,' Bùnmi tried begging, getting her pleas in as quickly as possible.

'You interrupt me,' the older woman hissed. Her tone didn't change, but Milúà felt a chill run down her spine.

'Ah! Ẹ̀ẹ̀wọ̀ – gods forbid. Ìyá, I just –' Bùnmi said.

Milúà grabbed Bùnmi's hand, pulling her back and stopping

239

the words from pouring out. Bùnmi still didn't know Ìyá-Ayé well enough to know when she wanted words and when she wanted subservience.

Ìyá-Ayé rose, and the maiden guards that stood behind her followed suit. These were sisters of the House who were not assigned temple duties. The role of house maiden was one they all prayed not to have growing up. The black-clothed maidens never got to wear red or gold. They moved from white to black, sealing their fate and swearing allegiance not to priests or the Holy Order but to Ìyá-Ayé and Ìyá-Ayé alone. Who in the world wanted to be trapped at home with their mother? With *this* mother? Her ever-wandering eyes were always watching, piercing, burning.

Ìyá-Ayé walked straight to Bùnmi and lifted her chin with a single finger, staring right into her glassy eyes.

'My child. Bùnmi ọmọ ìyá mí.' Child of my mother. That was what Ìyá-Ayé called all the girls she trained because she was once like them, answering to a woman she'd also called mother.

'I can't show you mercy, my child. The Order has called for blood. Of course,' Ìyá-Ayé said, pulling out a cowrie shell from her cleavage and placing it in Bùnmi's open palm, 'while you did the right thing avenging the death of your Àlùfáà, you still killed a daughter of mine. So you see that your sin is unforgivable.'

Bùnmi let out a loud cry and held on to Ìyá-Ayé's feet, begging.

Ìyá-Ayé bent over and lifted the crying girl up to her feet. 'Wipe your tears, my daughter. Your sisters will take you now, but I give you my strength. Whatever happens, don't die – I am especially fond of you and will welcome you back with open arms,' she said, smiling.

Milúà closed her eyes to the screams as they dragged her sister out of the room.

'Now you,' Ìyá-Ayé said as she returned to her seat, and a new set of maiden guards dressed in black stood behind her, replacing the ones who dragged Bùnmi away to the place no one speaks of.

Milúà, still on her knees, bowed again, 'Ìyá.'

'Tell me your side of the story. I am particularly interested in how you defied the abomination.'

Milúà smelt the trap. She chose her words carefully, telling as close a story to Bùnmi's version as she could. As she spoke, Milúà tried to read Ìyá-Ayé's face for any sign that she believed the words she heard, but nothing. The priestess hid all her emotions behind the wrinkles on her face.

'Now, tell me about the ice crystal,' Ìyá-Ayé said, leaning forward. The older woman's grey hair shone brightly against her warm brown skin, adorned with gold trinkets and red rubies. 'What did it feel like? What did you feel as you brought it down with your bare hands?'

'I only did what any daughter of Oru and this noble house would have done.'

'Yes, but they didn't, or couldn't. From what I heard, you weren't even afraid to touch it,' Ìyá-Ayé replied.

Milúà shifted uncomfortably, not knowing how much of the truth to tell.

'You taught us that fear was the enemy. To be afraid is to be weak, and we aren't weak. We are maidens of the Holy Order. We burn like the sun. The ground beneath us will crumble to dust before we crack.'

Ìyá-Ayé smiled as Milúà quoted her own words back to her. 'Come closer.'

Closer now, Milúà saw Ìyá-Ayé's dark brown eyes that looked like they held centuries of secrets. She wondered how long it would take for her mother to pass on all she kept hidden when she reached her deathbed. Why was Ìyá-Ayé more interested in this debacle with the ice structure than the fact that the prince was missing? She could feel herself walking into a trap but didn't know how to avoid it.

'Tell me,' the older woman said, 'did you see the face of this mysterious girl at the temple?'

'No, Ìyá, she wore a hood over her head, and in the dark of night, none of us could see her face.'

Milúà hadn't meant to lie, but there was no turning back now. She didn't know whether the girl's face was seen or not because she wasn't there. She'd used the distraction to dig out information in the temple library that was forbidden to maidens. However, any recanting on her part and Ìyá-Ayé would find out exactly where she'd been.

'Hmnnn . . .' Ìyá-Ayé muttered under her breath. 'Show me.'

'Ma?' Milúà asked. 'Show you what?'

Ìyá-Ayé leaned forward. 'Do you mean to tell me that a maiden of this house, trained by my hands, came in contact with a new kind of magic and didn't bring the evidence of it home?'

Once again, Ìyá-Ayé proved no one could outsmart her. Milúà sighed and brought out a piece of the ice crystal. A small black mist still churned within the clear shard.

Ìyá-Ayé's wide smile lit up her fair skin. She clapped to herself, 'That's my girl!'

Milúà cringed. When she'd stolen a piece of the ice shard, it hadn't been to please her mother. At that moment, she couldn't remember why she'd taken it. It somehow felt important. Maybe it was her mother's training that took over.

Ìyá-Ayé walked over to Milúà and took the crystal from her. She observed it, peering inside it, cursing it, and then burning it with her agbára. Dark mist oozed from it, the way steam rose from a pot when its cover was removed. It cracked, and she screamed, throwing it to the ground. Milúà ran to help her mother, but the woman shoved her off. Ìyá-Ayé's palm was trembling, the centre of it blackened as though it was diseased.

'Ìyá! Are you okay?' Milúà asked, surprising herself at how concerned she was, but at the same time, Milúà wanted to be the thing that hurt her.

'I'm fine, child, stop shouting,' Ìyá-Ayé spat back, wincing in pain. 'Move out of my face.'

'Ìyá, please,' Milúà said. 'Let me help you.'

Ìyá-Ayé summoned her agbára, and a soft red glow radiated from her palm. The same healing fire had scorched and healed her many times before. A skill she taught none of her girls.

Ìyá-Ayé exhaled slowly as the pain seemed to ease, and the dark spot disappeared. She turned to Milúà with a smile back on her face as if the last few moments hadn't happened. 'Now show me what you did.'

Milúà wanted nothing more to do with the ice crystal. She wished more than anything that she'd never taken it. The pain that surged through her as she brought down the wall still thrummed in her bones. It'd taken everything in her spirit and body to fight against the magic in the crystal.

'Show me or meet the same fate as your sister,' Ìyá-Ayé said, all smiles wiped off her face instantly.

Milúà swallowed slowly, trying to dispel the thickness in her throat. Gently, she picked up the ice shard from the floor. She closed her eyes and stretched out her hands. Her agbára burned brighter with every breath she took. Her eyes remained closed the whole time. All she could hear was sizzling, and then she felt the viscous liquid smear over her palm. An icy shiver ran through her, and she felt as though the liquid in her hand also smeared over the agbára in her core, dulling its light and chilling it. In a few heartbeats, there was nothing left of it. Milúà inhaled, breathing deeply for the first time since she held it in her hand.

Milúà opened her eyes, and locked her gaze on Ìyá-Ayé, whose eyes were wide in awe. The room was silent, waiting for Ìyá-Ayé to speak first.

'Your stupid mother! How could I have missed this? Even from the grave, her recklessness haunts us all.'

Milúà took a step back from Ìyá-Ayé. Then another, feeling the sudden need to sit or hold on to something. Her mouth went dry, and nothing came out when she tried to speak. The room suddenly felt small, the fire from the lanterns suffocating her.

Ìyá-Ayé's eyes were like the depths of a well, dark and hollow. She reached for Milúà's face with cold hands and said, 'I don't know how Àdùnní managed to conceive or birth you, but you are my little miracle from the gods.'

A few days before, Milúà hadn't even known her birth mother's name. As she rummaged through the temple's hidden library during the temple break-in, she had learned that her mother, Àdùnní, had been born to a family in Ìlú-Idán. Àdùnní had volunteered herself to Ìyá-Ayé after seeing ten first suns and was one of the first temple maidens who attained gold status even before being matched with a priest. That was all the information Milúà got from the library before the alarms were raised and her chosen one was stolen from her. The papers she saw said nothing of death, and so for a period that perhaps lasted longer than it should have Milúà had hoped her birth mother was alive. Now, it seemed Àdùnní of Ìlú-Idán was dead. It took every ounce of strength Milúà had to hold back the tears that pricked at her eyes. Somehow, she had desperately wished, prayed even, that among those musty scrolls lay a trail that would lead her to her mother somewhere far from here. That hope crashed as quickly as it had blossomed, leaving her breathless.

The words 'from the grave' kept echoing in Milúà's mind, and she felt her head nearly explode with grief.

'My mother –' Milúà started to say.

'You need no other mother but me,' Ìyá-Ayé sneered at her.

When Milúà was younger, she'd asked Ìyá-Ayé about her birth mother and could still feel the burn of the backhand slap she received that day. Milúà bit her tongue to keep from saying anything she might regret.

'Leave me. I will deal with you later,' Ìyá-Ayé said.

Milúà bowed and left the room without saying a word. When she got to the room she'd grown up in, she closed the door and fell to the ground, weeping quietly. In a little corner of her heart, Milúà had hoped that she too might one day stumble upon the woman who birthed her in the market square, the way Bùnmi had found hers. It was a long shot – but she'd hoped. But now she knew her mother was dead. Maybe she didn't even abandon her, perhaps she wanted to keep her, but death had other plans. Someone had other plans.

She still had so many questions. No maiden could bear a child. They all drank the same herbs that made them barren from the moment they saw their first blood. To seal their bonds, maidens gave their bodies to their priests. Her birth mother shouldn't have been able to get pregnant – how did she? And how did she hide being pregnant long enough to give birth? Milúà's head throbbed as she cried into her palms. The Holy Order could never allow a maiden that bore a child to live.

Milúà gasped out loud as the realization hit her. Her gaze fixed on the wall towards Ìyá-Ayé's throne room. Only one person could permit the killing of a maiden of the Sun Temple – the woman she called Mother.

The old gods do not shun their scions,
they answer all who call, all who know them
by their true names.
They have but one rule:
Do not call upon more than one of the
gods at a time.
Make your choice and stick to it.
Those who are wise call upon only one of the Òrìṣà
for as long as they live.
Call upon many, and none will ever hear
your cries again.
Perhaps that is why the scions of the old gods
live in chains today.
I do not know.

20

Ìlú-Ọ̀pọ̀, Third Ring,
Kingdom of Oru

L'ỌRẸ

L'ọrẹ was exhausted and sleep-deprived by the time she and Alawani reached the border of Ìlú-Ọ̀pọ̀, the third ring. They'd kept off the King's Road just as Baba-Ìtàn suggested, riding through Ìlú-Ìmọ̀ on a horse Alawani stole. When they got close to the border wall, they traded the horse for passage through the main gates.

And that was how L'ọrẹ found herself stuck underneath the floorboard of a wagon, struggling to breathe as it slowly inched towards the guard checkpoint. It helped that Alawani was right next to her, although it didn't help that his elbows were crushing into her side with every shake of the wheels. Among the crowd of voices that echoed into the small wooden compartment, L'ọrẹ could hear the guards questioning the drivers, and she could feel a chill coming in through her sweat-soaked shirt. She formed fists with her palms and felt Alawani's hand reach for her gloved ones. She was taking no chances with her new powers.

Alawani squeezed slightly. 'We'll be all right.'

L'ọrẹ barely had space to nod. If she moved more than a few inches, her head would knock against the floor of the cabin. She inhaled deeply, nearly choking on the dust of plantain flour that hung in the air. She squeezed Alawani's hand and hoped they wouldn't get caught before even leaving her home ring.

'Reason for crossing the border?' the guard's voice boomed from outside the wagon.

'I'm returning to my farm,' the driver said confidently, with a hint of annoyance.

There was a brief silence, then the guard said, 'With a wagon full of èlùbọ́? Were you not supposed to sell them?'

'My customer wanted èlùbọ́ iṣu not èlùbọ́ ọ̀gẹ̀dẹ̀, so back to the farm it is.'

L'ọrẹ could picture the driver's face and hoped the man's prickly tone wouldn't aggravate the guard. The last thing they needed was anyone searching the wagon.

Pay him, L'ọrẹ urged. When guards asked too many questions, they wanted sun coins. Everyone knew this. She'd added to the driver's fee in anticipation of this moment, so she couldn't understand why the driver was dragging the conversation. L'ọrẹ strained to look at Alawani, and his eyes met hers. If the guard tried to search, they'd have to fight their way through.

As L'ọrẹ prepared her mind to fight, she heard the clink of coins, and the wagon started moving again. Alawani exhaled next to her. Relief eased all the muscles in her body. The wagon bumped into a hole in the road, and the bags of flour puffed out a cloud of white powder and Alawani sneezed so loudly that the cabin shook with force.

'Curse the sun, Alawani!' she whispered.

'Sorry.'

'I swear if you get me killed, I'm taking you with me.'

Alawani coughed softly.

L'ọrẹ shoved him again, 'Shh . . .'

'I think we're all clear. I don't hear anything,' Alawani said.

248

Only then did L'ọrẹ realize that the wagon had stopped moving again. Her eyes widened, and just as she was about to speak, someone lifted the top cover of the compartment, and L'ọrẹ squinted at the sunlight that broke into the dark space.

'You're both the worst cargo I've ever carried. Not worth any amount of coin. Why in the gods' names are you making noise?' the angry driver scowled at them.

L'ọrẹ pursed her lips and eyed Alawani, who was clearly now suppressing a cough.

'Get out. Now!' the driver said, pulling off the rest of the top layer.

L'ọrẹ and Alawani got out of the wagon and watched the driver mumble as he drove off into the city. The first thing L'ọrẹ noticed was that her feet sunk slightly into the uneven ground. The sand was much darker than at Ìlú-Ìmọ̀, which was red, hard and cracked, covered with an ever-moving top layer of sand and dust – and different from the ground in the capital with its well-designed cobbled streets. This earth was dark and soft, and as she gazed across the horizon, she could see the result. Lands of green spread as far as her eyes could see, interrupted only by the border wall in the distance that led into Ìlú-Ìmọ̀, the ring they'd just escaped. Her home state. The wind in her face was cool and smelled like rain, and when she inhaled deeply, there was no dust clogging her nostrils.

'It's so beautiful,' L'ọrẹ breathed, spinning around slowly, taking in the cluster of trees, hundreds of animals flocking along the hills and the neat rows of cultivated land on the terrain in the distance.

Unlike the capital's houses with their constant sparkle of gold and white limestone towers, or her own home which was covered in a constant hue of red clay dust, the houses in Ìlú-Òpo spread out in a commune of humble bungalows surrounded by large farms.

They'd agreed that the first thing they'd do was take Máyòwá's àṣíri to his family, who lived here in Ìlú-Òpo. L'ọrẹ had been carrying his àṣíri – such as it was – since she'd knelt by his side as he died. The passing on of secrets by the dying was necessary to gain access to the afterlife.

This practice, thought L'ọrẹ, kept legends alive and sought justice for past wrongs – nothing must be hidden under the sun. That was her people's way. There must always be some-one alive who knew the truth to tell. No secret could be lost forever.

Everyone in the kingdom was named in a specific enough way to be easily tracked down. The combination of a per-son's Àmútòrunwá, the name unique to the circumstances surrounding their birth, their Oríkì, the praise name that described their personality, and their Orile, their family name, when combined with their tribal marks which told where they were born, made each person as distinctive as could be.

Máyòwá's full name was Máyòwá – the one who came with joy, Àjàgbé – the one who they fought to have, Onílè – owners of land. They were already in his home state, so all they had to do was to ask the first person they saw for the home of Máyòwá Àjàgbé Onílè, the Àlùfáà of the third ring.

Máyòwá's parents sat across from L'ọrẹ and Alawani on the large mat that filled the living area. The mat was thin and felt like sitting on dry grass. L'ọrẹ shifted uncomfortably, trying to find the perfect spot. They all glanced at her in unison when the shuffling became too loud, and she stilled herself.

'Sorry, if we'd known we were having guests, we'd have made more suitable arrangements,' Máyòwá's father said.

L'ọrẹ put her hands together, rubbing away at her nerves.

Alawani shot her a quick glance, and she understood his meaning. They had no time to waste, and there was no point in making them uncomfortable in their home. 'No, Bàbá, the fault is ours. We've come a long way and we're grateful for your hospitality.'

L'orẹ observed the older man as he moved around the chewing stick in his mouth, exposing stained teeth. Máyòwá's mother sat quietly next to him with a hand on his lap. L'orẹ felt a tightness in her chest, like a hand squeezing the truth out of her.

'Any friend of Máyòwá's is welcome at our home,' the older man said, gesturing with his calloused hands. Máyòwá had had the same farm-worn hands. L'orẹ noticed how the man's faint smile made him look just like his son.

L'orẹ and Alawani had introduced themselves as Máyòwá's friends the moment they arrived, but intentionally left out Alawani's true identity. They'd received a warm welcome, and although L'orẹ had rehearsed what to say, she still stalled.

'How is my son?' Máyòwá's mother finally asked.

Next to L'orẹ, Alawani sank back, allowing her to carry the conversation, and the inches between them felt an ever-growing distance. He wanted L'orẹ to tell the truth – but L'orẹ had promised Máyòwá she would not.

'The stripping ceremony was a few days ago,' L'orẹ said, and she saw hope fill their eyes. Máyòwá's father adjusted. 'Máyòwá didn't wake up,' L'orẹ said, and watched as the hope in their eyes went out like a light snuffed out from a candle.

Máyòwá's father stared at L'orẹ, his face pale and ashen, his red eyes piercing into hers. Máyòwá's mother closed her eyes, and tears rolled down her cheeks. L'orẹ lowered her head, unable to keep looking at their faces. Máyòwá's mother couldn't hold in her sobs and fell into her husband's arms, crying for her son.

The older man kept the tears from falling, but the stick in his mouth shook as his lips trembled. He held on to his wife as she heaved into him, holding on tightly to his clothes, ripping the delicate and faded embroidery around his neckline. L'ọrẹ found herself face to face with grief and was strangely aware of every breath she took. She could feel their pain, much more than she thought possible. Next to her, Alawani's eyes watered too.

Máyọ̀wá had been right to tell her to lie – the news she'd relayed was bad enough. The truth would have crushed his parents forever.

L'ọrẹ tried to speak and soothe their pain but couldn't find the words. Alawani got up and pulled her to her feet, and together they walked out of the house. The feel of the cool night breeze on L'ọrẹ's face made her inhale deeply. The smell of fermented corn filled the air as they stepped into the cornfield outside Máyọ̀wá's house.

Alawani grunted and let out a low groan as he bent over, holding his stomach. He paced, trying to calm himself, wiping the tears from his eyes. L'ọrẹ went to him and embraced him. She felt his tears soak into her shirt, and she hugged him tighter.

After a few moments, Alawani peeled himself from her embrace and exhaled, looking around the farm. L'ọrẹ wiped her own tears and scanned the field. Quietly, Alawani moved towards a tall tree a few feet away.

He crouched at the roots, trailing his fingers over its bark. 'It's here.'

'What is?' L'ọrẹ asked.

Alawani shifted and motioned for her to join him. She stooped low and saw it. On the tree's trunk was a carving: Àlùfáà.

'Máyọ̀wá told me he wrote this on the day he got the call,'

Alawani said with a sad smile as he rubbed the carving. 'He wanted to mark the very spot he was in when the gods looked upon him with favour and granted him a destiny so great his name would forever be remembered.' Alawani sobbed as he pressed his fingers into the tree, feeling out every letter. 'Now, no one will know his name.'

L'ọrẹ reached for Alawani's hand. 'We know his name. We won't ever forget it.'

A drop of water landed on L'ọrẹ's forehead, and as she moved to wipe it, another one dropped. Then another. L'ọrẹ hadn't felt rain in many first suns, and she wished it hadn't picked this moment to fall. Soon, the rain was pouring down on them. Alawani remained crouched at the tree, staring at the word, rubbing at it as if he was trying to scratch it off. L'ọrẹ didn't know what to do or say. She'd gone to the temple to save a life but had caused the death of another. She should never have taken Máyọ̀wá out of the tower. That was her greatest mistake, and she knew she'd never forgive herself.

L'ọrẹ placed her hand on Alawani's shoulder. 'I'm sorry,' she whispered.

'It doesn't matter.'

L'ọrẹ frowned, but when she saw his face taut with grief, she sighed. 'I shouldn't have forced him to find you.'

'No, you shouldn't.'

'I know, I thought –'

'Why did you lie to them?' Alawani said, his voice loud in the downpour. 'He was Àlùfáà, you know. After the stripping, he was first to recover, moving around as if nothing had happened. We all knew it. They knew it. If anyone were to survive the Red Stone, it would have been him,' Alawani pointed at Máyọ̀wá's house, 'And you lied to them!'

'Máyọ̀wá asked me to. This is what he wanted. You know that,' L'ọrẹ seethed.

Alawani scoffed. 'What he wanted was to live!'

'Do you think they won't turn us over to the Holy Order if we tell them the truth?' L'ọrẹ asked.

'You have all the answers, don't you? You know everything.'

'That's not fair.'

'What's not fair is Máyòwá dying.'

'Don't you think I know that? Do you think I don't think about him every single moment? I know this is my fault. I don't need you to remind me,' L'ọrẹ shouted back at him. The rain had now soaked through her clothes, and the shiver she felt only enraged her. Frost pricked at her fingers, and she formed tight fists at her side. 'You talk about not wanting to be a coward. You were being a coward, walking into a fate that you knew wasn't yours. The gods didn't call you, your grandfather did. I shouldn't have had to save you. You should've had the sense to never give in to something you don't even believe in!'

'You don't know what I believe in,' Alawani said coldly. 'I didn't ask you to save me! All of this! You did all of this on your own. And of course I had to come with you; I couldn't let my grandfather kill you the way he did your mother.'

L'ọrẹ's words caught in her throat. Her face fell, and her open mouth refused to speak or shut. This was her greatest fear. She could handle anything else, but what she couldn't deal with was him telling her that all this was a mistake. Like a statue, she stood still, allowing the rain to pour over her.

She raised her hand to her neck, looking for her pendant out of habit. The bare skin sent a rush of panic over her as she watched him walk away. She fell to her knees and wrapped her hands around herself, desperately wishing for her father's arms to be holding her. She placed her hands on the wet ground to steady herself, and the cold from the grass seeped into her body, chilling her bones. Around her, she could feel every drop of rain even before it touched her. This was how she'd felt before – when she'd killed the rhino, when she was frozen in the staircase. She squeezed against the ground, forcing down the agbára fighting its way to the surface. *Not now.* She gritted her teeth, fighting the pain of keeping down this thing inside her.

L'orẹ flinched as someone's arms touched her, and for a moment, she thought she'd conjured her father, but when she looked up, she met Alawani's wet eyes, looking at her remorsefully. 'I'm sorry, I didn't mean any of that,' he said, wiping her tears despite the rain. 'I wish more than anything that the Order did not know my name.'

Rain seeped through the leaves of the tree, soaking through her clothes to her bones. Thunder exploded in the air around them, and L'orẹ flinched as lightning streaked through the sky. They stood quietly in each other's embrace, shivering under the tree until the rain subsided. L'orẹ felt her anger seep away as she held on to her best friend and wished with all her mind that things were different.

By the time the rain cleared, L'orẹ and Alawani were seated by the tree, quietly leaning on each other. L'orẹ sprang up at the sound of muddy footsteps behind her. She walked to meet Máyòwá's mother a few feet from the tree, leaving Alawani behind.

The woman regarded them both, then sighed softly. 'Thank you for bringing news of my son. You're kind to have come all this way.'

'Mama, I'm so sorry to have had to bring you bad news. Your son was an amazing person, and I knew him only briefly, but I know he loved you so much,' L'orẹ said. This wasn't a lie. Only someone who loved their parents would use their dying breaths to send a final word to them.

'Thank you,' Máyòwá's mother said plainly. 'When Máyòwá

was chosen, we knew what it meant. We prayed and hoped that the gods who chose him once would do so again, but it seems . . .' her voice trailed off. She picked up again, 'It's not your fault. There's nothing you could've done.'

L'ọrẹ bit her tongue.

'I have his last words. He gave me his secrets to pass on to you. His àṣírí.'

The woman's eyes lit up, and L'ọrẹ smiled faintly, knowing that this was a consolation in some ways. L'ọrẹ leaned close to Máyọ̀wá's mother and repeated the words Máyọ̀wá had said to her so quietly that the wind couldn't carry them away. The woman smiled, and she closed her eyes in gratitude. Máyọ̀wá's last words revealed precisely the person he was, and it was exactly what his mother needed to hear. L'ọrẹ had done her duty and would never again utter those words in her lifetime. They were now for another to carry. With any luck, she'd forget them altogether.

'My son rests peacefully in the afterlife because of you. Thank you, L'ọrẹ,' Máyọ̀wá's mother said, embracing L'ọrẹ in her arms and kissing her cheek. 'You should go before the Holy Order comes for you. You and the prince aren't safe here.'

'Ma?' L'ọrẹ asked, stunned.

The woman eyed Alawani in the distance. 'The entire kingdom knows the prince was called too, and that boy looks too much like his father to go around thinking he won't be recognized. The town criers did not stop talking about him for days since the call. So if he is here, then something is wrong. I'm old, but I'm not foolish. My son did not die on the Red Stone. Whatever it was, my Máyọ̀wá is gone, may his soul find the city of light.'

'May his soul find the city of light,' L'ọrẹ responded grimly. 'He was too good for the Holy Order; they did not deserve someone like him.'

The woman smiled and continued, 'You have brought my son's àṣírí to me, so I am grateful. But if the prince is here, he's broken his oath, and soon, the Holy Order will come to claim what is theirs. You can't stay here.' Máyọ̀wá's mother pointed at a shed in the distance. 'Take our horse and leave.'

L'ọrẹ stood before her, too shocked to speak.

'I –' she tried to explain, but she didn't even know where to start.

'Child.' The older woman leaned closer. 'I don't know how you got yourself in the middle of this. Or how you were at my son's side in his dying moment. But this journey with the prince can't end well. The Called cannot be Uncalled. For as the gods have spoken –'

'So their will must be done.' L'ọrẹ wasn't a believer, but even she knew those words.

'May the gods of the sun and sands guide your path,' Máyọ̀wá's mother said and walked back into the house.

L'ọrẹ led Alawani to the shed and saddled the horse. The rain started drizzling again as they rode away, leaving behind the ghost of their friend.

Èèyàn boni lára j'aṣọ lọ; Ẹni tó l'áṣọ
tí ò l'éèyàn, ìhòhò ló wà
*People provide better cover than clothes; whoever
has clothes but has no one, is naked*

21

The Home of the Maidens, The Capital City, First Ring, Kingdom of Oru

MILÚÀ

It had been two days since Milúà and Bùnmi returned home to Ìyá-Ayé. Milúà hadn't expected mercy the way her sister maiden had, but even she was unprepared for their mother's plans for them. Redemption came only after punishment in the home of the maidens, so night after night, Ìyá-Ayé had made Milúà and Bùnmi punish each other. After the first night, when Ìyá-Ayé went in to heal Bùnmi's wounds as was the custom in their house, she'd been disappointed to find no broken bones. Ìyá-Ayé punished Bùnmi herself that day and then healed her just in time to show Milúà exactly what she expected someone sent to the weeping hall to look like. Bùnmi broke more bones in Milúà's body than Milúà thought possible. She had awoken the next morning blinded in both eyes. It took several light beads for Ìyá-Ayé to fix her. So this morning, Milúà walked out of the weeping chamber leaving Bùnmi hanging from her ankles, a few feet in the air, bleeding out and waiting for Milúà to return to her by nightfall.

All Milúà wanted to do now was sleep after a night of screams that still echoed in her ears. But her mother had summoned her and so now, she stood out of sight by the doorway, watching as Ìyá-Ayé paced across the throne room: the room in which she received guests and handed out orders.

Ìyá-Ayé wore an emerald-coloured gown that trailed just a few feet behind her. Its material clung tight to her curvy body and was cut below her neckline, her bare collarbones covered with layers of jewellery that matched her dress. It always surprised Milúà that Ìyá-Ayé didn't flaunt her cowrie shells the way maidens did. Milúà knew that Ìyá-Ayé was proud of her kills, yet whenever she was fully adorned, there was never a cowrie shell in sight, all skilfully hidden beneath her clothes.

Ìyá-Ayé stormed back and forth in front of her throne. Milúà could see the woman flare her agbára, her palms glowing brightly and dimming in intervals. Her mother was angry.

'Why don't you slap me?' Ìyá-Ayé scoffed. 'Èmi Ìyá-Ayé, the mother of maidens, the dark side of the sun. You want to shut me out. How? How can you do what no other before you dared? Àlùfáà-Àgbà, you think because you lord yourself over that temple that you have power?' Ìyá-Ayé took the crown from her intricately woven hair and flung it across the room. 'I will show you what power is!'

Milúà took a step back from the doorway and froze. At first, Milúà had thought Ìyá-Ayé was talking to her. But when her mother didn't turn in her direction, her heart eased. Still tensed, Milúà peered in to see if Àlùfáà-Àgbà was in the room with her, but there was no one there. She would not have been surprised if he was, as most conversations between the two of them ended in a fight, despite having been bound together many first suns ago. And while it was difficult to consider her mother to be a woman scorned, these common moments of distorted reality happened so frequently that Milúà wondered if there was more to their fights than Ìyá-Ayé let on.

Milúà kept her eyes down, waiting for Ìyá-Ayé's episode to

260

pass. She could never tell if Ìyá-Ayé wanted her to respond or not, to look her in the eye or not. Either choice would anger her mother when this mood came over her. So Milúà just stilled herself.

'Milúà! Are you deaf?'

Milúà nearly jumped out of her skin. She rushed in and fell to the floor.

Milúà could almost hear her ears ring from the slap that would come if she spoke out or told her mother that she was clearly losing her mind, speaking to herself in an empty room. But she was already in more trouble than she could hope to get out of.

'Is your sister awake?' Ìyá-Ayé hissed.

'Yes, Ìyá,' Milúà said softly.

'I hope you didn't show her any mercy. I can't stand weakness in my house.'

Milúà shook her head again.

'Good. You know it'll be her turn tonight, and whatever softness you have, she doesn't.'

Ìyá-Ayé started pacing again. 'That man thinks he can sit in his temple, take my daughters and then keep me out of the game? Ah! Kò tó bẹ. He's asking for trouble!'

Milúà flinched and took a quiet step back. At least once every blood moon, Àlùfáà-Àgbà did something to vex her mother, something they all had to pay the price for. Milúà wondered how the old High Priest and Ìyá-Ayé were ever bound to each other. Or how they ruled together when he was regent. Milúà hadn't been alive when Ìyá-Ayé ruled Oru as the High Priestess of the Sun Temple and right hand of the Regent, but if her reign within the four corners of their home compound was anything to go by, then Ìyá-Ayé was not missed by anyone in the kingdom.

Ìyá-Ayé stopped pacing, and Milúà risked a glance at her

mother. Ìyá-Ayé had knelt on the floor near the stairs leading to the throne. There used to be a rug there. Ìyá-Ayé seemed to have her eyes fixed on a brown stain on the otherwise spotless floor.

Ìyá-Ayé simmered and cursed at the blemish on the floor. Milúà had sliced through enough necks to know what the spray of blood would look like. It wasn't uncommon for Ìyá-Ayé to bring her enemies before her throne room and have them killed, but it was the first time Milúà had seen blood stain her mother's precious floors and she wondered who it was that died at her mother's hands.

Ìyá-Ayé screamed, placed her hands on the spot, released her agbára and burned the floor, turning the blemish coal-black.

Were those tears? Milúà was stunned – this she hadn't seen before. What in the world was happening to her mother? Instinctively, Milúà wanted to rush to her side but thought better of it as Ìyá-Ayé yelled out again, scorching the floor one more time.

Milúà froze, questioning herself. This woman had either killed her birth mother or known who killed her . . . yet, Ìyá-Ayé had been the only mother Milúà had ever known. She inched closer, watching Ìyá-Ayé heave, holding on to her chest, her hair loose and obstructing her face from view. Ìyá-Ayé was the reason Milúà knew pain as well as she did, but she never let Milúà go on suffering for too long. She did always heal Milúà – eventually.

She crouched and helped Ìyá-Ayé to her feet. Another maiden walked silently into the room, and just like Milúà, rushed to their mother, picking up the crown and helping Milúà lift Ìyá-Ayé to her feet. Ìyá-Ayé stared at Milúà, her eyes red from tears.

Milúà eyed the maiden who'd helped her. She wore gold

armour that clung tight to her slender figure – Mikún, a warrior maiden. She wore a gold piece that started as a pendant in the middle of her forehead and draped in three strands each on the sides of her face, leading to her ears, where large gold earrings sat comfortably. Her neatly braided hair glittered with gold threads, one big braid and two small ones interchangeably throughout the front of her head, leaving a huge puff of hair that fell past her shoulders.

Milúà lowered her eyes, observing her own blood-red ensemble. A hooded tight-fitted leather-like top that flared at the waist with matching trousers and her dagger on one side of her hip and her compressed staff on the other. She yearned for gold, and if Ìyá-Ayé had been fair, Milúà should have earned her warrior's uniform many blood moons ago.

'Ìyá,' the warrior maiden said, 'Aya'ba Oyíndà is here to see you.'

'What does that woman want?' Ìyá-Ayé said.

Milúà wondered the same. Aya'ba Oyíndà was one of the five wives of the Lord Regent and mother to the crown heir and had never come to the house of maidens before.

'She didn't say, Ìyá,' Mikún said quickly. 'She insisted that what she had to say was only for your ears and the gods. She's the mother of our crown heir, Ìyá. I couldn't question her.'

Milúà clenched her teeth. Why did everyone seem only to say the wrong thing to Ìyá-Ayé? While she was erratic, one thing remained constant – her pride. Keep her ego gratified, and Ìyá-Ayé wouldn't be happy exactly, but at least you'd avoid a slap or two. Mikún was another wrong word away from a heavy slap.

'Bring her in,' Ìyá-Ayé hissed.

As soon as Mikún left the room, Ìyá-Ayé walked through the false wall behind her throne. Moments later, she reentered, wearing a new, much more expensive, embroidered outfit. A few heartbeats later, the Queen Mother walked in, dressed in a full-length royal-blue gown that sparkled with every movement. Ìyá-Ayé moved to meet her guest in the middle of the room. Her new ensemble was dripping in gold, reminding everyone who she was before she took on the role of mother.

Ìyá-Ayé adjusted her crown as she slowly approached Aya'ba Oyíndà.

Aya'ba Oyíndà stood in the middle of the throne room, defiantly refusing to meet Ìyá-Ayé halfway. Her attire was ostentatious, from the remarkably tied gèlè that stood a few inches tall, to the flamboyant sleeves and embroideries that ran the full length of the striped aṣọ-òkè she wore. The mother of the crown heir wore five outfits a day, her colours coordinating with the five stages of the sun's rising and setting from dawn to dusk. While Ìyá-Ayé looked like the midway sun draped in gold, to match the morning sky, Aya'ba Oyíndà's ensemble was accessorized with red coral beads that hung low from her neck and layered atop them was a chunky gold necklace with sapphire stones that aligned down the middle of her neck, in line with the gold piece she wore across her forehead, centred by a ruby. As she got closer, Milúà noticed how her mother wrinkled her face at the apparent show of wealth the younger woman displayed. As though she'd not done the same thing.

Aya'ba Oyíndà was even more beautiful than people described. At moments like this Milúà envied women like the Queen Mother, who were chosen whether through political influence or fate to be wives to a High Priest with the single job of birthing an heir. Lavished with titles and more wealth than could be spent in generations, all for the price of their freedom. Their bodies cursed to kill any man they laid with who was not their husband. And a husband who had four other wives and a temple maiden all bound to him in the same way. In the end Milúà looked away, realizing that all she envied was a prettier cage not unlike the one she was already trapped in.

As Ìyá-Ayé reached Aya'ba Oyíndà, they both began the usual display of respect common among many women in the kingdom of Oru. Ìyá-Ayé pretended to curtsy, reducing her height by a few inches, and Aya'ba Oyíndà pretended to dispute this show of respect by holding her in place to stop her from going further down and meeting her at the same point. Together they rose to their full height. In this way, Ìyá-Ayé had shown her the respect Aya'ba Oyíndà deserved for birthing their next king, and the Aya'ba had shown Ìyá-Ayé the respect she deserved simply for being who she was.

They both smiled, satisfied with their theatrics.

'What brings you to our side of town?' Ìyá-Ayé asked. 'We know we aren't worthy of hosting the Aya'ba, or you'd have come years ago,' she added coyly.

'I need to speak privately,' Aya'ba Oyíndà said, shooting a glare at Milúà.

'This is my house, Aya'ba. Say what you want to say here and now,' Ìyá-Ayé said.

Milúà quietly moved to the edge of Ìyá-Ayé's throne and stood at attention.

The room was silent for a moment, then finally, Aya'ba Oyíndà said, 'I know you've heard about the incident in the temple. I need your help handling a delicate and very private matter.'

The younger woman stretched out her palm and revealed a cowrie shell.

'Hmnn . . .' Ìyá-Ayé hummed. 'And who does the Aya'ba want to kill?'

'The girl who broke into the temple,' Aya'ba Oyíndà said.

'The girl?' Ìyá-Ayé asked. 'How do you know her?'

'I can't tell you that,' Aya'ba said. 'Will you do it or not?'

'The girl isn't my problem, Aya'ba. That is for your husband to fix,' Ìyá-Ayé said. 'And my girls aren't mercenaries. You can't just request them to fix your personal issues. Don't you have royal guards?'

'If that girl is who I think she is, royal guards wouldn't stand a chance. I need a maiden. A warrior maiden.'

Milúà fought the urge to look at Ìyá-Ayé. Surely she wasn't considering this. Maidens were not hired assassins. Although, if Alawani was still with the girl, it could be the perfect opportunity for Milúà to redeem herself. To kill the girl, bring him back and save herself from the trouble she was in. She'd do anything to have just one night off from the weeping hall.

'She's your problem too,' Aya'ba Oyíndà said.

'What are you saying?'

Aya'ba Oyíndà started speaking in a dialect Milúà didn't understand. It almost sounded like the woman was singing as opposed to speaking in a tongue that was closer to that used for old magic incantations. Milúà could pick out only a few random phrases. A word similar to 'death' was used many times. Then she heard two names that made her heart stop. Mọremí and Àdùnní. Milúà didn't know who Mọremí was, but she sure knew her birth mother's name. She clenched her fists and slowly breathed out, returning her gaze to Aya'ba. This woman had known her mother too.

The two women continued their conversation in the old tongue, and Milúà tried unsuccessfully to make sense of what they were saying. At some point, Ìyá-Ayé raged towards Aya'ba Oyíndà, who shrank back in defence.

'There is so much at stake here, Ìyá-Ayé. If you don't believe me, ask Àlùfáà-Àgbà,' Aya'ba Oyíndà said in the common tongue.

'I believe you. What I can't believe is how you could allow this to happen!' Ìyá-Ayé barked.

'Me? What could I have done?'

'Oyíndà, you could've told me!' Ìyá-Ayé raised her hand, and from where she stood, it looked to Milúà like Aya'ba Oyíndà flinched.

Titles were everything in Oru, hard to earn and near treasonous to erase from one's name. Aya'ba Oyíndà seemed to find her courage again, and she scowled at Ìyá-Ayé.

'Aya'ba,' Ìyá-Ayé said, correcting herself. 'Have you told your husband all this?'

'No!' Aya'ba Oyíndà said briskly. Then added in an even tone, 'I already killed the midwife, and did everything Àlùfáà-Àgbà told me to do. The truth about the night can never reach the Lord Regent's ears. He can't know my involvement in this.'

'In what you did or what you're about to do?' Ìyá-Ayé asked.

Even when they spoke in the dialect she understood, Milúà couldn't figure out the puzzle. However, from their countenances, Milúà knew Ìyá-Ayé had the woman cornered.

Ìyá-Ayé smirked, 'I didn't know you had this in you, Aya'ba.'

'I'll do anything for my son.'

'And, of course, anything to keep your crown,' Ìyá-Ayé said, but Aya'ba Oyíndà ignored her.

She continued, 'Consider it done. But first, I'll be risking the life of one of my darling daughters for your son. What do I get for this service, Queen Mother?'

Milúà felt her hands sweat, and she rubbed it off on her clothes. Her heart thumped in her chest. She didn't want to be a pawn in whatever politics Ìyá-Ayé was playing, but she hoped her mother wouldn't take away from her the chance to redeem herself and bring back the prince.

'What do you want?' Aya'ba Oyíndà asked through gritted teeth.

'When your son takes the throne, he'll marry a woman of Oru, any of his choice. His eyes will wander through the kingdom, but they will land on this house. In my house and on a girl of my choosing,' Ìyá-Ayé said.

Milúà's eyes widened. Ìyá-Ayé often told Milúà and her sisters how being maidens saved them from being married to men who'd use them and toss them aside. The bond a priest shared with his maiden was more sacred than marriage, although the girls shared their beds to seal their bonds. The difference was that the maidens got power for this bond as opposed to the burden of children.

'You want the king to marry one of your barren daughters? You want my line to end?' Aya'ba Oyíndà asked, unable to hold in her anger at the request.

'Maybe you should ask someone else to help you, Aya'ba,' Ìyá-Ayé said calmly. 'Anyway, what do you need grandchildren for, if they'll have no title or claim to the throne?' she laughed.

'Do you dare mock your king, Ìyá-Ayé?' Aya'ba Oyíndà barely concealed her disgust.

'Those are my terms, Aya'ba,' Ìyá-Ayé said plainly. 'You have nothing else to offer that I don't already have.'

Aya'ba Oyíndà was visibly uneasy. She looked around the room as if thinking of another solution. 'I agree to your terms,' she breathed. So quietly that Milúà nearly missed it.

In a loud voice, Ìyá-Ayé remarked, 'Perfect!' Then she collected the cowrie shell and called out to the door, 'Ẹnìkan! Who is there?'

'Bọ́lá ni,' a maiden responded, running in and kneeling before their mother.

'Our guest is leaving,' Ìyá-Ayé said, then smiled at Aya'ba Oyíndà. 'Thank you for coming. Let me get to work.'

Aya'ba Oyíndà turned to leave as Ìyá-Ayé said, 'In the story you've told me, Aya'ba, five of you hid this secret. Three are dead. Remember that when you return to your royal island and sit next to your husband. It was his wife that you all killed. I don't have to tell you what he'll do when he finds out about your involvement. He won't hear it from me, but as you know, the walls have ears. If you were ever going to confess, the time is now.'

Aya'ba Oyíndà didn't look back; she stormed out of the room, and Milúà saw the faint glow of agbára peeking through her clenched fists.

'Take this,' Ìyá-Ayé said, handing the cowrie shell to Milúà. 'Bring back your Àlùfáà and bring me that girl's ashes.'

The story of the day of the First Sun is one of
betrayal among friends:
Blessings born of broken oaths.
There was one who knew the tongue of the gods
who did the one thing that was forbidden.
He called upon the gods – all the Òrìṣà
and for a price, a price too steep, as he would
come to know,
they granted his request and sent down a drop of
the sun to all who stood in his presence.
That day would come to be known as the
Day of the First Sun.

22

The Royal Palace, Royal Island, Kingdom of Oru

TOFA

Tofa stood at the entrance to the Royal Court, awaiting the tune of the talking drum. He shifted and adjusted his agbádá – a beautiful royal-blue outfit woven from aṣọ-òkè. When he folded the extra-long sleeves over his shoulders, the gold damask hiding underneath was revealed. His mother had ordered this agbádá for him. It had threads of gold embroidery that ran from his neck down his full length – the designs a nod to his birthright and agbára. He checked his wrists and neck for his coral beads, ensuring he had two rows on each hand, including his time beads on the left hand. Outside the court doors, he heard the royal announcer's drumming. When it was his turn, each thud on the flat surface of the drum would produce a tune that echoed the sound of his name and title. The rhythm now told him that a meeting was still in session.

Next to him, his twin sister moved restlessly. She hated being called to court, but she'd never leave his side. Except, of course, when he had to go into the Sun Temple. Kẹni would never set foot inside the temple.

'Stop fidgeting. You're making me nervous,' Tofa said.

Kẹni sighed, frustrated. 'What are they talking about in

there that the crown heir can't hear? I don't know why the Lord Regent does this all the time.'

Tofa raised an eyebrow, 'You mean Father?'

Kẹni shrugged, 'I said what I mean.'

Tofa knew better than to pick at that wound. So many things bound him and his sister. He was Táíwò – the first twin to be born, and she was Kẹ́hìndé, born ten heartbeats after him. She was his shadow and best friend, bound in life and in death.

One decision by a greedy man centuries ago doomed his sister to a life even he pitied. The history he'd learned said that a long time ago, the king's twin brother killed the king and took his place. After all, as twins, they had the same strong connection to the gods, making them nearly equal in their power. After that incident, the high council and Holy Order set the rule: all Kẹ́hìndés must die at birth – and all had until now. The Lord Regent had pleaded on her behalf, arguing that as a girl, there was no chance for history to repeat itself. They had accepted his request but attached a long list of conditions. The most important being that Kẹni took on the name and role of Ab'ọ́bakú – the one who dies with the king. When Tofa died, she died.

Thus, Kẹni was both a warden and a prisoner, with her fate tied to his. Tofa doubted his sister would ever forgive their father for the decision to keep her alive. But to Tofa, she was the very air in his lungs.

Kẹni eyed Tofa's outfit, noting he was wearing agbádá with the royal emblem and not his usual armour. 'I thought you said you didn't care about politics.'

Tofa frowned, 'I don't.'

'You could've fooled me,' Kẹni scoffed.

Tofa sighed. 'Our father summoned me, and I'm here. What politics is there?'

'So wearing that has nothing to do with wanting him to see you as his son and heir and not a warrior? So he doesn't send you to bring back the runaway Àlùfáà?'

'You can say his name, you know? He's still our friend,' Tofa said, not meeting her gaze. 'Anyway, this meeting could be about anything.'

Kẹni scoffed again. 'He's your friend.'

Tofa sighed, unwilling to argue the point with her. She and Alawani had their own odd kind of feud that he never got in the middle of. 'I wouldn't have to resort to coy politics if our father could simply realize that I shouldn't have to go. He shouldn't be asking me to do that.'

'If I were you, I would go after the intruder and the deserter and bring them back here to face the council.'

'Why? Unlike Father, my position on the throne doesn't include any priestly duties. My duty is to the crown and not the Sun Temple. Following his own orders, I've spent the last six blood moons travelling every state in this kingdom, and I can tell you there are bigger problems than temple politics.'

Kẹni shook her head. 'You should go.'

'Why?'

'At the next First Sun festival, you will become the Aláàfin,' Kẹni said in her usual whispering tone. 'This kingdom will be yours to rule and protect. This incident at the Sun Temple makes you look incompetent. And apart from all that, one of these chosen ones could be your successor. The kingdom needs Àlùfáà. You know that.'

'I didn't know you were planning my death,' Tofa said jokingly, then immediately hated himself.

Kẹni's mouth parted, and her gaze fell. She stiffened, and her hands balled into fists.

How could he be so callous? His death was the one thing they never spoke about.

'I'm sorry. That was stupid,' Tofa said, reaching for her, but she slid out of his grasp.

'It's fine,' Kẹni said, straightening her sandy brown outfit and adjusting her turban.

The red string around her wrist caught Tofa's attention, and a pang of familiar guilt ate at him. The way the midwife who attended to their mother told the story, at birth, Kẹni had put her hand out first into the world, and the midwife had tied the red string around her wrist, but Kẹni had pulled back her hand. That single move changed the fate of their lives as Tofa was then born first and named the heir.

Tofa straightened too, instinctively mirroring her move-ment, adjusting his agbádá again. As heavy as the crown he was about to inherit felt in his heart, he knew it was nothing compared to his sister's burden. He couldn't imagine being forced to remain as small and restrained as was required of her. When he shone, they expected her to hide. Few people outside the palace ever saw her face. It had taken years of his begging for the mask she'd worn across her nose and mouth to be taken off. She couldn't ever leave the royal island. When she had seen about twelve first suns, their father sent her to be trained by the general of the army in Ìlú-Òdì at the edge of the kingdom. His best friend returned a stranger. The part of her that wanted a life untethered to him was gone. Everything she was – her person, her strength, her agbára – was all in service of her brother. Now she perman-ently stood by his side, waiting and watching. His life was in her hands, and he knew no one could get close enough to harm him except her.

'Sorry, I shouldn't have said that,' Tofa apologized again.

'Don't be daft. I'm not an egg. And you're right. The only way anyone from this stripping would inherit this throne is if you die. And since I have to die with you, I won't allow it.

274

I intend to see a hundred first suns, brother,' Kẹni said with a smile that didn't reach her eyes.

When the time was right, Tofa planned to convince Àlùfáà-Àgbà to remove the rule and separate her life from his. He hoped that he could, and yet a small part of him knew that he was being naïve.

The gilded doors to the courtroom cracked open, and Tofa heard the tune of the drum announcing him. Kẹni let him lead the way. Tofa felt the beat in his bones, like a voice singing in his head.

The drum said, 'Welcome, Táíwò Tofaratì Aládé Adékùgbé, crown heir of Oru, firstborn of the sun, the one whose agbára rivals the gods, protector of the six rings, light of the continent and Supreme Lord of sun and sands. May the sun find you even in the dark of night. May your heart burn like the sun, bright, hot, and undying.'

After repeating this three times, the drummer changed the rhythm, and the drum said one time only, 'Kẹ̀hìndé Ab'ọ́bakú.'

The room fell silent. Tofa marched past the tall pillars and empty marble steps that surrounded the courtroom and moved through the curtains into the inner chamber where the Lord Regent sat atop an elevated dais. Using his agbára, he cooled his body temperature, drying off the sweat beading across his forehead. No need to appear any more nervous than he was. He'd hoped this meeting would be a private audience with his father, but seated along both sides of the rug were the last three remaining members of the late king's high council, some priests of the Holy Order, and, of course, Àlùfáà-Àgbà. Next to the former High Priest was his maiden and former High Priestess, Ìyá-Ayé – the mother of maidens. Up on the dais, one step below the Lord Regent's throne, were two golden chairs. Tofa's mother, Aya'ba Oyíndà, sat on the left, and High Priestess Àṣá, the Lord Regent's maiden, sat on the right. Tofa's other sisters, Àríké, Àníké and Àbèní – who would soon comprise Tofa's own high council – sat at the base of the steps. The girls wore multicoloured àdìrẹ fabric sewn in different styles, each with a nod to their mothers' home states of Ìlú-Oníṣòṇà, Ìlú-Ọpọ and Ìlú-Idán. Like the other women in the room, they adorned their hair with coral beads and were bathed in gold from their wrists to their ankles.

The precious stones and jewellery of the court's outfits glittered in the light. Everyone had the same idea as him: one's outfit, when chosen carefully, relayed messages that didn't need to be spoken out loud.

Tofa prostrated himself before his father. Behind him, Kẹni knelt and bowed. Tofa held the position with his forehead on the ground until his father asked him to stand. As he stood up, his eyes met his father's and his heart ached the way it did every time he was in his presence. Tofa missed him. The Lord Regent's downturned brown eyes peered back at Tofa. His white crown emphasized his round features, making him look less intimidating than he was, despite his sunken cheeks and well-moulded beard. The crown had taken much from his father.

The Lord Regent's parents had died, last laying eyes on their son the moment he left for the Sun Temple at sixteen. Tofa's father had now seen forty-four first suns and four blood moons. That was a long time to be without one's family. But the law was the law, and it decreed two things: that all must bow to their knees before the ruler of the land and that parents must never bow to their children. And so, in a wicked twist of fate, his parents lived and died without seeing the man he'd become.

Soon, Tofa would be king and never again fall before his

father, never again set eyes on him, never again be near him as he was now. So even though his father was right in front of him, Tofa couldn't shake the feeling of missing him, of grieving him, as though he were already dead.

'I've asked you here to discuss the prince Àlùfáà and the incident at the temple,' the Lord Regent said, loud enough for the room to echo his voice.

Tofa nodded, thinking of how best to say he didn't want this mission. 'It's been three days since the incident and the warrior maidens have searched every corner of this island to no avail. The royal guards are searching this ring and the next where the exiled priest lived but there is no news on the girl and all this stealth and secrecy is wasting our time. If the girl uses her evil powers on our people, the secret will be out either way. We need to contain this. We must summon the Lord General's army from the sixth ring and have their portraits on every state wall, ordering a full search of anyone crossing any borders. We built this kingdom to protect itself. I'm unsure what the prince's plan is, but Alawani can't expect to escape through all six rings of Oru.'

The Lord Regent slowly swayed the horsetail in his hand as he listened to Tofa. 'Àjànàkú tells us that the girl who took Alawani is more dangerous than we know.' The priests shifted in their seats by Àlùfáà-Àgbà, who remained still. His father was still angry if he was calling the old man by his first name – something no one else in the kingdom could do. 'This requires greater precision than an army. You need to go after them, Tofa. You have the most powerful agbára in the kingdom.'

Tofa clenched his fists – it was exactly as he suspected. 'Why is the girl with the strange magic so important? Who is she?' he asked.

'She's a direct threat to our kingdom and a mockery of our

gods. We will bring forth their wrath if we allow her to live,' Àlùfáà-Àgbà said, his anger palpable.

The room echoed, 'Àṣẹ.'

The Lord Regent shifted on his throne. 'More to the point, we can't allow Alawani to abandon his duty. The Call to be Àlùfáà is a sacred oath we've made with our gods, our connection to the source of our agbára. Whatever the reason for his cowardice, I want him found. This is a dangerous precedent.'

'And the girl?' Tofa asked. 'What is her name? What else do we know about her?'

'Her name is L'ọrẹ,' Àlùfáà-Àgbà jumped in. 'She was raised by the defect priest in the second ring. Find her and kill her on sight.'

The name rang like a bell, and his old friend's face flashed before his mind. Alawani had sat with him until the sun was high in the sky. They had reminisced about the days long past, and most of all, he'd told Tofa about the girl who had won his heart. L'ọrẹ.

'He loves her,' Tofa said. 'If it's the girl he told me about, he won't return without her. Alawani is in love with her.'

'Bring her to me alive,' the Lord Regent contradicted.

'Àdèlé Ọba – Lord Regent, permit me to speak,' Ìyá-Ayé said, and the room turned to look at her. The Lord Regent nodded, and Tofa caught the flicker of a smile on his mother's face as she looked at Ìyá-Ayé. 'As your firstborn, the gods have indeed blessed the crown heir with the most powerful agbára in the kingdom,' Ìyá-Ayé said.

Praise. A good way to start before asking the crown for anything. Tofa didn't know Ìyá-Ayé very well, but her reputation preceded her. In the game of politics, she was second to none.

'But, my Lord,' Ìyá-Ayé continued, 'we shouldn't waste the

blessing of the gods. How can we send a mountain to crush a termite? The crown heir is a few blood moons away from becoming the Aláàfin of our great land. We need his attention here in the capital. Let me send my girls to bring back the prince and this cursed girl. I can assure you, there's no power she can possess that my maidens can't handle. They are the sharp edge of this great kingdom. They are yours to command.'

'You overestimate your maidens,' Àlùfáà-Àgbà said, sneering.

'You underestimate them – and me,' Ìyá-Ayé said, not once taking her eyes off the throne.

Just as the Lord Regent was about to speak, Aya'ba Oyíndà turned to him and said, 'Olówó orí mi. My husband. She is right. Our son's place is here. Learning from you. Not chasing after Prince Alawani, who has brought as much shame to this kingdom as the late king once did.'

Tofa almost smiled. His mother had planned this. She wasn't as subtle as she thought she was.

The Lord Regent grunted and then looked at High Priestess Àṣá. The woman didn't turn, but somehow knew he was asking for her opinion. He'd seen his father interact with his mother and other wives, and Tofa was sure that what people said was true. The bond between a priest and his maiden was something different.

High Priestess Àṣá cleared her throat and said, 'Send the crown heir after them. The gods blessed him with the agbára to protect this kingdom. This is his destiny.'

Behind him, Kẹni shifted. She'd been so still, Tofa had nearly forgotten she was there.

Aya'ba Oyíndà seethed in her seat. If looks could kill, Tofa knew High Priestess Àṣá would already lie cold on the floor.

'I have sent a maiden to find them, my Lord. I expect her to return soon with good news,' Ìyá-Ayé said.

The room went quiet, and Ìyá-Ayé straightened, confident in her decision.

'Without my permission?' the Lord Regent asked.

'My Lord, I only did what I would've done in my time as High Priestess, seated on that throne. My oath was to protect this kingdom. I'm only doing my part to keep that promise.'

'How will your maiden find them?'

'One of my girls saw the invaders moments before they entered the temple. And don't you worry, she's being punished for that oversight. She recognized the boy who broke in with L'orẹ. He's called Kọ̀yà. Brother to one of the royal guards. They are both in the temple dungeons as we speak, and my Milúà will have all she needs to find the prince.'

'What instruction did you give this maiden? To kill them?' the Lord Regent asked.

'To kill the girl and bring back Alawani,' Ìyá-Ayé said.

'Surely the prince's crime is punishable by death?' Àlùfáà-Àgbà said.

The Lord Regent shot him and Ìyá-Ayé a look and turned back to his son. 'I want Prince Alawani *and* the girl brought back here alive to face this council. We'll decide their fates here before the gods, not recklessly on the streets of Oru. As the words have left my mouth –'

The room echoed after him. The Elder Priest concluded, 'So let it be done.'

The Lord Regent faced Ìyá-Ayé, 'Never do something like this again. And instruct your maiden to capture the prince and the girl. Provide their location and await the crown heir's arrival. And don't waste time sending another maiden or a messenger bird. I want you to go to her yourself in her dreams and make sure she hears my words.'

'As you've said, Lord Regent,' Ìyá-Ayé said, bowing her head.

'One more thing,' the Lord Regent said to his maiden. 'I

want the prince's mother and their entire family out of this palace and off the island before nightfall.'

'Ẹ̀ẹ̀wọ̀,' Àlùfáà-Àgbà said. 'Abomination.'

Tofa straightened at this. Alawani's mother, Ìyáàfin Olorì Atinúkẹ́, was the queen who had been married to Àlùfáà-Àgbà's son, the late king. Tofa was not at all surprised by the old man's outrage. Àlùfáà-Àgbà had five children from his time as High Priest, the other four having ruled as the council for their brother and the new regent for many first suns. They were set to retire from the council and their positions as governors of their home rings once the new council, formed of Tofa's siblings, took over from them. With his father's latest declaration, Tofa wondered if the Lord Regent intended to banish the late king's council as well? They were still Alawani's family after all.

One of the council members stood; from his tribal marks Tofa knew the man was the governor of Ìlú-Òdì – the sixth ring. 'Lord Regent, you cannot banish the late king's wife from this island. She is our queen. Her children are of royal blood,' he said with his arms folded before him, showing respect even as he challenged the Lord Regent.

Tofa noticed how none of Àlùfáà-Àgbà's children, serving as council to the late king, ever looked in his direction. They all had their eyes fixed on the Lord Regent.

'And royal blood means nothing,' the Lord Regent said, 'or have the laws of our land changed?'

The council member held his ground, 'For hundreds of first suns the sovereign's family has lived in the royal palace for as long as they want. This is not the way. Our brother the late king would be turning in his grave.'

'I will not debate this. You are lucky I don't have them put in the dungeons for what their son has done. Alawani has brought disgrace to this palace and spat in the face of our gods. I want Olorì Atinúkẹ́ and her children out, and I will not discuss this again.'

'You are making a terrible mistake,' Àlùfáà-Àgbà seethed. His sunken eyes blazed with fury.

The Lord Regent slammed his staff on the ground and rose. The sound sent a wave of energy through the room. 'As the words have left my mouth.'

Slowly, in unison, the room said the words in response. And finally, after a long moment of silence, Àlùfáà-Àgbà said, 'So let it be done.'

'The crown heir will wait until we have a location,' the Lord Regent said, then walked through the curtains behind the throne.

The room bowed in unison as the Lord Regent disappeared from sight. The high council and the priests of the Holy Order filed out, leaving Tofa standing there before an empty throne. 'Are you coming?' Kẹni asked.

'Give me a moment,' he said.

His sister nodded her understanding. 'I'll wait for you by the door.' Leaving him alone was not an option.

As he stared at the throne, Tofa sighed in relief that his father wanted the prince alive. Despite this declaration about Alawani's family, Tofa knew it was just another of his father's mistakes that he'd fix once he took the throne. They shouldn't have to suffer for Alawani's folly. Tofa wasn't sure what kind of king he wanted to be but hunting down Alawani, someone he'd once called friend, wasn't how he wanted to start. Broken oaths or not, he wanted nothing to do with the death of the prince of Oru.

Tofa heard footsteps approaching and lifted his head, expecting Kẹni, but instead noticed Àlùfáà-Àgbà walking back into the chamber, shooting Kẹni an irritated glance as he passed. His face softened as he set eyes on the crown heir.

Tofa felt a rush of warmth towards the old priest, although he disagreed with his tough approach to Alawani's cowardice. The old man had taught him things his father would never teach him; things like old magic, politics, and an understanding of the delicate balance that kept the kingdom together. But it was more than that: the man had been there for Tofa in so many ways. When he needed a father, and his own was too busy ruling the kingdom, it was Àlùfáà-Àgbà who heard his concerns and wiped his tears. It was he who promised Tofa that he would be the greatest king who ever lived, and he'd always be there to show him the way.

Tofa moved closer to Àlùfáà-Àgbà and placed a hand on his arm. 'It's good to see you, Bàbá.'

Tofa didn't know anyone else who called the old man Bàbá. He wished that people saw the same nurturing and protective man he saw when he looked at the Elder Priest. Even the high council's indifference towards their father was always uncomfortably obvious to Tofa. He didn't know what had happened between them, but he didn't ask. It was a shame that none of them could see the heart of the man who loved him so much.

'Come here,' the older man said with arms wide open, embracing Tofa in a tight hug. 'It's good to see you too,' Àlùfáà-Àgbà said quietly, holding Tofa's face in his palm. 'Have you lost weight?'

Tofa smiled and moved out of his grasp. 'I'm fine, Bàbá, you worry too much.'

From the corner of his eye Tofa noticed Kẹni, her eyes like a hawk's, watching the old man's every move. She had more reason than most to hate Àlùfáà-Àgbà: he'd been the one to insist on her taking on the title of Ab'ọbakú – the condition that whenever he died, so would she. Tofa on the other hand was grateful for every moment his sister was alive and he had the Elder Priest to thank for that.

Àlùfáà-Àgbà's voice dropped so low that Tofa had to lean in to hear his words. 'Your father underestimates the powers this girl of Òtútù has. You mustn't. He can afford to be careless with his reign as it draws to an end, but if this girl lives, the repercussions will be yours to bear. I don't want that for you.'

'My father has ruled on this, Àlùfáà. There's nothing I can do.'

The older man leaned in with intent. 'I'm telling you, your father knows nothing. This L'ọrẹ of Òtútù is a threat to your throne and our kingdom! The guards have just brought in a battle rhino, frozen to death from the inside. Crystals crawl over its body like a disease. She did this. She must die.'

Tofa shivered at the thought – but that didn't change his orders. 'I can't disobey my father. He said to bring her back alive.'

'I taught you better than this, Tofa. You need to stop thinking like a boy and think like a king.' Àlùfáà-Àgbà leaned even closer. 'It is you who will sit on that throne as king and Aláàfin. This is your kingdom, and there has never been a war in this land. Do you want to be the first Aláàfin in our history to change that?'

'War?' Tofa said. 'She's just a girl. Even if these powers she has are dangerous, she can't be more powerful than I am. And nor can this kingdom of Òtútù be as powerful as Oru.'

Àlùfáà-Àgbà did the thing he does where he thinks he's smiling but instead looks like an animal ready to pounce. 'Her kind are born of darkness, born of the void deep within the night sky. They move from shadow to shadow like ghosts. They drain the life of anyone they touch, channelling that life and power into themselves. The extent of their evil is unknown, but, Tofa, we don't need to know any more. We know enough to know that they can't live on this continent with us.'

284

Despite himself, Tofa felt a chill settle deep in his heart at this. 'Why would they want war with us, anyway?'

'They seek vengeance for the justified massacre of their people a thousand first suns ago,' Àlùfáà-Àgbà said. 'They are coming, Tofa. The girl will be the catalyst they need.'

Tofa's eyes widened. 'There's no such thing as a justified massacre.'

'There is, when they threatened to wipe us out. And by the gods we won that war.'

'What are you not telling me about this girl, Bàbá?' Tofa said. 'Did you know that she was the one Alawani had been in love with and protecting all this time?'

'I often wonder what I ever did for the gods to curse me with a grandson like Alawani. No, I did not know that he had allied himself with the enemy. I should not have let him stray so far from the island. I know now that Ẹniìtàn has filled his mind with lies. Even after all I told him about his purpose in this kingdom after the stripping, that he would do something as foolish as running from his destiny is beyond me.'

'His purpose? Did you call him to the Order, Bàbá? Did you break the rules for him? Why?'

'Do you trust me?' Àlùfáà-Àgbà asked, placing a firm hand on Tofa's shoulder. Tofa frowned, considering the question. The old man gripped his shoulder tightly, forcing him out of his thoughts. 'Have I ever lied to you?'

Tofa shook his head slowly.

'Then trust me when I say, if you want this throne,' Àlùfáà-Àgbà pointed at the throne, 'the daughter of the Òtútù needs to die by your hand.'

Tofa stared at the gilded throne, surrounded by fire torches even in the light of day. No one had ever asked him if he wanted the throne before. He'd never considered the option of not wanting it. In truth, there was no choice to make.

Nothing to decide. He was oathbound to do all within his power to protect his kingdom from anything that threatened it. Unlike the king before him, he was no oath-breaker.

If the girl had to die? Then the girl had to die.

Àwòdì n fò ferere, ó l'óun fé m'Olúwa. Ibi tí
yóó fò dé, kò yé mi
*Àwòdì (a species of eagle that flies high) says it wants
to meet the Most High. It has no idea
the heights it will have to reach*

23

Ìlú-Òpọ, Third Ring, Kingdom of Oru

L'ỌRẸ

L'ọrẹ sat across from Alawani in the inn they'd stopped at when the rain got too heavy. She was glad of the chaotic energy in the farm bar. In the corner, a man drummed while a few women danced in front of him, singing above the cheers of the drunk audience. Between them and the gambling table in the corner, L'ọrẹ hoped she and Alawani were invisible. As soon as the storm cleared, they'd leave. They were only a few miles from the border of the third ring and she wanted to put as much distance as possible between her and whoever the Holy Order had sent after her.

L'ọrẹ felt Alawani's lingering gaze, but she ignored him. Àmàlà and gbẹ̀gìrì were staple meals for farm hands to build up strength or recover from a full day's work, so when the serving girl offered it to L'ọrẹ, she took it gratefully, unsure when she'd have her next full meal. Alawani opted for a light, peppery soup with goat meat and a small mound of bread instead. He finished his meal first, and washed his hands in the bowl underneath their table, then slowly moved to stand.

L'ọrẹ slammed her hand on his. 'Where are you going?' she whispered.

'I'll be right back. The storm is getting worse. We might

need to stay the night.' Just then, the winds crashed the door shut as someone ran out of the bar.

'Baba-Ìtàn had told me about the rainstorms in the third ring, but I never imagined anything like this could happen in a desert kingdom with nothing but cracked earth and dry harmattan. Not one drop of this gets to Ìlú-Ìmọ̀ and we're just one ring over,' L'ọrẹ said.

Alawani shrugged. 'Old magic. Without Ìlú-Ọpọ, Oru would starve.'

'Yes, but how is it done?' L'ọrẹ said.

'Shh . . . not here,' Alawani said, pulling out his seat. 'I need to pay for a room upstairs before this place gets booked out. I think the owner's just walked out.'

'Okay, I'm coming with you,' L'ọrẹ said, pushing her food aside.

'No, finish your meal. I'll be right back,' he said, shoving the bench underneath the table. 'Don't talk to anyone. Keep your head down.'

L'ọrẹ sighed, 'Hurry.'

She cautiously glanced around the room. No one seemed to pay attention to either of them. Her eyes lingered on the two hooded figures in the corner, but she quickly looked away. If they weren't looking at her, then she shouldn't be looking at them. She washed her hands in the bowl beneath her table, too anxious to finish her meal.

One of the men nearest to her stood abruptly, raising a small gourd of palm wine. 'To Máyọ̀wá, son of Ìlú-Ọpọ, our Àlùfáà and chosen priest of the third ring.'

The room echoed, 'To Máyọ̀wá! The chosen of the chosen.'

L'ọrẹ shrank in her chair. She needed to get out of this room.

The man continued, 'It's been decades since an Àlùfáà from our great state has survived the stripping ceremonies.

But I've heard on the grapevine that our Máyọ̀wá has sur-vived the first stripping!' The room cheered louder.

Alawani burst in through the door, soaking wet from the rain. 'Let's go,' he said quickly as he reached for her.

'What's happened?'

The words had barely left her mouth when a middle-aged man burst in after Alawani, his frown so deep it further dis-figured his scarred face. 'I'm talking to you, Ọmọ'ba.'

The man's words slurred as he moved to corner them, 'You think I won't recognize the son of our king?' he hiccupped.

The music stopped. The room quietened and the buzz that had lingered in the air floated away. L'ọrẹ could feel her chest grow cold as panic rose to her throat. They backed away from the man until they were leaning against the bar top.

'We don't want any trouble,' Alawani said, his hand out-stretched to the man. 'What do you want?'

L'ọrẹ glanced from Alawani to the man inching closer to them, his eyes bloodshot. How had their night turned to this in mere moments? At least this wasn't about her. The people of the third ring seemed less concerned with fulfilling their civic duty to harass the coward's daughter and instead, were more enraged by the presence of the prince.

'Gbẹ́kẹ̀, go home,' a deep voice came from one of the hooded figures in the corner.

Gbẹ́kẹ̀ croaked and spat on the floor, 'Mẹ́fà, stay out of this. I only asked this young man a question.' He turned to Alawani, 'Are you or are you not the Ọmọ'ba? The oath-breaker's son.'

'He's not the prince,' L'ọrẹ said, squeezing Alawani's hand even tighter.

'Then he only needs to take off his hood and prove it,' Gbẹ́kẹ̀ said.

Eyes roamed and the room went silent. Their gazes settled on Alawani and L'ọrẹ felt the hackles on the back of her neck rise.

'You're drunk,' Alawani said sternly.

'Even so,' Gbẹ́kẹ̀ said and hiccupped, pointing at the wall. 'I may be drunk but I'm not blind.'

Curse the sun. Right there was a sand portrait of the late king next to the Lord Regent. Right on cue, Command was in her head: *Another fight?* L'ọrẹ nearly spoke out loud defending herself and telling the voice that none of this was her fault.

Whatever you do, don't use those blades or agbára. The secrets you hold will turn this crowd on you quicker than you can imagine.

L'ọrẹ stepped forward. 'I told you, he's not the prince,' she said above the man's voice.

Gbẹ́kẹ̀ glanced at L'ọrẹ. 'Why don't you stop talking before I make you stop talking.'

'Touch her, and there'll be nothing left of you to bury,' Alawani growled.

Get ready now. This is going to turn into . . . The sound of Command's voice was drowned out by the loud cry from Gbẹ́kẹ̀ as he lunged for Alawani, reaching for his hood, trying to pull it off.

Alawani lit his agbára and punched the drunk man with a blast of energy that flung him back against the entrance door. The bar erupted in a frenzy with men rushing towards them.

L'ọrẹ picked up the stool nearest to her and broke it over the head of the man who approached her with a raised cutlass. She held on to one of the chair's broken legs and swung at the next man's face. Behind her she heard a crunch as Alawani crashed his fists into one man's jaw and slammed another face down into the bar top.

By now, most people who'd come for some peace and quiet had run out of the bar, leaving the angry people defending the man Alawani had blasted off.

Gbékè finally found his footing. He strolled towards them with charred clothes. 'So you are, after all . . .' Gbékè said, slurring his words and pointing at Alawani, whose hood was now uncovered, '. . . the son of that bastard.'

L'orẹ saw the anger rise in her friend.

'Gbékè, I said get out,' the cloaked figure in the corner shouted again.

'And I said shut up. His father is the reason we're starving in this ring. All our food ends up in the capital city, and we beg for scraps of what they could not have produced without us,' Gbékè shouted back. 'Oath-breaker. Just like his father. Did the Holy Order not announce that the gods broke their own rules and called the prince to the Red Stone? So what is he doing here?'

'Those were just rumours, Gbékè,' the bar owner called out to him. 'The gods cannot call the prince to be Àlùfáà – it is forbidden, and you know this. Just get out of my bar.'

Gbékè spat and slurred his words, 'This bastard may have turned his back on the gods but I tell you now, our Máyọ̀wá is destined for greatness, and the gods have told me he will be our next High Priest.'

'Èèwọ̀,' came a soft whisper from the corner. 'Abomination.'

Alawani took advantage of the distraction and lunged at Gbékè.

'No!' L'orẹ shouted, but the words caught in her throat. She couldn't speak. She could hardly breathe; her hands grabbed her neck, and she reached out for Alawani as he collapsed.

One of the figures in the corner stood and pulled off his hood to reveal a bald head and a severe face, tribal-marked cheeks, deep-set eyes, and something bulging in the middle of his forehead like a large stone beneath his skin. When he stood up, everyone in the bar fell to the ground.

'Mẹ́fà!' the young woman he'd sat next to called out to him. 'Leave him.'

L'ọrẹ noticed the woman's cloak was identical to Mẹ́fà's. She didn't look as sullen as he, and the fullness of her cheeks made her appear younger. She had the same tribal marks as Mẹ́fà and most of the people in the bar – six horizontal dashes.

Mẹ́fà glanced at the woman, 'To speak such things is treason,' he said in a low gruff voice.

'We don't need this att—'

Mẹ́fà didn't wait for the rest of his partner's sentence. He turned towards Gbẹ́kẹ̀, who was now looking up at him in shock, a hint of fear on his face, his hand also holding his neck.

The older man turned slowly without saying a word. Then the lanterns in the room grew brighter, and the room got so hot that L'ọrẹ felt herself growing even more faint. A few feet from her, Alawani was breathing heavily, and she crawled towards him. The man's agbára boiled the air in the bar and every person except he and the woman next to him was gasping for air.

Alawani stretched his hands towards L'ọrẹ's face, his agbára taking away some of the heat in the air around her so she could breathe.

The man's agbára glowed so bright L'ọrẹ squinted to see him and watched in horror as he punched his fingers into the drunk man's mouth and burned out his tongue.

The younger woman sprang to her feet and shouted, 'Mẹ́fà, stop it! Now!' She gathered her things and stormed out of the room – Mẹ́fà following in step behind her. The room cooled as soon as Mẹ́fà crossed the threshold, and everyone exhaled in unison.

Half the bar emptied after that. The air was no longer hot but heavy with delayed panic.

'Gbẹ́kẹ̀, you idiot! No one in this entire state is foolish enough to pick a fight with Mẹ́fà. You're lucky he didn't burn us all alive. I'm warning you for the last time. Don't come back to my house,' the bar lord said, ignoring the drunk man's pain-filled groans as his friends carried him out of the bar.

L'ọrẹ looked at Alawani, eyes wide with panic. She whispered, 'What in the cursed names just happened?'

Alawani helped her to her feet. 'Let's go up.'

The storm raged on, so they had no choice but to stay in the room they'd paid for.

In moments, they were up the stairs and in the room. Once in, they barricaded the door with the single bed.

'Curse the sun, Alawani. Why did you let that man pick a fight with you?' L'ọrẹ said. 'You might as well tell the Holy Order where we are.'

'You heard what he said about my father.'

'It doesn't matter what he said. Staying alive is all that matters,' L'ọrẹ spat back.

Alawani turned away from her, and she sighed, frustrated.

After a few moments, she slumped onto the mat and took off her shoes. The room was small and stuffy, and a hint of animal dung floated around in the air. Apart from the bed against the door, the furniture consisted of one chair on the opposite side of the room and a mat in the middle of the floor. Still, anything was better than the wet desert night soaking all corners of her body.

'That man would've killed us all. He burned that man's tongue!' she said in hushed tones.

Alawani shrugged and sat opposite her. 'Good thing whoever that woman was stopped him.'

'Why did he say Gbẹ́kẹ̀ committed treason?' L'ọrẹ asked. 'Were they not all cheering for Máyọ̀wá, may his soul find the city of light.'

'May his soul find the city of light,' Alawani repeated the death call and said, 'Lucky all Mẹ́fà took was his tongue. In the capital, that man would have lost his head for what he said.'

'What did he say?' L'ọrẹ frowned. 'I don't understand.'

'He said that Máyọ̀wá was going to survive the Red Stone and become the High Priest. That's treason,' Alawani said, his voice low as though he worried that the walls would echo his words.

'What? Why?' L'ọrẹ asked, realizing how little she knew about the workings of her own kingdom.

Alawani leaned in closer. 'The crown heir will inherit the throne on the next day of the First Sun. So there's no need for another High Priest for as long as he's alive. To speak of choosing a new High Priest now is like wishing the crown heir dead. And that's treason.'

'Wait, you were risking your life just to be a random priest of the Holy Order?' L'ọrẹ's frown deepened and she let out a bitter laugh. 'So you didn't even leave for crown or glory, you left to be what exactly? Is the Holy Order just hoarding survivors of their bloody trials until they need one of them to pluck out in . . . what? A hundred first suns?'

Alawani lowered his gaze. 'No one from this stripping ceremony was ever eligible to be High Priest. We all knew that. Only the survivors of the last stripping ceremony before the crown heir's death can be considered for the role of High Priest.'

L'ọrẹ screamed into her hands, 'This was all for nothing!'

She stroked the healing scar across her palm where she'd cut her oath. 'I wish I could reverse this. I wish I knew how.'

'Blood oaths can't be undone,' Alawani said.

L'ọrẹ laughed dryly. 'Oh, so you know that. You know that, and you broke it anyway. You walked into that temple knowing that breaking a blood oath is bringing a curse upon us both, and you did it anyway. And – And at Máyọ̀wá's house, you had the nerve to tell me that all this is my fault?'

Alawani placed his hand on hers. 'I didn't mean that it was your fault . . . I . . . Doesn't matter. Our oath stands. I shouldn't have said those things back at the farm. I know none of this is your fault, I just meant,' he sighed and placed his hand across his chest, 'seeing you standing there in the temple ruins, my heart dropped. I knew I had to get you out. You'd broken the cardinal rule – nothing else mattered but saving you. And I just wish you hadn't been so reckless.'

'Reckless? Reckless?' L'ọrẹ could hardly hold back her anger. 'What else was I supposed to do, Alawani? I was fighting for our lives. For your life! Your world has everyone and everything you'll ever need. My world had three people: you, Command and my father. And in one fell swoop, you took half my world.' L'ọrẹ paused, choking on her words as she fought back the tears. 'You broke my world in half and gave it to the godsdamned Holy Order! Yes, I was reckless, and I'd do it again and again and again. Because I chose you, and you chose death!'

Alawani shifted closer to her and placed her trembling hand on his chest. 'Tèmi, you aren't just a part of my world. You are the entirety of it. I'm here with you now. The oath stands. I'm not leaving you. We're getting out of this kingdom together.'

L'ọrẹ's breathing was heavy and she tried to calm her shaking hands, but now even her lips trembled. Before her was the boy she'd loved for as long as she could remember. At that moment, as his brown eyes pierced her soul, she hoped with all her heart that he was still the boy she knew and loved. That she hadn't made a mistake in risking everything for him.

Alawani moved in even closer, 'You have no agbára oru, and I didn't know. I've spent most days in the past – I don't know how many first suns with you – and I never realized this secret you kept from me. And I'm not angry about that or anything –'

'What's there to be angry about? I was protecting myself.'

'From me?' Alawani asked, his hand across his chest. 'You think I'd have turned you in?'

L'ọrẹ sighed, 'I don't know,' and his hand slowly pulled away from hers. She cast her gaze to her feet. 'I don't know why I didn't tell you. Maybe part of me wanted you to notice?'

The silence returned, stretching between them until Alawani spoke first. 'I'd never have turned you in. You know that, right?'

Her treacherous heart fluttered, and she smiled despite herself. 'So you say.'

The knock on the door broke the moment. She blinked, restarting her brain from the fixed glare she had on Alawani's face.

Alawani pulled back the bed from the door, and when he opened up, she heard the inn owner's angry voice pour into the room, 'You can't stay here. I don't want any trouble.'

'Ahan Oga, we bring no trouble. I promise you won't see us again tonight and we'll leave at first crow,' Alawani said in a calm baritone. He emptied his pouch of sun coins into the man's hands. 'For your inconvenience.' L'ọrẹ could hear the smile in his voice. Baba-Ìtàn always said that the prince could charm an ant into giving him its last piece of sugar cane.

After a few moments of coin clashing against coin, Alawani returned from the door with a large gourd of palm wine.

Alawani passed the gourd to her, and she took a large gulp. The milky liquid tasted sweet before settling into a more sour and yeasty aftertaste. She chugged down a few more gulps and burped, giggling. 'Baba-Ìtàn would be so angry if he saw this.'

Saying her father's name made her chest tighten with guilt, and she had to fight between thinking of him and moving forward on this journey he had set her on. If she let her thoughts linger, she would return home by dawn. It helped to remember that the kingdom would never kill an Àlùfáà. It helped to hope that they wouldn't.

Alawani did the same, smiling. 'What he doesn't know can't hurt him.'

L'ọrẹ smiled. She was tired of being angry. But she'd held on so tightly to anger because it kept fear at bay.

'How do you do it?' Alawani asked.

'Do what?'

'Not break the head of everyone who calls you a coward's daughter?'

L'ọrẹ frowned instinctively, her body reacting to the name before taking a deep breath. 'It's hard but you get used to it.'

'I don't think I could stand one more person calling me the oath-breaker's son,' he said quietly. 'I mean, I know they have a right to. At his coronation, he made oaths to all six rings and broke every one. To the priests, he promised official political positions in the kingdom.

'The second ring was supposed to get funding for public schools for children without families, the third ring asked for a fraction of the food they produce for the kingdom, the fourth ring had asked for the ban on old magic to be removed, which he never made a royal decree, leaving them unprotected. The fifth ring asked for reduced hard labour for the prisoners there, and the sixth ring wanted to make it mandatory for royal children to join the army.'

L'ọrẹ frowned, the image of the last execution she witnessed still fresh in her mind. 'I can't imagine giving the Holy Order any more power.'

'Granted, some of these oaths did not deserve to be fulfilled,' Alawani said, 'but some, like this ring, just wanted to survive. Three-quarters of every harvest is the price they pay for being located here in the third ring, and within the magical barrier that protects the inner rings from hail storms and everything else that ravages the rest of the continent. They begged and begged for generations for fairer terms. My father was the first king to say yes.' Alawani sighed and took a big gulp from the gourd. 'The more I learn about my father the more I realize he was never going to do it. Not this, nor keep any of the other promises he made to the kingdom. There wasn't an oath he made that he kept his word on.

'Every time I close my eyes, I hear his voice, and sometimes, I wish I could do something to fix the damage he caused. But what authority does a mere prince have to fix his father's legacy? With no authority and no inheritance, born nothing more than a commoner. I think that's why I accepted the call. I thought maybe as a priest, I could do something good for this kingdom. Anything at all. Even though I didn't know what I agreed to when he made me commit to a fate I was too young even to understand. I just . . . I don't want his legacy following me all my life like a curse. I mean, I loved him. He was my father after all. My memories of him are fading with time, but I remember that he was tall, and when I looked up at him, his eyes always shone like the sun, and it was like looking into the eyes of a god. I remember his laugh as he carried me in his arms and when he held my head close to his,

I remember the smell of kola nut that I hated then but miss now. But there are parts to him that I didn't know and when I woke after the Red Stone trial, my grandfather told me some of what my father did in his final days and the life they had planned for me from the moment I was born, and I can't reconcile what I remember with what I know. With what people say about him, I am terrified of becoming him.'

L'ọrẹ moved closer to him. 'Look at me.' She held his chin and slowly dragged it to face her. 'I'm still angry with you, and you're still an idiot, but you're nothing like your father. Do you hear me?'

Alawani never spoke about his father unless it came to honouring his wish to accept the call. So when the corner of his lips tilted into a smile, she mirrored his expression.

The room fell silent – only the sticky floorboards creaked beneath their weight as they shifted in place. L'ọrẹ sighed and stared out the window, mulling over what to say, hating the tightness in her chest.

She turned to see Alawani looking at her. Still fighting the mixed emotions in her guts, her lips twitched as she noticed the way the moonlight fell on his face, making his brown eyes shine brilliantly in the dim room. She had more to say but something made her stop, her words hooked like an arrow pulled tight, waiting to be released.

He stretched out and touched her thigh. 'I'm sorry for what I said back at the farm. I know none of this is your fault, and I shouldn't have said it was. I am truly sorry.' By this time, the drink had slowed his words. She stared at his hand on her thigh. She liked the feeling, even though it made her heart nearly burst out of her chest. Her eyes met his, and he quickly removed his hand, and she smiled.

'It's fine. You say stupid things sometimes. I can't blame you for having half a brain.'

He shoved her softly, and she fell off balance, landing on her back, giggling. Alawani shifted and lay down next to her, and they both stared at the ceiling. L'ọrẹ pulled out her pouch and took out the cowrie shell that Baba-Ìtàn had given her. 'This belonged to my mother,' she said.

'Did Baba-Ìtàn tell you about her?'

L'ọrẹ nodded. 'Not enough. I want to know everything about her and why she came here. She's always felt like a fading memory, but with this,' she said, holding out the cowrie shell, 'I feel like she's with me. I wish I could put it in my hair or somewhere I could see it, not hide it away like a secret.'

Alawani turned towards her and smiled. He slowly raised her top, revealing the beads strung in layers around her waist. L'ọrẹ's stomach nearly burst with the nerves that shivered in them as his hands found the end of the rope. He untied a string with his teeth, and she felt every part of her body come alive under his touch. He slid the cowrie shell in and tied it up. 'There,' he said, smiling up at her. 'She'll always be with you.'

L'ọrẹ was so flustered that she couldn't think of what to say. She just stared at him, smiling sheepishly. As they lay on the floor together, Alawani lifted his hand and, using his agbára, dimmed the lantern and made dancing shadows with his fingers. L'ọrẹ smiled, and then a thought crossed her mind. She sat up quickly and pulled him with her. They faced each other again. She pulled off her gloves and moved her hand closer to him, filling the space between them. 'Show me your agbára.'

He eyed her cautiously then slowly stretched out his hand and a warm glow filled the room.

'How do you do that?' she said, eyes wide, reaching for his palm.

He pulled away from her. 'No. I don't want to hurt you.'

'You won't,' she said. 'If you teach me how you do that, maybe I'll be able to do the same? I want to know how to use this agbára. I want to know how to summon it without facing certain death.'

Alawani hesitated but slowly moved his hands closer to hers and gently touched her fingers with his glowing hand.

As his fingers touched hers, a spark burst out from where they met, and L'ọrẹ flinched and pulled back.

Alawani withdrew his agbára immediately. 'I told you!' he said. 'Are you okay? Let me see,' he asked, leaning over and pulling her hand from her back where she hid it. He touched her arm, and she immediately let go, allowing him to move her fingers to his lips. He kissed them. Her racing heart seemed to stop at that moment, skipping many beats before restarting, taking the air out of her lungs. The shock of his agbára had stung, but this felt like something wild dancing in her guts. She forced out a breath and smiled.

'Let's try again,' she said, hoping the right spark would trigger her magic.

'No,' Alawani said. 'I won't hurt you again.'

He was talking about his powers. But that treacherous little heart took it to mean more, and she let it.

'I've always wanted agbára in the same way you have it. Now I have this, I'm terrified and I don't know what to do with it. What I'd do to have nothing at all again.'

He frowned. 'But . . . you didn't ever have nothing. I saw you use the blades Baba-Ìtàn gave you. I've seen you wield agbára oru in those blades better than most soldiers I know.'

'Old magic,' she said quietly, shame filling her voice as she spoke.

'What?'

'Baba-Ìtàn taught me how to use my blades when I started

training at Gbàgede. The power is in the blades and the words, not in me.'

'Old magic,' Alawani said, shocked. 'That's so reckless. Anyone could've caught you. My goodness, they'd have chopped off your head.'

'It was better than not having anything at all. You don't know what it was like to be the only one beneath the sun to have no agbára,' L'oré said. She felt the edge in her voice and the anger she'd forced down threatening to spark up again. She took a deep breath. 'I just don't want to hurt anyone. I want to control this without hurting myself, either.'

L'oré folded up her sleeves and revealed her arm. Streaks of black lines ran the length of her forearms. Again.

'What happened?' Alawani asked in shock, moving closer.

'I feel it all the time. Ever since the temple, I feel it buzzing beneath my skin, just waiting for the slightest trigger. It hurts keeping it down, and I'm always trying to keep it down. These appeared at the temple; they disappeared for a while and returned last night. I'm scared, Alawani.'

Alawani raised her hand to his eye level and softly rubbed against the marks. He shook his head. 'I only know how to use agbára oru – but I can try to teach you that, in case it helps. What did Baba-Ìtàn teach you?'

L'oré shook her head, 'Nothing. He taught me a few lines of old magic and that's it. Tell me everything.'

Alawani smiled. 'Well, the first thing we teach children is that agbára oru is the magic of the sun, and there are so many incredible things we can do with it. We all try to explore them but the most important thing to remember is, don't push too far. In the days of the First Sun when people first got agbára from the gods, they were reckless with this gift. Every other person died from the burn because they kept burning out their cores exploring new ways to use their agbára.'

L'ọrẹ's heart ached at how little she knew about these powers she'd been desperate for all her life. She'd have asked him about this much earlier if she hadn't been terrified of exposing herself. After all, these are all things people learn from their parents but if her last conversation with Baba-Ìtàn was anything to go by, he was proud of his decision to keep everything agbára-related from her. Surely knowing the history of the world she was forced to live in would have helped prepare her more than anything else but it was too late for what should or could have been now. She had to carve out her own path now. Starting with understanding this magic of the gods.

She lifted her gaze, 'I've seen you do crazy things with your agbára. Aren't you afraid of the burn?'

Alawani shook his head. 'The closer you are to a sovereign, the less likely you are to get the burn.' He paused, then said, 'As agbára flows from parent to child, it generally weakens through time except for the royal lines. Which is why everyone of royal blood is encouraged to marry a commoner. I mean, you've seen my sister train, and she's much older, yet her agbára is remarkable. She's married to a common man from the fourth ring, and their children are just a bit less powerful than she is, and that access to power that they got from my father will last many generations. Since every new sovereign is from a different family line, there are more opportunities for power to spread out more evenly in the kingdom. However, if there are any families in Oru that have not had anyone of royal blood mix with their line since the days of the First Sun, then their children will only be able to do basic things. People limited by their heritage in that way will surely burn out their cores the first time they try to do something that requires intense powers.'

'Command must be of royal blood. I've never seen anyone else do the things she does,' L'ọrẹ said.

'Exactly. She is,' Alawani nodded. 'But even without great powers, people can still do really cool things like manipulate heat and light. They can make flames hotter or snuff them out, some people can control how the flames move, and even the smoke. Or transfer heat from their bodies to an object. And some people, although very few, can heat up another person, burning them – in rare cases, without even touching them. But that doesn't come easy. That kind of agbára lies with the crown. Even I can't do that. The first thing my mother taught me was how to control my own body temperature in the heat of the desert, so as not to burn up in the sun.'

'I've never seen anyone sick with the burn before,' L'orẹ said.

'It's the worst thing you can imagine. Their skin turns black as though charred over a flame and breaks off, leaving raw flesh exposed. The agony is . . . it's brutal.'

Alawani paused, seeing her overwhelmed expression. 'We can talk about this later, let's start with something easy. Light.' He moved closer to her and said, 'Close your eyes.'

L'orẹ did as he asked, embracing the darkness and listening for his voice.

'Breathe in, deep and slow,' he whispered. She could feel his gaze on her and his breath as it fell upon her skin. She followed his every command.

'Clear your mind. Listen only to the sound of my voice. Imagine what you want to do. Follow the feeling that nudges at you, like walking towards a light at the end of a tunnel. Walk through that light and open your eyes.'

When L'orẹ opened her eyes, the room seemed brighter. The buzzing in her blood was still there, but the pain was dulled. No. It was gone. She felt tense and ready to burst, but somehow in more control than she'd ever felt before.

'Don't force it down. Let your body be a vessel, not a

prison. Allow the energy to flow back and forth through you until you're ready to use it,' Alawani said.

L'ọrẹ looked at him, and his eyes widened. 'Your eyes are glowing,' he said. 'They're blue.'

'What?' L'ọrẹ asked and immediately noticed the soft glow of white light that radiated from her palms. It looked like she'd pulled the rays from the moon's light and hidden them in her body. Different from the warm glow of yellow light that reflected agbára oru. Her hands felt lighter than usual. She felt cold, but not like she would do in the night's breeze. This cold almost felt like a warm hug, which made no sense, but nothing happening in this moment did.

'It feels different,' she said, smiling. 'This doesn't feel like fear or death. It feels – I don't know how to describe it.'

'It should feel like a part of you. Like the air in your lungs or the blood in your veins,' Alawani said.

She smiled, amazed and excited, and tried not to panic as she examined her palms repeatedly. Slowly, the black marks on her forearms faded, and she let out a deep sigh of relief. Could someone be happy and terrified at the same time? Elated and scared? She was everything. She felt every-thing. As she mulled over what Baba-Ìtàn had told her about agbára òtútù, she clung to the tiniest hope that these powers wouldn't be the death of her.

Alawani brought out his hands, and they shone with agbára oru. 'Let's try it again,' he said, moving his palms closer to hers. They met in the middle, and this time L'ọrẹ did not flinch. She felt nothing. No pain, no burn. Nothing. Not nothing exactly. A jolt of energy flowed through her, and she could feel her body come alive. It was as though her agbára protected her from his touch. A mist rose from where their fingers connected. Hers cold and his hot. They let their fingers linger, and the mist grew and filled the room.

L'ọrẹ couldn't hold back the smile that filled her face as Alawani grinned, entranced by her light.

'You are incredible!' he said, eyes wide in awe.

That perfect moment faded quickly as Alawani's light dulled. L'ọrẹ yanked her hands away, breaking their connection.

'Am I hurting you?' she asked, worried.

Alawani shook his head. 'It's the stripping ceremony, not you. My agbára will only keep fading. I shouldn't have used it in the bar.'

L'ọrẹ frowned and sighed. He seemed to not only know so much about the agbára of the gods but to love it. Love having it.

'Don't worry about it,' Alawani said, one side of his lips curving into a half-smile. 'I'll be fine.'

But he wasn't fine. Every time he used his agbára it was draining away even faster. And if his powers drained away entirely, there was a good chance he would die. L'ọrẹ fought back the tears that stung her eyes, her joy completely disintegrating.

Before I continue, do you know the names
of the old gods?
Do you know how they came to be on earth?
Do you know their story?
Well, it all begins with Olódùmarè, the all-knowing.
It is in search of this being that mankind discovered
the Òrìṣà.
For who are you to speak directly to the Supreme One?
The one who comes in three:
Olódùmarè, the Creator; Ọlọ́run, ruler of the
heavens; and Ọlọ́fi, the conduit between Orún
(Heaven) and Ayé (Earth).

24

Ìlú-Òpo, Third Ring,
Kingdom of Oru

MILÚÀ

Milúà had seen ten first suns when she earned her first cowrie. Taking a life was a privilege given only to the mother's favourite daughters. She'd cried then and thought that the face of her mark would hunt her all the days of her life. It didn't. By the time she'd seen fifteen first suns, her cowries were long enough to make the waist beads she wore beneath her dress. Now nearly nineteen first suns past, she wore two anklets made of cowries, and she remembered none of the victims' faces. As she raced after the girl she now knew was called L'orẹ, she expected to forget about her, just like she did the others.

She tightened her grip on her battle rhino as it thundered through Ìlú-Ìmò, heading towards the north gates leading into Ìlú-Òpo. Her thighs were sore from the hard ride from the capital, but she was determined to catch Alawani and L'orẹ before they got too far. Every moment away from the temple and Ìyá-Ayé was one more moment that she didn't know who exactly killed her mother. Before this incident, all she'd wanted was to know more about her mother. Now she desperately needed to remain a temple maiden. A title she hadn't been fond of in the past but was now the only thing keeping her alive. Milúà didn't enjoy killing although she was quite good at it. However, earning another cowrie for ending L'orẹ's life would be a reward for all the pain the girl's actions had caused her.

'Steady now,' she said, patting the beast as it grunted again, no doubt exhausted from the chase. 'We're almost there.'

The rhino huffed in response, and she patted it a couple more times. 'I don't want to be here either,' she said, trying not to slip off as the beast sped up.

Alawani's disappearance wasn't something Milúà had antici-pated and she questioned herself on how she had missed the signs. He had been reluctant at first, but she'd gotten her hopes up after the stripping, thinking he actually might sur-vive all the trials to come. And then he was gone. She ought to be in the temple figuring out who killed her birth mother. Instead, she was here, on a hunt for a foolish and ungrateful prince. She sighed. He thought the Red Stone was painful. Just wait until she got her hands on him. Memories of her nights in the weeping chamber flashed through her mind, and she grimaced. Ìyá-Ayé had healed every wound before Milúà left home, making sure she was equipped for this errand, but somehow the memories brought phantom pain that felt real enough to make her wince. She tightened her grip on the reins. *Curse you, Alawani.*

Milúà had waited for Ìyá-Ayé to return from the Regent's court before leaving on her hunt, so even though Ìyá-Ayé had told the Lord Regent that Milúà was miles away from home, she had in fact been waiting patiently for her mother's final word as instructed. Once their meeting was over, Milúà followed Àlùfáà-Àgbà into the temple to the dungeon where they kept the boy L'orẹ and Alawani left behind. Why would anyone be so foolish as to bring a friend along on such a dangerous heist? Why would anyone be so foolish as to have friends at all? She couldn't imagine making herself so vulnerable as to put her life in another's hands. Not even Bùnmi, whom she'd grown up with, was her friend.

Kọ̀yà was the friend's name. Milúà wondered if he was still alive. She winced as she remembered hearing his screams. She didn't know where they'd found him, but she knew the priests had tortured him for a full day, getting nothing from him before, as usual, calling her to do what they couldn't.

Milúà hadn't expected to learn that it was the boy's own brother holding the seven-tailed whip that lashed across his back. And it surprised her even more that although the brother held and swung the whip, it was he who wept as flesh tore from Kọ̀yà's broken skin. She could not remember the last time she cried for any of her sisters in the weeping chamber. Her mother would not stand for such senseless displays of weakness. She would instead really give her something to cry about.

Àlùfáà-Àgbà had not been able to control his anger during his interrogation. 'You dared to come into my temple, to defy the gods, to defy me!' He had held Kọ̀yà's face in his hands in a short pause between the whippings, and the boy groaned. 'Where is the girl?' he shouted.

That was when Milúà knew she had to step in. The old man was wasting time. 'I think it's time to try something else,' she said.

Àlùfáà-Àgbà shot her a dirty look when she ordered the whipping to stop.

'He can't speak if you keep torturing him,' she said firmly.

The Elder Priest's eyes burned with anger, but he conceded, stepping back as the palace guard cut off the ropes that held his brother's arms up and guided him to the floor.

She observed as Kọ̀yà struggled to stand upright in her presence. *A strong one*, she thought.

Milúà bent down beside him and moved her lips to his ears. 'Tell me where they went, and I promise the pain will stop. At least for today.'

He remained as he was, eyes closed and head hung in despair.

She leaned in closer. 'You know they won't stop at just you,' she said, distancing herself from the people who inflicted pain on him. 'They'll kill your brother. They already know he helped you. That's why he's been made to do this. They'll find your parents, parade them through the capital, and chop off their heads in front of everyone.' She paused for a response, then sighed when he still didn't move. 'If you make Àlùfáà-Àgbà feel the need to use old magic, there'll be no coming back from that.' Nothing. Not even the soft whimpers from earlier. 'They'll kill the old man, too,' she spat out, frustrated. 'The girl's father.' If, after several light beads of torture, he still held his tongue, perhaps she could play on that sense of loyalty that often got people like him killed.

Nothing.

Milúà lost her patience and thrust her hand into his chest and squeezed against the bruised flesh. Her hand glowed with agbára, and Kọ̀yà screamed so loudly the walls seemed to echo after him. When she removed her hand, Kọ̀yà's chest was bruised and bleeding but . . . not burnt.

Milúà blinked, unable to believe her eyes. His chest wasn't any worse than before she'd touched him with her agbára. That wasn't supposed to happen.

She glanced back at Àlùfáà-Àgbà, who took a brisk step closer. Then she again thrust her hand at Kọ̀yà's chest, nearly breaking a rib, and allowed her agbára to shine bright and hot. Smoke oozed from the touch, simmering off the sweat from Kọ̀yà's body, but when she removed her hand, there was no burn or blister. Just raw skin torn by the whip.

Àlùfáà-Àgbà's eyes grew to double their size, and Milúà could see the whites of them for the first time. Nothing ever shocked the old priest. But this . . . this was impossible. Agbára oru burns all but the wielder.

'What evil magic is this?' Àlùfáà-Àgbà slapped Kọyà across his face, and the boy groaned.

Milúà's gaze shifted to the boy's brother, whose eyes were red with tears. She moved fast and cornered him against the wall. Before he could speak, she slammed her palm against his chest and poured out her agbára. He screamed just as loud as his brother. Louder. When she removed her hand, flakes of burnt skin clung to her fingers. She brushed them off. *So, it's not a family thing.*

She turned to Àlùfáà-Àgbà, 'He's immune to agbára oru. Did you know this?'

'How can I know what isn't possible?' Àlùfáà-Àgbà shouted at her. 'Burn him again. Burn his tongue! That way, he won't whisper any incantations to the old gods.'

Milúà shook her head. 'He didn't speak a word. I would've heard if he did.'

'Get out,' Àlùfáà-Àgbà said. Kọyà's brother slowly and reluctantly walked out of the cell, hunched over in pain. Àlùfáà-Àgbà turned on Milúà, 'You too.'

Milúà raised a questioning look to Àlùfáà-Àgbà. The fury that burned in the old priest's eyes gave a glimpse of what he had planned for the boy.

Milúà knew pain as well as she knew how to breathe. So, it wasn't often she felt pity for anyone who had to endure it. Even the stripping at the Red Stone, while agonizing, felt bearable. At least some of those boys survived. She shot one last glance at Kọyà and, perhaps for the first time in her life, felt pity. This was why one didn't have friends. It didn't matter what brought Kọyà to the Sun Temple. He was

313

never getting out. Mercy wasn't something Milúà was taught so it shocked her every time she even considered it, much less acted upon it. She shook all thoughts of Kòyà from her mind, another thing she'd have to explain to her mother. She should've killed him.

Milúà slowed her battle rhino to a halt as she approached the border gates that led into Ìlú-Òpọ, blocking off the memory of the boy held deep within the darkness of the earth beneath the Sun Temple. The mighty beast huffed, grunting as it slowed, its pin-sharp horn slicing the air before it.

'Don't be grumpy now. Just a bit longer,' she said, patting its thick armour. 'We're almost there.'

She had got nothing from Kòyà, but figured her first stop on the hunt should be the home of the boy who nearly escaped with them but got killed in the crossfire. Máyòwa.

Before her, the people cleared out of her way, and she could hardly hide the smile that crept onto her face. People hadn't moved nearly as fast when she was a red maiden. Her fingers trailed over the gold bracelets she wore. The gold was worth the wait. She wore golden sandals with thin straps that ran crisscrossed all the way to her thighs, where they met with the thick bands she had firmly secured around her upper thighs, one for a dagger and the other for her staff. Her solid gold bracelets were wide and long, covering half of each hand, and further up, she wore matching gold arm rings in layers.

The warrior's statement outfit was the gold armour on top of the flowing white gown. It sat atop her chest and started from the top of her neck to her waist, moulded to fit every curve of her body. The white dress underneath had very high slits on each side for when she had to kick someone in the face, and she kept her long braids in a high ponytail, held by a gold band; when the hair fell, it reached low, sweeping below her bottom. Everything a warrior maiden wore was a distraction. Behind every glittering accessory was a blade visible only when needed to kill. The ensemble's last piece, perhaps the most important, was her retractable gold staff strapped firmly to her right thigh. When it blossomed on her command, it was almost twice her height with spears on both ends, and when she channelled her agbára through it, it lit aflame.

Milúà came to a stop a few yards from the main gate. She rubbed the inner part of her thighs, wishing she'd carried some ointment to help with the blisters that would no doubt sprout in a few days. As she rode through the gates, the people, even the guards, turned away from her as she moved. She could get used to this. As soon as she crossed the border, she quickened her pace, pushing the rhino back to full speed. It growled but obeyed and raced through the empty sparse lands towards the settlements.

It was easy to find the prince. She only needed to close her eyes, breathe and channel her agbára into her eyes.

Although it could be useful, true sight wasn't an ability she used too often. Since everyone around her had agbára oru in varying degrees, it could be overwhelming. But as she'd grown up, she'd learned to concentrate on only one person at a time. This made hunting easy because if the gods had blessed her prey with agbára oru, she could always find them. Their agbára appeared to her in threads of gold, leading to the glowing orb in their chests. Weaker people had a soft yellow glow in their core. Stronger ones had orange, and those who could make her sweat in a fight had a pinch of red, nothing more than a dot. Those were scarce.

Milúà was grateful she had studied Alawani's heat energy the moment she met him. His red-tinged core made him stand out among the sea of yellow threads that filled her eyes as she opened them with true sight activated. Her eyes were on fire and stung as though she'd rubbed pepper in them. The light from the hundreds of agbára threads that appeared before her was almost too much to bear. But this was the quickest way to find him.

At first, everything was too bright, like a wash of sunlight, but as it filtered out, she could see a reddish-gold thread curving left and disappearing into the distance.

Got you.

He must be close. She followed the pull she felt, racing faster as the thread started fraying and shedding its glow. Her rhino galloped beneath her, feeling her urgency as she drove her legs into its sides.

The sky was dark, and the rain had started by the time the thread Milúà followed grew fuzzy like a cloud. She slowed, patting her rhino as he eased to a walking pace. No longer able to tell which direction to travel, she jumped off the rhino and strolled around. Alawani had to have spent time in the area she was in. She didn't know why he'd stopped in a corn-field, but – she spun around again and saw something in the distance. The thread was nothing more than a fog now, like a puff of powder dancing in the air, but it clearly went through the house a few yards from her. Milúà moved towards it immediately. She stormed into the house.

Inside the house, in a small four-cornered room, she found an older couple seated on a mat having their evening meal. They rose to their feet immediately, bowing before her in greeting. Milúà ignored them and searched the two other rooms in the house before returning to them.

'The prince was here,' she said in a cool steel voice.

The couple looked at each other, and Milúà assumed that meant yes.

'Where did they go? Where are they going? Why did they stop here?' Milúà couldn't decide which question was most relevant, so she asked them all.

The older woman spoke first. 'Our son was Máyòwá, the chosen one from this land. They brought news of his death and his àṣírí and left. We know nothing else.'

Milúà sighed and sat on the mat, squeezing the rainwater from her dress onto the floor. Even her thick braids sagged and dripped, making her hair feel twice as heavy. The couple sat back down opposite her.

'What did they tell you about your son's death?' Milúà said.

'Nothing,' the woman said hurriedly.

Milúà allowed the silence that followed to stretch on.

Then the man shifted on the mat and said, 'They said he died on the Red Stone.'

Milúà knew mothers well enough to know they knew everything. She turned to the older woman. 'What else did they say to you?'

The woman looked at her husband and sighed. Without taking her eyes off her husband, she said with tear-filled eyes, 'Our son didn't die on the Red Stone.'

The old man frowned, his lips quivered, but he remained quiet. His eyes never left his wife's.

'What else?' Milúà said.

The woman closed her eyes and let the tears fall. She shook her head. 'That's all. They didn't stay long.'

Thunder boomed outside the house, and the old woman winced and shuffled closer to her husband.

'Which way did they go? Are they walking or riding? How long ago did they leave?' Milúà asked.

The woman's voice wasn't as steady as before. 'They took our horse. They left a few light beads ago. Going north, I think.'

Lightning flashed outside the window, and a cool breeze rushed into the house.

'Do you have anything else to say?' Milúà said quietly.

The old man didn't seem to get her meaning, but the woman did because she propped up and stared at Milúà, eyes wide with fear.

'But we told you everything we know,' she said, sobbing.

'And for that, for your son, I'll make it quick.'

Then the man got her meaning, and he grabbed on tight to his wife's hand.

Milúà rose to her feet.

'Wait!' the woman shouted. 'Take our àṣírí please, maiden, I beg you. Don't send us into the darkness.'

Milúà considered mercy. Then she thought of how she'd explain to her mother that she let people who knew the secrets of the Order live. Without fail, Ìyá-Ayé would appear to her in her sleep tonight as she did to every maiden on assignment to know their progress. As images of the weeping chamber flashed before her, Milúà made her decision. 'The things I know will take many blood moons to pass on. I can't take on another,' she said flatly.

They couldn't live. They knew their son didn't die on the Red Stone, they knew the prince was gone from the Sun Temple. They simply knew too much to be allowed to see the next day. She was still a maiden of the Holy Order, and mercy was a privilege she didn't have to spare.

'Please,' the old man croaked, and Milúà wasn't sure if it was the tears that flowed from his eyes or the way he held on tightly to his wife's trembling hands, but something made her say, 'Fine. Write it down, and I'll make sure someone reads it.'

The following moments were memories Milúà hoped to the gods of the sun and sands that she'd forget the way she did the others. The couple handed her a crumpled piece of paper, heavy with words that would keep them from the city of light if not passed on, and then held on to each other in a tight embrace. The next time lightning flashed outside the window, Milúà summoned her agbára to life. Drawing on her core energy, she pulled the lightning from outside into her hands. Sparks danced along her fingertips as she formed orbs of energy. In the moment between breaths, she shot firebolts into their beating hearts. Another shot at the raffia baskets in the corner, and they sparked a fire. Milúà filled the room with heat energy, holding her ground until the fire engulfed the house. Then walked out of it, watching the fire roar even as the rain poured in streams down her face.

Milúà stood before the blazing house, watching the fire blossom and spread into the farm. Moments later, the rain slowed to a drizzle, and a young woman came running towards the burning building but fell to her knees at the sight of Milúà. Trembling, she tried to run away, but Milúà called out after her, 'Take another step, and you'll meet the gods tonight.'

The woman stopped in her tracks, going still as a statue.

Milúà went to meet her and handed her the piece of paper with the couple's last words. 'Read it.'

The young woman peeled it open and started to speak when Milúà said, 'No! Read it in your mind. I don't want to hear it.'

The young woman nodded, trembling where she stood. Her eyes went back and forth until she was done.

'This is your àṣírí now,' Milúà said.

The woman nodded, still shaking with fear.

'Go,' Milúà said, taking the paper from her and burning it with her agbára.

Milúà rubbed her forehead, and her hands moved along her braids. She stopped and counted the cowries hanging from them – one, two, five. What were two more? She pulled two cowries from her cleavage and attached them to her wet hair as she whispered the last words the dead hear, 'May your souls find the city of light.' And with that, she turned away from the house towards her rhino, summoning her agbára. Blinking hard to awaken her true sight, she waited for the thread that led to Alawani to reveal itself again.

Bí ó ti lè wù kí oòrùn mú gangan tó,
bó pẹ́ bó yá, ó n bọ̀ wá fi àyè sílẹ̀ fún òṣùpá
*No matter how hot the sun is up above, eventually it
will leave room for the moon*

25

The Royal Palace, Royal Island, Kingdom of Oru

TOFA

Every morning at four light beads past midnight, all who lived in the Aláàfin's palace journeyed from their beds to the gilded throne to bow before the crown. The Lord Regent didn't need to be present for this ritual. Tofa couldn't remember the last time his father was on the throne when the entire court came out to bow before him. But now, as Tofa bowed before the throne, his forehead gently touched his father's feet, and he knew something was wrong.

'As long as the sun remains in the sky, so long shall the crown live,' Tofa said quietly, allowing the voices of others crouched behind him to echo the prayers.

Tofa lifted his head and glanced back when he heard a familiar voice. A voice he hadn't heard at the morning gatherings since the last time his father attended one.

Ìyá-Ayé rose to her feet, dusting off her hands and raising her voice above others. She recited the old praise names for the throne, the Lord Regent, and even Tofa as crown heir. Pausing every other sentence for the room to say, 'Àṣẹ.'

What was she up to? How did she know the Lord Regent would sit on the throne this morning when he hadn't for many blood moons? Tofa returned his gaze to his father, who waved over the crowd three times, accepting their greetings and sending them off to start their days. Slowly, the hall emptied. Even his mother and sisters left at the Lord Regent's request, all bowing out one by one until only Tofa, Kẹni, High Priestess Àṣá, Àlùfáà-Àgbà and Ìyá-Ayé remained before the throne.

They all sat quietly at the bottom of the dais, waiting for someone to speak first. Tofa noticed his father's slumped shoulders and reddened eyes, and at first, he'd thought it was because of the time of day, but as the silence stretched on, the Lord Regent's gaze narrowed on Àlùfáà-Àgbà. Something was very, very wrong.

The sound of the hall doors cracking open broke the silence. A palace guard marched in, and then another and another. The last guard walked in with a long iron chain in his hand, leading in a man who, by the change in countenance on his father's face, was someone the Lord Regent recognized. Many first suns ago, Tofa had seen the man's face on sand portraits hung all around the kingdom, reminding everyone who the coward was. Still, the matted grey hair and bloody, bruised face did not disguise the only Àlùfáà to have left the Holy Order and live to tell the tale: Ẹniìtàn – the one born with history on his lips.

Àlùfáà Ẹniìtàn, as the man was once called, had done the impossible. The rest of the council didn't know, but Àlùfáà-Àgbà had once, in a bout of anger, mentioned to Tofa that after surviving the Red Stone, the man had been his choice for High Priest but he'd turned it down, rejecting the Elder Priest and their gods. All priests would risk death to be chosen as High Priest and Lord Regent, but somehow, for some mysterious reason, this man chose a life of shame and humiliation instead. That decision had put Tofa's father on the throne and him in line to inherit the crown. This man's single decision was why Tofa would one day be the Aláàfin of Oru. Tofa didn't know if he was grateful or not.

Unfortunately, Ẹniìtàn's actions helping this L'ọrẹ of Òtútù had given Àlùfáà-Àgbà reason to throw him into the dungeons, as he had wanted to for a very long time.

The Lord Regent's voice cut through the air, sharp as a blade, 'Ẹniìtàn.'

The man raised his head, straining as the iron around his neck weighed him down. His eyes were bloodshot, and his lips cracked. He matched the Lord Regent's steel gaze.

'Tell me everything,' the Lord Regent said, his voice softer after staring down the man.

Tofa imagined surviving the Red Stone together must have created some bond between them. They could easily have been friends.

Baba-Ìtàn shifted where he stood. 'Your guards stormed my house, destroyed everything I own, and dragged me here to your dungeons.'

'You brought that upon yourself,' the Lord Regent said, agitated. 'I let you live, and you repay your Order by giving refuge to an enemy of Oru. Where in the world did you find that girl?'

'Is that what he told you? That she's your enemy?' Baba-Ìtàn said and scoffed, his chains rattling as he pointed to Àlùfáà-Àgbà.

'Ẹniìtàn, I want to help you. You're my brother. For whatever that is worth, you know more than anyone the position I am in.'

Baba-Ìtàn frowned. 'We are not brothers, Babátúndé –'

'Ẹ̀ẹ̀wọ̀! Gods forbid,' the members of the Holy Order present shouted in unison. They cursed the man for calling the Lord Regent by his first name.

The Lord Regent waved his horsetail again, excusing the blunder. Reluctantly, they quietened.

'Maybe once, we were something of the sort, but as the dust never settles too long in our land, so also time has shifted whatever we were. We are not brothers. We cannot be. Not while you sit on that throne, and I rot away beneath it,' Baba-Ìtàn said, stretching his hands and allowing the chains that bound him to shake as he moved.

'I don't want you in chains, and you know that. But the evidence of your transgression is permanently imprinted in the memories of those present for the attack from your . . . daughter. I can't justify your freedom.' The Lord Regent paused. 'Do you have nothing to say for yourself?'

'If I wanted to answer to you or the Order, I would not have left,' Baba-Ìtàn said plainly.

'And why did you leave? Was whatever you left your brothers for worth it?'

Tofa noticed the look that passed between Àlùfáà-Àgbà and Baba-Ìtàn. His father may not know why his friend left the Order, but Tofa could bet the crown that Àlùfáà-Àgbà knew every single detail of the truth.

Baba-Ìtàn, who looked like he was about to speak, withdrew after the glare from Àlùfáà-Àgbà. The Lord Regent must've missed it because he said, 'I remember the night you left. I remember begging you to stay like a child losing a sibling. You were supposed to stay!'

'Here? To be what? Your prisoner?' Baba-Ìtàn said.

'You chose this life. The life of a prisoner was your choice. You could've had this crown, you could've had it all,' the Lord Regent shouted.

Baba-Ìtàn scoffed, 'We're both prisoners. I'm bound in iron and you in gold. You're just too blind to see it.'

A guard struck Baba-Ìtàn across the face, and he bent over, groaning in pain.

Tofa looked away as the man spat blood onto the golden

floor. The morning sun had begun to fill the room, beaming its rays through the skylight above the throne, making the Lord Regent look like a god on his dais. His mouth formed a tight line, and his gaze darkened. 'Where is the cursed girl of Òtútù? Tell me now, and I'll spare your life. Lie, and you'll lose your tongue.'

'She's not cursed,' Baba-Ìtàn said.

Tofa almost gasped. Never in their history had their Àlùfáà been executed, but even then, Baba-Ìtàn did not seem to consider that these days, unprecedented things happened each new dawn.

Àlùfáà-Àgbà rose to his feet. 'Enough of this,' he said to Baba-Ìtàn, then turned towards the Lord Regent. 'My Lord, it is true that the gods forbid the death of an Àlùfáà away from the Red Stone, but this man has done nothing but mock the gods from the moment he joined the Order. With a heavy heart, we, the Holy Order of Oru, call for his execution. The punishment for harbouring an enemy within our walls is death, my Lord.'

Beside him, Ìyá-Ayé and High Priestess Àṣá nodded in agreement.

'So you ask permission to kill one of your own?' the Lord Regent asked.

'Not permission, Lord Regent. We don't need the permission of the Regency for this. He is one of us, and we'll do with him as we please.'

'He is a child of Oru and under the king's command. You are under my command.'

'You are not my king.'

'Èẹ̀wọ̀,' the room echoed, passing nervous glances at each other. Abomination.

That didn't stop the Elder Priest. 'You are just a regent,

and you do not have the right or authority to change our laws. Your word can't override me on this.'

The guards in the room slammed their rods firmly against the floor, and the sound of metal on metal boomed throughout the hall. The Lord Regent rose, and the room bowed before him.

'You forget I am still your High Priest, old man,' the Lord Regent said.

Tofa sat upright again, watching as realization hit Baba-Ìtàn. The law was a tool to be moulded in the hand of its beholder, and the fate of his life seemed to depend on who won the argument that played out before them. A battle of wills between the regent who once was and the one on his way out.

'He will remain in the dungeon until the next first sun. Then my son will decide if he lives or dies,' the Lord Regent replied. 'As the words have left my lips.'

'So let it be done,' the room said after him.

Tofa's heart dropped – another decision waiting for him when he took the throne. He locked eyes with Baba-Ìtàn.

'You dishonour your gods, Lord Regent! That girl he raised is an enemy of this kingdom!' Àlùfáà-Àgbà said.

'I have heard enough!' Lord Regent Babátúndé said, slamming his staff into the ground. The guards moved in unison, pulling Àlùfáà-Àgbà away from the dais and forcing him back to his seat.

'Take the prisoner back to the dungeons. Get the girl's location,' the Lord Regent said, sitting back on his throne. 'I wish it hadn't come to this, old friend.'

Baba-Ìtàn said with a resolved expression, 'I don't care what happens to me.'

Tofa believed him. He knew the look of a man willing to

die for something, making him even more curious to discover whatever secrets Àlùfáà-Àgbà was hiding.

Baba-Ìtàn moved closer to the Lord Regent's dais, 'Who did Àlùfáà-Àgbà tell you the girl was?'

'Don't you dare!' Àlùfáà-Àgbà shouted at Baba-Ìtàn.

Tofa saw the Elder Priest's mouth move silently and frowned.

'What did he tell you to do if you found her?' Baba-Ìtàn continued, ignoring the older man.

'Who is she?' the Lord Regent asked.

Tofa heard whispers of incantations from Àlùfáà-Àgbà. His eyes widened. He wasn't . . . he couldn't be using old magic to stop the man from revealing the truth.

Baba-Ìtàn spoke slowly, 'If you kill her, you kill –'

Baba-Ìtàn slumped to the ground as Àlùfáà-Àgbà's incantations stopped. The guards rushed to the storyteller. Up on the dais, his father was on his feet too, walking down the stairs. The Lord Regent wouldn't have heard the chants that caused Baba-Ìtàn to fall, but Tofa certainly had, and from their side looks, so had the women. What could Baba-Ìtàn have said that threatened Àlùfáà-Àgbà so much he would use old magic in front of the court?

Who was this girl?

'Is he dead?' the Lord Regent asked.

The guard closest to Baba-Ìtàn lowered his face to the man's chest. 'He's alive, Lord Regent.'

The Lord Regent slowly turned to Àlùfáà-Àgbà. 'You did this.'

'My Lord,' Ìyá-Ayé said quickly, 'the priests interrogated him before bringing him here. It is not unusual for him to faint. We had no hand in it.' As his maiden, she was always implicated in anything the old priest did.

'Stand up!' the Lord Regent commanded, and they all rose.

'Take him to the chamber next to mine,' he instructed the guards, before glaring at Àlùfáà-Àgbà. 'When he wakes up, my face will be the first he sees, and as the gods live, he will finish that sentence.'

The Lord Regent stormed out of the hall, the guards following him with Baba-Ìtàn in their arms.

High Priestess Àṣá was the first to leave, exchanging knowing looks with the others as she hurried out of the hall. Àlùfáà-Àgbà and Ìyá-Ayé walked out, too, using another exit.

Tofa hurried towards Kẹni. 'Did you see that? Àlùfáà-Àgbà used a spell on him.'

Kẹni rolled her eyes. 'What else do you expect?'

'That man knows something devastating. He must. There's no way Father buys Ìyá-Ayé's excuse.'

A young maid walked through the servant's entrance with a bucket and cloth to wipe Baba-Ìtàn's blood from the floors. The girl glanced at them, and smiled. Tofa frowned. He didn't know her, and – then he saw Kẹni smile. His sister had a friend. He wasn't sure what surprised him more, the friend or the smile.

Kẹni turned to him. 'If it's that important to you, follow them. I'll stay back. If you sneak up on them, maybe you'll overhear something important.'

He looked at the girl and back to Kẹni. 'But we're supposed to stick together. You're . . . not trying to get rid of me, are you?' he smiled.

'I told you, I don't care. Go or don't go. I'll be fine. I'm not the one dying to find out everyone's secrets.' But from the way her eyes flickered to the girl, Tofa could tell she definitely was trying to get rid of him. Well, he'd always wanted more independence for her – and what was a few minutes of separation, really?

Tofa smiled and nodded. 'I'm glad you're making friends!' Then turned away without waiting for a response.

Tofa almost ran into the old priest and the High Priestess as he sped through the corridors and down the stairs. As they came into view, he slowly took a few steps back, leaning around a wall to see them huddled in a corner, talking in hushed tones. He could see their lips moving but couldn't hear anything. From where he stood, he should be able to hear even whispers, but it was dead silent. Then he figured they were masking their voices – old magic.

Luckily, Àlùfáà-Àgbà had taught him a few tricks. He only needed to figure out which old gods were being summoned. He pulled at his collar to take a deep breath, then noticed he couldn't feel the morning breeze blow past him as it had just moments before. He got it. They were using the wind to channel the sound of their voices in a different direction. He closed his eyes, and called upon the old goddess of wind, Ọya. Focusing on the right spell to use, he softly whispered the incantation to summon a gentle breeze towards him, allowing him to make out the voices, faint and distant.

He heard Ìyá-Ayé say, 'You lied to me, Àjànàkú.'

Tofa supposed if anyone could call Àlùfáà-Àgbà by his first name, it would be his maiden.

'I told you what you needed to know,' Àlùfáà-Àgbà said in response.

'So, when were you going to tell me that Mọ́remí's child lived?'

'I had it under control.'

Ìyá-Ayé laughed, and her voice echoed. She looked around, and Tofa scrambled out of sight.

'You have nothing under control. You've let your silly fights with that man on the throne distract you from your true purpose. Even the little you had in your hand, you've lost.' Ìyá-Ayé sighed, and Tofa had to lean in closer to hear the rest of what she said. 'I don't understand why you didn't trust me with this. Have I not proved myself to you? Yet you hold this failure close to your chest.'

'Failure?' Àlùfáà-Àgbà said, and Tofa could imagine the look on his face.

'If you had told me who Mọ́remí really was the moment you found out, she would've been dead before she could birth the trouble she did. My Àdùnní would've been more than happy to see her end,' Ìyá-Ayé said.

Tofa searched his mind for the name Àdùnní. He hadn't heard it before. Probably just another maiden, he decided, then focused back on the whispering pair.

'This again,' Àlùfáà-Àgbà said, frustrated. 'Mọ́remí and Àdùnní would have destroyed themselves, and this kingdom would have been nothing but collateral damage lost in their feud.'

'Yes! This again,' Ìyá-Ayé said. 'It was your job to kill Mọ́remí and her child. And clearly, you did not. You forced me to kill my Àdùnní for the *future* of this kingdom, yet you had our greatest enemy living in this kingdom raised by a priest you chose to join the Order. Or did you forget that it was you who brought Ẹniìtàn's name to us? You who claimed the gods chose him?'

'Ẹniìtàn is my greatest mistake, and I do not need you to remind me. The fact remains that Àdùnní had to die, and you know it. She broke the rules. She should never have been with a child, and definitely not of the man she chose.'

'In that case, then why is Mọ́remí's child alive? Why are we hunting L'ọrẹ down when she should have been buried with her mother?'

'I did not know that the child lived! When we found Mọ́remí after she escaped from the temple, she was alone, and she told me she buried the child with her own hands to keep it from me.'

'And you believed her?' Ìyá-Ayé scoffed.

'All that is past. What matters now is that I will find L'orẹ, and she will die. By my hands if I must,' Àlùfáà-Àgbà said. 'But don't you dare question me. I know that it was no mistake that a maiden of our Order under your care got pregnant. I often wonder if you made that mistake intentionally.'

'I fed Àdùnní the infertility herbs myself, as I do for all my maidens,' Ìyá-Ayé said, her voice laced with anger.

'And what is your excuse for keeping Àdùnní's child alive?' Àlùfáà-Àgbà seethed.

Then there was quiet. Tofa had to move a couple of paces forward to see if they were still there.

Àlùfáà-Àgbà's words came slowly and quietly, 'Did you think you could hide Milúà in plain sight? To be just another random maiden? With agbára like that?'

This name Tofa recognized. Milúà was the warrior maiden Ìyá-Ayé had sent after Alawani and L'orẹ.

'Kill her,' Àlùfáà-Àgbà said in a single breath, and Tofa adjusted again.

'No,' Ìyá-Ayé gasped. Her voice took on a menacing undertone. 'We both let children who ought to have returned to the sands live among us. Mine is a warrior maiden serving the gods and the Holy Order. And yours will be the end of our kingdom as we know it. So if we are counting mistakes and errors, look in the mirror, Àlùfáà, and don't throw stones, lest they crack the image you put up.'

Àlùfáà-Àgbà sighed. 'It wasn't just for Àdùnní's crimes that her child had to die. Milúà's father –'

'She doesn't know who her father is,' Ìyá-Ayé quickly jumped in.

There was a brief silence. Then Tofa heard Àlùfáà-Àgbà

332

say, 'Milúà is just as much a threat to this kingdom as L'ọrẹ. The day she discovers who her father is, she dies.'

Tofa heard their footsteps and rushed out of the corner and down the corridor. He ducked into another corner, then stopped, confused about what he'd heard and whose fate had been sealed for death. He sighed. He really shouldn't be skulking around in his own palace. As he leaned against the wall, thinking of what to do about this enemy from the north, he considered his position in his own kingdom. When he took the throne on the next day of the first sun, who would be at his side? His father would have relinquished his role as the regent, and returned permanently to the Sun Temple to lead the Holy Order as their High Priest. Àlùfáà-Àgbà – the Elder Priest – would likely spend the rest of his days grumbling as he did now, longing for the power his previous posts had afforded him. And Tofa would be the king and supreme leader of the land of Oru. His sisters would be his council, but if they were anything like their predecessors, they would always steer him in favour of their birth rings. He was naïve enough to imagine that after granting Kẹni her freedom, she'd want to remain at his side the way she'd been compelled to. He needed the Order of the Secret Twelve.

*Those who seek strength and the spirit of a
warrior call upon
Ògún – the god of iron and war.
Those whose anger boils for justice call
upon the dragon-like
fire-breathing god of fire and thunder – Ṣàngó.
Those with desires that cannot be spoken
aloud call upon
Ọya – the goddess of wind, storms and the rebirth,
while those who yearn for family call upon
Ọṣun – the goddess of love, fertility and beauty.*

26

Ìlú-Òpọ, Third Ring, Kingdom of Oru

L'ỌRẸ

L'ọrẹ's dream was always the same. Pillars on both sides of her. Winds that moved in a loop. The same fixed line across the horizon. The same sand dunes and hills and the blistering sun above that burned her skin raw. Once, she'd been terrified of this dream, but now, all this was normal. So when a figure appeared in the distance, a black spot floating towards her with what seemed like many arms floating in the wind, and she started to sink into the sand beneath her, she screamed and forced her eyes open.

They were heavy, and it felt like prying open old heavy doors whose hinges hadn't been oiled for ages. She tried raising her hands to her face when she realized she couldn't move; she couldn't feel her arms, legs, or any part of her body. Panic seized her breath, and her mouth wouldn't open when she tried to speak. She forced her eyes closed and opened them again. Easier this time, but no other part of her body could move. She tried shifting in the bed to wake Alawani, but it was as though the part of her mind that made her body move was gone. Her breaths came in short bursts of white mist, and her mind flooded with terror and panic. What in the gods' names was happening to her? *Move.*

Move. Move, she commanded her body, but it remained stuck to the bed.

She tried to relax, but her breathing was shallow, her chest refusing to rise. She would die in this bed beside Alawani, and he wouldn't even know. There was no calming her now. She tried to scream, but the voice in her mind couldn't break through her frozen lips. Suddenly, Alawani stirred, and hope flared in her chest. He shifted towards her and placed his hand over her stomach but didn't wake up. She strained her eyes in frustration. The only movement she could make.

She kept struggling to move, to break out of this cast, but despite the battle raging in her mind, her body didn't hear her pleas. A few agonizing moments later, a tingling sensation spread over the area where Alawani's hand rested. His arm seemed to thaw whatever had frozen her in place. She flexed her torso, and it moved. She focused on every part of her body, every limb, and every movement she wanted to make in her mind, then fought with everything in her to move. Finally, something shifted, and slowly, her body came back to life. Every stretch and crack ached, but she was glad to feel anything. She was glad to take a full breath again. She sprang and crawled on her knees. Her legs were still recovering from their stasis.

She stretched to wake Alawani but the black lines that had disappeared the night before were re-forming across her hands. Was this what dying felt like? Watching your body rot from the inside? She'd have gotten off the floor and run home to Baba-Ìtàn if she could run fast enough. She placed her hand over her face and groaned, 'Help me.' She wasn't sure who she was talking to. Definitely not the gods of the sun and sands. Not the old gods, either. She didn't know them enough to dare. Still, she whispered again to whichever one of them would listen, 'Help me.'

Alawani stirred again and sprawled across the bed. He couldn't help her. There was no point worrying him about what had happened. He was losing his own agbára. He had enough to worry about. She realized how often she chose not to bother him. She supposed she'd been so happy to have a friend that over the years she'd decided it was best not to overwhelm him with things he couldn't do anything to change. Or maybe it was so that she didn't scare him off. Whatever the reason, as she sat on the floor deciding not to tell him she was dying, she realized how much she'd kept from him since they became friends.

Somehow, they'd managed to avoid any difficult conversations, never having to confront the hard truths of their life. Not about Baba-Ìtàn's sentence as an outcast and not about Àlùfáà-Àgbà, his grandfather, who was responsible for her mother's death and was the one sending them into this exile. All that was too much for what she was now seeing as too fragile a bond. She realized the man she loved, with every breath she had, might only know the side of her she'd revealed to him, and she couldn't help but wonder what parts of himself he might have kept from her too. She jumped at the bang on the door, followed by a loud cry, 'Prince Alawani!'

At that moment, everything around her seemed to come into focus. The smoke seeping in from beneath the door filled her nostrils and started to choke her. Outside she heard faint cries of people and hooves of animals as they raced out of the building. The pounding on the door got louder until eventually, the door rattled against the bed. The bed wasn't strong enough to withhold the force and as the door gradually opened, the smell of smoke and the crackle of fire filled the room. L'ọrẹ shrieked as Alawani leapt off the bed, allowing the door to crash open.

The figure in the doorway moved quickly. 'Get up. Now!'

'Who are you?' Alawani said. He groaned as he channelled his agbára, a dull orange glow lighting his outstretched hand. L'ọrẹ imagined how much it'd hurt to pull on his waning powers.

The figure removed their hood and L'ọrẹ immediately recognized the young woman from the night before. 'It's you,' L'ọrẹ said, 'from the bar. You were with that man, Méfà.'

'There's a fire downstairs and the royal guards are nearly here. I imagine you don't want to be here when they arrive.'

Alawani reached for his blade and L'ọrẹ did the same, as they moved closer to the woman who raised her hands in surrender. 'Gbẹ́kẹ̀ called those guards and while I don't know what kind of trouble you are in, I know that you,' she pointed at Alawani, 'are supposed to be in the Sun Temple as Àlùfáà.'

Voices shouted from beneath them. The royal guards were in. The fire was just a distraction; most people in Oru could control the intensity and movement of flames as well as the smoke they produced. They'd be on their floor in no time.

L'ọrẹ smashed her blades together and sparks flew as they crashed against each other. The woman looked at them and scoffed. She channelled her agbára and formed an energy orb, and threw it at the brick wall, blasting a hole through it.

The woman jumped and L'ọrẹ watched as she used short bursts of hot air to slow her falling speed until she gracefully landed on the ground. L'ọrẹ looked back at Alawani. She couldn't do that.

'Just go!' Alawani shouted, going back for his sword.

A royal guard grabbed on to his hand and held on like a feral beast as Alawani thrashed, trying to get free. 'L'ọrẹ, jump. Now!' he shouted through the chokehold. L'ọrẹ grabbed on to a pole hanging out of a window a few feet below her before landing on the ground. She looked up, hoping to see

Alawani at the hole in the wall, but instead, a royal guard sneered at her, and as soon as he stretched his hand to blast them off, the woman pulled L'ọrẹ behind her and shot at the room. Smoke and dust filled the hole which had doubled in size and the sounds of screams from within the building made L'ọrẹ's heart ache with every beat.

'What are you doing?' L'ọrẹ shouted at the woman. 'Alawani is up there, you could've killed him.'

'That guard would've killed you,' the woman replied sternly.

'I'm going back for him,' L'ọrẹ said, trying to climb in.

'No, you're not,' the woman said, holding her in a locked grip.

'Don't touch me!' L'ọrẹ said. 'I don't know you.'

'Okay, calm down,' the woman said, raising her hands. 'My name is Márùn, and I'm here to help.'

'Why? What do you want?'

Márùn sighed and turned her back to L'ọrẹ, raising her hair to reveal the back of her neck. There at the base of her skull were three tongues of flames, dark as coal, inked into her skin.

L'ọrẹ gasped, 'Life debt.'

'Yes,' Márùn said, facing her again. 'I owe a life debt to the prince's mother, so I promise you, I can and I will get him out, but not with you running around in there.' She glanced around the building and pointed at the barn in the corner. 'Take two horses, wait in the tree line and we'll meet you there.'

'I can't,' L'ọrẹ said, 'I can't just leave him.'

'We need a way to get out of here fast once I get him. So go!'

L'ọrẹ looked towards the barn. 'Tell him to light up the sky if you can't find me in there, I'll find you both.'

'What does that mean?'

'He knows what to do,' L'ọrẹ said and ran for the barn.

'Run!' Márùn shouted as the guards started shooting blasts of energy at them.

L'ọrẹ rode her own horse and managed to lead Alawani's by its reins as she made her way through the chaos of animals that raced to the tree line for shelter from the fire. Behind her she saw Alawani and Márùn fighting the royal guards on the ground, and so much of her wanted to go back but Márùn was right. If they made it to where she was, they could be out of the third ring long before the royal guards caught up with them.

She tied the horses to a stump and ran back to the tree line to watch. She crouched when she felt the earth moving beneath her. Slight vibrations she recognized. Alawani. She peered through the branches, and from a distance, she could see the glow of agbára oru radiating from his hands and the tattoos on his skin. He slammed his hands firmly on the ground. When the guards charged at him, covering the ground between them, the earth cracked open, and magma flowed out of it. The burst of red liquid spread quickly and burned their feet. Only one or two of them were quick enough to use their own agbára to remove the heat from the magma. Not that they were quick enough to avoid being burned. L'ọrẹ flinched against the guards' screams as the earth's heat engulfed them in flames. At that moment, L'ọrẹ realized that Alawani had been even more powerful than she thought before the stripping, since he could do this even when weakened.

Alawani and Márùn used the moment of confusion to race towards the tree line. L'ọrẹ sighed in relief, then yelled as someone grabbed her hair and dragged her across the forest floor, releasing her only when they reached a clearing. From the clash of cowries in her assailant's hair and the strong scent of temple incense, L'ọrẹ knew exactly who had caught her.

L'ọrẹ tried to stand and met the heavy blow of the maiden's fist on her face that sent her crashing to the ground. Blood filled her mouth and black spots danced across her vision.

'Oath-breaker,' L'ọrẹ heard Milúà say.

She lifted her head to see Alawani's image swimming in her blurry vision, hands raised as he ran towards them in the clearing. L'ọrẹ spat out blood and mud and tried to lift herself off the ground only to be struck down again, this time with the maiden's golden staff across her back.

L'ọrẹ yelled and fell back into the wet ground, grabbing hold of the mud as the ground swallowed the sounds of her scream.

'Stop!' Alawani shouted, running to hold L'ọrẹ.

Milúà grabbed a fistful of his hair and dragged him to his feet. 'I can't believe you did this to me,' she said.

'I didn't do anything to you, Milúà,' he said. 'I left.'

L'ọrẹ saw the slap coming before Alawani did. 'Exactly,' Milúà said, her nostrils flaring.

L'ọrẹ struggled off the ground, breathing heavily and trying to blink away the spots that still dimmed her sight. She glanced back at the way she'd come into the forest. Where was Márùn?

Don't do it, Command's voice whispered in her mind – but what choice did she have? Milúà wasn't going to let her live, that much was sure. The maiden would kill her and take Alawani back to his death. No. L'ọrẹ couldn't fail now, not when she'd gotten so far, and sacrificed so much. She clenched her hands in tight fists and released them, allowing her agbára to shine through her hands – the blueish-white light tinted by the warm ray of sunlight from above. Cold seeped deep into her core and she felt the dark veins on her hands grow, stinging with every inch of skin they claimed. The last time she used these powers, she'd killed something. She didn't want to leave a trail of dead bodies in her wake but if it came down to Alawani or Milúà, the maiden had to go.

'Let him go!' L'ọrẹ shouted at Milúà as the maiden pressed a knife to Alawani's neck.

Milúà tossed a pair of black cuffs at L'ọrẹ's feet. 'Put those around your hands and come with me, and I promise I won't accidentally slide my knife across his throat.'

L'ọrẹ picked up the chained cuffs and poured her agbára into them, freezing them until they became brittle like glass, then shattered them on the ground. 'Let him go, and I will spare your life.'

Milúà laughed. 'You think you can kill me with party tricks? What will you do? Build a wall here? Please go ahead. It's a shame you didn't get to see what I did to the last one you built.'

'She won't kill me,' Alawani groaned. 'L'ọrẹ. Just go.'

Go? Go where? Did he think she'd leave him after all they'd been through? After everything she'd done to get him out?

Milúà scoffed, and she pressed the dagger, cutting the skin and allowing Alawani's blood to flow down his neck.

Anger flared up in L'ọrẹ's chest. The energy in her buzzed as if responding to her emotions, fighting its way out. She stretched her hands towards the trees that surrounded them. Dark mists danced around the edges of the light that shone and oozed from her hands, and like a spreading disease, everything in the surrounding clearing froze over. The grass, the trees, and even the small animals scurrying around froze mid-jump.

Milúà tossed her knife to the ground and held Alawani in a tight lock with one forearm. With her free hand, she poured out her agbára oru, sending a beam of burning fiery energy towards everything L'ọrẹ's agbára had frozen over. Turning round in the same spot, she cleared it all, leaving a pool of mucky liquid drooping on the ground where the tall trees once were.

L'ọrẹ hoped she didn't look as frightened as she was on

342

the inside. The maiden was powerful. Perhaps even more powerful than Alawani had been before his stripping.

'You're going to have to do better than that,' Milúà said, panting and smiling. Her eyes were dark and her breath heavy.

'You can't kill an Àlùfáà,' L'ọrẹ said, grasping at straws.

'Do you want to bet on that?' Milúà asked with a coy smile.

L'ọrẹ turned off her agbára. Milúà had leverage, and she knew it. Alawani was weakened from his earlier burst of agbára and she couldn't risk hurting him with her powers if she tried to fight Milúà.

The maiden thrust her hand at Alawani with agbára-ignited hands and burned him. He screamed and fell to his knees and Milúà kicked his jaw, sending him to the ground in a thud. She raised her staff over his head and a sharp spear sprung out from its end. L'ọrẹ screamed.

In the next moment, an energy blast exploded near Milúà, sending her back into the mud. L'ọrẹ had never heard a maiden scream before, no matter how much pain they were in. L'ọrẹ swirled to see Márùn behind her, her glowing hands pointed at Milúà. L'ọrẹ noticed how the maiden's dark skin seemed to sizzle, the sweat drying off her and her skin nearly melting off. Márùn was burning her alive. Through the screams, Milúà tossed a blast at Márùn, who easily dodged it. Milúà's agbára glowed through her hands and every mark on her skin, her eyes flaming red, burned in agony.

Changing her moves, Márùn pulled the same trick Méfà had the night before, heating up the air around the maiden's face. Milúà clawed at her neck, trying to use her agbára to cool the air, but Márùn kept moving closer, narrowing her hands and closing the invisible bubble of hot air around the maiden's face. Milúà fell to her knees. She held on to her neck, choking, unable to breathe. Her eyes bulged, and she slammed her hands onto her chest to clear her airways. She wasn't breathing.

'Run,' Márùn shouted.

L'ọrẹ had been stuck in a stupor watching Márùn do things she'd never seen anyone do before. She ran to Alawani, pulling him away from both of them.

'Stop!' Alawani shouted at Márùn.

L'ọrẹ gaped at Alawani in surprise. What was he doing? If Milúà had had one more moment, she'd have run him through with her spear.

'She wouldn't have killed me. She can't! Stop it. You're killing her!' he shouted, running to Milúà, who was now lying limp on the wet, muddy ground.

L'ọrẹ broke her silence. Her mind struggled to understand what she was seeing. 'Stop! Let's go,' she shouted at Alawani.

'L'ọrẹ, we're not killing her!' Alawani shouted. 'Márùn, stop it now!' His voice boomed, and Márùn released her hold on the maiden.

Milúà's breath hitched as she inhaled sharply. She squeezed her chest as she forced in deep breaths, trying to tear off the armour she wore, which no doubt was hot enough to burn through the sheer white cloth beneath it.

Alawani finally stood up when Milúà seemed more stable. L'ọrẹ didn't hear what the maiden said to him, but as Alawani approached L'ọrẹ and stretched out his hand to her, she slapped it away and stormed off. She found their horse a few paces away and climbed on, giving Márùn a hand to join her.

'Find your own way to the border,' she hissed at Alawani and galloped away.

L'ọrẹ was so angry, it had taken everything in her not to slap him across the face. Hot tears burned in her eyes as she rode through the winding trail. Even so, she glanced over her shoulder and saw him galloping towards them on the horse, and a wave of relief washed over her. Who was this maiden, and why – why did he care about her so much he'd risk his life to save her?

The thick forests gave way to sparse land, and by the time they reached a deserted part of the wall, the ground was hard and sandy, like the rest of the kingdom. Márùn steered L'ọrẹ away from the King's Road and towards the east side of the wall, about half a mile from the guarded gates. She used her agbára to freeze the locks on the door, and together they smashed it open, revealing a tunnel cutting through the stone wall.

Only then did they notice the group of guards in the distance behind Alawani racing towards them, leaving a cloud of dust in their wake. Márùn ran through the tunnel without looking back. L'ọrẹ hated herself for waiting for Alawani. But still, she waited impatiently, bouncing on her feet until he reached her. He jumped off the horse and they ran into the tunnel, leaving their horses behind. Once in, L'ọrẹ used her agbára to seal the entrance. Stretch and shoot. It wasn't hard to summon her agbára when she could feel panic tight in her throat. Even in the heat of the tunnels, she shivered as her agbára rose to the surface, filling her fingertips with dark mists and hands with streams of dark veins. Ice crystals poured out of her and covered the entrance as she'd wanted to. But then it started to grow, consuming the tunnel nearly faster than she and Alawani could run. They made it out just moments before the crystals filled the tunnel and began crawling up the exit wall.

L'ọrẹ was surprised to find Márùn still waiting for them at the other end. Although she noticed a look of fear that flickered across the woman's face.

Alawani sighed, 'What now?'

'You don't have a plan?' Márùn asked.

'We do,' L'ọrẹ said, bringing out the letter her father had given her from her boot. 'My father sent us here to his friend.'

'How will we find her?' Alawani said. 'We don't know where to start.'

'He said once we got into Ìlú-Idán, we only need to call her name to the wind, and she would find us.'

'Fine, what's her name?' Alawani said.

L'ọrẹ read the name on the letter, 'Àdùkẹ́.'

A cloud of dust appeared in the distance.

Tó bá kù díẹ̀ kí ọmọ olóore jìn sí kòtò,
mànàmáná á ṣiṣẹ́ imole fún un
*Just before a good person trips and ends up in a ditch
in the dark, lightning would light up their path*

27

Ìlú-Idán, Fourth Ring,
Kingdom of Oru

L'ỌRẸ

Àdùkẹ́ looked at the ice that covered the exit, which now seemed to have grown a few inches climbing up the wall. She turned to L'ọrẹ and said, 'Ọmọ Mọ́remí. Mọ́remí's child.'

Àdùkẹ́ said those words as fact. Not a question. Nothing about her firm gaze made L'ọrẹ think the woman was asking if she really was Mọ́remí's child. So she nodded in agreement – too stunned to speak.

L'ọrẹ couldn't take her eyes off the woman, who walked slowly and confidently before them. Step by step, she led them through the city of Ìlú-Idán, walking past soldiers and guards who didn't seem to recognize any of them.

The woman spoke softly without turning back to them, 'Keep close, and my shadow will hide you from their eyes.'

L'ọrẹ, Alawani and Márùn picked up their pace. Àdùkẹ́ – loved by many. That's what the woman's name meant. She considered Àdùkẹ́'s small figure and brisk steps as she paced through the town, each step hardly touching the ground. Over the woman's hair was a finely wrapped satin head tie the colour of blood, and over her silk gown, across her waist, was a single row of cowrie beads. A woman who wanted the world to know how many people had died by her hand. As they moved through the busy streets with buildings almost as tall as those back at Ìlú-Ìmọ̀, L'ọrẹ noticed the men they passed tilt their heads in the briefest of nods, and the women bend their knees ever so slightly, neither actually uttering a word as they breezed by. Who was this woman Baba-Ìtàn had sent them to?

They walked through the sandy streets of the home of old magic, passing by residents whose ancestors were the first to join the new kingdom of Oru all those first suns ago. Although L'ọrẹ had never been to this ring before, it was just as Baba-Ìtàn's stories had described: there was a visible drag in their steps, a solemness familiar to anyone scorned by the kingdom. The people whose execution she'd watched back in the capital city were all from this ring. The home of old magic. Descendants of the old Idán tribe, filled with the innate strength of old magic but forced to turn away from their old ways.

L'ọrẹ wondered when the tides had turned. At what point in their history the magic that made these people special had turned into something outlawed by the Order? Many of them prisoners awaiting death. Those who believed in the gods of old, the myths and tales of their scions. Those who still knew the old dialect that was now restricted to be spoken only as incantations. Incantations only to be uttered by priests of the Holy Order. There were more soldiers in Ìlú-Idán than L'ọrẹ had ever seen in any other state. They clustered in a large group, all on edge, ready to pounce, their hands on their blades. Some even kept the warm glow of their agbára permanently on for others to see. The air around the city was thick with tension. L'ọrẹ stilled and gasped at a figure in the distance, a woman amid a group of soldiers a few yards from them. Àdùkẹ́ stopped, glared at L'ọrẹ, then turned and continued walking after L'ọrẹ sheepishly whispered, 'Sorry.'

L'ọrẹ peered through the crowd to catch the face again, but it was gone. Had she seen Command? No. It couldn't be. Not this far from home. Not coming after her.

L'ọrẹ was just about to look away when she noticed the familiar glitter of gold, and there Milúà was, her white dress stained with blood, her gold armour scorched with flame, and her face an angry scowl. L'ọrẹ froze and pulled Alawani to a stop next to her.

Àdùkẹ́ turned on them. 'What is it?'

'We know that maiden. She's trying to kill us,' L'ọrẹ replied frantically.

Àdùkẹ́ held her hand in a firm grip. 'As long as you are with me, they cannot see you. Even if the gods open the skies to look for you, they will find the face of another. Follow me and keep your head down.'

Àdùkẹ́ stopped walking when she noticed L'ọrẹ hadn't moved from her spot. 'Enough of this foolishness,' she sighed as she waved her hand in a flowing motion, as if controlling something. L'ọrẹ soon noticed as loose sand from the ground rose, swaying in the same direction as the woman's hand, back and forth repeatedly. Àdùkẹ́ pointed a finger and spun it. And what had first felt like a bit of wind was now a raging cyclone spinning through the town. People rushed indoors. Others hid their faces under their scarves. Even Milúà and the soldiers choked inside the storm. The heavy wind ended abruptly, but thick dust filled the air, making it hard to see.

The commotion that ensued was the perfect distraction. The entire street corner was in a frenzy.

'Hold this and follow me,' Àdùkẹ́ said, handing L'ọrẹ a long piece of cloth that was attached to her waist. Alawani held on to L'ọrẹ's other hand and Márùn's, and with noses and mouths covered, they walked into the storm, past Milúà and further into this strange land her father had sent her to.

They reached the woman's house, and L'ọrẹ couldn't help but think it was the ugliest house she had ever seen. The outside of it smelled like medicinal herbs, the rotten kind. The walls were filled with dried vines and sharp thorns. They walked inside and met a dark hallway. *Why would anyone live like this?* She instinctively gripped Alawani's hand, and he held on tight, matching her wariness of the stranger. She only let go when she walked into the light, and the darkness gave way to a stunning room – filled with flowers and colours she'd only ever seen streaked across the sky at the first light of dawn. It felt as though the sun had chosen this room to display all the hues of its golden shine. Her eyes widened in awe as she slowly paced around the space, which seemed to come alive with each step she took.

'Make yourself at home,' Àdùkẹ́ said plainly.

Inside, the house was much bigger than L'ọrẹ could have imagined. There were desks, chairs and shelves of books. If not for the glowing flowers, L'ọrẹ would've thought she'd been transported back home. Above her the flowers formed chandeliers and lines of lower hanging lights that swung from wall to wall.

L'ọrẹ brought out the letter Baba-Ìtàn had given her and handed it over to Àdùkẹ́, who raised her brows in curiosity. She took it from her and opened it. The next moment, the letter burned in the woman's palm, and the ashes fell to the ground in a slow puff of cloud. It happened so quickly that L'ọrẹ almost missed the light of Àdùkẹ́'s agbára as it came on and off in seconds. Did she even read the letter? L'ọrẹ remembered the look in her father's eyes, the earnest desperation with which he spoke when he gave the letter to her. She did not know what was in it, but it was important. It had to be. And this woman just burned it?

The woman didn't even look at where the ashes fell.

The three of them lined up before Àdùkẹ́ and L'ọrẹ stared in disbelief, mouth open as her father's words swayed to the ground like burnt feathers off a message bird.

'Who are you?' asked Àdùkẹ́, pointing at Márùn.

Márùn removed her hood.

'I am Márùn. Five of Twelve,' she said, standing upright.

What does that mean? L'ọrẹ thought.

In the third ring, the man who nearly killed them all was Mẹ́fà. That name meant number four. Four and Five. Who was this woman really?

'Liar,' Àdùkẹ́ said firmly.

Márùn removed her scarf and unbuttoned her shirt to reveal five short vertical lines across her chest, then hit her palm against her chest five times. 'I am Márùn,' she said again.

'She saved our life,' L'ọrẹ added.

Àdùkẹ́ frowned, 'Márùn is dead.'

'And I am Márùn,' Márùn said sternly.

Àdùkẹ́ paused and, after an awkwardly long moment, she hit her palm against her chest just as Márùn had done but instead she did it seven times.

L'ọrẹ looked from one to the other and then at Alawani, who shrugged. He was as clueless as she was.

Àdùkẹ́ observed L'ọrẹ and Alawani as though seeing them for the first time. 'You're wounded,' she said, looking at the bruises on L'ọrẹ's stomach and arms, the cut on her brow and the muddy state of her wrapper. Alawani wasn't any better. His trousers were torn and his shirt was scorched where the maiden had burned him, leaving behind a hole and blistered skin. Àdùkẹ́ brought out a vial from her turban and placed it in L'ọrẹ's hands. 'Drink.'

L'ọrẹ frowned. 'What is this?'

'Do you think I brought you to my house just to poison you? Drink.'

L'ọrẹ drank the liquid, slowly and apprehensively. If her father trusted Àdùkẹ́, then so would she. It smelled and tasted like fermented sap from an old tree bark. She bent over and heaved loudly.

'Don't you dare throw up on my floor,' Àdùkẹ́ said firmly.

L'ọrẹ forced the liquid down and it felt like something exploded inside of her. Making her body so heavy, she could hardly stand. Her ears rang and for a moment, a flash of white crossed her vision, blinding her, and then it was gone. Her senses dulled. Even the putrid taste disappeared from her lips. She felt stronger, her aches eased, the gash on her forehead hadn't healed but it no longer stung and for the first time in a long time she stood upright without pain.

'Give it to him,' Àdùkẹ́ said, pointing at Alawani, who looked even more worried than L'ọrẹ had been.

'It's fine, take it,' L'ọrẹ said, handing the vial over to him.

Alawani drank it in a single gulp and didn't as much as flinch.

Àdùkẹ́ raised a brow. 'You've had this before then.'

Alawani didn't respond, he only nodded and returned the empty vial to the woman. Where had he ever taken anything like this?

Àdùkẹ́ eyed Alawani warily then moved on. 'Your rooms are this way,' she said, leading them to stairs that led to a landing above them. 'Leave your clothes at your door and the girls will fix them by morning.'

On the stair railings were bright yellow flowers that ran all the way to the top. They blossomed as she approached them, slowly awakening as her presence drew nearer. L'ọrẹ had seen nothing of the sort before. She had grown up thinking that old magic was a cheap replacement for the agbára she didn't have. Most importantly, it was something that had to be hidden, so watching this house clearly and proudly filled with old magic made her heart flutter with anxiety. She couldn't shake the feeling that the Holy Order would sense such a surge of power and track them down. On the other hand, if she'd known that a place far from home would have been more accepting of her using a little bit of old magic she'd have moved to the fourth ring a long time ago.

With every step that L'ọrẹ took, the flowers around her turned a light shade of blue, deepening until they mirrored the colour of the sky. She stopped and glanced back, shocked to see the blue spread to the top of the landing. She turned to look at Alawani; the flowers on his side of the stairs had changed colour too, creating a crimson background behind him.

L'ọrẹ turned to Àdùkẹ́, silently asking for an explanation, but the woman only said, 'They won't harm you. They only recognize what is in you.'

Àdùkẹ́ pointed to two rooms, one on the right and the other on the left.

'We would like to stay together,' Alawani said in a low tone.

L'ọrẹ's cheeks burned with embarrassment. In truth she didn't want to share a room with him, not after that stunt he pulled with the maiden.

'We're fine with the arrangements,' she spoke up.

Àdùkẹ́ gave a brisk nod, and L'ọrẹ did the same, responding with a weak smile.

'Get washed and come down for your meal. We have a lot to talk about. Márùn, come with me,' Àdùkẹ́ said, going back downstairs.

After a few restless moments in her room, L'ọrẹ decided to draw more answers from this woman her father had sent her to. She'd only got as far as the landing when she saw Àdùkẹ́ on the floor below, staring at the burnt remnants of the letter on the floor.

L'ọrẹ crouched by the top of the stairs, hiding behind a post. She leaned over to watch the woman. Àdùkẹ́ sobbed softly, wiping the tears from her eyes. L'ọrẹ didn't know Àdùkẹ́ very well, but the woman's set features, grim eyes and tight lips did nothing to show that she was the kind of woman who cried over anything. L'ọrẹ watched quietly as Àdùkẹ́ scooped up the ashes in her hands and said a few words of incantation softly into them. There the letter was. In its original form, without burn or scorch.

'Curse you, Ẹniìtàn. Curse you for sending this child to me. May your gods and mine and those whose names are long forgotten curse –' Àdùkẹ́'s voice hitched, and she sobbed into the note.

L'ọrẹ frowned, confused.

Àdùkẹ́'s hands shook as she tried to open the letter. She stopped and turned towards the stairs, and L'ọrẹ fell back. Too fast. Her elbow slammed into the post behind her, and L'ọrẹ placed her hand over her mouth to silence the cry that forced its way to her lips.

'Kàá fún mi. Read it to me.' Àdùkẹ́'s voice cracked, and L'ọrẹ peered out again to see what was happening.

The letter in Àdùkẹ́'s hand hovered in the air, and obeying her command, a voice read the words out loud. His voice. Baba-Ìtàn's voice. L'ọrẹ's eyes widened. Her experience with old magic had been limited to the words that ignited her blades and lit her time beads.

'Àdùkẹ́ mi. I have no right to ask this of you. It breaks my heart that after all these years, this is what reconnects us. The same thing broke us. But I pour my heart out to you, and I beg you in the name of the gods, yours and mine, known and unknown. This is L'ọrẹ. You know who she is. You know

355

what she is. Protect her, give her safe passage out of Oru, show her the way to her people, and I'll forever be in your debt. I sign this with my blood, Ẹniìtàn.'

Tears welled up in L'orẹ's eyes as her father's voice trailed away like a soft breeze. She missed him so much. She wondered what he'd done after she left? Was he safe? It broke her heart to realize how much he knew about her. Her powers, her curse, her mother. Her life. How much he knew and kept hidden. She let out a forceful breath as tears rolled down her face. Every step towards safety was another away from him, and she didn't want to be away from him. She wanted the home she grew up in more than she wanted to be safe outside the walls of Oru.

Àdùkẹ snapped her fingers, and the floating letter fell to the floor, returning to ash. She scoffed and swept the ashes with her foot. 'You are already in my debt.'

L'orẹ flinched back as the woman's words echoed through the hallway.

'If you want to eavesdrop, have the decency to be quiet.'

L'orẹ scurried back to her room.

When evening came, a young girl called her and Alawani out to dinner. The entire time, she practised her apology for eavesdropping, hoping not to be kicked out into the hustle and bustle of the town that she could hear rumbling outside her windows. As they sat at one end of the long rectangular dining table, L'orẹ ran her lines in her head once more, waiting for the perfect time to break the silence. Opposite her, Alawani ate his meal of freshly baked bread and goat meat pepper soup, too occupied with filling his stomach to notice the tension in the air. Knowing him, he was more likely pretending not to notice. No one avoided confrontation like her best friend.

'The first rule of staying in my house is that you must not walk out that door without my permission,' Àdùké said, breaking the silence. 'Márùn will go on patrols twice a day to see what's happening outside and let us know when the maiden and royal guards have moved on from this side of town.'

Márùn wasn't at the table with them. L'ọrẹ hadn't seen her since they got to the house. She tried to ask about the woman but Àdùké went on, 'I can't keep you here indefinitely, so what's your plan?'

L'ọrẹ glanced at Alawani and back at Àdùké. 'My father said you'd get us out. You are our plan,' she said, conscious of the way her voice cracked with worry.

Àdùké scoffed and returned to her meal, suckling on the bones and spitting them out on the table.

'Baba-Ìtàn said –' L'ọrẹ started to say, but Àdùké cut her off.

'Your Baba-Ìtàn is not here! I'm not going to risk my life for you again.'

L'ọrẹ quietened. Again? Her father had never even mentioned this woman's name until he put that letter in her hands. L'ọrẹ returned to her meal, not even looking at Alawani, who was still quiet the whole time. He was smarter than her. He knew not to poke the beast.

Once again, only the tearing of bread and the chewing of bones could be heard in the room. L'ọrẹ silently mulled over the challenge of winning the woman's trust, hopefully avoiding her short fuse. She opened her mouth to speak but then realized she didn't know what to call the woman. Aunty Àdùké or Ìyá-Àdùké or Mama Àdùké. L'ọrẹ figured the woman was younger than her father. Her satin turban kept her hair hidden, so L'ọrẹ couldn't tell by the number of grey hairs. But she looked like someone who'd seen nearly forty first suns.

357

'Aunty Àdùkẹ́,' L'ọrẹ said in a soft whisper.

'Call me Ìyá-Idán,' the woman said plainly. 'My oríkì is reserved for those who earn the right to say my name.'

Ìyá-Idán – mother of magic. L'ọrẹ stifled a gulp and bowed her head. Ìyá-Idán nodded, accepting the unspoken apology.

Far into the passageway that led deeper into the mysterious house, L'ọrẹ thought she could hear voices of girls chattering and laughing, but as soon as she tried to focus on them, they disappeared as fast as they came.

'Ìyá-Idán,' L'ọrẹ started softly, 'what did my father mean by you know who and what I am? Do you know about my agbára? Can you help me?'

'Baba-Ìtàn, is that what he goes by now?' Ìyá-Idán said, ignoring L'ọrẹ's questions.

L'ọrẹ nodded. 'He tells tales by moonlight under the tree in our compound. The children started calling him the father of stories. He tells the best ones in the entire city, maybe even the kingdom,' L'ọrẹ said with pride.

She thought she saw the hint of a smile on the woman's face as she said, 'Yes, he does.'

L'ọrẹ hoped Ìyá-Idán would say more. She was dying to ask about her mother, to ask what connection she had with Baba-Ìtàn. To know more about where she'd come from and where she was running to. But she had to wait for the right moment. It didn't seem like that moment would ever come. L'ọrẹ considered what to say next, and just when she convinced herself she could wait until morning to ask, the question came tumbling out of her mouth.

'How did you know my mother?'

Ìyá-Idán shot her a menacing look, her eyes growing dark and stormy.

L'ọrẹ braced herself but continued, 'It's just that when we

were at the city wall, you called me Mọ́remí's child. How did you know? How did you know her?'

Ìyá-Idán slammed her fist onto the wooden table, rattling everything. The plates, the soup, and even some bones came flying off. 'Let that be the last time you speak Mọ́remí's name under my roof.'

'Why? What did she do?'

'She brought darkness into my life. I owe you no explanations and I am not here to tell you midnight stories like your father. So stop asking.'

L'ọrẹ finished the rest of her meal in silence.

Ìyá-Idán rose from the table. 'You leave in two days.'

'Two days?' L'ọrẹ said. 'We don't –'

'If Àlùfáà-Àgbà knows who you are,' Ìyá-Idán cut her off, 'then he knows who your mother was, and that means he'll know where you've gone. Because when he hunted her down all those first suns ago, this is where she ran to, and this is where he found and killed her.'

There are still those who call upon
Ọ̀rúnmìlà, the grand priest, sage and
custodian of the oracle,
the god of wisdom, knowledge and divination.
And still, some call upon Oba'lúayé, the god who
heals with one hand
and delivers sickness with the other.
Others yearn for the ocean and call upon the protective
energy of the feminine force,
Yemọja, the goddess of the seas and rivers.
And finally, those who seek chaos call upon Èṣù,
the trickster and divine messenger.

28

Ìlú-Idán, Fourth Ring, Kingdom of Oru

L'ORẸ

The unchanging scene L'ọrẹ's subconscious stumbled into every night had become a sort of solace to her. Nothing could scare her here because she knew this place as well as she did her own bedroom. So when a figure started walking towards her, dressed in white, wearing a crown with a curtain of cowries, hiding its features from view, she knew she was dreaming. But she didn't know how to wake up from it.

As the figure approached her, L'ọrẹ tried to run away. But just like every time she'd tried before, the pillars that kept her safe also kept her trapped.

'Who are you?' she asked, hoping her brashness would hide her fear.

'You stole from me,' the person said as they circled her. The sound of their voice curled around her like a slither, low and menacing.

L'ọrẹ still couldn't see the face, but she recognized that voice. The last thing she'd heard that voice say as she tried to flee the temple was, 'Kill them.'

Àlùfáà-Àgbà. Alawani's grandfather. How was he in her dream? In her mind. She forced her eyes closed and whispered,

'Wake up. Wake up. Wake up.' Whatever was happening to her at that moment had to be magic. Old magic.

She opened them to find the pitch-black eyes of the priest staring into hers. She screamed and fell back. 'What do you want from me?'

'Bring my grandson back to me,' Àlùfáà-Àgbà said, his voice echoing in her mind. 'Come back with him, and I will show you mercy.'

'How are you here?' L'orẹ shouted, banging against the invisible shield that kept her inside the platform. 'Get out!'

'I'm not here to fight with you, child. Nor to tell stories. Return to the capital with my grandson, or their deaths will be slow and painful.'

'Their?' L'orẹ asked, her heart buzzing in her chest like an angry hornets' nest.

The old man's face crept into a wicked smile. 'Your father — oh, and the boy you left behind. Kọyà.'

'No,' L'orẹ gasped.

Àlùfáà-Àgbà waved a hand, and something like a window appeared before her, and through it, she could see her father. Bruised and hunched over in the corner of a dark cell. With another wave of the priest's hand, she saw Kọyà's bloody body slumped on the floor of a much darker and smaller cell than her father's. And unlike her father, he wasn't moving.

That should've been her. That would've been her if she hadn't run away like the coward she was. There her friend was, a shadow of himself, because of her.

L'orẹ lunged at the Elder Priest. She summoned her agbára and threw her hands at him, willing her powers to burst forth and strike him in the heart. Nothing happened. Her body hit an invisible barrier, like it always did.

Àlùfáà-Àgbà laughed, 'You're just a child after all. Slow and foolish.'

She screamed at the priest, but no words formed in her mouth. *Curse you.*

'If you return to the capital I will grant them a quick death,' Àlùfáà-Àgbà said.

'You'll kill me if I come back. Just the way you killed my mother,' L'ọrẹ said, the words a hoarse whisper.

'Yes, I will,' Àlùfáà-Àgbà said so calmly that she could only stare back.

L'ọrẹ's mouth dropped open, and he moved closer to her, his face leaning against the invisible barrier. 'You thought I'd lie or hide the fact that I killed Mọ́remí? To lie, one must be afraid of the person they're speaking to. Afraid of what they'll do or think. Do you think I'm afraid of you, child of Òtútù?'

L'ọrẹ just stared at the man before her, unnerved by his resemblance to Alawani. *Wake up. Wake up.* Her heart was beating so fast that she could feel the heavy throbbing all over her body. It was one thing to know the name of the man who murdered your mother. It was another to look into his eyes as he admitted it. Anger brewed inside her, rising to her skin, fingertips and lips. Her whole body trembled from the force of it. Fear. It wasn't anger. It was fear. Her hands grazed her chest, looking for her pendant. It wasn't there. It hadn't been there for a while. Her head throbbed like it was being kicked into a wall, again and again, and again. She crashed to her knees, clawing at her chest, trying to breathe, slamming her fist to her chest, begging it for release, begging for air. She looked up into the eyes of her best friend's grandfather, and the smile across his face told her all she needed to know. Death. It wasn't anger or fear. It was death. She was dying. He was more powerful than whatever was trying to keep him from entering her space, and he wanted her dead.

But he didn't kill her. Not yet.

Air rushed into her lungs, and it burned like she'd inhaled a room full of smoke. She coughed and spluttered, heaving as Àlùfáà-Àgbà circled her. 'Until you return to the capital, I'll be here. Every time you fall asleep. Every time you close your eyes for the briefest of moments. You'll see my face, and you'll feel my wrath. And I'll show you what I'm doing to those you love. Return, and your death will be much quicker than your mother's.' He drew himself up and pressed his face to hers. 'I *will* have your powers,' he hissed.

Your powers. Suddenly it clicked: *that* was what he wanted.

She sucked in a long breath. *Wake up! Wake up!* But she couldn't drag herself out of this nightmare. She reached into her mind, clawing for something, anything. She searched for Command's voice, hoping for a way out, something to help her save her father and Kòyà. She even screamed for the god of fire and thunder. Nothing. Her mind was heavy with fog and her throat was still tight, her sight dimming. He'd kill them, just like he did her mother, and it would all have been for nothing. She had no choice. She could only hope to find a way out of any trap he had planned for her.

'I'll give you –' she choked out the words, 'I'll give you what you want.'

L'orẹ didn't often think about her mother. She didn't have the slightest clue what Móremí had looked or sounded like. L'orẹ had only had one piece of information: her mother had been a maiden. But even that turned out to be false. Her mother hadn't been a maiden. She hadn't even been born of Oru. She'd come from somewhere far away with powers that scared the Holy Order and died for it. L'orẹ wondered if Àlùfáà-Àgbà had offered her mother a similar deal, and what did the fact that her mother was now dead mean for how that bargain turned out? Regardless, L'orẹ

decided her agbára was not worth the loss of Baba-Ìtàn or
Kòyà. She'd come this far without it. She could go much
farther.

She choked out a question. 'I'll return to the temple. But
how will you take my powers?'

Àlùfáà-Àgbà's eyes narrowed. 'The Red Stone.'

Of course. *Of course.* A stripping. A gamble. There was no
way to know if she'd survive. But if she could save her father
and Kòyà . . . 'Swear to me that if I give you my agbára, you
won't kill me, and you'll let them go free.'

Àlùfáà-Àgbà grinned. 'You have yourself a deal. I swear
by the gods of the sun and sands, by the light of agbára oru.
Your agbára for your father and your friend.'

The clouds lit up with bolts of lightning, followed by a
rumble of booming thunder. L'ore felt her heart grow heavy
in her chest, and then a sharp pain surged through her, and
she screamed.

'Hold her down,' she heard a voice say as someone's hands
pinned her to the floor.

The sound of her own screams filled her head.

'L'ore, calm down, L'ore, I'm here. It's me. L'ore!'

L'ore opened her eyes to see Alawani above her, and for
half a heartbeat, she saw the flicker of his grandfather's
face in his, and kicked him off. She jumped off the bed and
crawled to the wall. Eyes closed. She whispered, 'Wake up,
wake up, wake up.'

A figure knelt before her, and only when L'ore heard Ìyá-
Idán's voice did she slowly open her eyes and look around
the room.

On the bed, Alawani still held his stomach. Groaning, he
asked, 'What happened?'

L'ore couldn't stop the tears from falling. She crumbled

into the woman's arms, wailing and sobbing. 'I – He – I thought I was going to die.'

'Shh . . .' Ìyá-Idán said, rubbing her head and holding her close. 'It's over now. It's over. You're safe.'

Alawani joined them on the floor, and L'ọrẹ moved to his side.

L'ọrẹ's lips trembled, and her eyes filled with tears. She tried to speak, but the words would not come. She broke into sobs, heaving in his arms as he embraced her. 'What have I done? What have I done?'

'It's going to be okay,' Alawani breathed.

'No! It's not.'

'Who did you see?' asked Ìyá-Idán.

L'ọrẹ placed her hand on her chest, feeling the pain thudding in her heart as fear and panic raced through her veins. L'ọrẹ met the woman's gaze and wondered if the mother of magic could feel the magic that had been used on her.

L'ọrẹ turned to Alawani, 'It was your grandfather.'

'What did you see?' Ìyá-Idán asked frantically.

L'ọrẹ shook her head. 'He showed me Baba-Ìtàn and Kọ̀yà,' she sobbed. 'He hurt them.'

Alawani wiped her tears. 'I'm sorry. I'm so sorry.'

'What did he want?' Ìyá-Idán said as she rose from the floor.

'He said he'll spare Baba-Ìtàn and Kọ̀yà if . . .' L'ọrẹ said, turning away from Ìyá-Idán.

'If what? What did you agree to?' Ìyá-Idán said knowingly.

L'ọrẹ shook her head but didn't speak.

'That man would never offer something like that without a heavy price. What did you say?'

L'ọrẹ opened her palms, and the blueish-white light of agbára òtútù glowed through. 'I offered this for my father and Kọ̀yà,' she said, looking up at this woman. 'It's my powers he wants, stripped from me on the Red Stone.'

366

'No!' Alawani shouted. 'I won't let you do that. You can't.'
He glanced from her to Ìyá-Idán and back to her. 'L'orẹ, you
can't trust him. You're not going back. And most of all,' he
let out a dry laugh, 'you're not going back to the stripping
ceremony you saved me from. This is ridiculous.' He turned
to Ìyá-Idán. 'Tell her she can't do this.'

'You didn't see them, Alawani. Beaten and broken. In
chains. We have to do something,' L'orẹ said.

'Something. We'll do something. We'll do anything, but
you won't go back there. You won't submit yourself to be
stripped. You can't, please,' Alawani begged.

There was something about the way Alawani begged her.
The tone of desperation she recognized from the time they
sat by the fire in her house making a blood oath, swearing to
be together for as long as the sun was in the sky. She knew
that fear of losing the one you thought you'd grow old with.
Only now did she realize how hollow her pleas sounded to
him then. When everything was on the line, the sliver of hope
that the Red Stone didn't claim all the souls who climbed it
seemed like a chance worth taking. And she almost forgave
him for breaking his oath. Almost.

'Won't you say something?' Alawani said to Ìyá-Idán. 'She
can't go back. He'll kill her. This is crazy. Tell her this is crazy.'

Ìyá-Idán's eyes narrowed as she gritted her teeth. 'And
whose fault is that?'

Alawani choked. 'I had nothing to do with this. I didn't
choose who I was born to.'

'But you knew who you were, who your family was when
you selfishly became a part of her life,' Ìyá-Idán said.

Alawani's shoulders dropped.

Ìyá-Idán adjusted her robe. 'I stood in this room and
begged her mother not to go to that temple. I told her what
they'd do to her. What did she think would happen if she set

foot in that cursed place? She didn't listen. I see that same defiant look in your eyes. Do whatever you want. I don't care.' Ìyá-Idán locked eyes with L'ọrẹ. 'You must leave as soon as possible. If he's in your dreams, then he knows you're here in the fourth ring and it's only a matter of time before his magic finds this house. Deal or not, he's coming for you.' And with that, she stormed out of the room.

L'ọrẹ let the silence in the room settle over them like a heavy blanket. Her nose stung, and tears pricked at her eyes. What had she done? Her mother had trodden this path and failed. What made her think she could win? No woman had ever been to the Red Stone.

Alawani cupped her face, wiping the fresh tears that rolled down her cheeks. 'I was so scared when you wouldn't wake up. I thought – I thought I'd lost you.'

L'ọrẹ leaned into his embrace. 'It was horrible. He was horrible. He's killing them, Alawani. I can't – I have to go back.'

Alawani shook his head. 'I know we have to save them, I know we can't leave them there, but you can't protect them by giving up your powers. You can't believe anything Àlùfáà-Àgbà says.'

L'ọrẹ noticed how he distanced himself by not calling the man his grandfather.

Alawani pressed on, 'We are on this path because you knew accepting the call was wrong. You knew that the Red Stone was not the answer. You saved me from certain death. I can't let you go back. I can't let you do this. If you die – I can't live with that, L'ọrẹ. I don't want to live in a world without you. I won't.' He pulled her into a hug, and the feel of his breath on her neck, those words she'd longed to hear, felt like a balm over her aching heart.

L'ọrẹ let out a shaky breath, her shoulders slumping in defeat. 'I don't know what else to do.'

'We don't talk about who he is and everything he's done to you,' Alawani said, 'but I want you to know that I'm sorry. I'm sorry about your mother. I'm sorry Baba-Ìtàn and Kòyà are suffering for what I did. I'm sorry for coming into your life and putting you at risk. Maybe Ìyá-Idán is right,' he said, looking towards the door. 'I should've stayed away.'

L'orẹ considered his words. The first time she met Alawani, prince of Oru, she hadn't realized who he was. She'd only been glad not to have died at the hands of the boys who cornered her in the dark after her training that night. She'd run away from him and hadn't seen him again for at least two blood moons. When he finally introduced himself to her in the light of day, she didn't let down her guard for a very long time. L'orẹ couldn't remember when she finally did. She only knew that his presence in her life had changed everything. Knowing she walked alongside the prince somehow gave her a little reprieve from the town's violent attacks on her and Baba-Ìtàn. It didn't make the stone-throwing or the assaults stop altogether, but it made them think twice before hunting her down at night like prey. Regardless of who Alawani's family was, he'd saved her life long before she saved his.

L'orẹ shook her head. 'I'm glad you didn't. I needed you.'

Tears glistened in his eyes. 'I need you a lot more than you need me.'

Alawani guided her to the bed and lay next to her. She nestled into his side, breathing in his scent as he stroked her hair. 'I'll protect you,' he whispered and kissed her forehead. 'Everything will be all right.'

L'orẹ focused on the rhythm of his heartbeat as it drummed fast against her temple. She exhaled slowly, allowing herself to get lost in the beat. Then her body grew tense, and she had to make a conscious effort to keep her eyes open, too scared to find out what she'd see in the darkness.

Ìyá-Idán's words played back in her mind, and L'ọrẹ couldn't help but wonder if her mother had slept on the bed she lay on. If she had walked the same steps she did.

Alawani stirred beside her, and she softly whispered, 'Are you awake?'

'Yes, yes,' he said, straightening up and wiping his eyes. 'Are you okay?'

L'ọrẹ nodded. 'We need a plan.'

'We have a plan,' Alawani said. 'We keep moving. No matter what happens, we get you out of the kingdom.'

L'ọrẹ studied the depths of his eyes. He was determined to keep going.

'It's hard, I know it is,' he continued, 'but you need to remember that whatever his crime, they'll never kill Baba-Ìtàn. In the same way Milúà wouldn't kill me. Your father cannot be killed. He is Àlùfáà.'

'What about Kọ̀yà?'

Alawani didn't have an answer for her. That was all she needed to know.

She decided she would return to the Sun Temple, just like Àlùfáà-Àgbà demanded. But first, she'd learn to control her agbára. She'd trade her powers for Baba-Ìtàn and Kọ̀yà if she had to. Maybe she was like Mọ́remí after all.

But unlike her, she'd be prepared for the fight.

Ọgbọ́n ọdún yìí wèrè èmíì
Today's wisdom may be tomorrow's madness

29

Ìlú-Idán, Fourth Ring, Kingdom of Oru

L'ORẸ

L'ọrẹ found the room too small to breathe in. So she sat on the staircase while Alawani slept. She sat halfway down the stairs; overlooking the open foyer with morning light spilling through the windows was the next best thing to leaving the house, which she couldn't do. Around her the sapphire flowers bloomed, casting shades of blue against her skin. L'ọrẹ was lost in thought when Márùn walked in from her patrol. She seemed to be the answer to the question she'd been asking herself: how would she get back to the Sun Temple?

She called Márùn over and the woman sighed before settling down next to her on the stairs. 'What's happening out there?' L'ọrẹ asked softly, noticing how drenched in sweat the woman was.

Márùn exhaled deeply as if catching her breath. 'There are several platoons of soldiers and royal guards patrolling the city. They're searching every house, burning buildings and arresting anyone they think knows anything about you. They don't know where we are, but they seem to know we're close – and the people are suffering for it.'

L'ọrẹ avoided Márùn's gaze, guilt eating at her for being there at all.

'It's not your fault,' Márùn said, noticing L'ọrẹ's expression. 'This happens in Ìlú-Idán more often than you think. The Holy Order keeps a heavy hand pressed on their necks to make sure they never revolt against them. The people of the fourth ring are descendants of the old Idán tribe, the scions whose call the old gods will always listen to. Unlike agbára oru, the strength of old magic is determined by the power the Òrìṣàyou call upon, not by the strength of the core in your physical body. So as they should, the priests fear what would happen if people with agbára oru learn to use old magic. They'll be severely overpowered, and they know it. They're not just here for you. You're simply the excuse this time.'

Márùn leaned forward to tuck her blades into her boots and L'ọrẹ noticed the mark at the base of her skull. 'Your mark,' L'ọrẹ said. 'It's fading.'

'Thank the gods,' Márùn said. 'When it's gone, my debt will be repaid in full.'

'How many first suns have you seen?'

Márùn raised an eyebrow at her and smirked.

'I just mean, back at the farm inn, you said you owed a life debt to Alawani's mother. You seem a bit young to have made such a commitment to serve out your days bound by old magic to someone else.'

Márùn shrugged. 'I've seen twenty-five first suns but I inherited this debt from my father long before I knew what it meant to be bound to the will of another.'

'But how . . . what did he do?'

'I won't stop you from telling me your secrets but don't ask me to tell you mine.'

'The ink is nearly faded. You'll be free when it's gone, right?' L'ọrẹ asked.

'Say what it is you've come to me for, L'ọrẹ. What do you want?'

L'ọrẹ sat up as she filled Márùn in on the deal she had made with the Elder Priest. After a few moments of silence from Márùn, L'ọrẹ added, 'I want to go back.'

Márùn was quiet for a moment longer, playing with the rings on her fingers. 'You think he'll really do it?'

'I don't know but I have to try,' L'ọrẹ said.

'And I imagine you're not taking the prince with you, that's why you're telling me?'

'If you come with me, you'll be saving him too,' L'ọrẹ said, grasping at straws. 'You might pay off your debt.'

'When do we leave?'

L'ọrẹ could hardly believe her ears. 'Thank you. Thank you so much.'

'When?' Márùn asked again.

'Tomorrow. At dawn. I'll be ready.'

Alawani appeared at the top of the stairs. 'What's going on?'

'Just catching up on the news from outside,' L'ọrẹ said, surprised at how convincingly she lied.

Márùn nodded to L'ọrẹ and Alawani and walked into the dark hallway. Voices drifted from somewhere deeper in the house.

L'ọrẹ watched her go and decided to follow. She wanted to see where the voices were coming from.

'Come on,' said Alawani, following her eyes with a smile.

L'ọrẹ and Alawani trailed Márùn down the corridor, into a part of the house they hadn't seen before. The narrow passage grew darker with each step but soon there was light. L'ọrẹ noticed how the same flowers that bloomed in her room were growing along the ceiling. They shone brightly, lighting up the way until they entered a large airy room.

Here, ten girls sat behind tables dressed in what looked like a uniform, but each with a different colour. Their tables were arranged in a circle around the centre of the room, where Ìyá-Idán stood, surveying their work.

L'orẹ wasn't sure what she expected to see in the mother of magic's inner chambers, but it was so far from anything she could've imagined. To her right, one girl moved her hands in the air and stared at the flowerpot before her. The girl spoke in a dialect of Yoruba that L'orẹ didn't understand even though she recognized its rhythm; the dialect her father had taught her to light up her blades.

'Old magic,' Alawani said quietly. He held out his arm, blocking L'orẹ from moving further into the room.

Soon, a green-coloured mist danced along the girl's fingertips, and the plant sprouted from the pot. Its colour was identical to her uniform's shade of green. Although no one was taught old magic in Oru, everyone knew the names of the old gods. Listening to the incantations, L'orẹ realized the girl was channelling the old god of the earth, Erinlẹ̀. She pushed a surge of green smoke into her plant, and it died. Her face fell as she looked at Ìyá-Idán. The woman's face remained blank but stern. 'Again,' she said in a flat, dismissive tone. The girl picked up another pot with a different plant to repeat the spell.

Across the room, L'orẹ noticed another girl channelling the old god of resurrection, Ọbàtálá. She was trying and failing to make the dead frog on her table move to the rhythm of her hands. Another girl summoned Ògún for metal manipulation, and L'orẹ recognized the name of the old god Ṣàngó as another burned objects to ash then tried and failed to return them to their original state. One girl at the far end of the room, challenging Ọya for air manipulation, had successfully turned her clay pot into red sand and was trying to form a small cyclone. L'orẹ took another step back, in awe of the impossible things being conjured in her presence. She had only ever summoned Ṣàngó to ignite her blades and activate her time beads, but this was nothing like that. These girls were manipulating nature like it was agbára.

L'ọrẹ stared wide-eyed at the twist of sand growing between the girl's hands and recalled the sandstorm Ìyá-Idán started in the town to escape the guards. Just as L'ọrẹ was about to speak, the girl lost control of the storm she'd conjured, and it exploded with a loud bang, filling the room with sand. But with a single snap of her fingers, Ìyá-Idán reversed the girl's spell, and a wind picked up in the room, gathering all the sand and tossing it in a single heap on the girl's head as punishment for failing whatever test this was. The other girls snickered and laughed among themselves. What shocked L'ọrẹ more than the display of old magic was that when Ìyá-Idán used the magic of the old gods, she didn't hear her say spells or incantations.

How could she be teaching these girls old magic? It was one thing to practise it knowing the risk to one's own life, but to teach children the thing that would have their heads severed from their bodies?

'Aren't you afraid they'll get caught?' L'ọrẹ asked Ìyá-Idán before facing the girls. 'I thought only a few sacred institutions in Ìlú-Idán could research the magic honed for the priests of the Holy Order?'

'Look at you. Spewing back to me the words of the people trying to kill you,' Ìyá-Idán said, and L'ọrẹ felt her cheeks flush with shame and glanced away.

'L'ọrẹ thinks she is better than you,' Ìyá-Idán told her girls. 'She thinks practising the old gods' magic is wrong.'

L'ọrẹ noticed the girls glaring at her from behind their tables. Alawani grabbed her hand as though ready to pull her out of the room at a moment's notice and run.

'What L'ọrẹ here doesn't know is that we, the people of

Ìlú-Idán, are the life source of this great kingdom. Without us, there would be no food, no life, or sustenance. This forbidden magic from our land – from our ancestors – feeds into Ìlú-Òpọ and, in turn, feeds the entire kingdom. So before you come in here all high and mighty, know your history and show respect where it is due!'

L'ọrẹ bowed her head and continued to listen, sensing Ìyá-Idán was only just getting into her stride.

'Tell me what your Baba-Ìtàn told you before he sent you here for refuge?' she asked, a scowl on her face. Ìyá-Idán didn't wait for L'ọrẹ to reply. 'Did he tell you that the Holy Order turned our homeland into a power source for this kingdom and repaid us for our blood with chains around our necks? Forcing us to work tirelessly to find ways to substitute the agbára they so willingly gave up for the crown? We are descendants of the first High Priest of Oru – the man who, by order of the old gods, blessed this kingdom with agbára. How does the Holy Order repay us? How does this kingdom repay us? By stealing our children, draining them of their blood and using it to wield magic they have no right to.'

'What?' L'ọrẹ's voice was weak. She couldn't understand what she was hearing – she glanced at Alawani but his expression was equally confused. *Draining them of their blood?*

Ìyá-Idán continued. 'Old magic needs two things to work. The blood of a scion of the old gods and the words of the old tongue spoken by the gods themselves. So do you know what happens when someone who is not a descendant of the old gods calls upon them? They die. A slow painful death. So to avoid that, the priests cut open our children and drink their blood to be able to call upon our gods.'

L'ọrẹ felt sick, remembering the bloody chamber she had stumbled across when they'd broken into the temple. Could this explain its purpose?

'They kill us for using old magic, but they would be nothing without us.' Ìyá-Idán was raging now. Every word was like thunder striking against the earth. 'Without the incantations they force out from our lips, and the blood from our veins, they would be nothing. Nothing! Agbára oru was supposed to be the great equalizer. Putting everyone on the same level. But the old gods did not abandon their descendants. So in addition to agbára oru, we the children of Ìlú-Idán have the magic of our gods on our tongues. They fear what we might become if we are free to use the magic of our ancestors. The magic that built this kingdom. Every day, someone's head is separated from their body, reminding us that without their permission, we are forbidden to use what is as much a part of us as the agbára in our blood. Every girl here has felt the agony of watching someone they loved being punished with death for not following the rules of the Holy Order. We hide because they have their foot on our necks, and we cannot breathe.'

L'orẹ noticed that the stern glares on the girls' faces had now fallen into solemn looks as their gazes fell to the floor, and her heart broke for them. She remembered the woman at the execution in the capital who defiantly died with her àṣírí unspoken and wondered if any of them knew her. Ìyá-Idán was right. L'orẹ hated the Holy Order. But even now, on the run from them for being different, she hadn't realized how much their ideas were ingrained in her mind.

'I'm sorry,' L'orẹ said in a soft voice.

Old magic, forbidden or not, had saved her more times than she could count. Old magic was the only reason she was alive. And that meant somehow, she was one of them. A scion of the old gods.

L'orẹ turned to the girls. 'I'm sorry.'

'We don't need your apology. We need only for you to understand the consequences of your prejudice,' Ìyá-Idán said. 'You come here with the oath-breaker's son, and you think it is easy for them to see you together? Knowing his spineless father is why we are still bound in chains today.'

L'ọrẹ turned to Alawani and his face was twisted in a mix of humiliation and fury.

'My father –' Alawani started to say, his voice low and hoarse.

Ìyá-Idán turned on him. 'Your father, the oath-breaker, promised to remove the ban on old magic. His words were nothing but rotten seeds, yielding nothing but lies.'

L'ọrẹ knew that Alawani's father had broken the oaths he swore on his coronation day to all six rings of the kingdom. Much like he hadn't judged her based on her father's reputation, she'd afforded him the same grace. Even back home in the inner rings, the people seemed to allow him the luxury of forgetting, but here, everyone mentioned the broken oaths as though there was anything a prince without authority could do to ease their suffering.

'It wasn't his fault he died before he could –' Alawani started to say, but Ìyá-Idán cut him off again.

'He died knowing that his oath was not fulfilled!' she shouted. 'He had decades to fulfil his oath, but no, he allowed his father to control him. Even with the power of the crown, he was a coward. He broke his oath to us and may his soul rot in the dark beyond forever.'

The only sound after her outburst was the sound of Alawani's frantic breathing, filling the room. His eyes brimmed with tears, his gaze turning a fiery shade of red. She'd never seen him so angry. He stormed out of the room, slamming the door behind him. L'ọrẹ moved to chase after him, but Ìyá-Idán shouted, 'Let him go!'

L'ọrẹ froze on the spot. Ìyá-Idán dismissed her girls and slowly the room emptied. Márùn was the last to leave, turning her back only when Ìyá-Idán gave her a firm nod.

When they were alone, Ìyá-Idán faced L'orẹ, who noticed for the first time the seven short vertical marks on her chest. The marks were similar to the five Márùn had on hers. L'orẹ noticed Ìyá-Idán watching her stare and quickly looked away.

'The prince is on a different path from yours. You can't keep chasing after him,' Ìyá-Idán said.

L'orẹ looked at the door Alawani had left through, and it took everything in her not to go after him. She forced her gaze back to Ìyá-Idán and nodded reluctantly. Ìyá-Idán still needed to teach her how to control her powers. She may not have them for much longer, but as long as they were inside her, she needed to learn to control them.

'I need to show you something,' L'orẹ said quietly, pushing thoughts of Alawani to the back of her mind. 'I don't know what's happening to me.'

Ìyá-Idán raised an eyebrow, and L'orẹ lifted her sleeves to reveal the black marks like vines growing from her wrists to her forearms.

Ìyá-Idán sighed. 'That man really didn't teach you anything about these powers, did he?'

L'orẹ knew she was referring to Baba-Ìtàn. She shook her head.

Ìyá-Idán sat on a bench and patted the space next to her. 'Tell me everything.'

L'orẹ started from the first moment, when she felt a strange sensation in the temple, and described every time she'd used her agbára since that moment. Ìyá-Idán listened carefully, her face unreadable as L'orẹ described even the most terrifying parts of her experience with agbára òtútù. She told her about the temporary paralysis she'd experienced in Ìlú-Ọpọ. All the while, Ìyá-Idán's expression remained blank, almost like she'd heard it all before.

'When did these start?' Ìyá-Idán said, referring to the marks on L'ọrẹ's skin.

'I don't know,' L'ọrẹ said. 'They burn every time I use my agbára. They aren't too painful, but I'm scared.'

'You should be. You're killing yourself.'

'How do I stop this?' L'ọrẹ asked, frightened.

'Show me your agbára,' Ìyá-Idán said, stepping back from her.

L'ọrẹ sighed. 'I – I don't like to use it,' she said, then noticed the woman's raised eyebrows. 'Uh – I don't know how to control it,' she added. 'I just point and shoot.'

Ìyá-Idán gestured towards the wall as if to say, *Go on.*

'I don't want to hurt you,' L'ọrẹ said.

Noticing the smirk on the woman's face, she added, 'Or anyone else.'

Ìyá-Idán chuckled. 'You couldn't hurt me even if you tried, my dear.'

L'ọrẹ felt like she'd stepped on a stage and could feel her audience's anticipation, eagerly awaiting her performance. She steadied her breathing and tried remembering how she felt with Alawani in the room back at Ìlú-Ọpọ. That was the only time she'd used her agbára but hadn't felt like she was being consumed from the inside. The convergence of fire and ice clashed in a storm that raged on constantly inside her. She couldn't explain where the heat was coming from, but she felt it as hot as she felt the ice that bled out of her fingertips. She didn't have to reach far for her agbára. It took more effort to keep it in than to use it. Her agbára was always there. Always just a deep breath away, waiting to be called, summoned, unleashed upon the world.

She opened her eyes, and they burned. This, she now knew, meant they'd turned blue. She raised her hand, and out of it came rushing a mix of white light and a flurry of black smoke. In a heartbeat, the wall froze over. All four walls of the room glittered with ice. Then they crystallized and started to grow. Immediately, Ìyá-Idán summoned her agbára and sent a wave of heat energy around the room, consuming every last bit of frost, leaving nothing behind. Not even a drop of water.

L'orẹ watched with admiration as the woman demonstrated her incredible power. 'Does it hurt when you do that?' L'orẹ asked.

'No,' Ìyá-Idán said. 'Because agbára oru creates energy.' Ìyá-Idán spread open her palms. A glowing orb buzzing with energy formed in her hands, filling the room with her light. 'Agbára oru creates light and heat. I create this energy from my own being. Of course, the downside of that is that if I use more than the gods have blessed me with or stretch beyond the boundaries of my own powers, my agbára will burn me from the inside out until I turn to ash. Your agbára is the opposite. Agbára òtútù is the power of darkness, cold, void and shadow. You cannot create energy. Your agbára manipulates everything around it to provide the energy it needs. In your case,' Ìyá-Idán said, holding L'orẹ's hands, 'you've been taking energy from your own body. Killing yourself every time you use it.'

'Curse the sun!' L'orẹ blurted out. Ìyá-Idán eyed her, and she sighed. 'Is that what happened with the rhino?'

Ìyá-Idán nodded. 'You said Alawani's light also dimmed when you touched him?'

L'orẹ nodded.

'You were siphoning his energy. That's why the next morning, the black marks on your skin were gone,' Ìyá-Idán said. 'I suppose this means you can take someone's agbára as well as their life force.'

L'orẹ's eyes widened.

'If you keep using your own energy, you'll die. It's that simple.'

'Help me, please?'

'I don't know enough about your agbára to help you survive having it. I can only show what I know based on agbára oru, which might be the wrong way to go about this.'

L'ọrẹ clenched her fists. 'Then I don't want this agbára.'

'It's not about what you want. It's about dealing with what you already have. It's who you are. You can't change it, the same way you can't decide to be a tree.'

L'ọrẹ eyed her curiously. 'Back at the temple, I created a wall of ice crystals, and Àlùfáà-Àgbà used old magic to make fireballs, but they didn't melt the wall. They didn't do anything.'

'He's not as smart as he thinks,' Ìyá-Idán said casually. 'Old magic is as delicate as it is versatile. Say the wrong word or the right word with the wrong accent, and the spell fails. The tongue of our ancestors is sacred, and the incantations are as complicated as they are exquisite. One must build upon simple phrases like the one that wakes your blades in order to see the full strength of the old gods. Àlùfáà-Àgbà has spent most of his life learning the old tongue, and even then, he cannot know it like the direct descendants of this land. In the days before the day of the First Sun, the king who formed this kingdom did not understand the old dialect. Much like the priests now, he wanted power he could wield without spells or rituals. It was his disdain for our tongue that birthed agbára on the day of the First Sun.'

L'ọrẹ thought about every time she'd panicked when her blades or time beads didn't obey her and glow when she summoned the power in them. How many times had she had to whisper the same phrase over and over in a fight before they finally listened? It made sense now. The incantation had to be perfect.

'Why can I do old magic if I'm not born of the sands like you?'

'It's true that you're of Òtútù, but the history your Baba-Ìtàn should've told you is that your mother's line dates back to when Òtútù was still part of Oru, and in those days, her family hailed from Ìlú-Idán – the home of the old gods and their magic,' Ìyá-Idán said plainly. 'Come here, I'll teach you how to use the energy around you, so you don't kill yourself on my watch. Now close your eyes and listen to the sound of my voice.'

L'orẹ frowned but did as Ìyá-Idán asked.

'Take deep breaths. With every exhale, I want you to push out your agbára,' Ìyá-Idán said. 'As it rises, feel the heat in this room, feel the energy in the air, everything that has life. Your agbára will look for something to pull on before it looks inwards, so give it something else.'

L'orẹ did as she said, breathing deeply and slowly. She could feel a warmth deep inside her core. It spread to every part of her body. She felt a prickly feeling against her skin, coming from the inside of her. She could feel the hairs on her body stand at attention. Her fingers tingled as they did when she'd slept on her arm and the blood was rushing back into it. She felt like life was rushing inside her, filling up every part of her body. It was such an intense euphoria; she struggled to keep her balance.

'Keep your eyes closed and focus. What can you see? What can you hear and feel?'

L'orẹ frowned, concentrating on Ìyá-Idán's voice. When her words died down, L'orẹ could hear something. Water – the splashing of water.

She opened her eyes and couldn't believe what was happening around her. It looked like she had pulled all the light from the moon and trapped it inside her hands. The cool white light filled every corner of the room. Dark mist danced around her fingers, and she looked at Ìyá-Idán, who seemed to shiver and smile at her. Around her were specks of white ash floating in the air. L'orẹ smiled at the view and threw her head back, allowing it to fall on her face. Each tiny piece sent a cold shiver through her, making her feel even more alive than ever. She could feel the burning sensation at the back of her eyes.

'Enough, or you will freeze me to death,' Ìyá-Idán said through chattering teeth.

L'orẹ dropped her hands, but the light didn't fade. The cold didn't stop growing. Even she could feel it seeping into her skin now. What felt like a calm flow moments ago was now choking her. The light tingling feeling she welcomed turned to what felt like knives piercing her skin from the inside. She screamed in panic, 'I can't turn it off!'

'You can, Mórẹmí!' Ìyá-Idán said, then quickly corrected herself. 'L'orẹ, just breathe, breathe.'

L'orẹ only screamed more, 'It hurts. Help me!' She felt her throat closing up. With her hands clutching her throat, she felt her lungs tighten as she struggled for air, and the darkness crept in around her vision. She could feel Ìyá-Idán's warm hands on her face and see pieces of her through the spots, but soon the darkness grew, and she felt her legs give way under her. Around them the cold fell away like a spell.

'I'm sorry. I didn't mean to hurt you,' L'orẹ wheezed.

'I have told you, child. You couldn't hurt me even if you tried,' Ìyá-Idán smiled. 'We'll try again.'

L'orẹ smiled back faintly. Too exhausted to keep her head up, she allowed it to fall slowly to the ground. She had so much more to learn about her agbára, but she'd also learned more than she thought possible. She knew exactly what Alawani's grandfather was afraid of, and he was right.

She would become his worst nightmare.

What about Ọbàtálá, Odùduwà, Aganjù and Erinlẹ̀
And all the other Irúnmọlẹ̀ – the principal divinities?
If you do not know them, find one whose wisdom
sparks from their grey hairs
and sit at their feet to learn from them.
I do not have the time to tell you the things you
should already know.
What you may not know, though, is to be careful
when seeking the gods.
It's best to call upon the gods of your fathers
and their mothers before them.
Do not call upon a god that does not know your name.

30

Ìlú-Idán, Fourth Ring, Kingdom of Oru

L'ỌRẸ

When night fell that day, L'ọrẹ found herself counting the stars that blinked across her vision. Using all the will she could muster to avoid falling asleep and into the desert dream where Àlùfáà-Àgbà waited for her. She tapped her index finger against her thumb in a steady rhythm to keep from drifting off. She considered her options. She was confident that Márùn could get her to the temple; what she wasn't sure of was everything that would happen when she got there. She found herself wishing Command were with her. She'd have the right answers. She'd know exactly what L'ọrẹ needed to do, and how to get out of this alive. She wondered if her old commander was thinking about her too. Worried for her, as she always was but often pretended not to be. L'ọrẹ wished she could've explained everything to her before she had to leave. She curled into a ball, and her heart ached for everyone she'd left behind. Back then she'd felt like she had no one, and now she was far from home, she realized how much she'd had to lose.

This thing between her and Alawani, this unspoken thing that was long overdue to blossom, was cocooned in a web of lies and secrets, and her heart broke at the thought that it would never happen. Maybe she should have kissed him back at the palace when he'd tried. No, it was all wrong. She didn't want her first kiss to be tainted with the bitter tears of grief. Yet every excuse she'd given herself as to why they couldn't have explored this thing between them seemed irrelevant in the face of death. Now they were on the run for their lives, every day a gift, every day full of danger and uncertainty. Could she really die not knowing what it felt like to have his lips upon hers?

She rolled over on her bed and screamed into her pillow. She sprang up as the door to her room cracked open. She raised her hand and shone a beam of light at the door, and Alawani grimaced. 'It's me.'

L'orẹ lowered her hand and reduced the glow of her agbára to a dull shine.

'I heard you shouting. What's wrong?'

'You heard me from your room?'

Alawani looked away shyly and scratched his head. 'I heard you from the door.'

L'orẹ raised an eyebrow. 'You were out there?'

He nodded and sat next to her on the bed. 'I was deciding whether or not you'd want me to come in.'

'And?'

'And, well . . .' he said, smiling, 'I'm here.'

L'orẹ glanced back at the door. 'How long were you there for?'

'Doesn't matter.'

L'orẹ sighed, and then her eyes widened. 'Have you been there all night? Did you sleep on the floor?'

'Doesn't matter,' Alawani brushed off. 'Did something happen in your sleep? Is that why you screamed?'

L'orẹ couldn't believe it. Had he camped at her door all night? She couldn't help the smile that crept onto her face. 'Did you get any sleep at all?'

Alawani shook his head. 'Nightmares. I can't stop think-ing about my father, those last moments with him. I think I just feel guilty for leaving what he'd dreamed for me and wish I could tell him why it's not the path for me.' He sighed, 'And the moments of peace I get, my grandfather comes to me –'

'What? Curse the sun! Why won't he leave us alone? What does he say?'

'Pretty much what he says to you. To come back.'

'This will be over soon,' L'ọrẹ said as she pulled him in and wrapped her arms around him in a tight hug. He winced, and she pulled back. 'What?'

He grimaced and put his hand over his chest.

'What is it?' L'ọrẹ asked, her voice rising with worry.

He sat upright and pulled his shirt over his head, revealing a bloodied piece of cloth stuck to his chest right above his heart. L'ọrẹ gasped. 'In the name of all that burns, Alawani, what happened?'

Alawani stopped her hand from touching the cloth. 'Wait, I'll show you.'

Slowly, he peeled it off to reveal a tattoo inked into his skin. L'ọrẹ exhaled slowly, recalling everything he'd taught her about how his agbára worked. She reached into her core and cautiously pulled out a beam of light that glowed through her palm. She would never get used to that. She'd craved this her entire life, and now, she could summon light at a whim. Although different from his powers, she was still awed by her own ability. Her agbára brightened the room, and there it was, etched into his skin. A replica of her tattoo. She looked at his face and back at his chest repeatedly until he said, 'Say something, please.'

Tears brimmed in her eyes. She couldn't find the words. She reached for it, and he flinched. 'Still hurts.'

L'ọrẹ nodded, wiping her tears. 'I can't believe you did this.'

'I should've done it when you did. This is you,' he pointed at one of the blazing circles on his chest, 'and this is me,' he said, pointing at the other one that cut through it.

L'ọrẹ choked out a sob. 'How did you do this?'

Alawani nodded towards the training room. 'I asked one of the girls to do it for me. All it cost was all my sun coins and cleaning their rooms.'

'You did that?' L'ọrẹ chuckled. 'I'm surprised Ìyá-Idán allowed that.'

'I waited until she left the house.'

L'ọrẹ laughed. 'Did it hurt?'

'Not really,' Alawani said, smiling.

'Liar,' L'ọrẹ said, tapping his arm. He winced and laughed.

'Mine isn't complete like yours,' she said, turning to show him her back. She loosened the wrapper tied across her chest and shifted her hair to reveal her bare skin.

Alawani trailed his finger over her skin, and it felt like a thousand thunderbolts running through her body. 'It's perfect.' His touch sent a wave of pleasure rippling through her body. He moved closer to her and whispered, 'Hand to flame, we burn the same,' and as she said the words back to him, he kissed gently on the spot where their bond had been etched into her skin. She felt an overwhelming surge of emotion as her heart swelled with passion.

L'ọrẹ turned off her agbára, and darkness swallowed the room. She pulled Alawani into bed with her, and he spread out to his full length. His legs were longer than hers, and she tucked hers between his, and pushed her body against him, removing every inch of space between them. His chest rose and fell, pushing and pulling her deeper into his embrace. Every hot breath sent waves of pleasure through her. His body temperature rose beneath her touch, and his agbára glowed softly through all the tattoos on his body, creating a warm glow of light around them. His agbára didn't burn her. Instead, it was like a gentle hug that enveloped her from the inside out, calming her worries with a passionate fire. She looked up at him, and his beautiful brown eyes shone with sparks of gold within. He softly murmured her name into her ears, and his deep, husky voice sent shivers down her spine.

'I have so much to say to you, so much I should've said before. But now, at this moment, it feels like nothing else matters.' As he spoke, she could feel herself getting lost in the sound, the way his words flowed together in a powerful and soothing way.

The intensity in his eyes made her flush with heat, and she lowered her gaze.

'No, don't look away,' he said, using his finger to raise her face to his. They were so close to each other now that their noses touched, and their breaths collided. The intensity of their connection was overwhelming, and she could feel herself melting into him.

'I've wanted to do this for a very, very long time,' he whispered.

'Why didn't you?'

'I was scared. I – I don't want to mess this up. Our friendship means everything to me.' He sighed. 'I thought – it doesn't matter what I thought. We are here now, and I don't think I could ever let you go.'

His fingers trailed the length of her body past her waist and back, all the way to her lips. 'Can I kiss you?'

This was what she'd wanted, what she'd wanted for as long as she could remember. Not a rushed goodbye, I'm dying tomorrow kiss. Not a first and last kiss wrapped up in one fleeting moment. But this. This was hope. A lover's kiss. A survivor's kiss. She nodded and felt his fingers graze the corners of her lips. She closed her eyes, savouring every moment, and when his lips touched hers, something exploded in her. Their kiss was passionate and urgent, each of them desperately wanting more. As he deepened the kiss, she could feel his hands exploring her body, igniting a fire within her she'd never felt before. She moved to the rhythm of his body, mirroring his every move. They broke to breathe. They'd both forgotten to inhale for a moment, taking in each other, hungry for more with each kiss.

'I wish we could be together forever. I wish there were nothing and no one in our way. I want to do this with you, explore you, and explore this world with you,' he said through heavy breathing.

Breathless, she moved to climb on top of him. She laughed as he helped move her into place. 'Shhh . . .' he whispered, placing his hand over her mouth, 'you'll wake the house.'

She winked at him and loosened her wrapper's last grip around her chest. His eyes widened, and he reached for her hand, holding it in place just as the wrapper was about to fall. She slowly removed his hand, and the wrapper dropped to the bed. The corner of her lips curved upwards in a sly grin as his mouth hung open in awe. He placed his hand on her waist and pulled her close, kissing her again, even more passionately. His fingers gently ran through her long, curly hair, creating a gentle sound of rustling. She moved in sync with him, consumed by a passion hotter than the sun.

Alawani flipped her back onto the bed, his hands roaming her body as if trying to find a hidden treasure, and when he got to the place between her thighs, he stopped and pulled away from her. 'I –' he said, but she cut him off.

'There is no one I would rather do this with, Alawani.'

There was nervousness in the air, a feeling of excitement

mixed with apprehension. For so long, they'd been dancing around their feelings, uncertain of where they stood with each other. But now, as they gazed into each other's eyes, L'ọrẹ knew that she'd been right to fight for him. This was worth fighting for. He was worth holding on to forever.

Maybe it was his eyes that glowed with pleasure. The way his body moved against hers or the way her name sounded like a song on his lips. All her fears melted away in the heat of his presence. She loved him and wanted to show him how much he meant to her. She said it with her touch, her kiss, the swing of her hips. Everything she wanted to say but couldn't find the words to. That night, she said it all through deep moans and shallow breaths. Nothing was left unsaid.

The next morning L'ọrẹ woke up to frozen fingers and stiff legs again. Àlùfáà-Àgbà had kept his promise and tormented her with images of her broken father every time she closed her eyes. He terrified her but she didn't lose her nerve now that she knew he wanted her alive.

She rolled out of bed and walked over to the bathing chamber in a corner of the room, and she was glad that she had fetched buckets of water the night before. She'd need every drop. She was still sore in the place she had taken him in – she had never done that before, and it couldn't have been any more perfect. As the bowls of water streamed down her body, memories of the night before washed over her, and she could feel the tingling sensation she'd become quite familiar with running throughout her body.

Everything was perfect for a few moments longer until the loud bang at the door startled her. She rushed out of the bath to find Ìyá-Idán, her voice thundering as she hurled a bowl of water at Alawani. He leapt out of bed.

'Downstairs! Now!' Ìyá-Idán shouted and stormed out of the room.

Alawani dressed hurriedly, and L'ọrẹ did the same, trying to fit one leg after the other into their pants. Alawani tripped and fell, and L'ọrẹ burst out laughing.

'Don't make me count!' Ìyá-Idán shouted from the stairs.

L'ọrẹ covered her mouth, still snickering. Alawani winked at her and led the way out of the room. When they reached the dining table, Ìyá-Idán was still fuming.

They sat across from each other on either side of the woman whose frown grew deeper with every passing moment. Finally, she said to L'ọrẹ, 'I warned you.'

Alawani stepped in, 'It was me that –'

Ìyá-Idán raised a hand to silence him without even look-ing at him.

'I know your father must have taught you better than this. Better than whoring yourself –'

Alawani cut in, 'I love her!'

L'ọrẹ gasped. Love. The corners of his lips twitched into a quick smile. 'I love her,' he said again, smiling at her, and somehow, everything else paled compared to that moment.

The woman hissed loudly, breaking the moment they shared. 'You cannot love an Àlùfáà,' she said to L'ọrẹ. 'Trust me, I speak from experience. No good can come from this. Of that, I am sure. I know Ẹniìtàn told you as much. There's no way he would approve of this nonsense.'

'I *was* Àlùfáà. Not anymore. I've rejected the call. I left,' Alawani countered.

'Once an Àlùfáà, always an Àlùfáà,' Ìyá-Idán leaned in as if the louder L'ọrẹ heard the words, the sooner she would be convinced. 'He accepted the call. His powers are dying. He's been to the Red Stone. Do you think the gods let go so easily? They will come for what is theirs.'

'I am not theirs. I left. I chose her. I choose her, and I will remain at her side.'

'Then why did you accept the call at all, Prince of Oru?' Ìyá-Idán said.

'Why do you hate me so much? You don't even know me,' Alawani asked her.

For the first time, L'orẹ noticed as Ìyá-Idán's turban slipped backwards slightly that she had full lines of her tribal marks on her temples. She had three short vertical lines over three short horizontal lines, which meant she was an indigene of Ìlú-Idán. L'orẹ studied them. She noticed that the horizontal lines looked newer, fresher somehow. They hadn't darkened into the woman's skin the way the top lines had. L'orẹ knew only one thing strong enough to make someone change their home state and alter their birth tribal marks.

'Is that what happened with you and Baba-Ìtàn?' L'orẹ said. 'Did he break your heart when he accepted the call to be Àlùfáà?'

She'd mulled over it ever since meeting Ìyá-Idán. Who this woman was to her father. Why they both said each other's names with tears and broken hearts. They must have been lovers once before.

Ìyá-Idán leaned back in her seat. 'He broke many things, and just like your prince, the oaths they swear to their Holy Order are the most important thing to them in the world. So this thing you think you have here, this love,' she said the word with disgust, like it tasted bitter in her mouth, 'forget it and move on with your destinies. Nothing good comes from one touched by the Red Stone.'

L'orẹ and Alawani stared at each other for a while, only breaking eye contact when L'orẹ said, 'I'm sorry that my father hurt you, but that's not what is happening here. I've known Alawani my whole life, and I believe him when he

395

says he loves me.' She turned to him. 'Because I love him too.' She reached for Ìyá-Idán's hand and held it. 'I know you want to protect me, but I risked my life for him. So please trust me, trust us.'

'Pack your bags. You leave once the sun sets tomorrow,' Ìyá-Idán said, pulling her hand out of L'orẹ's. 'Just remember that if he can forsake his gods, he can forsake you.' She angrily slammed the door behind her as she stormed out of the room.

Alawani moved over to her. 'She'll come around,' he said, pulling her up from the chair and embracing her.

'I hope so,' L'orẹ said quietly, eyes still fixed on the door.

'She will,' Alawani said, gently turning her gaze to him. 'I meant it. I love you.'

L'orẹ's lips curved up in a weak smile. 'I love you too. I loved you first.'

He leaned in and kissed her, and she let him. This time softly, slowly savouring every moment their lips explored each other's mouths.

He pulled her in further, this time more intense. He led her backwards until she reached a hard stop as her back went against the wall. She shuddered as his gaze wandered down to her cleavage. 'I want more of you,' he growled into her ears, and she could feel her knees buckle beneath her. He held on to her waist and lifted her. She wrapped her legs around him and smiled, glancing between his eyes and the doors. He kissed her and said, 'We can take this upstairs.'

She gave a slight nod, her face flushed. He carried her up the stairs and shut the door with a quiet creak.

Dúrógbadé tó ń dẹ isà ejò, bí kò bá dúró
gba adé, ọmọ míì yóò gbàá

A royal heir who unconscionably exposes himself to risk,
hunting snakes, may find that someone else has been
crowned king in his stead

31

Ìlú-Idán, Fourth Ring, Kingdom of Oru

L'ORẸ

At first light, L'ọrẹ slipped out of bed before Alawani woke. Exhausted from trying to keep from falling asleep and terrified from the nightmares Àlùfáà-Àgbà plagued her with, her body felt weary, but her spirit was more determined than ever to learn more about her agbára. She wished she'd spent more time trying to get Ìyá-Idán to speak with her. To have had more time to learn about her mother. She'd spent the rest of the previous day watching the girls practising their old magic spells and even learning a few more ways to summon the god of fire and thunder. But as much as she wanted to stay, she couldn't leave Baba-Ìtàn to die.

She glanced back at Alawani before leaving the room.

It surprised her how easy it was for her to keep things from him. Even as she questioned herself she knew she couldn't tell him the kind of damage her powers could cause. She couldn't tell him anything that'd threaten the bond they shared. Was it so fragile, or was that all in her head? Was she so desperate to keep him that she'd keep parts of herself hidden from him?

L'ọrẹ walked down the stairs and found Ìyá-Idán and Márùn waiting for her. Immediately, she knew something was wrong.

She curtsied low and greeted Ìyá-Idán as she reached the table.

'I asked you to leave tonight, I didn't tell you to get killed trying to return to the Sun Temple,' Ìyá-Idán said plainly.

L'ọrẹ glared at Márùn. 'You told her?'

'Just listen to what she has to say, you'll thank me.'

She heard footsteps behind her and swung back to see Alawani approaching, stumbling as he pulled on his clothes in haste. Her mouth hung open, and before she could speak he said, 'I'm coming with you.'

L'ọrẹ turned on Márùn, 'Did you tell everyone?'

Márùn raised her hands, 'I didn't tell him.'

'I heard you get out of bed,' Alawani said. 'If you're going back, I'm coming with you, Tèmi.'

L'ọrẹ let out the breath that had caught in her throat.

'You will not make it out alive, Tèmil'ọrẹ,' Ìyá-Idán said, rising from her seat. 'You won't even get as far as the royal island. Àlùfáà-Àgbà made the mistake of letting you live the first time. He won't make that mistake again. And you,' she turned on Alawani, 'you think that if you appear in the capital again, your grandfather will let you out of his sight?'

'I need to do this,' L'ọrẹ said, pleading.

Ìyá-Idán's face hardened, and she walked out of the room through the dark hallway and returned with a box in her hand. The stony expression was replaced with something sorrowful. She sat in her chair and opened the box, and the lid creaked as it fell backwards.

'Your Baba-Ìtàn asked me to get you out of this kingdom. I will tell you how to get out – afterwards, it's your choice where you want to go. But remember that your Baba-Ìtàn is one of the gods' chosen, a survivor of the Red Stone protected by the gods and their laws, whatever his crime. You on the other hand, they will cut down without mercy.' She pulled out an hourglass and placed it on the table before L'ọrẹ.

'What is this?' L'ọrẹ asked, surveying the miniature hourglass.

'This is how you get out of this kingdom. This is how you go home,' Ìyá-Idán said, pushing the hourglass to L'ọrẹ. 'Getting through the fifth ring will be the easiest part of your journey north. The people in the fifth ring of Ìlú-Oníṣọ̀nà will give you no trouble. They have their own problems. As long as you don't get caught, you can ride through in a day or so. If you go with Márùn, she can get you through the magic barrier and all the way into the last ring leading out of Oru. Ìlú-Òdì – the sixth ring – is the stronghold of this kingdom. The home of the Lord General, the most ruthless man in this kingdom.'

Next to her Alawani nodded slowly. L'ọrẹ remembered how he had begged Command to take on his training, releasing him from his mandated training with the Lord General who nearly broke him.

'The Lord General won't make any deals with you,' Ìyá-Idán said. 'So your job is to not get caught. The sixth ring also has the highest number of guards and soldiers in the kingdom since it's the first ring that any invaders would encounter when entering Oru. With Márùn you will get far, but there's a sparse mile-long stretch of land called the graveyard. The graveyard sits between the last fortress in Ìlú-Òdì and the border wall leading out of Oru. It's heavily guarded and littered with the bodies of people who try to enter or leave this kingdom without the crown's permission. That is where this comes in,' she said, picking up the hourglass.

She turned it upside down, and the sand still flowed in the other direction, flowing upwards. Ìyá-Idán carefully placed it before L'ọrẹ. 'There's a sandstorm that rages through the outer rings not protected by the magic barrier. It comes without warning and is as spontaneous as the will of the gods. But I've enchanted this hourglass to predict it. When the sand runs out, the next storm will reach the outer ring. The soldiers will go underground to protect themselves from the hailstorm that follows, so that's your chance to run. Keep running until you find somewhere to hide in the caves beyond the wall. The storm will build slowly, from heavy winds to sandstorms then hail. Don't be caught in the storm in its peak. You won't survive that either.'

L'ọrẹ felt as though she should've been writing notes as the woman spoke instead of staring endlessly at the magical hourglass that dripped sand before her. No matter which way Ìyá-Idán held it, the sand always trickled slowly in the same direction. There was just about a quarter of sand left in the upper chamber. 'How much time do we have?' she asked, finally considering that Ìyá-Idán might have been right about what Baba-Ìtàn would have wanted, and that if there were truly a relatively safe path for her to freedom, maybe she ought to take it.

'Two days,' Ìyá-Idán said, pointing to a series of delicate marks in the side of the glass. 'See these markings? Each one represents half a day. You should go as soon as you can to catch this storm – the next one may be too late.'

For the first time since she had left home, it felt like a path out of the kingdom had been carved for her. She closed her eyes and remembered her father's words, urging her to keep going no matter what happened. No matter what she heard or saw. He wanted her to keep going north until she found her mother's people. Her people. Tears filled her eyes. Her heart ached in her chest, throbbing without rhythm.

Ìyá-Idán brought two bead bracelets from the box. One was a time band similar to the one L'ọrẹ wore. But where her time beads were red and gold, these ones were obsidian and white. The first row was all black with a single white bead and the second row was all white with a single black bead. 'This belonged to your mother. Everything in this box did.' She paused and closed the box.

L'ọrẹ couldn't take her eyes off the beads as Ìyá-Idán placed them in her hand. She slipped the beads on her wrist onto the table and replaced them with the ones Ìyá-Idán had given her. Immediately, all the beads glowed. The white ones glowed like the moon, the dark ones looked like a starless night.

'The obsidian beads will help you walk through time,' Ìyá-Idán said. 'I think the white ones are time beads that your people use.'

L'ọrẹ couldn't believe her eyes. Time beads that worked without agbára oru, words or spells. Her hands trembled as she stared at the lights until they dimmed. Only one bead glowed. Four to noon. She looked around the table, glancing from Alawani to Márùn, who gave her a firm nod and the hint of a smile. Then her gaze settled back on Ìyá-Idán and the beads. 'She – my . . . my mother? How? When?' L'ọrẹ didn't know what questions to ask, but she wanted to ask them all. Her words just refused to be coherent, and she kept asking, 'How?'

Ìyá-Idán sighed. 'I wish Ẹniìtàn had told you the truth. I wish I didn't have to be the one to sit here and break your heart, dear child.'

'I thought you hated my mother?'

Ìyá-Idán gave a subtle nod, her lips lifting slightly in a sombre smile. 'Mọ́remí was my best friend, my sister. I loved her once. But like everyone else in her life, I was a means to an end.' She stared L'ọrẹ in the eyes. 'You've been running blind, and it's time for you to know the truth.' She brought out a small scroll from inside the box. 'Many years ago, when we were just girls, the woman who built this house – the Ìyá-Idán before me – created this spell for your mother when she needed to return home. She never got to use it.'

L'ọrẹ opened the scroll. It was written in a dialect she could not read. 'I don't understand the words. What is this for?'

'I'll teach it to you. You'll need to learn the words and commit them to memory. Pronounce them exactly as you hear them. The scroll activates the obsidian beads, but it cannot leave this house. The spell and the beads will quicken your steps and hasten your journey. Whenever you say the words, your every step will be like a hundred steps, and a week's journey on foot will only take you half a day.'

L'ọrẹ tried to take in what Ìyá-Idán was saying. The hourglass before her kept pulling her attention, the slow dripping of sand making her stomach churn. They were already running out of time.

'What's the price?' Alawani asked Ìyá-Idán. 'Old magic always comes at a price – so what is it?'

The woman eyed him, her mouth set in a tight line, then turned to L'ọrẹ. 'Time cannot be cheated. This is only a loophole. If you use this, your physical body will get you where you need to be. But your dream self will walk that entire journey. Every time you close your eyes to sleep, you will walk back all the steps you stole from time, and you won't rest until all the steps are accounted for in the spirit realm. You can go about your day as you wish, but until your steps are collected, every sleeping moment is where you repay the debt you owe time. You will wake with the exhaustion from covering back your distance, so whatever you do, best not to use this when going to battle because you will wake even more tired than before you lay down to sleep – until your debt to time is repaid.' She added quickly, 'This will only work for one person at a time.'

'That's terrible magic,' Alawani replied.

L'ọrẹ watched as the two of them glared at each other. Alawani was wary of old magic. She'd have felt the same way if it wasn't the only thing that had kept her alive her entire life.

'There's more you need to know,' Ìyá-Idán said as L'ọrẹ studied the words on the scroll. 'When I was young, I was betrothed to my life's greatest love – your Baba-Ìtàn. And just like your prince here, when the gods came calling, he welcomed them with open arms. It was his duty, he would say then. It broke my heart. I lost the will to live. This man I had built my whole world around chose death over me. And even if he didn't die, you know the responsibilities of the priest. He would be forbidden to marry anyone. And if by some grace he survived and was chosen as High Priest, he would be duty-bound to his maiden. Inseparably joined in body and spirit.' She darted a glance at Alawani. 'He would also have to go through the marriage ceremonies. He would marry a wife from each state, bed them and sire the next heir of our kingdom. It was all too much for me. The thought of all those women being with the man I loved – I could not handle it. Even after his duties, even if he had become regent and then handed the crown over to his child, even then, the gods would never let him go. He would never again be mine.'

L'ọrẹ felt her heart pounding, the tightness constricting her chest with each beat. As she listened to Ìyá-Idán, it was like hearing someone speak her worst fears. This was a glimpse of what her future would be like – or would have been like if she'd not saved Alawani from the Sun Temple. The woman's reddened eyes made L'ọrẹ's heart ache. Of all the people in her life, even Alawani, only Ìyá-Idán seemed to know what L'ọrẹ felt on the inside. What she'd felt since the moment she saw Alawani bowing before the fire, praying to the gods and accepting their call.

'So I ran away from home. I ran here, and this is where I met your mother for the first time. We lived together in that room for six blood moons.' She pointed to L'ọrẹ's room. 'This is where we learned the magic of the old gods. Then one day, she volunteered to be one of the handmaidens who lived in the temple and taught the priests the magic of Ìlú-Idán. At the time, all we knew was that she desperately wanted to get close to the priests of the Order. My Ìyá-Idán was furious and forbade it, but your mother was relentless. You have the same look in your eyes that she did the day she left. By then, Ẹniìtàn was already a priest in the temple, so I sent her to him. I wrote to him, asking him to protect her and keep her safe.' She laughed wickedly. 'That was my greatest mistake.'

'What happened?' L'ọrẹ asked slowly when Ìyá-Idán's silence stretched.

'So many things happened in this kingdom the night the king died. Some are still a mystery to me. The king died at sunset, and by midnight a new High Priest was chosen. In the few light beads between the death and the announcement, the state leaders cast their lots and pitched their daughters to be the wives of whoever would be chosen. There's no moment more chaotic in our land than when a king dies. Those moments before a leader is crowned are as sensitive as the moment a child's head crowns in labour. I received a message from my father that evening to say I'd been chosen as the bride to represent Ìlú-Ìmọ̀, the second ring, where I was born.' Ìyá-Idán paused, then explained, 'My father was a high-ranking member of the scholar's guild in Ìlú-Ìmọ̀. My mother was from here in Ìlú-Idán. My father's order was easy to follow because I hoped that if the gods willed it and the odds fell in my favour, Ẹniìtàn, who was already an Àlùfáà representing the second ring, would be chosen as High Priest, and we'd get to be together. I knew I would have to share him, but I didn't care anymore. I just wanted him. But when morning came, the night after the king's death, Àlùfáà Babátúndé was announced as the High Priest, and Ẹniìtàn was nowhere to be found.'

Ìyá-Idán paused again, and stared blankly at the box before her, lost in thought. Of all the stories Baba-Ìtàn had told L'ọrẹ in her lifetime – hundreds of stories and tales, old and new – this was the one she'd have killed to hear.

'Ìyá-Idán,' L'ọrẹ probed quietly, reaching for the woman's hands.

That shocked her back to life, and she let out a deep breath. 'Hmnn . . . I never thought I would tell this story again.'

'Please, I need to know,' L'ọrẹ replied.

Ìyá-Idán nodded silently, and continued. 'Sometime between the king's death and my wedding to the new High Priest, I learned Ẹniìtàn had broken his oath and returned home. Whatever heartbreak I thought I felt when he accepted the call was nothing compared to the shattering feeling of betrayal when he left. Something made him leave the Order, and it wasn't for me that he left. It couldn't have been; he didn't even tell me before he did. He just left, and I was trapped. I had no choice but to marry the chosen High Priest.'

'You married the Lord Regent?' L'ọrẹ blurted out.

'I did not get the chance. For two first suns, they had lived in the Sun Temple together and on my first night there, I knew the moment I saw Ẹniìtàn with Mọ́remí that she had filled the space I once had in his heart. There was no denying what they felt for each other. At first, I thought he had left the Order for Mọ́remí. That he did for her what he could not for me, and believe me when I tell you, it nearly killed me. But that wasn't it – at least not for Mọ́remí. Because on my wedding day, your mother gave me sleeping herbs and took my place, marrying the High Priest and taking my place in our bed.'

L'ọrẹ gasped. Even Alawani looked like his eyes would bulge out of their sockets. She couldn't believe what she was hearing about her mother. Not the version of the woman who was murdered for being different, but the woman who lied and stole and cheated her way through the kingdom. And for what? Why could her mother have possibly wanted to destroy the lives of so many people? People who offered her sanctuary.

Ìyá-Idán ignored their expressions. 'When I woke up, it was already too late. The Lord Regent Babátúndé did not know any of his brides nor had he ever seen them. In the days after the king's death, the mourning queen had been the one to oversee the brides and prepare us for the wedding. We were to be veiled for the entirety of the ceremony, ordered to unveil our faces to the High Priest only when we got to his bed. I was so angry I could barely understand it, but I knew I had to remain silent. Of course, Mọ́remí's trickery was discovered by the Holy Order the very next morning, but it was too late. She had bedded the High Priest and there was no way to break that bond, nor would he have wanted to. Babátúndé realized his unrequited love was now his bride before the gods and the entire kingdom, and he could not have been more pleased. He and Ẹniìtàn were like brothers, bound by their trials as survivors where many before them had fallen, and that meant he couldn't interfere with whatever Ẹniìtàn had going on with Mọ́remí. Maybe he felt none of them would have her in the end because if all had gone according to plan, one of them would have become the High Priest, married and bound to their wives and priestess, while the other would have been a regular Àlùfáà bound only to their maiden. But with Mọ́remí's intervention, risking her life to be his wife like that, I just know he

407

took that to be a sign from the gods themselves. Like all before him, he had fallen hopelessly in love with her. My family barely survived the aftermath of Mọ́remí's deceit. I don't know how she managed to, but she produced documents and a witness that proved she had been born in the second ring, which was all the High Priest needed to shut down the council's call to remove her. She married the most powerful man in the kingdom and, within a month, was pregnant with his heir. She was untouchable. My family, on the other hand, wanted nothing to do with me. The stench of my shame was too much for them. I was forced to return here and this has been my home ever since.' Ìyá-Idán scoffed, 'I had fallen in love with my best friend, and he in turn fell in love with Mọ́remí, who claimed to love him only to drop him the moment he turned down the chance to become High Priest, and married *his* best friend instead. To have loved Mọ́remí was to destroy your life with your own hands.'

L'ọrẹ was still stuck on the part where her mother married the Lord Regent. 'My mother married Lord Regent Babátúndé?'

'Yes, she did,' Ìyá-Idán sighed, 'and you are the fruit of their union. The Lord Regent is your true father.'

'That's not possible,' L'ọrẹ said, standing from her chair. 'It's not true. My birth father is dead. He was a royal guard killed before I was born. That's what my fa— Baba-Ìtàn told me.'

'No word I have said here today is a lie.'

'That means,' Alawani said quietly. 'That means she is one of the high council.'

'No.' Ìyá-Idán rose to her feet. 'It means that you are the firstborn of High Priest Babátúndé and Mọ́remí of Òtútù. You are the firstborn of the sun.'

Once again, L'ọrẹ was speechless. Then she laughed.

Ìyá-Idán looked at her, then curtsied low to the ground.

408

'L'ọrẹ, you are the true heir to the kingdom of Oru. You are our queen.'

L'ọrẹ wanted to launch herself at the woman to stop her from bowing to her. No one should bow to her, much less this older woman who'd given her refuge in her time of need. She didn't know why Ìyá-Idán wanted this story to be true, but it simply couldn't be. Baba-Ìtàn would never have told her that her true father was dead when he lived in the palace, just one ring over from them. Would he?

The look on Alawani's face reflected precisely how she felt about everything she had heard this morning. His face was contorted with confusion, and he, too, was speechless.

'Àlùfáà-Àgbà wants you dead not only because you have this agbára òtútù but because you are the heir to this kingdom, and the Holy Order has made it their mission to rid the world of your people. To them, someone with agbára òtútù could never rule Oru.'

'He killed my mother for this? Because she gave birth to me?'

'You are a glitch formed within a loophole. When parents with agbára oru and agbára òtútù sire a child, that child has no agbára. The hidden texts written in the blood of the children born that way and slaughtered say as much. But when your mother chose to bed the High Priest, she did so with one born of the sun but also void of agbára oru because of his stripping. If he hadn't been stripped, you would have had no agbára at all, but because of that, you were born not just of your parents but of the Red Stone as well. The whole reason the priests strip themselves of power and bear children afterwards is so their first child will have direct access to the gods, making them the most powerful in the kingdom. So you, L'ọrẹ, whether you understand it or not, are the most powerful person in this land. And that is what Mọremí died for. She made a mockery of the Order. Her mere presence was a threat to the kingdom. Her powers were skilfully hidden and just like you, she used old magic to conceal the truth. Very few people in this kingdom know about your people in the north. That secret is worth more than any life to them.' Ìyá-Idán lifted the scroll. 'I think she was coming back here for this. She wanted to get you home. I saw her get killed outside this house and dragged away by the priests, and I mourned for you both. But then, one day, you called my name, and there you were, the child of the north, the queen of Oru.'

'You can't go back,' Alawani said quickly. 'If this is true, Àlùfáà-Àgbà will kill you and anyone who protects you, no matter what he has promised. I know he will.'

L'ọrẹ could feel her world tilt on its head. Her vision grew blurry, and her breaths came in short bursts. How could Baba-Ìtàn have kept this from her? She closed her eyes to ground herself, and in her mind's eye, the pillar for Baba-Ìtàn, the one that had protected her all her life, cracked in half, the top of it slipping and sinking into the sand beneath. Her world wouldn't recover from this.

Ìyá-Idán's voice cut through the haze in her mind.

'I've told you all this so you can know your true enemy. There is one more determined than the Holy Order. One who will fight you even until death. The one whose seat your presence threatens, the one whose crown you will wear. Your brother, Crown Heir Tofarati. As long as you draw breath, he will come for you.'

Don't go, did you think that was all? Sit sit,
get comfortable.
Now, where was I?
Many things happened beneath the sky on
the Day of the First Sun.
The sun did not set until the next dawn arrived
and when it set, the moon was red with blood.
The blood moon appears every thirty days
twelve times, then the Day of the First Sun
repeats itself.
It has been many First Suns since I walked the earth.
Too many to count or remember.

32

The Royal Palace, Royal Island, Kingdom of Oru

TOFA

Tofa felt his twin's absence as keenly as he would a missing limb. He surveyed the throne room every other heartbeat, checking over his shoulder for her in the shadows, but she wasn't there. He wondered if their father had ordered her to stay away from the meeting. Earlier that day, the Lord Regent's mouthpiece had brought a message of whispers summoning Tofa to a private audience with his father. As he looked around the hall, it seemed he wasn't the only one to receive the summons. Next to him, his mother fidgeted with the hem of her sleeve. He noticed she was more dressed up than usual. He peered at her, trying to figure out why her bejewelled ruby dress looked so familiar. She turned to him and gave a weak smile. The dress was made of tulle and lace and embroidered with stones that glittered in the moon's light. Her wedding dress. She was wearing her wedding dress.

Next to him, Ìyá-Ayé scoffed, 'Oyíndà, do you really think that flimsy dress will help you?'

His mother's face twisted into a deep scowl. 'It's Aya'ba to you.'

Ìyá-Ayé pursed her lips and gave a mocking smirk.

Tofa was confused. Obviously, they knew more about

this midnight meeting than he did. What was Ìyá-Ayé talking about? Why was his mother dressed in her wedding attire? And where in the godsdamned names was his sister?

'Enough of that,' Àlùfáà-Àgbà's voice boomed in the empty throne room.

Tofa watched his mother's face redden with rage. She was about to speak when the Lord Regent stormed into the throne room, his maiden on his heel.

All four of them fell to their knees and bowed before the crown. Lord Regent Babátúndé took his place on the throne, and just as they were about to rise and sit, he spoke in a voice that sent cold shivers down Tofa's spine. 'Do not stand up.'

The four of them looked at each other, trying to figure out who the command was for. Tofa glanced at his father and could hardly recognize the man he saw. The Lord Regent was shaking with anger, and it burst out of him with the force of a pot boiling over. His breaths were heavy, his chest rising and falling, rattling the loose gold beads that decorated his crown.

They froze in place as Lord Regent Babátúndé spoke with a roar, his eyes blazing with rage. 'I'm talking to you all.'

They all bowed with their foreheads to the ground.

'Tofa, come here,' the Lord Regent said, his voice still booming through the room.

He walked over to the spot near the edge of the throne where his father had pointed and waited quietly.

The Lord Regent glared at Ìyá-Ayé, Àlùfáà-Àgbà and Aya'ba Oyíndà with bloodshot eyes. 'Which one of you will say the truth first? And before you think of lying, I've spoken with Ẹniìtàn and sent Command to bring the girl to me. Alive.'

Tofa was still trying to figure out what his father was

413

talking about when a loud screeching sound erupted from the throne. His father was on his feet, his eyes nearly crimson, his hands shaking uncontrollably, and he spoke in the old tongue. As the Lord Regent spoke his incantations, the metal bars around the throne ripped apart, turned into sharp points like spearheads, and hurtled towards the three on their knees.

'No!' Tofa shouted and ran to stand in front of his mother.

'Get out of the way!' the Lord Regent bellowed.

Tofa didn't realize when his agbára burst out of him, shooting down two of the metal heads with a blast of heat energy. 'Father, please. What is going on? What's happened?'

Tofa's voice seemed to get through to him.

'Let her tell you herself,' the Lord Regent said as he returned to his seat, keeping the remaining metal head hovering over the room.

Tofa turned to his mother, but she moved past him. Crawling to the bottom of her husband's throne, she placed her crown on the floor and fell flat before the Lord Regent, weeping. After a few moments, she dragged herself up the dais, past High Priestess Àṣá and collapsed into his lap.

'My Lord,' she began, wiping away the quick tears that had formed and rolled down her face. 'Olówó orí mi. Forgive me. I was young, naïve and stupid, but I had nothing to do with this. I don't know what that old witch said to you, but you must believe me.'

Tofa looked at Ìyá-Ayé, who seemed less afraid than even Àlùfáà-Àgbà in the face of death. What had she done this time? He'd never seen his mother this way before. Even when she'd vexed his father in the past, she'd never, ever begged for forgiveness.

The Lord Regent seemed unmoved by her tears. 'I have only one question for you, Oyíndà. Did you know that Mọ́remí's death was not as a result of childbirth, as you had told me all those first suns ago? Did you lie then or are you lying now about what happened to my wife?'

His mother stopped sobbing immediately and jerked her head from his lap. 'What? She – I, I – what?' She turned back, and Tofa noticed her eyes locked on Àlùfáà-Àgbà's. He knew that look. It meant, *Be quiet.*

'Tell me the truth! Did you kill my Mọ́remí?' the Lord Regent said, and she flinched back.

'I beg for mercy, my Lord. Be gracious to the mother of your child.'

'Oyíndà, I want the next words out of your mouth to be the truth. I want to know what happened to Mọ́remí, and I want to know what happened to my daughter. Both of whom you three told me died from birthing complications.'

'Daughter?' Tofa eyed the room looking for some explanation from the group. No one met his gaze. The story of Mọ́remí was one that had circled the palace when he was a boy. The bride from Ìlú-Ìmọ̀ who won their father's heart. The one who died giving birth, along with the child. So what was this about a daughter?

'Ah – hmmm,' Àlùfáà-Àgbà cleared his throat.

The Lord Regent slammed his hand on the edge of his seat and the metal head hovering over him vibrated with the sound of his voice, 'Don't you dare say a word.'

Àlùfáà-Àgbà recoiled under Lord Regent Babátúndé's anger.

'It was all the Àlùfáà-Àgbà's doing, my Lord. He forced me to lie to you,' Aya'ba Oyíndà said quickly. 'That night, Mọ́remí had her child before me – but only mere moments before me, my husband. The timing was so close they could've been twins.'

415

'This woman is a lia—' Àlùfáà-Àgbà said, and before he could finish saying the word, the metal head hovering over the throne shrunk to the size of a long needle and went right through his arm and into one of the doors at the far end of the room. The old man shrieked in pain and slumped to the ground, and Ìyá-Ayé ran to him. Holding the old man in her arms, she summoned her agbára and hovered her glowing palms over the wound. Her eyes shot daggers at the Lord Regent, but she dared not say anything.

'Father, what's going on? Stop this, please,' Tofa begged.

'Not another word!' the Lord Regent shouted at him, then turned to his mother and said, 'Continue,' in a voice so calm it was scarier than his outbursts.

When she spoke, her voice was filled with fear, trembling with every syllable. 'It was a strange night, my Lord. One moment Àlùfáà-Àgbà was taking our son from my arms, and the next, Mọ́remí had disappeared into the night. I didn't know what to think. Àlùfáà-Àgbà had sent maidens after her, but they didn't find her. That night, he returned to tell me what Mọ́remí had done to the midwife. He said he knew from the marks she left that she had the cursed agbára – the abomination. He said that she was part of the scourge once removed from our blessed lands, and they threatened a return that could destroy our kingdom, and I believed him. So when he asked me where she might have gone, I told him about Mọ́remí's relationship with Ẹnìítàn, the coward priest. And Àlùfáà-Àgbà hunted her down and killed her. Until now, my Lord, he made us all believe the child was dead too.'

'What?' the Lord Regent said.

What? Tofa thought as he listened to his mother say things he couldn't quite grasp. Oh gods, did his mother have a hand in the murder of a rival wife? He turned to Àlùfáà-Àgbà,

416

whose wound was healing under Ìyá-Ayé's flame. Did Àlùfáà-Àgbà kill an innocent girl?

The Lord Regent's eyes burned with fury. 'This man told you that he killed my wife and child and you kept this from me for eighteen first suns? Ah, Oyíndà?!'

'My Lord husband, I had to consider that the child might not even be yours. Mọ́remí was not faithful to you, my Lord, and you deserved more than to be forced to raise a bastard as your own.'

The Lord Regent shifted uncomfortably in his chair, and she moved back promptly but continued to speak. 'We all know that Mọ́remí was sleeping around. It's no secret in this palace that she bedded Ẹniìtàn, your best friend at the time, I might add. I figured if she was innocent, why would she run? Even if she had broken her marriage vows why would she not come to you, our husband, and beg for mercy, even as I do now. After all, she was your favourite.'

'This girl is my daughter!' he cried.

Tofa's eyes widened. In shock at his mother's audacity, in horror at the secrets she spilled. He stepped onto the dais, shielding her with his body, and keeping her away from his father's crimson gaze. He was done being kept in the dark. Done being silent. 'Someone needs to tell me what's happening right now,' Tofa said. His booming voice filled the room, bringing a sudden hush of stillness.

'Your mother conspired to kill the mother of my firstborn child,' the Lord Regent said. 'L'ọrẹ – the girl who broke Alawani out of the temple, was my Mọ́remí's daughter. The one Àlùfáà-Àgbà, Ìyá-Ayé and even your mother have been urging me to hunt down and kill. Just like they killed my Mọ́remí.'

Tofa now realized why Àlùfáà-Àgbà had wanted the girl dead. This L'ọrẹ was his sister and a threat to the kingdom and his throne. He could not help but wonder if this was the secret Alawani had refused to speak when he visited him that morning?

Before Tofa could fully process all that he'd been told, his mother spoke again. 'My Lord husband, please forgive my naïvety. But how can we be sure L'ọrẹ is your child? We have no proof. The fact that Mọ́remí kept a lover outside of her covenant to you, Lord Regent, leaves room for speculation to anyone who hears of this. What will the kingdom think?'

'The kingdom will think what I tell them to think!'

'That girl may be the firstborn, but she is not born of the sun and sands. That evil power she has is a curse meant to destroy us all,' she said, pursing her lips.

'You told me Mọ́remí and her child died. I buried them. I mourned them! Who did I bury, Oyíndà?'

'I did it for you, my Lord husband.'

'You did it for yourself. So your son could claim this throne!'

'He is our son! And this is why we didn't tell you,' she spat back. 'You were so blinded by Mọ́remí's cheap charms. Following her around like a lovesick puppy. Even now, her ghost still holds on firmly to you. Isn't that why, even now, you don't want to harm the girl? Knowing full well that she may not even be of your loins.'

Tofa felt like the floor had dropped out from beneath him as he pieced together the vague and disorienting confession. *You did it so your son could claim the throne.* Claim the throne.

He was the son who claimed the throne.

Had the crown rejected him even before he could claim it? For as long as he could remember, his mother had called him Àkọ́bí Oru. The firstborn of Oru. She taught him who he was before he knew who she was. His eyes locked on hers. His mother wouldn't lie to him. She wouldn't kill others so that he could be king. Aya'ba Oyíndà was many things,

418

but she was not a murderer. He looked at everyone in the room, meeting their eyes. He could read their side glances and sighs. Ìyá-Ayé stared back at him as Àlùfáà-Àgbà looked away. Even High Priestess Àṣá, who was quiet the whole time, standing behind the Lord Regent, glared at him. They knew. They'd always known.

'The child is mine. Ẹniìtàn swore to me by the gods of the sun and sands that he never took Mọ́remí to bed.'

Aya'ba Oyíndà scoffed. 'Didn't he forsake his call, his oath and his gods?' She laughed scornfully. 'He swore to you in the name of gods he doesn't serve.'

'I believe him,' Lord Regent Babátúndé said.

'My husband, why would this man risk his life and raise a child that was not of his own loins? He is in the dungeons now because he will not forsake her, even for the crown. Even as you have commanded him as Lord Regent, and he faces the executioner's axe, yet you think he's protecting your daughter from you? To what end? Does it not make sense that he would do all this for his own daughter?'

Tofa led his mother down the dais and away from the throne. Away from his father, and the council. He held her face in his palms. 'Tell me this isn't true. Please tell me you didn't do this?' His voice broke, tears filling his eyes. 'Tell me that all this is a lie. Tell me I am the Àkọ́bí Oru. Màámi, please tell me this isn't true.'

His mother only frowned and sighed, unable to meet his gaze. That broke his heart more than the truth itself. This was his mother. His everything. She breathed life into him. She moulded him into what he was. Into the king he would be. The king he was born to be. It was her voice he heard in his head when he saw the crown. And all of it was a lie?

The Lord Regent shot a menacing stare at Àlùfáà-Àgbà. 'You killed my wife. You will die for this.'

The Lord Regent's face contorted with anger. Ìyá-Ayé stepped in front of her priest, shielding him. 'Will you kill a priest of the Holy Order, Lord Regent? Will you do what no other before you has done? Are the Àlùfáà not sacred, born and killed only by the will of the gods?'

The Lord Regent walked towards her, 'I am the High Priest of the Sun Temple, the chosen Àlùfáà of this land, and ruler of this kingdom. I can do and undo as I wish. So don't test the boundaries of my reach, or I'll show you just how far it goes.' He pointed at Àlùfáà-Àgbà. 'Did you know what he did?'

Ìyá-Ayé nodded. 'Mọremí had to die. You know that. She was an imposter – she took the place of the woman who was to be your wife. This anger you feel is not because she's dead, but because you were so easily fooled. You fell for this kingdom's greatest enemy. Your anger cannot erase your guilt.' She glared at Tofa and said, 'As far as this kingdom is concerned, Tofaratì is your firstborn, the firstborn of the sun, the one whose agbára rivals the gods, protector of the six rings, light of the continent and Supreme Lord of sun and sands. He is the crown heir. And when the day of the first sun comes, you will yield that crown to him. Whether or not the girl lives is up to you, but you can't think that a child of Òtútù will ever rule this kingdom.'

Aya'ba Oyíndà's crown scraped the floor as she pulled it towards her. The Lord Regent turned on her. 'Do not touch that.'

'My Lord?' she asked, confused.

'I strip you of your crown and title. Get out of my sight. Return to your father's house. Don't let my eyes ever fall upon you again.'

'My Lord! Please. I'm your wife, the mother of your son, your king!'

The Lord Regent turned to his High Priestess Àṣá, 'Arrest her.'

Aya'ba Oyíndà unleashed her agbára, eyes burning, palms aglow with a light so bright they all squinted and covered their eyes. 'Touch me and turn to ash!' she screamed at the maiden.

'Try it, Aya'ba. Just try it,' Àṣá said, seething.

Ìyá-Ayé joined the fight, using her agbára to heat up the room. 'Lord Regent, if your wife touches my daughter, she'll meet her ancestors tonight.'

Tofa flexed his hands. His agbára shone brightest in the room. A moment ago, he'd thought to scare them with the limitless power the gods gave him as his birthright as first-born, but now, all he could do was hope they couldn't see through his glassy eyes to the terrified and heartbroken boy he now was. 'Anyone touches my mother, and I'll burn this palace to the ground.' He couldn't hope to be more skilful with agbára than two maidens of the Holy Order, but he wouldn't let them hurt his mother – his liar of a mother.

The door to the temple swung open, and Kẹni ran scream-ing through. Four guards on her tail. They caught up with her as she approached the throne, pulling her by her hair and torn clothes. She screamed so loud the glass windows sur-rounding the throne hall shuddered.

Tofa ran towards his sister. 'Leave her alone.' He shoved the guards holding her, and they let go. Kẹni ran past him and fell flat before their father.

'What's the meaning of this?' the Lord Regent said.

'Please, Father. I beg you. Spare her life,' Kẹni begged, hands clasped together.

'Spare who?'

As the Lord Regent asked, the room echoed with the sound of chains rattling against the floor and the shuffling of feet. In came a servant girl dressed in the white robes of those heading to the grave. Bound from neck to ankles in heavy black chains. She was the girl Tofa had seen Kẹni talking to the other day.

The Lord Regent edged forward. 'What is her crime?'

'Old magic, my Lord,' said a guard.

Tofa's heart sank as Kẹni sobbed louder, 'Father, please.'

Tofa realized, looking around, that his mother was gone. And so was her crown – she must have used the distraction to sneak out. Everything that could go wrong had gone wrong. His place on earth had shifted with just a few words.

He rushed to Kẹni's side and picked her off the floor. She wailed into his arms. The one person she'd befriended would die, and Tofa couldn't do anything about it. And neither could their father.

'You know the rules, child,' Àlùfáà-Àgbà said, and Tofa couldn't believe the venom that laced the old man's words. 'The magic of the old gods is not to be played with. It's forbidden to mix the gifts of our gods with things of old. The decree in this kingdom is death, a law which has been set by every king and queen to sit upon the throne.'

Tofa didn't miss the emphasis Àlùfáà-Àgbà placed on the word *king*. As Regent, his father had no authority to change the laws set by a sovereign, and that included the ban on anyone outside the Holy Order from using old magic.

The Lord Regent glared at Àlùfáà-Àgbà. His gaze warned the old man not to say another word.

'She is my friend, Father. She didn't mean to –' Kẹni's words caught in her throat.

Father. She'd never called him father before this moment. Not since they were children. She put aside her rage and pride to save this girl's life. Tofa glanced at the servant girl and wondered how in the world their lives had collided.

'Please, Father, she'll swear an oath, a blood oath, never again to use the magic of the old gods.'

Lord Regent Babátúndé looked at the girl in chains. The servant girl trembled so much that a constant rattling of iron filled the throne room. Ḳ̣eni had never asked their father for anything before, and Tofa knew that if it was something he could do, he would.

'The law demands death by beheading and burning,' the Lord Regent said to the servant girl. 'But my daughter pleads for you, and while I can't save your life, you may choose the way you go to meet the gods, and may they welcome you into the city of light with open arms. You may speak your àṣírí.'

Àlùfáà-Àgbà grumbled under his breath.

The Lord Regent raised his hand, silencing him.

Ḳ̣eni embraced Tofa, 'Please, brother, save her. You were born to be king. It doesn't matter if you wear the crown today or blood moons from now. Your word stands. Please help me. Save her.'

A heavy, hollow sensation in Tofa's chest weighed him down. He was without power, without a birthright, without his place in the world. Had she asked this just a day before, even just a few light beads before, he would have climbed the throne and decreed her friend's release. But who was he fooling? Everyone else in this room knew the throne wasn't his. His words had no power or authority. Not anymore. So he shook his head. 'I'm sorry, Ḳ̣eni, I can't.'

Ḳ̣eni pulled away, and his stoic sister, who never smiled or cried, crumbled before him. Her eyes, filled with betrayal, pierced his heart like a dagger.

The Lord Regent prompted the servant girl, 'What will it be, child?'

Ḳ̣eni shoved Tofa and ran to her friend. They held each

other for a long moment, whispering to each other, and then the servant girl said, 'Poison herbs, my Lord.'

'Then you will meet your gods tonight,' the Lord Regent said.

Kẹni hugged the servant girl, squeezing her tight as the girl sobbed her àṣírí in whispers.

Lord Regent Babátúndé nodded to Ìyá-Ayé. The mother of maidens stepped forward and leaned over the servant girl crouched on the floor. 'It'll be quick,' she said, pulling out a small pouch from her breasts.

The guards forced Kẹni away from the girl as she took the contents of the pouch and lay down on the floor. Kẹni screamed at Tofa, 'You killed her!'

Kẹni held on to the girl until she breathed her last, and when she looked into her brother's eyes, he saw fury. A rage so wild and hot her agbára glimmered from beneath her palms. Tofa had never seen Kẹni's agbára before. It was a condition for her survival. He wasn't afraid; he knew she'd never hurt him. He took a step forward, hand across his chest, tears in his eyes, hoping she could see his heart breaking. She did not. She crawled off the floor and lunged at him.

The world slowed, paused, and then cracked wide open in the next few moments. How could she forget? She knew the standing order all the guards in the kingdom had. She was Kẹ́hìndé, Ab'ọ́bakú. She knew that her life would be over if she ever attacked him or even looked like she would attack him. She'd known her whole life the terms of her survival. Yet, she lunged at him, and the guard nearest moved quickly. Tofa rushed to Kẹni, reaching out to pull her away from the dagger heading for her chest. But he was too late.

Agbára burst out of him. His hands glowed, and heat crawled through every inch of his body, consuming him and turning the brown of his entire arms golden. The blast that shot out of him didn't just burn all four guards. It eviscerated them, leaving nothing behind. He ran to Kẹni's slumped body on the ground. 'Kẹni, Kẹni, wake up, please. Wake up!' He looked up to Ìyá-Ayé, 'Help her!'

Ìyá-Ayé looked to the Lord Regent as if asking his permission.

Tofa's rage was a scorching fire, searing through him and making every muscle in his body burn. 'I am your king, and I command you to heal her now!' He flared his agbára, and Ìyá-Ayé complied.

Tofa held on to Kẹni's body as Ìyá-Ayé worked her healing flame through the wound. 'I'm sorry, sister,' he whispered.

Kẹni's breath hitched as she tried to speak, blood pouring from her mouth. 'I'll never forgive you for this,' she coughed, and closed her eyes.

Tofa's shoulders shook with silent sobs. He'd never forgive himself, either.

Àjùmọbí ò kan t'àánú; Ẹni orí
rán sí'ni ló ń ṣe'ni lóore

*To be related to someone by blood does not guarantee
receiving favour from them; help comes
only from those divinely sent to one*

33

Ìlú-Idán, Fourth Ring, Kingdom of Oru

L'ỌRẸ

L'ọrẹ had a hard time deciding her next move. Márùn had gone out for one last patrol before they left the house at nightfall. So while they waited for the sun to set, L'ọrẹ had to decide what to do. The hourglass in her pocket kept her stomach in knots, and she pulled it out to check the time every other heartbeat. She struggled to keep her mind from breaking as anger flared in her chest. Her heart raced, and her mind reeled from the shock of it all. She felt a myriad of feelings, each one blending into the next.

She wanted to free her father. Well, not her father – Baba-Ìtàn.

Her birth father was Lord Regent and High Priest of the Sun Temple. There was no way he didn't know what Àlùfáà-Àgbà was doing. No way he hadn't sent the maiden and his guards after her. He wanted her dead just like everyone else. She shouldn't even have felt any hurt about the actions of a man she had never even seen before. But her heart was broken, and everything hurt. The father she did know and love had lied to her all her life and her world just didn't make sense anymore.

L'ọrẹ thought about Mọremí. The woman she'd placed on

427

a pedestal her whole life for defying the Holy Order. Baba-Ìtàn had told her stories of how strong, kind and brave her mother was, and she'd lived every moment hoping that her mother was looking down at her, pleased to see her daughter as formidable as she once was. But now, that dream, too, was reduced to nothing more than a faint whisper of what once was. Mọ́remí hadn't been kind at all. She had been deceptive, cunning, and wicked to those who cared for her.

In the box Ìyá-Idán had given her, she found a scarf with cowries sewn into every corner. The box had two other items: a small journal half-filled with writings and a slick, lightweight dagger. When L'ọrẹ held it in her hands, the dull metal turned bright blue. She'd thrown everything on the floor at the foot of her bed, the sight of it too much for her to bear.

She glared at the darkness until her eyes burned. When she closed her eyes, she saw Alawani somewhere in the distance, too far to reach. The faster she ran towards him, the farther he seemed to be. She heard Ìyá-Idán's voice repeating her story. Her voice went on like an endless echo in her head. L'ọrẹ held her palms to her temple, begging the voices to die out, crying herself to sleep.

The door to her room opened, and although she didn't look up, she knew it was Alawani by the familiar way his feet dragged across the floor. He climbed into bed with her and hugged her tightly. Kissing her forehead, he said nothing at all. Just what she needed. She couldn't face her demons alone.

As dusk rolled in, and the sky turned dark, Ìyá-Idán insisted they eat with her one last time, so they sat silently together around the dining table, eating a meal of móín-móín and ògi – steamed bean cake and fermented corn pudding. L'ọrẹ kept her bag, which now contained her mother's box, close to her.

After the meal, Ìyá-Idán pulled L'orẹ to a corner of the room, out of Alawani's earshot. 'Have you decided what you will do? Are you going back or going north?' she asked.

'I don't know,' L'orẹ said, her voice choked with tears.

'Whatever you decide, you will need this,' Ìyá-Idán said as she brought out a pouch of herbs and shoved some of it towards L'orẹ's mouth.

L'orẹ shirked her outstretched hand.

'Swallow it!' Ìyá-Idán said sternly, shoving it in her half-open mouth.

'What is it?' L'orẹ said, spitting it out.

'It'll keep you from getting pregnant!' Ìyá-Idán said. 'I know Ẹniìtàn wouldn't have told you this, but you must know that when people with agbára oru and agbára òtútù bear a child, the result is a child with no agbára at all. This was one of the reasons for the massacre of your people. I told you to stay away from that boy. You didn't listen. Now swallow!'

L'orẹ took the pouch from her, stunned and confused.

Suddenly, a voice came from the walls of the house. 'Méje!' L'orẹ looked around the room, but there was no one there. The voice seemed to echo through the flowers that crept along the ceiling – old magic.

The voice called out again, 'Méje, open the door!'

Ìyá-Idán rushed to the main entrance, and with the swipe of her hand, the door flung open, and a man flew in carrying a woman in his arms. Márùn.

Ìyá-Idán closed the door once they were through the threshold and rushed to the man. Alawani was already helping him lay Márùn on the table. She had bruises and cuts all over her bloodied body. Her scorched clothes revealed burnt skin beneath.

L'ọrẹ gasped at the wounds.

'Méjọ, what is going on?' Ìyá-Idán said to the man.

By looks alone, L'ọrẹ figured he was about Baba-Ìtàn's age with streaks of grey snaking through his plaits. The sides of his hair were shaved off, leaving three long braids across his head. His burnt clothes clung to his skin, which was slick with sweat and blood, and his breath came in quick bursts. He coughed, and a smoky scent hung in the air as he tried to speak. Ìyá-Idán fed him a cup of water. She held his face in her palms and sighed. She hugged him, and L'ọrẹ thought she was dreaming again.

Méjọ. That name meant the number eight. L'ọrẹ now had four people named after numbers. Márùn and Méfà, her partner back at the farm inn, were Five and Six. This man called Ìyá-Idán Méje – seven. And she called him Méjọ – eight. What was going on and who were these people?

Ìyá-Idán pulled out a vial from underneath her clothes, opened it and whispered into it in the old tongue. L'ọrẹ recognized one word – Oba'lúayé. She was summoning the old god of healing and biological manipulation. She fed the vial into Márùn's mouth and L'ọrẹ could see her skin slowly start to heal almost immediately.

In her usual fashion of being short and abrupt, Ìyá-Idán wordlessly placed the half-filled vial into L'ọrẹ's hands. L'ọrẹ didn't say anything at all, she just put it into her pocket. She couldn't tell when she'd need a vial of healing potion.

'No,' Ìyá-Idán said firmly. 'Put it in your hair. Wrap it into your braids. Keep it safe.'

L'ọrẹ obeyed. She pulled out the blade she had in her hair and replaced it with the vial, ignoring Command's voice that told her she was better off killing anything that threatened her with the knife than hoping to recover from any wounds.

Méjọ looked at L'ọrẹ and Alawani as if noticing them for the first time, then turned to Ìyá-Idán. 'Méje, what have you done? Why is the prince in your house? The city is on fire. Every house is being searched looking for him. Márùn was nearly killed. Someone said they'd seen them together. If I wasn't there to save her, she'd be dead!'

L'ọrẹ sucked in a breath of shock. How did anyone know to connect Márùn to them? They had been careful. L'ọrẹ stepped away from the woman, her steps heavy with guilt, crushing her from the inside.

Ìyá-Idán said calmly, 'There's a lot to explain, Méjọ. Come and sit.'

'Méje, you can't open yourself to danger like this,' Méjọ said, still frowning.

'Why do you keep calling her that?' L'ọrẹ asked.

'It's her name,' he replied, irritated.

'Okay, everyone, sit down!' Ìyá-Idán said, taking her usual seat at the head of the table.

'First, tell me what happened?' Ìyá-Idán said to Méjọ.

Méjọ sighed. 'I was at a bar house when a warrior maiden came in asking for anyone who had seen the prince,' he glared at Alawani. 'I was about to leave when she noticed Márùn and said she recognized her. Márùn put up a much better fight than I could have, but still, the maiden nearly killed her. I stepped in and only managed to escape because the entire bar turned on the maiden. They only attacked the maiden as an act against the Holy Order; still, without the chaos of their rage, we'd have never gotten out alive. It was horrible. The maiden killed them all and set it all ablaze. It's mayhem outside.' He paused. 'They need to leave now. The entire city will burn you alive if they discover they are losing their homes and loved ones because you're protecting the oath-breaker's son.'

L'ọrẹ saw Alawani look away, and she understood his shame.

'I am not protecting him,' Ìyá-Idán quietly said. 'I am protecting her.'

'And who is she?' Mẹ́jọ spat back.

'Look at her and tell me.'

Mẹ́jọ frowned, squinting his eyes for a moment, then sighed. 'We don't have time for this. I've never seen this girl in my life.'

'Yes, but whose eyes are those?'

Mẹ́jọ peered again, straining his neck as if trying to see inside her.

L'ọrẹ knew the exact moment the realization hit him. She noticed his eyes growing wider and his lips parting in surprise.

'Mọ́remí,' he said the word like he'd seen a ghost. 'It's not possible.'

'This is L'ọrẹ. She is Mọ́remí's firstborn,' Ìyá-Idán replied slowly.

Mẹ́jọ swung his head so fast that L'ọrẹ thought it might fall off his neck. He brought out a cigar and lit it with his fingers as if he couldn't comprehend what he was hearing without taking in a swag. He let the smoke pour out of his mouth and said, 'Queen from the north. I'll be damned.'

'Queen of Oru,' Ìyá-Idán said, standing to her feet.

Mẹ́jọ shook his head. 'No, no. Don't do that. I'll not swear allegiance to this girl. The Holy Order will find her tomorrow, and what then? I will have to jump in front of the sword headed for her neck? Duty or not, I don't want to die for the wrong heir.'

'Your life is hers whether or not you pledge it,' Ìyá-Idán said. 'You don't get to choose who wears the crown, but you must protect them, as we all must. She is our queen.'

Méjọ got up from his chair and threw it against the wall. He let out a deep groan, hands on his knees. 'I'm too old for this,' he said, looking to Ìyá-Idán.

L'ọrẹ could only watch as they discussed her. She didn't understand what was happening. Why did this man feel he had to pledge allegiance to her? She'd asked him for nothing. She'd never ask him to die for her or ask anyone to. This bloodline meant nothing to her other than all she'd lost even before she had it. The crown meant nothing to her. With Baba-Ìtàn and Alawani by her side, she'd never return to these cursed lands.

'I don't understand. What's happening?' L'ọrẹ said to Ìyá-Idán.

'My father named me Àdùkẹ́. My girls call me Ìyá-Idán, but my duty to this kingdom is to be Méje. I am Seven. This is Méjọ. He is Eight. We are twelve. We are –'

'Don't tell her!' Méjọ shouted.

'She is our queen,' Ìyá-Idán replied. 'She is our duty.'

'We reveal ourselves only to the sovereign after the coronation and never in front of another living soul!' Méjọ said, eyeing Alawani.

'We don't have time for that, Méjọ. Without us, that crown may never sit on her head. And she refuses to part with the prince – they are in love,' Ìyá-Idán added almost mockingly.

'This just keeps getting better!' Méjọ laughed. 'The others will never believe this or accept her as their queen, and you know that.'

'We will make them believe,' Ìyá-Idán replied firmly.

Méjọ shook his head. 'Heads will roll for this.'

'So they must,' Ìyá-Idán proclaimed, her body radiating confidence.

'I don't want your pledge of allegiance. I just want to save my father and my friend,' L'ọrẹ said.

'The path before you no longer allows you to save one man. Your kingdom is dying,' Méjọ said intently.

'I don't want your crown. I'm not your queen!' L'ọrẹ shouted back.

Suddenly, there was a loud knock on the door. 'Open this door! Who is in there?'

L'ọrẹ felt a chill run down her spine, and her body went rigid. How did they find them? Ìyá-Idán said no one could find them in this house. Did Méjọ lead them here? Had Milúà found them? She wasn't ready. She had more to learn about her agbára. More to learn about controlling it. The safety bubble she'd created in her mind when she'd stepped into this safe haven burst open, and panic flooded in. Her eyes met Ìyá-Idán's and then Alawani's. They stood frozen in place, waiting to hear if the knock returned. It did.

Méjọ pulled out the embers from his cigar and turned them into a ball of fire in his hand. Ìyá-Idán waved a hand, and all the flowers that decorated her house turned to long, sharp thorns pointing towards the doors. Even the house seemed to get darker.

'No one should be able to find this house,' Ìyá-Idán said, looking at Méjọ. Her face was flooded with fear, her eyes wide and wild.

'I don't know how they found it,' Méjọ replied.

The next knock was even louder, and the hinges on the doors shook, threatening to come apart.

The girls ran out, their voices bouncing off the walls as they anxiously waited for their leader to tell them what to do. Ìyá-Idán looked overwhelmed and panicked – emotions L'ọrẹ never thought she'd see the woman wear.

Suddenly, Ìyá-Idán fell to her knees before L'ọrẹ. 'On this day before the sun in the sky and the sands beneath our feet, I swear loyalty to you, Queen Tèmil'ọrẹ of Oru.'

L'ọrẹ felt like she was drowning in the chaos of it all. Now? Was she doing this now? Before L'ọrẹ could shout, telling them that this wasn't the time, the girls fell to their knees one by one, repeating Ìyá-Idán's words. Even Márùn, who'd just opened her eyes, the old magic working incredibly quickly through her body, was still weak yet fell to her knees.

L'ọrẹ's panic flared her agbára, and she fought to keep it in. Too afraid to hurt these people bowing to her. Bowing to her while the enemy was breaking down the doors. This was madness.

'Open this door in the name of the gods!' the voice called.

L'ọrẹ looked at Mẹ́jọ. 'Please stop this. Tell them to stop,' she pleaded. 'We need to run or hide or fight. We need to do something! They'll soon break down that door.'

L'ọrẹ shut her eyes, feeling hopeless and terrified with each word that made her feel responsible for these girls' lives. This wasn't what she had imagined being royalty would feel like. The emotional burden of it was like a crushing force around her. She didn't need this. She didn't want it and most definitely wouldn't accept it.

She followed Alawani's eyes to where Ìyá-Idán still knelt. He raised his gaze to her, their eyes locked and for a moment she thought he felt the same way she did as the dread that crawled up inside her seemed reflected back to her on Alawani's face. His mouth hung open as the realization of what was happening dawned on him. His eyes pooled instantly, and he kept shaking his head as though disagreeing with them. But just as she moved to hold him, Alawani fell to his knees before her too, and her blood ran cold as he said, 'On this day before the sun in the sky and the sands beneath our feet, I swear loyalty to you, Queen Tèmil'ọrẹ of Oru.'

'Alawani, I am not your queen. What are you doing?' she

said when the doors broke open, and a squad of four royal guards rushed into the house.

Ìyá-Idán rose quickly, and at her command, the vines in the house raced like snakes, tangled into each other, and formed a barrier between them. Ìyá-Idán shouted to Márùn, 'Go with them. Protect your queen. Get her to the sixth ring. Go now!'

The girls and Méjọ gathered around Ìyá-Idán, mists mirroring the colour of the elements they channelled hovering over their hands. Their incantations rang in the air, and they readied for battle, calling their old gods to come to their aid. The guards on the other side shot energy blasts at the magic-woven barrier, and it was weakening. Ìyá-Idán lifted her hands to hold it, but L'ọrẹ knew it wouldn't last long.

L'ọrẹ looked around. She wasn't worth dying for. She wanted to stay and fight.

Ìyá-Idán's voice broke through her thoughts. It was as if the woman could hear the questions that raced through her mind. 'Don't worry, child, go. They couldn't hurt me even if they tried.' She smiled.

L'ọrẹ felt a sting in her heart. The next thing she knew, her legs took off the ground, Alawani grabbed her with both hands and hurled her over his shoulder. She saw Márùn leading the way, running ahead of them as they disappeared into the hallway, and Ìyá-Idán controlling a bunch of vines, sealing the passageway behind them. Just before they were out of sight, she saw the barrier separating Ìyá-Idán and her girls from the guards fall and heard the thunderous roar of chaos and screams of terror.

The exit was blocked with a heavy metal door that had no lock or key. Just a block of steel. Márùn ignited her agbára and placed her glowing hands on the door. She punched, ripped and pulled, melting the steel and creating a hole big enough for them to go through. The light and heat emanating from Márùn and the melting door nearly blinded and choked L'orẹ. Whatever Ìyá-Idán had given Márùn had replenished her strength faster than L'orẹ thought possible.

The exit led into a tunnel within a hill a few yards from the house. Inside, Márùn's light guided them through the passage, which felt longer with each step they took. After what felt like a whole light bead later, the trio stepped out into the sun. There Milúà was, standing a few yards away. No guards or soldiers, just the maiden and her battle rhino almost twice her height, its golden armour gleaming in the sunlight. Ìlú-Idán – the fourth ring – didn't have nearly as many trees as Ìlú-Òpọ where it rained often. It was more like the rest of the desert kingdom with stones and rocks as high as hills across the terrain. L'orẹ took one step back and the maiden turned and locked eyes on her. Márùn had a shield up quicker than L'orẹ could blink. Before them, emerging from Márùn's hand was a shimmering light glowing like glass in fire. Even from this distance, Milúà wasted no time attacking the trio with blasts of energy as she raced for them, her face the portrait of scorn.

L'orẹ and Alawani hid behind Márùn and her agbára shield. 'When she gets closer, we attack at once,' Márùn shouted to them.

Behind her, L'orẹ heard the blast of energy soaring towards her before she saw it. It was as though the sun had left the sky and was pummelling towards them. There was nowhere to run. The impact crashed through Márùn's shield and flung all three of them against the rocks behind them and knocked them to the ground.

L'orẹ's ears rang, and pain flashed through her head. She blinked furiously to clear the light from her eyes but couldn't see properly. Her mind was hazy and disoriented, unable to focus on anything. Her skin stung where the blast had exploded. She grunted as she forced her body off the ground. Her legs trembled beneath her, and she clenched her jaw and winced as she pulled out a sharp stone that had lodged itself in her arm.

'Alawani,' L'ọrẹ called out through the dusty haze in the aftermath of the attack.

Silence.

Panic surged through her. 'Alawani! Márùn. Can you hear me?'

Her head throbbed, and her vision dimmed intermittently as she searched for them.

Then the dust cleared, and there they were, slumped on the ground. Not moving. She ran to Alawani, shaking him, calling his name. She placed her face to his, checking for breath. He was alive. Márùn was the same. Between Alawani's waning agbára and Márùn's recent attack, L'ọrẹ wasn't surprised that they took longer to wake. But being alone terrified her, and so she kept calling their names, waiting for them to hear her.

Her voice didn't wake them. But it woke Milúà, who L'ọrẹ noticed was also caught in the blast. That meant Milúà hadn't caused that explosion – someone or something else did. L'ọrẹ jumped to her feet as quickly as her shaky feet would allow. Milúà moved slowly towards L'ọrẹ like a being half-alive, dragging her leg and holding on to her visibly dislocated shoulder. L'ọrẹ watched in horror as Milúà leaned against a rock and popped her shoulder into place. As usual, the maiden didn't let out a sound; she clenched her jaw and glared at L'ọrẹ with the most sinister reddened eyes that L'ọrẹ had ever seen.

'I'm going to kill you,' Milúà said through gritted teeth, blood dripping from the gash on her head.

438

L'ọrẹ's fingers trembled as she reached for her agbára. It felt as though she'd forgotten all she'd just learned. An icy chill flowed through her, and L'ọrẹ knew she was doing it wrong. Something about being alone, cornered by the maiden she knew could and would kill her, made her tremble with fear. She stood up and reached for her blades. She called upon Ṣàngó in the old tongue. The old god who always heard her after the new ones had forsaken her. But nothing happened. Her blades did not glow. She'd either said it wrong, or he had grown tired of her. L'ọrẹ clashed her blades together – gods or no gods, she wasn't going down without a fight.

'Don't take another step, maiden,' a voice called out, and Command walked out from behind a cluster of high rocks.

Milúà swayed and glared at the figure, releasing her frown only when Command came into full view. Then she bowed slowly and stepped out of her path, a glare still fixed on her face.

L'ọrẹ watched her commander stride into the clearing and her heart raced in her chest. Seeing Milúà's bow confirmed that the maiden acknowledged Command's rank and would not attack. So L'ọrẹ ran towards Command, crying as she crashed into her. She hugged her so tightly, she feared she would crush the woman in her own armour. L'ọrẹ wept into her arms, her heart so full every word out of her was incoherent; she sobbed, unsure of what she wanted to say while trying to say everything all at once. Command held her just as tightly, holding her head like a child she hadn't seen in a long time. Her voice softer than anything L'ọrẹ had ever heard from the woman, she whispered, 'I'm here.'

'Stay out of this, Command,' Milúà said, the edge in her voice not as firm as it had been when she was speaking to L'ọrẹ a few moments ago. 'I have orders from the Temple to bring the Prince Àlùfáà and the girl back to the capital.'

Behind her, L'ọrẹ heard the maiden's blade shoot out of her staff. She turned to see Milúà advancing. Command moved L'ọrẹ out of the way and pulled out her sword from the sheath strung to her back.

'I won't tell you again, Milúà, I don't care what you do with the prince,' she said, nodding towards Alawani, still slumped on the floor. 'You're not taking L'ọrẹ from me.'

'Command,' Milúà said with a shaky curtsy, greeting the woman before rising again with a stern glare. Being at war with each other was no reason to discard respect in Oru. Milúà spun her spear and pointed its steel end at Command. 'I don't want to fight you.'

'Where are the palace guards? The king's army?'

Milúà scoffed, 'My mother sent me. I don't need guards to find my prey.'

Command chuckled. 'The Lord Regent sent me, and that overrides whatever the Elder Priest and his maiden have ordered you to do.'

'It doesn't,' Milúà seethed.

'What do you know, you child of the temple,' Command said. With her outstretched hand glowing bright in the sunlight, Command used her agbára to grab hold of Milúà's spear. Like a magnet, Command's agbára pulled the spear and she turned it around mid-flight and flung it back at Milúà, who jumped out of the way. The spear sank deep into stone.

'Don't die,' Command said softly. 'Is that not what Ìyá-Ayé tells you girls? I'm telling you for the last time, L'ọrẹ is coming with me. One more attack from you and you'll join the souls in my hair.'

Milúà was up quicker than L'ọrẹ thought possible, her hands aglow with agbára. The girl didn't know when to give up.

Command launched a throwing star at Milúà. The four-sided

spiked steel blade flew in an arc towards the maiden, who dodged it easily, but L'ọrẹ knew this trick. Milúà only realized her predicament when she felt the sting of the second and the third and the two that came after it. Command's stars seemed to multiply with each throw. Milúà ducked and danced through each strike, trying and failing to avoid getting hit. Finally, the last one came hurtling towards the maiden – right in the middle of her forehead. L'ọrẹ had thought that there was no way Milúà could avoid the hit from the awkward position the previous stars had left her in. To her surprise, Milúà raised her hands, and used her agbára to stop the red-hot star mid-flight. L'ọrẹ gaped at Milúà as she mirrored Command's previous move. L'ọrẹ had never seen anyone push and pull steel the way Command did. Milúà shoved the star right back at Command, who slowed it to a stop and plucked it from the air like an unripe mango. And smiled.

'You have your mother's will,' Command said.

Those words seemed to knock the air out of the maiden more than anything Command had done to her.

Milúà gaped at Command, panting like a dying ox. Her eyes were still red but with much less fury than a moment before. For the first time, L'ọrẹ considered that there was a person beneath those layers of gold and steel.

'This is what I've been trying to teach you, L'ọrẹ,' Command said, turning to her. 'When you fight an enemy stronger than you, learn their tricks and use them against them. Never stop moving until there is no life left in you.' Then she turned to Milúà, who was bruised and bleeding, the crimson staining her midnight-dark skin, 'Very well done.'

L'ọrẹ could not believe it. Now? Command chose this moment to teach her lessons?

Command looked from L'ọrẹ to Milúà and back, a grim expression on her face. 'In another world you'd have been sisters, yet here you are fighting each other at the whims of the same people who led your mothers to their deaths.'

Sisters? L'orẹ nearly scoffed. But how did Command know Mọ́remí? Why had she never mentioned it? Was that why Command risked her life to train her?

'You knew my mother?' L'orẹ and Milúà said at the same time, then glared at each other.

'You follow Ìyá-Ayé's orders like a trained dog, just like Àdùnní did,' Command said, pointing to Milúà, and then she turned to L'orẹ. 'And you blindly follow your father's wishes. Both of whom got the girls they claimed to love killed. Their fight is not your own.'

Milúà took a step closer and L'orẹ's heart skipped a beat. She thought she saw the maiden's eyes brim with tears, but she must have been imagining it because Milúà turned her back to them and walked towards Alawani in the distance.

'Don't touch him,' L'orẹ shouted, moving to stop Milúà when she felt the heavy blow of Command's hilt strike her across her head. Pain flared in her mind and then she was falling. Falling into darkness.

*The treaty that bound the continent
was signed in blood.
Six kings laid down their crowns and yielded to the
Aláàfin – the ruler of the newly formed
kingdom of Oru.
In exchange for a drop of the sun
all but one yielded their throne
and till this day, the kingdom to the west,
hidden in the caves and cliffs,
lives at the edge of the continent, separated
from the gods' blessing.
They remain as scions of the Òrìṣà, untainted
by the gods of the sun and sands.*

34

Ìlú-Idán, Fourth Ring, Kingdom of Oru

L'ỌRẸ

L'ọrẹ opened her eyes to the bright sunlight, and felt its heat radiating off her skin. She moved to sit up, but her body was too heavy and too sore. She slumped back, and her head hit a wooden panel. Groaning, she rolled to her side. She was in the back of an open wagon. The taste of dust and sand on her lips told her she was still in Oru. Gathering all her strength, she heaved her body up and looked around. She was in a clearing surrounded by rocks on all sides. In the distance, a horse was tied to a tall shrub; farther past it, she could see the mighty wall that divided the rings. L'ọrẹ hoped that the wall she saw was the border into the fifth ring, and that Command hadn't taken her farther from her destination.

'Alawani,' she called out, straining her voice. 'Alawani, where are you? Command, are you there?'

L'ọrẹ climbed out of the wagon and roamed the stony grounds. She checked her pocket, quickly tossing everything out to the ground until she found it. She held the hourglass up to her eye level. The sand had reduced significantly. A wave of panic surged through her as the looming boulders surrounding her seemed to inch closer. Her breath stopped short, and her entire body tensed when she heard her name.

She swung round to see Command's tall figure coming towards her. L'orẹ heard the chimes in her hair before she saw her face.

'Good, you're up,' Command said flatly. 'Now let's go. I can't drag you all the way to the capital on this thing.'

'The capital?'

'I'm taking you home.'

'Command, I can't go back,' L'orẹ said.

'If you turn yourself in, they will release your father and Kòyà,' Command said briskly.

L'orẹ stepped back from her. 'Àlùfáà-Àgbà will never release them.'

'It's not up to him. The Lord Regent sent me to bring you home. It's his word that matters, not the Elder Priest's.'

A few light beads ago, L'orẹ might have said yes. She trusted no one more than she trusted Command. But Àlùfáà-Àgbà hadn't told Milúà to stop hunting them, even after the deal to give up her agbára. He wouldn't even give her a chance to honour her side of the bargain. She wasn't going back. Not now. Not when she was so close to doing what her father had begged her to do. Escape and survive.

'Where is Alawani?' L'orẹ said, breathless. 'Did you leave him with Milúà? She'll kill him.'

'You think a maiden of the Holy Order whose life is bound to her priest will kill an Àlùfáà? L'orẹ, please, you're smarter than this,' Command said. 'Anyway, my mission is you. And you need time apart from him to understand the situation you're in. You need to come with me.'

'I need to go back to him. He needs me.'

'Do not move from that spot, L'orẹ. That boy does not need you,' Command replied firmly. 'We need to talk.'

'Did you know my mother?' L'orẹ said abruptly. 'If you want to talk, that's what I want to talk about.'

Command's shoulders slumped and before she could speak L'ọrẹ went on, 'You knew my mother and you didn't tell me. I've spent nearly every day for gods know how many first suns with you. Every night you could have told me, and you didn't.'

'I chose not to tell you. To save you from walking the same path she did,' Command said, fuming. 'Your mother had friends in high places, and enemies in even higher places, and when she chose to defy the gods, she died by their hands. I didn't want that for you. I was trying to protect you. I am trying to protect you now. I love you. Can't you see that?'

L'ọrẹ's eyes stung with tears. Those were words she never thought she'd hear. 'I love you, Command,' her voice hitched, 'but I can't do it. I can't go back. What if you come with me?'

Command's eyes darkened. 'The Lord Regent didn't give that option.'

'So you're not helping me. You're kidnapping me.'

'L'ọrẹ, you've caused so much damage,' Command's voice shook with anger.

'You don't understand!'

'What is there to understand? Your father is in a dungeon awaiting the executioner's axe.'

'He is not my real father!'

'Of course he's not your father, L'ọrẹ – not by blood. But he is your father in every way that matters.'

'You knew?' L'ọrẹ said, her voice a mere whisper. 'You knew who I was this whole time.'

Command's jaw clenched, 'I don't care what you found out. Whatever that man did, he did to protect you. How can you not see that? You're alive now because of him. I look at you now, and I don't see the warrior I trained, I see –'

'Everyone in my life has been lying to me. I didn't think you would too!'

446

'Our lies saved your life,' Command said and unsheathed her sword. 'You're coming with me back to the capital.'

'They'll kill me.'

'Come with me and I promise the Lord Regent will keep you, your father and Kòyà safe. He assured me of this.'

'Command, please listen to me,' L'orẹ begged.

'You've changed the fate of so many because you couldn't accept that boy's destiny. When you became his friend,' Command grimaced as though the word was bitter in her mouth, 'I told you. I warned you and begged you to let him go, but no. You always have to be right. Everything always has to be on your terms.'

As Command spoke, her words stirred the air around her. L'orẹ felt the pain and anger pouring out of her commander.

'They'd have killed Alawani,' L'orẹ said, her voice shaking.

'And how do you know that? I'm starting to think you were never even afraid he might die. You were afraid he would live and you wouldn't have the chance to be with him.'

'That's a lie!' L'orẹ shouted back.

'Are you in love with him?'

L'orẹ lowered her gaze and Command roared, launching herself at her. L'orẹ jumped out of the way. She realized that she couldn't reach her blades, which were in the back of the wagon. She was in trouble.

L'orẹ weaved and dodged Command's attacks, and her muscles burned with each step until her vision grew hazy. Feeling at a disadvantage, she channelled her agbára. She remembered her training with Ìyá-Idán this time and tried to focus on the heat coming off the surrounding rocks, not the heat coming off Command. After moving as far as she could from Command, she closed her eyes for a single heartbeat to concentrate on challenging the energy around her.

Eerily, it was still Command's voice she heard in her mind

447

when she fought. Even now that she fought the woman in the flesh, the voice in her head directed her moves as it always did. *Watch out!*

Command's strike came quickly, and L'ọrẹ caught the edge of the blade in her palms just before it struck. She screamed as the blade tore through flesh, and she poured her agbára into it. The blade froze over, turning brittle. It shattered in her hands.

Command stepped back, her eyes wide with disbelief. 'Gods, you are one of them.' She took another step back. 'So this was Mọ́remí's secret.'

L'ọrẹ inched closer and withdrew her agbára but didn't get the chance to reply before Command punched her right in the face, and she fell back flat. The sharp, searing pain made her face feel like it was being pierced by needles. *You should've seen that coming. Focus*, the voice in her head said.

Command lifted her by her collar, and L'ọrẹ's feet dangled beneath her. She struggled to break free, and Command threw her against the ground. L'ọrẹ heard a crack, but as heat and pain spread throughout her body, she couldn't tell what had broken.

You're losing. Always losing. Get up and fight. She wouldn't survive this by evading the fight that was clearly not going to be over until Command had her back on that wagon. L'ọrẹ struggled with the decision to fight Command. Her Command. The closest thing to a mother she'd ever had. But Command wasn't backing down, and L'ọrẹ wasn't ready to give up. Even as Command leered at her now, she realized she was right. She wasn't behaving like the trained warrior she was. She hadn't for a long time now. A fight had come to her, and she was nothing if not well-trained. If Command's remarks to Milúà were anything to go by, even she wasn't expecting L'ọrẹ to give up, no matter how hard the fight became.

As Command prepared to take her on with her fists, L'ọrẹ shuffled around the clearing. With high rocks on all sides, it felt much like the pits of Gbàgede. If nothing had changed, this would have been the fight she'd have to win to be declared ready for Ogun. And she was ready. L'ọrẹ faked a blow, and as Command ducked, she struck the side of her face with her foot.

Good! Go now, hit her again before she's ready! the voice prompted.

Command stumbled back but didn't fall. She spat out blood from her lips and cracked her neck. 'Now we are talking.'

L'ọrẹ's heart raced as she saw the blood, and she felt her determination slipping away. 'Please, Command, I don't want to fight you.'

But Command wasn't listening. She launched at L'ọrẹ again, throwing high kicks at her.

Jump. Get out of reach! the voice shouted.

L'ọrẹ felt the world slow as she bobbed and slid out of each kick's reach. Her feet shuffled through the loose rocks on the ground. She was panting heavily by the end, her arms aching with exhaustion as she blocked each strike.

'Surrender, L'ọrẹ, don't make me ask you again!' Command said.

'I – I can't. They won't spare him if I go back. They will kill us both! You don't –' she heaved, 'you don't know the truth.'

Command lunged again. L'ọrẹ's reflexes had slowed, so when Command reached for her, she caught her hair, pulled her close, punched her stomach, and tossed her to the ground. L'ọrẹ groaned and attempted to stand, the sound of her pulse pounding in her ears as she tried to keep the world from spinning.

Move, L'ọrẹ, move, the voice said, and L'ọrẹ hit her hand against her head to stop the disorientating noise that echoed in her mind. 'Leave me alone!'

By the time her sight cleared, Command's dagger was coming down on her. L'ọrẹ put up her hands in front of her and screamed. She didn't realize what had happened until she saw Command stagger and whimper, gasping for air. In her panic, she'd channelled her agbára and shot a blast of frost into Command's core. The ice blast had sunk deep into Command's chest, oozing dark mists, spreading quickly over her body. L'ọrẹ rushed to grab her, holding her head in her arms.

Command's lips trembled, her words fluttering as she tried to speak. Stuck on the first letter, she repeated, 'I – I –'

'Shh, don't speak. You'll be all right. I'm sorry. I'm so sorry.' L'ọrẹ used the dagger to tear through the woman's clothes to see the impact on her bare skin. The dark streaks across her chest spread out like webs from her core. L'ọrẹ desperately brushed off the flakes of ice forming over Command's skin. They only grew faster.

'Channel your agbára. Let your heat warm you up!' L'ọrẹ pleaded. Command didn't respond, her gasps ebbing away slowly. 'Command! Wake up! Curse the sun, please, please, wake up!' She shook her vigorously. 'Help me! Somebody, help me, please! Command, wake up!'

Command opened her eyes slowly, and L'ọrẹ leaned in close, her ears to her mouth to catch every word. 'I wasn't going to kill you.'

'I know, I know, I'm sorry,' she rubbed her face, 'I'm so sorry, I panicked.' She placed her hands over her head, confused and more scared than she'd ever been in her life.

Command coughed, and L'ọrẹ hugged her tighter. 'Please, please, somebody help me! Aunty Títí, please get up!' she

450

screamed at the top of her lungs. Command hadn't let L'ọrẹ call her by her birth name since she was a child. L'ọrẹ couldn't bear to call her Command in this moment. She couldn't lose her.

'You fought well,' Command struggled to say with the briefest smile across her face. Then she said, 'Save your father,' and she went quiet.

Tears poured out of her eyes as she held on tightly to the woman who had loved her and trained her. She was hysterical, 'No, no, Aunty Títí, please! Wake up! Wake up! Open your eyes! Help me! Wake up! Wake up! Open your eyes! Help me! Somebody help me!'

L'ọrẹ screamed, her voice echoing through the air until her throat was raw, and her sobs came in strained gasps. She jumped at the sound of footsteps crunching on the ground nearby. She looked up to find Milúà staring back at her.

L'ọrẹ's shoulders fell and she hunched over Command's body, too exhausted to run or fight. Too tired to do anything but cry.

'Is she dead?' Milúà said in an even tone, looking at the ice crystals covering half of Command's body.

L'ọrẹ looked up at her, frowning, then shook her head. 'Can you help her?' She noticed the warm glow of agbára in Milúà's hands and knew the maiden was there for her, but she couldn't do anything about that now. She just wanted Command to live. 'Please help her. Use your agbára to warm her up. There's ice inside of her.'

L'ọrẹ stepped back in shock when she saw Milúà kneel beside the woman, her face filled with emotion. Ice had formed around the corners of Command's lips, and her breath came in slow bursts of dark mist.

'I don't think anyone can help her,' Milúà said, glaring at L'ọrẹ. 'What did you do?'

'It was an accident. I love her,' L'ọrẹ sobbed.

'So you killed her? A commander in the king's army? What is wrong with you?'

'It was an accident!'

Milúà scoffed.

'Please, just try!' L'ọrẹ shouted, crying and sobbing.

Milúà channelled her agbára, sending a warm glow through her palms and placing them on Command's chest. The woman groaned softly, and the ice clinging to her chest melted away.

L'ọrẹ moved in closer and spoke softly to Command, caressing her locs. 'Tell me what to do, tell me how to fix this.'

Command gasped as the warmth seeped into her. 'Àṣírí,' she said in a coarse, strained voice.

Tears streaming down her face, L'ọrẹ cried out, her voice full of anguish, 'No, no. Hold your secrets. Tell me when you are better. You'll be fine, I promise.'

She met Milúà's gaze. 'She'll be fine, right?'

Milúà glared at her with a piercing stare. 'No, she won't,' she said, wiping sweat from her face and pouring her agbára into Command's body. 'If you don't want her to die two deaths, take her àṣírí.' Milúà leaned in close to Command's face. 'You know who killed my mother. Tell me. Please.'

That last word was something L'ọrẹ never thought she'd hear from a temple maiden. The ache in her voice as she begged was even more of a surprise.

'You need to focus. Use more energy, please don't let her die,' L'ọrẹ said to Milúà.

Milúà glared at her, her eyes brimming with tears. 'I need to know.' Then she returned to Command, crouching lower. 'Please tell me. Was it Ìyá-Ayé? Did that woman kill my mother? Who is my father? Command, please,' the maiden's voice cracked.

The ice was growing again – Milúa's agbára wasn't saving her.

'Our king was murdered,' Command's voice broke through their sobs, and with that, her haggard breathing stopped. There was no raspy sound coming from her, no more groaning. Nothing.

They looked at each other, shocked by the secret revealed.

L'ọrẹ's eyes widened. 'No, no, no,' she mumbled as she grabbed Command's clothes, shaking her cold body, calling her name, rocking her in her arms. L'ọrẹ wailed loudly, ran her hand through Command's hair and pulled out a cowrie, and pressed it into her palm. Her first cowrie. Her first life taken.

L'ọrẹ didn't recognize the voice that whispered in her head. It wasn't Command's. Command was gone. Her voice was gone. Forever. This voice was unfamiliar. Softer, calmer, sweeter. *Look up*, it warned.

L'ọrẹ moved to find Milúà standing before her with her spear pointed at her face.

'You killed her,' Milúà said, rising with her weapon. 'You killed her, and she was the only one who knew about my family.'

'She gave the only secret she had. If she were the only one alive who knew your parents she'd have told you. She didn't. So someone out there knows. Go find them and leave me alone. Find whatever answers you seek, and let her soul find rest in the city of light.'

'You killed her before she could tell me,' Milúà said, her voice so gritty and coarse with fury that L'ọrẹ was reminded who exactly the maiden was. Not someone worthy of pity, but a tool for murder. And in Milúà's eyes, L'ọrẹ saw blood.

L'ọrẹ poured out her rage and agbára in a blast of energy,

453

creating a crystalized barrier that formed a dome around the maiden – trapping her within it. The structure was so thick that L'ọrẹ could only see faint glimpses of the maiden's shadow within.

'You can't hide from me. I'll find you!' L'ọrẹ heard Milúà's muffled voice shout from within the dome, as she grabbed her bag and blades and ran as fast towards Command's horse as she could. She jumped on it and bolted out of the fourth ring.

As she raced towards the border wall, in the distance to her far right, she saw a beam of light shine from the ground up. A few heartbeats later it shone again, and again. Alawani. She knew that signal well. She raced towards it and hoped no one else had seen it, or at least hoped she'd reach him before Milúà did.

The sun had set when she finally found Alawani and Márùn waiting by the base of the tower-high stone wall a few miles from where she'd left Command's body. She leapt off the horse and ran into Alawani's embrace, her body shaking with sobs and tears streaming down her face.

'What happened? Where were you?' Alawani said, arms outstretched. 'We looked everywhere for you.'

He hugged her so tightly, she felt the pain from the crack around her ribs earlier. 'I thought I'd lost you,' he breathed.

L'ọrẹ shook her head, then pulled away. 'We need to leave now. Anyone could have seen your signal.'

'I told you not to do that,' Márùn said to Alawani.

'It worked, didn't it?' Alawani said.

'How did you get away from Milúà? Before I got knocked out, I saw her standing over you.'

'By the time we both woke up, no one was there,' Alawani said, squeezing L'ọrẹ's hand.

'She just left you there? Why would she do that?' L'ọrẹ asked.

'Whatever the reason, I'm glad she's gone,' Alawani said. 'Where were you? Who knocked you out?'

'I don't know. Someone from the capital, a senior guard maybe. I couldn't recognize them.' The lie came more easily than L'ọrẹ had expected. She caught the frown that flashed across Alawani's face and looked away. She hoped he wouldn't pry further.

'I'm just glad you're okay,' Alawani said after a brief moment.

'How will we get through?' L'ọrẹ asked, looking up at the massive border wall.

Márùn placed her hand through the stone all the way to her arm. 'This wall is protected by the magic of Ìlú-Idán. Hold on to me and don't let go. We'll walk through the stone.'

L'ọrẹ could hear her own gasp of disbelief as she looked around her. She'd expected a smuggler's tunnel like there was at the third ring border wall, but this was something wildly different. The stone wall had no holes or doors, and she expected her to walk into it?

'It's fine,' Alawani said to L'ọrẹ, 'I've gone through before.'

She gave him a weak smile. Blood still thundered in her ears. Her hands still felt cold and clammy from holding on to Command. Flashes of her commander's body kept flooding her mind. She wanted to tell him. But how would she explain? She killed Command. *She killed Command.* Her mind was breaking, her heart fracturing and splintering off in different directions. In her mind's eye, the roof over her head on the platform was gone, and the pillars swayed as the unforgiving storm rained sand over her, blistering her skin. 'I have to tell you something,' she blurted out.

'No time,' Márùn said, 'just walk through. Keep walking in a straight line until you see the sun.'

'And what happens if we don't see the sun?' Alawani asked.

'Then you get lost in there forever. There's a reason why this wall in particular uses magic. We're leaving the crown's protected lands and going into the outer rings. The Holy Order fully expects anyone entering or leaving without permission to get lost in there. So hold on and don't let go.'

'I've got you,' Alawani said, seeing L'ọrẹ's distraught expression.

L'ọrẹ stared at the wall, wondering if the stone would swallow her and keep her. Would it know what she'd done? Would the old gods punish her for murder? Was it murder if it was an accident? 'I'm scared,' L'ọrẹ whimpered, tracing the empty space on her chest as she instinctively reached for the necklace that she'd long lost.

'Here,' he said, offering her his hand. 'Hold on and follow me. I won't lead you to your death. I'm oath-bound to you now. You won't get hurt on my watch.'

At that, L'ọrẹ felt her heart swell with conviction, and her doubts quelled. She trusted him, more than she trusted herself at that moment. So she took his hand and let him lead her through.

'Whatever you do, don't use agbára in here, or none of us is getting out,' Márùn said as they took their first step through the stone.

Inch by inch, the wall swallowed them up.

L'ọrẹ closed her eyes in the darkness of the stones, the only light source being the little red spots that greeted her when she did so. The darkness was so thick she could feel the space they walked through push and close in on her. Her grip on Alawani's hand tightened. She felt her panic grow as the air left her lungs, and she found it harder to take a deep breath. The spots she'd focused on faded, and there was nothing but the empty yet suffocating blackness around her. When she tried speaking, to call Alawani's name, her voice wouldn't come, and that was when she lost it. The darkness overwhelmed her with a feeling of terror. Her body stiffened in response, and she made it through only because Alawani kept a tight grip on her hand and pulled her along.

The sun, although hidden behind thick layers of dust, smoke and ash, was still too bright for her as they walked out of the stones. She kept her eyes closed, only opening them slowly and for short periods of time until they adjusted.

Ìlú-Oníṣònà – the fifth ring, was like a ghost town. Huge black buildings, many stories high, stood in clusters of four, surrounded by barbed wire fences all over the land, back-dropped by a dismal grey haze. L'ọrẹ knew about the volcanic eruptions near the kingdom's outer states but wasn't expecting anything like this. Galvanized steel rooftops, chiselled stone walls and more rhinos than she'd ever seen in a single location, although these ones were used for load-carrying not battle. Ìlú-Oníṣònà's gloomy atmosphere was nothing like she'd read about in Baba-Ìtàn's books. Those books praised the state as the home of all artisan works, from blacksmiths to clay workers, builders and stonemasons. It was the home of creativity, but this just looked like an abandoned town. There was hardly anyone around, and those they saw avoided their gazes and trudged along as though they'd faint with the next step.

'What happened here?' L'ọrẹ asked Márùn.

'We've crossed from the land of the sun and sands to that of ash and smoke,' Márùn said, pointing to the grey skies and the ash flurries that danced in the air.

'What's causing this? I've never seen anything like it,' L'ọrẹ said.

'Ìlú-Idán's magic keeps everything within its ring safe from the ash plague,' Alawani said.

'What is the ash plague?' L'ọrẹ asked.

Márùn shrugged, 'You'll hear many things in these parts. Some moonlight storytellers say it's punishment for abandoning the old gods; others say it's the price we pay for our agbára. Whatever the reason, the volcanoes across the continent have spewed ash consistently for almost as many first suns as our kingdom has been alive.'

'How come it's so bad here and not a flake of ash in the inner rings?' L'ọrẹ asked, looking from one to the other.

'Because his father promised to extend the magic border to cover the entire kingdom – another oath he never kept. Instead, the outer rings continue to pay the price for something their forefathers did in the days of the First Sun. A crime they are forbidden to speak of to outsiders,' Márùn said, her voice venomous. 'It's up to the next ruler of Oru to right that wrong and extend the magical barrier to shield all six rings from the ash plague.'

Márùn glanced at L'ọrẹ, who quickly averted her eyes. The state was an image of despair, the sound of silence punctuated by the occasional gust of wind and ashen dust. How could any ruler let their people live like this? L'ọrẹ didn't blame Alawani for his father's crimes, but this was abysmal. It was a surprise anyone survived in this state at all – if the charcoaled earth didn't kill them, the air would.

'You could change everything, Queen of Oru,' Márùn said to L'ọrẹ, her eyes wide with hope.

L'ọrẹ stepped back as if to run from those words that had now become the backdrop of her existence. She could hardly keep the tiny family she had alive. How was she supposed to accept the responsibility of the thousands of people who lived in Oru? How could she ever make right the terrible things the past rulers had done? No. The crown was not hers to hold or claim.

L'ọrẹ brought out the hourglass; the sand remaining would not last two full days. It was unlikely to last even one before the storm arrived. They needed to be at the last wall of Oru before then. She tucked it back into her pocket. 'We need to keep moving.'

In the days before the Day of the First Sun,
kings birthed heirs who took their thrones
and from father to son, the crown passed
down a single lineage.
Then came the gift of agbára oru
and the curse to keep it strong in our blood.
Then came the need for High Priests and
stripping ceremonies.
Then came what is now and what will always be.

35

The Royal Palace, Royal Island, Kingdom of Oru

TOFA

Tofa had not left his sister's side from the moment the knife went into her until now. Many light beads passed, and there he lay next to her body, speaking to her to keep her mind alive while her flesh weaved back together. He told her stories from when they were young; he reminded her of their love, and their promise to each other – before the world tried to separate what the gods had bound at birth. In truth, he begged for forgiveness he did not deserve. Her breaths came slow and shallow and he knew, even if she could hear him from the deep slumber she was in, she wouldn't respond. It wouldn't surprise him that even if she woke, she would never again utter a single word to him.

Tofa rose from the bed and looked around Kẹni's room. It looked as bland as a dungeon cell. The dry grey stones had no cover, no curtains, just a single bed and a piece of rug on the floor. He'd tried many times to make it more like his, but Kẹni always refused. She spent her life determined to prove to the crown and order that all she wanted was life. Tofa strolled towards the flimsy wooden shutters that opened into the balcony. Kẹni's room was high enough that the kingdom spread out before him and he could see past the river and into the first ring.

The wind blew in his face, the light air cooling the nervous sweat that had built up as he waited for Kẹni to wake. On the ground below him, people moved around with purpose, the guards, the maidens, the rest of the court, all going in separate directions, doing different things but all in service of the crown. Every so often someone would look up high enough to catch a glimpse of him and kneel to the ground in respect before moving on.

There was a feeling of safety, of purpose and destiny when one knew who they were, what they were born for and how they would die. Tofa had grown up believing three things to be true. He was born to be king, his purpose was to rule, and he would die as king. Thoughts of the bastard daughter his father revealed threatened to waive his conviction. But no. The crown was always his. There were no games to be played in pursuit of the throne. It was his. And he was a fool to have not wanted it.

Now he was starting to see the truth. The crown did take, and it would continue to, but he could take from it too. Without it he was powerless to save those he loved, to defend himself against anyone and anything that crossed his path. He had been too meek, he saw that now. Floating through the palace like a ghost instead of the king he was destined to be. Pleading and begging for the things he wished for instead of demanding what was already his.

He turned back to see Kẹni's body lying still on the bed. He couldn't imagine ever again being in a position where he didn't have the power to protect her. To free her from the curse she was born into. At that moment Tofa knew he didn't have the privilege of backing down from this fight. Nor did he want to. For a moment, he worried that he was being wiped from the history books in a single swipe of ill fate. But then he remembered who he was. Who his mother always told him that he was. Àkọ́bí Oru. Raised for a single purpose. To rule the six rings of the great kingdom of Oru and nothing would stand in his way. The crown was his, and he would not yield. Not to this girl from the north, not to his father or the Elder Priest, and not even to the gods. He knew what he had to do and he knew exactly who he had to speak to.

Tofa chose a disguise as he walked out of the palace, across the golden bridge and into Ìlú-Ọba – the first ring of Oru. The home of the rich and poor alike. Long lines of royal families that yielded the throne of inheritance to the Holy Order as was demanded by the gods. Most importantly, it was here the mother of maidens built her home, and that was where he was headed.

Ìyá-Ayé had never knelt before Tofa before. At most, she'd do something that looked like a curtsy but wasn't. It never bothered Tofa in the past; after all, he wasn't king yet. So when he stood in the middle of her makeshift throne room, surrounded by a dozen maidens, and said in a low gritty voice, 'Kneel,' the old woman's brows rose in defiance.

Tofa often wondered what kind of king he'd become. He was sure that he was nothing like his father. He had promised himself and his sister that the crown would not strip him of his humanity. Yet at that moment, his agbára flared out of him so brightly that his next breath could have burned the maidens' home to ash. 'Kneel before your king, mother of maidens,' he said again, and this time, the woman went down quick, bowing low but keeping her eyes fixed on his. Her maidens fell in unison, heads bowed and hands outstretched, shining their agbára upon his feet. Submitting to him.

Tofa didn't have to prove to Ìyá-Ayé his power or authority, but he knew that when he became king, he'd need the maidens to fear him just as much as they did their mother. A few days ago, when he was still young and foolish, he had thought that he'd win their love and respect. But what did that get his father? No matter what the Lord Regent did, Àlùfáà-Àgbà all but spat in his face every time he spoke. Tofa finally saw their spats as they were: a defiance and ridicule of the crown. Something he would not accept from anyone in his kingdom. He would show no weakness.

He dismissed the maidens and Ìyá-Ayé rose to her feet, a wry smile on her face. Tofa didn't know what she was up to but no one in the kingdom was more cunning, more ruthless or had as many lives as Ìyá-Ayé and all the mother maidens who came before her.

Ìyá-Ayé straightened finally and said, 'If I had known that all it would take for you to see that you are king was putting a knife in your sister, I would've done it myself.'

'You had something to do with this. You reported Kẹni's friend, didn't you? You knew how much she loved that girl and would want to protect her. You forced her hand.'

'I did what I had to, for my kingdom, your kingdom. We are on the brink of collapse, infiltrated by the enemy, the girl from the north is claiming your throne and you were spending your days doing what? Nothing. Waiting for the crown to come to you. We do not have that kind of time. Nor do we have the time to wait until you realize what it means to be king. Something had to wake you up. If I didn't make you see what it was that you were giving up so easily –'

'And hurting my sister was the only way to get my attention?' Tofa shouted.

'My king, did it not work? Even with all your power as crown heir, you couldn't save the girl from the law. I knew Kẹni would beg your father for mercy and when he said no, she would turn to you, and you would know what it meant to be without power. Now imagine if this L'ọrẹ takes the throne from you. You'll have nothing. You'll lose even –'

'How did you do it?' Tofa said, cutting her off.

'Kẹhìndé made it easy. Too easy. Making friends was already against the rules of her life sentence. Then she befriended a child of Ìlú-Idán. All I had to do was wait to catch her in the act. Scions of the old gods can't help themselves but tap into old magic.'

'I could kill you here and now.' Tofa ignited his agbára and the room flooded with heat.

'You could kill me, or you could ask for whatever brought you across the river,' Ìyá-Ayé said, stepping back, and Tofa welcomed the fleeting spark of fear that flashed across her face. 'I'm the reason she's alive. I saved her. Despite the fact she broke the rules when she lunged at you with her agbára. It doesn't matter whether she'd have hurt you or not. The law is the law and she broke it.'

'She would never have hurt me!' Tofa shouted and flared his agbára.

Ìyá-Ayé fell to her knees again, 'Your sister will wake up, my king. I will make sure of it.'

Tofa withdrew his agbára and the room cooled quickly.

'I want to find this L'ọrẹ. She will not claim what is mine.'

Ìyá-Ayé tried to stand but Tofa said, 'Stay there.'

She knelt back down and said, 'I can get you to my maiden, and she will lead you to the girl. Find her and kill her.'

'This is what you wanted,' Tofa said. 'What you and Àlùfáà-Àgbà have always wanted. Blood on my hands. The blood of my blood, spilt by my hands.'

'Àlùfáà-Àgbà tried to tell you, but you wouldn't listen. Everything I have done, including the trial of Kẹni's friend, I did to show you the truth. Only the one wearing the crown has the power to do and undo, and you were letting your

465

claim to the throne slip through your hands by refusing to hunt down this child of Òtútù.'

'That's what you want me to become? A hunter and a killer?'

'I want you to become the king you were meant to be.'

Tofa eyed the woman before him. Was she really expecting him to be grateful? She'd ruined his life. She'd ruined him. He could feel himself spiralling and brought his thoughts back to focus. 'Tell me about Mọremí of Òtútù,' he said in the most even tone he could manage.

'As you wish,' Ìyá-Ayé said, and began the tale of the servant girl who snuck into the temple pretending to be one of the mages of old magic from Ìlú-Idán teaching the priests the ways of the old gods. A series of unfortunate events later, a child was born, and the servant girl was killed and a reckless decision by Àlùfáà-Àgbà not to find the child she bore led them to where they are now. Tofa listened carefully.

'Your maiden, Milúà,' Tofa said, 'how do I get to her?'

Ìyá-Ayé pulled out a set of obsidian beads from her breasts. 'I'm sure Àlùfáà-Àgbà taught you how to use time beads with old magic. You can cross all six rings in a single day but remember that with every sleeping moment you will walk back the real distance you've skipped past. I recommend very little sleep until your mission is complete. The last message I got from Milúà, she had clashed with Command, whom your father sent to retrieve the girl. They are in the fourth ring.'

Tofa took the beads and slid them onto his wrists. 'You were expecting me. You knew I'd come here. How?'

'You are a wise man. You know where the real power is.'

'When I get back, we have much to discuss.'

'As you wish, my king.'

'One more thing,' Tofa said. 'Go to Kẹni, and pray to the gods known and unknown that your fire heals her and she

466

wakes. Because if she doesn't, I promise you in the name of all that burns, I will destroy this house, and every maiden who ever stepped foot in it. As the words have left my mouth.'

'So let it be done, my king,' Ìyá-Ayé said, giving one final bow to him, then she walked over to a large box by the foot of her throne and brought out a map. She spoke in the old tongue and blew on it. A bright line appeared and she handed it to Tofa. 'This will take you to Milúà. It'll burn out when you reach her.'

Tofa had woken up unsure of his place in the world, unable to recognize his own reflection. Now, he was sure that he would not rest until he had destroyed anything and everything in his path that tried to take his birthright from him. He snatched the map from Ìyá-Ayé's hands and walked out into the world, to hunt his blood, his sister, his enemy.

Tofa had seen ten first suns when he had his first taste of palm wine. The sweet milky liquid went down with ease and he keenly remembered the feeling of going home in a drunken stupor, the world around him slow and fast at the same time. That was what using the obsidian beads to quicken his steps felt like but without the throbbing headache. With every step he took, the world seemed to pass by him in a quick haze; the houses, streets and people blew past him, and in blurs. He wondered how they perceived his movement, if they could see him speed through or if they couldn't see him at all. All he knew for sure was that after four light beads of walking the King's Road north, he found himself at the border wall of the fourth ring.

A warm glow snaked across the map Ìyá-Ayé had given him, and he followed its trail until he reached a clearing surrounded by rocks about a mile or two out from the border wall leading into the fifth ring. There on the ground, hunched over a crystallized body, was Milúà, maiden of the Holy Order. As Ìyá-Ayé had said, the map burned to ash the moment he laid eyes on her. Milúà didn't seem to notice him as he walked nearer to her. Her long braids fell loose around her face, accentuating her long features and sharp chin. This couldn't be the fearless maiden he'd heard so much about. Her reputation had well preceded her but this wasn't what he'd expected to find. Her armour was scathed, and charred, her white dress torn and burnt, her body scraped and blood-ied. But even with scrapes and cuts and a wound across her forehead, Tofa had never seen anyone more beautiful than the maiden before him and he suddenly became keenly aware of his own heartbeat. Something about the way her shoul-ders hunched over in despair when he found her made him want to hold her in his arms.

'Milúà,' he said softly.

Milúà jumped to her feet and turned her back to him. She moved her hands over her face and he assumed she was wiping tears she didn't want him to see.

'Crown Heir,' Milúà said firmly. 'What are you doing here?'

'Turn around,' Tofa said, and flinched at the commanding tone in his own voice.

Milúà stood straighter and turned in a single move.

Tofa looked down at the body on the floor, completely covered in a thick layer of crystallized ice. 'Who was this?' he asked.

'Command,' Milúà said. 'Commander Títí, leader of the –'

'I know who she is,' Tofa said, eyes wide. 'Who did this?'

'L'orẹ. The one who attacked the temple and stole the Prince Àlùfáà.'

'My father told me that Command trained her for Ogun. That was why he sent her to retrieve the girl in exchange for her life. Was he wrong?'

468

'I suppose this is how L'ọrẹ repaid her.'

'Where is this L'ọrẹ now?' Tofa asked.

Milúà pointed towards the border wall, 'She'll have crossed over to the fifth ring by now.'

'And why didn't you follow her in there?' Tofa said.

Milúà glanced down at Command's frozen body, and then back at Tofa. 'She trapped me with her dark magic and by the time I summoned the strength to break out, she was gone.'

Tofa watched as her face morphed from sadness to something else, more like the maiden he'd actually heard about. She spun and packed her hair into a tight bun. She whistled and the ground began to shake, and out from behind the rocks, a battle rhino came crashing in.

'I know how to find her,' Milúà said as the rhino came to a halt in front of them. She pulled out a set of fresh clothes from the bags attached to it. Without looking back at him, she pulled off her armour and undressed completely. Tofa turned around, clearing his throat. Milúà didn't say a word. He glanced back and saw her wearing a fresh set of robes and putting her charred armour back over it. She wiped her hands clean of blood and climbed onto the rhino.

'Follow me,' she said.

'Wait, stop,' Tofa said. 'We can't just leave her here.'

'I don't care what happens to her,' Milúà said.

Tofa sighed, 'Obviously you do.'

Milúà glared at him, and just as he was about to speak, she said, 'Command knew a secret that I wanted – that I needed to know.'

'What secret?'

'She knew who my father was,' Milúà said, glaring at the body on the ground, 'and she knew who killed my mother. Or at least I think she did.'

Milúà's words triggered Tofa's memory, and he remembered

overhearing Ìyá-Ayé and Àlùfáà-Àgbà whispering in the palace. Milúà was the daughter of Àdùnní the temple maiden. The one Ìyá-Ayé had promised to kill the moment she discovered who her father was. Tofa might not know who her father was but he remembered clearly as Ìyá-Ayé confessed to killing her mother and the deal the mother of maidens had made with Àlùfáà-Àgbà. Tofa was certain that if Milúà discovered the answers to those questions, either or both would get her killed. Tofa couldn't explain why he felt protective of this maiden he'd only just met but he immediately decided that he would never tell her what he knew about her parents.

'Tell me everything Command said. Tell me her àṣírí,' Tofa ordered.

Milúà nodded and stretched her hand to him. He raised his hand to hers, and she pulled him up onto the rhino. He held on to her waist as she kicked the rhino's side, and they began the hunt for L'ọrẹ of Òtútù as she spoke the commander's last words to him.

*Long before the day of the First Sun,
there was a prophecy.
The Elder Priests had said that one day, an evil
would invade the continent
and only those favoured by the gods would survive.
For centuries, this prophecy haunted the continent,
unsure of when their end would come.
The people fought and scavenged, waiting for the
darkness to come.
So when the Aláàfin and his priest
discovered agbára oru
it was an answer to a prayer that had gone unanswered
for many generations.
How could they have said no?*

36

Ìlú-Oníṣọ̀nà, Fifth Ring, Kingdom of Oru

L'ỌRẸ

L'ọrẹ's day had started in Ìyá-Idán's house, on the bed her mother had slept in, and in less than a day, she'd lost her refuge, been captured, taken a life and now at just a few light beads past midnight she was sleep-deprived and exhausted, dragging herself towards the sixth ring. L'ọrẹ's pulse raced as her heart hammered in her chest, driving her mad with fear. Her agbára prickled beneath her skin, threatening to burst as she grew even more anxious. Never again. Never again would she use her agbára. Whatever she thought she knew about it was a lie. It was nothing more than a curse, her mother's cruel gift to her. She felt a deep, aching shame in her heart, the sound of its throbbing reverberating in her chest. If the gods had ever favoured her, she'd have begged them to take the curse from her, but the gods had no ears, not for her.

The further they went into Ìlú-Oníṣọ̀nà, the darker and thicker the air got. Every attempt to breathe was a struggle; L'ọrẹ's lungs burned as she worked to fill them. Hoods up, scarves tied over their faces, and heads down. Those were Márùn's instructions as they followed her lead through the town. L'ọrẹ was grateful for the cloaks, which helped hide her tears from Alawani, who held on firmly to her hand. She'd killed Command. It was an accident. She knew that. And she wanted to tell him as much, but every time she pulled him back to speak to him, the words wouldn't come. *I killed Command.* The unspoken words tasted bitter in her mouth. Worse still, how could she tell him about Command's àsírí? How would she say she found out that his father was murdered? She'd have to explain everything that happened with their commander, and he'd never trust her again, at least not while agbára òtútù plagued her soul. For the first time in her life, L'ọrẹ was comforted by the night's darkness that cloaked them. The dusty haze they trod through would make it harder for anyone to find them. So even if Milúà was on their tail, she'd have difficulty finding them. And L'ọrẹ never wanted to see that maiden ever again.

As the moon's light struggled to break through, they ran into a small town with fewer giant clusters of buildings and more familiar bungalows forming rows of streets in all directions. They ran towards the buzzing noise in the distance and entered what seemed to be a sort of marketplace. Loud voices laughed and haggled over everything from roasted plantains to peppered goat meat to pottery and grains. The market had traders and blacksmiths alike. It felt like the midday market in the capital but all of this was in the dark of night. The people seemed more alive, although they all wore the same washed-out clothes and threadbare materials as the ones they'd seen closer to the border.

'Why is there a night market?' L'ọrẹ asked.

'People here spend daylight working for the overlords, so everything happens at night. Their day has just begun.'

'Overlords?' L'ọrẹ said, looking from Márùn to Alawani.

'I don't think this is the time for this,' Alawani said quietly.

'Those monstrous buildings you saw closer to the borders

were prison houses,' Márùn said. 'The fifth ring has hundreds of those all around the state from north to south. Each ward has an overlord.'

'Why so many? Who's in there?' L'ọrẹ asked, and noticed the glance between Márùn and Alawani. Again.

'Everyone and anyone. From those who dabbled in old magic to those who defy the crown or the Holy Order to those who can't pay their taxes or debt. Everyone sent here from any ring in the kingdom is serving a life sentence. They go in as people and return as dust.'

L'ọrẹ's eyes bulged in disbelief.

'How come you don't know this?'

'I'd never – never crossed the border of Ìlú-Ìmọ̀ before,' L'ọrẹ said, defending herself.

'Even then, don't you read? It is written.'

L'ọrẹ had read. Or at least she thought she'd read all there was to know about the kingdom of Oru, but every moment she spent outside of Baba-Ìtàn's library proved that reality differed greatly from the books back there.

'You didn't tell me about this,' L'ọrẹ said to Alawani, who had been to all ends of the kingdom on his adventures.

'There was no point,' he said plainly. 'It's just more people my father promised to help and didn't.'

'Don't they try to escape?' L'ọrẹ turned to Márùn.

Márùn snickered. 'Where would they go? They're trapped between the magic border of Ìlú-Idán that we just passed through and the heavily secured walls of Ìlú-Òdì, where we're headed.' Márùn pointed behind them in the direction of the wall they had come from. 'That wall has only two gates, and they are on the King's Road – one on this side and the other on the south side. As you experienced coming in, old magic protects that wall, and it's monitored by the Holy Order. Only those who know the words and the way can pass through.' She sighed. 'If that wall ever falls, it'll spit out the bodies that tried to cross and got lost in its stones. There's nowhere to run, so no one does.'

L'orẹ's life back in Ìlú-Ìmọ̀ suddenly seemed less brutal. At least she hadn't had to work for overlords till her bones dropped. Back home, if she stayed indoors protected by books and a father who loved her, she could always pretend that all was well in the world. Once, she thought she had the worst fate in all of Oru. Now, looking at these people hunched over from hard labour, she knew she was wrong.

Márùn pulled L'orẹ along as she slowed. 'This way, we need to get some food.'

'No, we can't stop,' L'orẹ said.

'Let me give you some advice. When you're on the run and you see food, eat it. You don't know when next you'll get a meal. And we don't know what army Milúà is bringing with her. I don't think the Holy Order is going for stealth anymore,' Márùn said.

'She's right,' Alawani added.

L'orẹ nodded and kept running alongside her. Everything was a blur in L'orẹ's mind. She couldn't tell what parts were real and which were nightmares she conjured in her head. She was moving and speaking, but it was like she was outside herself. Command's face kept flashing in her mind, and L'orẹ knew that face would haunt her for the rest of her life.

Márùn stopped a few times to buy food from different sellers. She returned with mounds of bread and balls of àkàrà – golden fritters made from blended beans, wrapped in paper from torn books. For their reserves Márùn got roasted yams which would last many days before going bad. They ate as they walked, not deviating from their mission.

L'orẹ grimaced at the oil-soaked sheets wrapping the food. She knew just how much work was done to get that single sheet from plant to book, and here it was, soaking in fried oil and serving as a plate. Baba-Ìtàn would be horrified.

Márùn led them to a small house at the end of a dark street. 'Wait here,' she said to them as she entered the clay roundhouse with a woven raffia mat at its entrance in place of a door.

'Hurry,' L'ọrẹ whispered as they watched her disappear into the darkness.

All around them were large clay huts and houses separated at even distances from each other. More than L'ọrẹ had ever seen in a single location. The fifth ring clearly saw very little of the kingdom's wealth. She wrapped herself in her cloak as the desert cold seeped into her bones. Peering into the house, she saw nothing but flickers of candlelight. Her fingers rubbed against the obsidian beads Ìyá-Idán had given her, and she wondered if she could still go back for Baba-Ìtàn and Kọ̀yà. She'd been more confident when all the Holy Order wanted from her was her agbára. She'd had something to bargain with. But now, with everyone thinking she'd magically transformed from the coward's daughter into the heir to the throne, L'ọrẹ knew if she went back, she'd never get out.

'Do you think we'll make it out?' L'ọrẹ said quietly.

'We will. I promise,' Alawani said, meeting her gaze. He placed a kiss on her forehead and she melted into his arms. 'Do you still have the hourglass?'

L'ọrẹ nodded and showed it to him.

'The storm will be here in a few light beads,' Alawani said, bringing the hourglass close to his eyeline. 'Definitely before sunset tomorrow.'

They heard raised voices and although L'ọrẹ couldn't hear what they were arguing about, she heard Márùn's voice and a word – Mẹ́sàn. Mẹ́sàn meant nine. Was this another member of their group? L'ọrẹ didn't understand how this group worked and it unnerved her.

The soft hum of the market they'd passed by still buzzed in the air. Suddenly the voices turned to screams and shouts. Márùn ran out of the house and then quickly disappeared behind it, returning with two horses.

'Climb. Now!' Márùn commanded.

A man came out shouting, 'The crown will have your head for this, Márùn!'

In the direction of the market, blasts of explosions lit the night sky as the screams intensified, and L'ọrẹ knew in her guts that Milúà was coming for them. They rode their horses fast and hard towards the base of the border wall leading into the sixth ring. A light bead later, they came to a stop about a mile away from the King's Road entrance.

'Here's the plan,' Márùn said. 'Ìlú-Òdì is a military stronghold. This ring is unlike any other in the kingdom. This wall is the only one big enough to be a garrison in itself and it has ten times more battlement stations built into the wall than others. Now is your best chance to get in. Just before first light, when the soldiers on night shift will be a little extra tired and less vigilant. More than half the population are soldiers, so once you're in, prioritize stealing armour or anything to help you blend in. All you have to do is get past this wall and make it all the way to the Lord General's keep that leads into the graveyard. If you get in there just as the storm picks up, the guards will have gone underground, and you can cross without being shot to death. You still have Ìyá-Idán's hourglass, right?'

L'ọrẹ nodded.

'I've spent a few blood moons in there with the Lord General,' Alawani said. 'I can get us in. I trained with him many first suns ago.'

477

'Perfect. Then you should know your way around,' Márùn said.

'Are you not coming with us?' L'ọrẹ asked, panic rising in her chest.

'I need you to listen first,' Márùn said as she unwrapped a package strapped to her horse. 'Alawani, make sure no one recognizes you. Moving through the ring should be easy with these cloaks. Blend in as much as you can, keep your head down. You already have a head start, so stick to the plan.'

'The Lord General's keep is at least two miles long. It's the longest castle in Oru, crawling with soldiers. There's a reason it leads out into the graveyard,' Alawani said.

Márùn turned to him, 'Yes, but the sandstorm will get bad enough to make the Lord General and the majority of his soldiers leave the fortress when the winds pick up. Last time I was there, the storms had destroyed huge portions of the forward-facing side.'

L'ọrẹ held up Baba-Ìtàn's map as Alawani and Márùn bounced ideas off each other.

'Here,' Márùn said, illuminating the map with her agbára and pointing at the line indicating the fifth ring. She slowly moved her finger through in a winding motion. 'On the other side of this wall is the soldiers' keep. It's not as big as the Lord General's, and so there's a way here leading into the servants' quarter.'

Alawani nodded, pointing at another spot within the sixth ring, 'This will be less guarded. This way, we can avoid the training grounds altogether.'

Márùn nodded in agreement, pulled the map closer to her face, and pointed at a curved line at the far end of the kingdom. 'There's no way to go around the Lord General's keep without losing half a day, but if you can cut through, you only need to hide out in the stables.'

478

Alawani shook his head, 'Stables will have guards, we can't risk being recognized. We can hide out in the kitchens.'

'Fine,' Márùn said, 'just be close enough to get out when the time comes.'

Alawani nodded and pointed at a spot a few fingers from where Márùn had indicated, 'We don't have to go all the way around. If we go slightly east and avoid the mid towers, we can still access the graveyard without risking the Lord General's battalion.'

'Good,' Márùn said and turned to L'ọrẹ. 'The graveyard is a mile long, the ground is hard and the air even worse. Stay close to him, and don't get killed. The graveyard is dangerous because there's nowhere to hide while crossing it. And the guards have the standing order to shoot on sight anyone who approaches the last wall without permission. But when the storm starts, they hide within the walls, some even going underground. So as long as you cross that path before the storm becomes deadly and eats you alive, you'll be out of the kingdom without anyone even seeing you. After that you'll have to find your own way north – I have no idea what's outside those walls.'

'And where will you be in all of this?' L'ọrẹ asked.

'I'll be right back,' Márùn said, walking away from them. 'I just need to find the way up. It's here somewhere.'

The night was so dark that in a few paces, she was out of sight.

'Is she gone? Márùn?' Alawani called out.

'I think she'll be back,' L'ọrẹ said, 'I guess if only for the life debt that has her following you.'

Alawani held on tight to L'ọrẹ's hands, looking around the darkness. 'I don't like this.'

'Alawani,' L'ọrẹ said in a soft voice, terrified of his response to her next words. She wanted to blurt out everything about

479

Command – they had promised each other, no more secrets – and standing so close to freedom made the guilt eating at her so intense she had to say something. He smiled at her softly, and her heart warmed at his touch and that was all it took for her to lose her resolve. She couldn't ruin this. Not now. Not when they were so close to freedom.

After a moment, she pulled out the other half of the map Baba-Ìtàn gave her and spread it open. Alawani's agbára lit a soft glow over it. The map to freedom. She wasn't free as long as her father remained in those dungeons, but she'd lost this battle with the Holy Order.

'It's just sand for miles out there,' Alawani said. 'We could get lost trying to find our way.'

L'ọrẹ shook her head. 'We'll use the stars to travel at night and rest in the caves in the heat of the day. Or at least that was Baba-Ìtàn's plan.'

'It's not a bad plan,' Alawani conceded.

L'ọrẹ shook her head, 'No, it's not. I just wish he were here to lead us himself.'

Alawani gave her a weak smile and held her shoulders. He placed a kiss on her forehead. 'It's almost over,' he said softly. 'I'll keep you safe.'

L'ọrẹ exhaled a shaky breath. The smart thing to do was to go north and hope to find something to help her win the fight for her family. She knew she couldn't return to the temple now, but when she did, she wouldn't lose.

Márùn returned a few moments later. 'Found it,' she said, signalling them over. 'Last time I snuck into the fortress, I left this rope here. It'll take you all the way to the top of the wall.'

'Why are you leaving us?' L'ọrẹ asked.

Márùn looked from L'ọrẹ to Alawani. 'I have something to tell you, L'ọrẹ,' she said, looking at Alawani.

'Whatever you want to say, you can say it in front of him. There's no one I trust more,' she said even as her heart skipped a beat, anxious about what Márùn had to say.

'Since the days of the First Sun, the Order of the Secret Twelve has protected the firstborn of the sun. I am Márùn, Five of Twelve, and I am oath-bound to protect whoever sits on the throne of Oru. While my journey started with fulfilling my life debt to the prince's mother, I continued this journey with you because of what Ìyá-Idán revealed about you, L'ọrẹ. My duty as Márùn forces me to protect you above all else.'

'You're working for the Lord Regent?' L'ọrẹ gasped.

'No,' Márùn said sternly. 'The Twelve have never served a regent. We serve only the sovereign. We exist outside of the court and its laws and we remain secret, revealing ourselves only to the true heir. We served the late king and everyone who wore the gilded crown before him.'

'I don't understand,' L'ọrẹ said. 'Ìyá-Idán is a part of this?'

Márùn nodded. 'She is Méje – Seven of Twelve. We live in pairs in each ring of the kingdom.'

'I don't want anyone oath-bound to me,' L'ọrẹ said. 'I don't want anyone dying for me or because of me. I can't take it. I can't lose anyone else. I don't want any of this, please.'

'I'm afraid that's not a choice,' Márùn said. 'We are as we always have been. When I die, another Márùn will take my place and so it will continue until the end of time.'

'I have never heard of this order before,' Alawani said.

'And you never would have,' Márùn said.

'We won't tell anyone,' L'ọrẹ said.

'Good,' Márùn replied. 'You don't need me here. Alawani knows his way around. Send me to the temple, and I will get your father and friend to a safe place. But I am yours to command, so I will do only as you ask.'

L'ọrẹ placed a hand on her chest, tearing up, 'You would do that for me?'

'My oath is to the crown, to the firstborn of Oru. To you.' Márùn smiled. 'Right now, most of the Twelve are still devoted to the crown heir. I'll do my best to convince the others of your true claim but if tonight with Mẹ̀sàn was anything to go by, it won't be easy. I need you to be far away from here where they can't kill you until we have a plan to bring you back to take your throne. I'll tell you what my father once told me. When you have a weapon, use it before your enemy learns how to take it from you. I am here, I am your blade, use me.'

L'ọrẹ felt her knees go weak and she could have fallen to the ground in gratitude.

'I should remind you that I've kept you safe since we met, and I can take care of myself,' Márùn said. 'I'm not risking much. This is not a hard mission for me, I promise. Mẹ́fà will go with me. You may remember him from the inn when he tried choking you all to death? He's my partner. And we've survived worse odds.'

L'ọrẹ hugged Márùn. Tears choked her words, so she just held on tightly, sobbing into her arms.

'Thank you,' Alawani said softly.

Márùn nodded in response. 'I need you to release me from your mother's bond. Otherwise, I can't leave you.'

'I don't know how to work the magic that'll remove the mark but as far as I'm concerned, you've already saved my life. So please go. Save them. I can get L'ọrẹ out of Oru. I release you from the bond formed with the blood of my blood.'

'Are there members of the Twelve that'll help us in the sixth ring?' L'ọrẹ asked.

'No. Captain Méjìlá is Twelve of Twelve. He is the Lord

General's right hand, loyal to the crown heir, and he will never accept your claim. And no one has seen his partner, Mọ́kànlá, in too many first suns to count,' Márùn said firmly.

A dot of sunlight cracked through the sky.

'Start climbing,' Márùn said, straddling her horse. 'May your heart burn like the sun, bright, hot, and undying, Queen of Oru.'

Then she was gone.

L'ọrẹ reached the top first. She climbed onto the roof and realized that it was so vast that calling what they had climbed a wall felt too insignificant. Behind her, she heard the rope slip from the hook it was tied to and rushed to stop it from falling. She held on with all her might. 'Alawani, climb faster! I can't hold on.'

She strained as the rope burned her palms, slipping further down.

'L'ọrẹ!' Alawani shouted from below. 'L'ọrẹ!'

L'ọrẹ bent over and reached for him. 'Closer, Alawani, I can't reach you. Grab my hand!'

The last of the rope slipped from her hands, and she felt the world slow around her. In the time it took her heart to beat once she saw him falling into oblivion, the darkness consuming him.

'L'ọrẹ, help me up!' Alawani shouted, pulling her back to consciousness. Hanging off the side of the wall, he groaned as he struggled to hold on. Her ears rang with blood, and her entire body strained against Alawani's weight as she tried to lift his body over the wall. She could feel his weak grip as he held on to her with one hand. The stripping he endured was causing him to lose more and more of his strength with every passing day. Her hands were slick with sweat, and he was slipping again. She leaned over the wall, inching closer to her fall as she tried to pull him in.

'L'ọrẹ, let me go!' Alawani said. 'You're going to fall over!'

'No!' L'ọrẹ shouted, gasping as her body started to spasm as she struggled to keep her feet grounded. 'I can do it. Come on, climb!' She couldn't hold him. She couldn't pull him in. She was falling. He was falling. They would die.

Suddenly, someone ran to join her on the wall top. She hadn't even heard the footsteps. The stranger leaned over and helped her pull Alawani onto the battlement. They all fell flat on the floor, heaving and gasping for air. L'ọrẹ crawled over to Alawani, who was hunched over, holding his arms. She froze as the sharp edge of a blade dug into her side.

'Turn around. Slowly,' said the stranger.

The man wore a uniform different from any L'ọrẹ had seen before. The black leather outfit was layered, making it look like it had serpent scales etched into its design. He wore a squared helm with a rounded face guard reaching just below the eyes, with two openings for his brown eyes.

L'ọrẹ held her hands up in surrender as the soldier now pressed the knife to her neck. Alawani stood next to her holding his hands up as well.

'Please, we mean no harm,' L'ọrẹ said softly.

'Who are you?' the soldier asked in a baritone voice.

By this time, dawn had broken, and it was significantly lighter on the wall top, and with that came sounds of chatter from the levels below.

'We are just trying to get out of the kingdom,' Alawani said, hands still up. 'Let us go and you'll never see us again.'

The soldier scoffed, 'There's no getting out of Oru without permission. The graveyard will be your resting place if you dare to try.' But despite his words, his expression was curious.

'Then it doesn't matter if you let us go,' L'ọrẹ said.

'You won't be able to get out,' the soldier said flatly.

'We have a plan,' L'ọrẹ said. 'No one has to know you let us go.'

The soldier tossed a pair of handcuffs to Alawani, continuing to hold a knife to L'ọrẹ's throat. 'Put those on. And don't try to escape; the old magic in these cuffs will turn your agbára against you and you will burn.'

As a second pair of cuffs closed around L'ọrẹ's wrists and the guard manoeuvred them both towards a set of stairs, she realized their journey was far from over.

As agbára oru flooded the hearts and
cores of the people
their hands glowed bright like the sun
and without having to speak the old tongue
they had the powers of the sun at their fingertips.
The celebrations on the day of the First Sun
lasted an entire blood moon,
for whatever darkness loomed beyond the ocean
the light of agbára would extinguish.

37

Ìlú-Òdì, Sixth Ring, Kingdom of Oru

TOFA

Tofa felt his energy draining away with each light bead that passed. He and the maiden had only been riding for half a day but he hadn't had a moment's peace or a good night's sleep since he left home. Every night, walking back the steps he stole from time. He was sleep-deprived and exhausted and had to grip on tight to Milúà as she held the rhino's reins and raced down the King's Road towards Ìlú-Òdì – the sixth ring of Oru.

Tofa hadn't yet decided what he'd do when he found L'ọrẹ. Seeing what L'ọrẹ had done to her commander only made him warier of this agbára òtútù and what it meant for his kingdom if he let it fester.

The border wall leading into the sixth ring was higher and thicker than all the others within the rings of Oru. It loomed high over them as they approached, each square tower like a spike decorating the wall top. An enormous gate with heavy metal doors, a drawbridge and strong defences was the only way in on the north side of the kingdom. The south side would have a similar single entrance.

As they approached the main gate, Milúà sped up the rhino's pace and screamed at the guards, 'Make way for your king!' They obeyed her command and quickly made a path for them.

Tofa watched her order soldiers that weren't under her command. She was a force of nature. Her gaze was so intense it was as if nothing else existed. Nothing and no one could stop her from finding her prince Àlùfáà. He wondered if it was more than duty that fuelled her anger and zest. It was always a thin line between love and loyalty with maidens and their priests. He knew that much from the relationship between his mother, father and his father's maiden. Looking at Milúà's rage now, he wondered how she lost her charge in the first place. Now that he'd met her, he wondered if she knew what the mother of maidens had planned for her.

As they entered the quad in the barracks, a squad of soldiers blocked Milúà from walking further in, forming an arc a few paces in front of the rhino.

'Let us through,' Tofa commanded.

'Hold!' a voice called out.

The imposing figure of the Lord General loomed over his troops, his broad shoulders draped in chain mail and his visage obscured by a blood-red helm adorned with a sun crest. As he strode through the ranks, his polished armour clanging and his sword slung at his hip, the soldiers fell silent, their eyes fixed on their leader.

The Lord General spoke in a voice that carried across the fortress, his words dripping with cold, unyielding authority, 'The gods have smiled upon us today, bringing our very own crown heir to us.' He turned to the soldiers. 'Men, today we feast!'

Tofa recoiled at the sound of the Lord General's voice. This was the man who trained every member of the royal family. The man Kẹni had spent a few first suns training under and returned from a shell of herself. Tofa had hoped

488

he wouldn't have to hear the old man's croaking voice for a long time. It had been only six blood moons since he finished his final training at Ìlú-Òdì, and he had sworn not to return until the man was dead.

Tofa climbed off the rhino. 'We're on a hunt. We don't have time for feasts.'

'Ah yes, the elusive prince and the mysterious girl. We've heard the rumours.' The Lord General looked around. 'You have journeyed far and fast. I'm afraid they must be behind you, Crown Heir.'

Tofa glared at the man. He could almost hear his father's words, reminding him that if a king ever needed to show a force of strength to gain respect, then he had already lost the kingdom. He'd always tried to live out this understanding, gaining respect through wisdom and not a reckless display of power. But as he stared at the face of this man, he wanted to hold his palm to his face and burn it off. He was the one who in the name of training sent Kẹni back home with broken bones and bruised flesh.

'We chased them through the fifth ring. People saw their group heading towards here. Everything they've done since the temple shows that they plan to leave Oru, so they have to be here,' Milúà said.

The Lord General barked, 'I suggest you calm down and listen to your elders, maiden.'

'Don't you dare tell me to calm down,' Milúà shouted.

'That's enough, both of you,' Tofa said.

Milúà closed her eyes as if calming herself and when she opened them, she flinched and covered her eyes as though something had got in them. Tofa moved to hold her but she slid out of his grip. 'What's wrong?' he whispered.

She looked up at him with strained eyes. 'They're here.'

Then the Lord General chuckled. 'As I said, Crown Heir,

you must all be tired. And clearly the journey has made your maiden . . . fragile. No one has come through these gates today. I can assure you of this. You are the first guest of Ìlú-Òdì since daybreak. Come with me, rest, wash your feet and eat good food. We have the most refreshing palm wine and the best women in all of Oru!'

The men cheered, and Tofa turned to Milúà. 'How do you know where they are? Are you tracking them somehow?'

Milúà glared at him, 'Just trust me.'

The Lord General laughed again. 'Crown Heir, what else do you expect from a maiden? They are more sly than they are warriors of any sort. Come feast with us. In the morning, we'll gather my best hunters. The prince cannot escape my clutches. I trained him, after all, and I can tell you now, he's as weak as they come.'

Tofa could tell that Milúà was hiding something, but if she wasn't going to tell him, there was nothing he could do but rely on his trained soldiers to do their job. He nodded, resigned.

'Fine. I'll find them myself,' Milúà said and reached for the reins on her rhino.

'Stop,' Tofa said. 'That's an order.'

Milúà froze, and he saw flecks of gold spark in her eyes. If he were not to be king, he knew he'd already be ash. Still, she obeyed his command, allowing the men to lead her towards the Lord General's keep. As its name implied, Ìlú-Òdì was the stronghold of the kingdom, formed of castle-like fortresses for the army garrison, massive estates for high-ranking army officials, and slums for those who didn't fit into either category. At the edge of the city, the Lord General had built a banquet hall rivalling the royal palace in his mile-long fortress that overlooked the graveyard. Thousands of soldiers lived in the keep, but the first twenty blocks in the middle of the row, the highest building with the most security, were reserved for the Lord General alone.

Inside, Tofa watched as the heavily adorned girls danced in the middle of the great hall, shaking every part of their bodies. The soldiers cheered, and the girls laughed, allowing their waist beads to vibrate in rhythm with the talking drums. The hall was lit with rows of chandeliers and intricate designs from raffia and goldwork decorated the walls. The room was filled with the smell of roasted meat, plantains, yams, fish and all kinds of pies and baked dough confectionaries. The smell of fried oil and savoury spices mixed uncomfortably with the body odour of the soldiers whose voices echoed and reverberated all over the hall.

The Lord General quickly got drunk on palm wine with his right-hand man, Captain Méjìlá, and Tofa could hardly hear himself think over the sound of their laughter.

He noticed Milúà's clenched jaw and knew she was still upset, sending scathing looks to the dancers and the men that cheered them on. After a few moments, she got up and bowed next to him. Her face nearly touched his. 'This is a waste of time. I have a mission to complete, and I need you to believe me when I tell you that I can find the prince and the girl. And I know they're here.'

'How?'

'Does it matter? Would you rather stay here in this filth?'

Tofa's eyes swept across the room, taking in the noise and the smell of sweat in the air. 'They could be anywhere in this state. There are thousands of people here. It'll be easier for them to hide. We need a more strategic approach than just searching the streets hoping to bump into them. The Lord General knows this ring, it's his domain. With him and his hounds tomorrow, we'll find them before sunset.'

'They can't hide from me,' she said with poison in her voice. 'They are harder to trace in this state. Every soldier is powerful, and the threads blur into each other. But I'll find her. Just trust me.'

Tofa saw a flicker of gold in her eyes, and at that moment, he realized why maidens weren't to be touched and why crowds parted for them. Her eyes looked like they were on fire and would scorch anyone who looked into them for too long. He blinked, nodded, and followed her.

'That's right, my king, show the maidens what they are missing!' the Lord General called after them.

Tofa ignored the drunk man, glad Milúà wasn't close enough to hear his remarks, or he'd have spent the night putting out fires.

Suddenly Tofa turned, only to see Milúà's spear flying right past him, sinking its sharp end deep into the Lord General's chair. The man jumped up and roared at her. He shook his hands, and a light, golden glow soon accompanied the gentle hum of energy buzzing around him. Milúà did the same, and the battle line was drawn. Tofa knew this couldn't end well, but he was willing to see what the warrior maiden was made of. It had taken him weeks before he won his first battle against the general.

Captain Méjìlá whispered in his ear, 'My Crown, you cannot allow this.'

Tofa looked at Captain Méjìlá, his personal guard in Ìlú-Òdì. 'Why do I have to? The Lord General deserves this humiliation.' He turned to see the pair fighting in the circle created for them, men all around them, cheering for their general, who was not winning. He couldn't help but smile at Milúà when she looked up, eyes filled with rage that seemed familiar to him. The soldiers had formed a fighting ring around them, and it was too late for either of them to back out. With a nod of encouragement from him, she sent the Lord General sprawling onto his back.

Captain Méjìlá urged, 'My Crown, in a few blood moons, these men will swear loyalty to you as king. Don't make enemies of the men who protect your kingdom. You may be their king, but that man is their god.'

Tofa sighed and shouted, 'Enough!'

His voice reverberated through the hall, bouncing off the walls and echoing in the rafters. Everyone froze. The cheering died out in an instant. He heard only the heavy panting of the two fighters. Tofa walked towards them, and the circle broke, allowing him to pass through. He walked over to the Lord General's body sprawled on the floor and went to Milúà. Blood poured from her lips, and there was a deep cut across her temple where the Lord General had smashed his head into hers.

He held her face, and she let her head fall into his palm. She looked exhausted, her face swollen and bruised, but she had won the fight. He yielded and she was the last one standing.

'The party is over. Shut this down. Shut it all down,' he said as he scooped Milúà into his arms and carried her out of the hall.

MILÚÀ

Milúà woke up the next day with a terrible headache. For the first few moments, she struggled to keep her eyes open. Then she turned to see Tofa sleeping on a mat a few feet from her bed, and she jumped at the sight of him.

He woke up startled and quickly rose to his feet, his eyes still heavy with sleep. Milúà raised the sheets to cover herself.

'You are not naked, maiden,' Tofa said, smiling and rubbing his eyes.

Milúà looked down, observing her body for the first time. He was right. She was still in her warrior's outfit. Only her armour had been removed. But the sheer material still made her feel naked as she sat before him, and she held on to the sheets even tighter.

'Why are you in my room?' she scowled.

'I'm not. You are in my room,' Tofa replied.

'Why am I in your bed?' she frowned.

'You passed out from the pain last night, maiden. You picked a fight with the Lord General in his house and won. It wasn't safe for you to be alone.'

'He wouldn't dare,' Milúà muttered, annoyed. Frowning made her head hurt even more as her skin pulled on the cut across her temple.

'Come, let me help –' Tofa said, but stopped when Milúà moved back from him.

He let out a long, weary sigh. 'I'll send the servants in to help you clean up. We must find L'ọrẹ and Alawani today,' he said as he headed for the door.

'Thank you,' Milúà blurted out. While she hadn't needed his help, he was still the crown heir, so when he turned to face her, she let the sheets in her hand drop and bowed to him.

He frowned and nodded and walked out of the room. She couldn't understand him. He walked and talked like a king. He knew what he was and who he was. She lay back in the bed, and as she closed her eyes, she could remember glimpses of the night before. The feel of his breath on her face when he cleaned the blood from her wound with water and herbs. Falling and thinking she'd hit the ground but landing in his arms, comforted by the solid build that held her up. She remembered the odd feeling of safety as he held her

494

close and sang to her, stroking her hair. That was when she'd drifted off. He'd sung to her. *What was his problem?* Her frown deepened, and she lifted her gaze when a servant entered the room. Before the girl could speak, Milúà shouted, 'Get out! I can clean myself.'

Milúà slumped in the bed and covered her face with her palms. Frustration made her head boil. She shouldn't be here. This hunt would have been over days ago if Ìyá-Ayé hadn't sent a message demanding that the Lord Regent wanted L'ọrẹ alive. She'd spent so much time tracking them, finding them and losing them because she couldn't just burn them all to ash. Her mission had been a failure from the start. She should never have taken her eyes off Alawani. It was her fault he escaped the temple.

Images of Command flashed in her mind, and she remembered every word the woman had said. She'd implied that Àdùnní knew L'ọrẹ's mother. She'd implied that there was more to the girl from Òtútù than Milúà knew. Milúà didn't care about L'ọrẹ other than the fact that she ruined her life. And it vexed her that she was no longer allowed to kill her. People had died for less by her own hands.

Milúà rubbed at her eyes. For many centuries descendants of late kings and queens moved to the sixth ring to join the army and so with so much agbára concentrated in a single place, every time she used her true sight, she was flooded with an influx of light that nearly blinded her. Still, she knew, she could feel it in her guts. They were close. They had to be.

Just before dawn, she walked out of the fortress to meet the Lord General, Captain Méjìlá and Tofa standing together.

Turning to look at her, Tofa said, 'Milúà will lead us to them. If they are in this city, we'll find them.'

The Lord General growled at the sound of her name and stepped towards her. 'Touch her and feel the burn of the sun,' Tofa growled back, placing himself between her and the Lord General.

Milúà didn't need him fighting for her. Did he forget she was a maiden of the Holy Order? She was the weapon used to cut down enemies, not a damsel in distress. As she glared at him, she noticed for the first time how handsome the crown heir was. He stood tall in his armour. He had five chunky braids with the sides faded off in a trim cut. His face was chiselled like the gods had created their chosen one. But ultimately, too thin for a king, she thought. She'd considered him much too meek, but now she was impressed by the raw venom that laced his threat. She wanted that kind of power. She needed it.

The Lord General spat on the floor near her feet and walked away. 'Let's just get this over with.'

Milúà was lost in thought, staring at Tofa, and didn't notice the group staring back at her.

Captain Méjìlá's voice pulled her back, 'Maiden, allow me to introduce you to my ward, Rèmí,' he said, slamming a heavy slap into the man's back, smiling with pride. 'He will join the hunt.'

Milúà eyed the man she hadn't even noticed before. He stood next to Captain Méjìlá wincing at the strike. Something about how Rèmí inched away from the man reminded her of herself when she stood next to Ìyá-Ayé. Rèmí bowed to her and his locs fell to frame his face. She nodded to him and looked away. She needed no reminders of her mother today.

'What's your plan, Milúà?' Tofa asked, and the group gathered in closer.

'We're not leaving this keep,' Milúà said, moving a few steps away from him and pointing at the large stretch of building before them, the ends of which faded into the horizon on account of how long it was. On the map of Oru the Lord

General's keep was marked as a long half-crescent line in the middle of the sixth ring. 'This is the last line of defence when leaving the kingdom. This is where we wait for them. Every inch of this building is crawling with soldiers, and with us here, they are not getting past. If they manage to do that, the graveyard will do what it's been made for. I imagine that your archers are poised on the last wall ready to strike as usual?' Milúà said to the Lord General, who grunted a nod. 'Good. Have the guards here on alert. We're looking for the prince Àlùfáà and L'ọrẹ. She's about my height, and her tribal marks are three lines for Ìlú-Ìmọ̀. Last I saw her, she was wearing a clay-red ensemble. The prince Àlùfáà has the royal seal inked into his arm. They're armed and dangerous.'

Milúà clenched her jaw, fighting the pain as she awakened her true sight. The light burned her, but she kept it on, trying to sort through the tangle of threads to find the bright-est. Her eyes stung, and she squinted, forcing herself to keep them open.

'What is she doing now?' she heard the Lord General ask.

She walked away from the group. Back at Ìlú-Idán – the fourth ring – the witch's powers had blocked them from her sight. But once they were out of the woman's house, she'd quickly found them. But now, the flood of threads and light was nearly unbearable for her. Oddly, back at the fifth ring, the light of L'ọrẹ's agbára core thread was brighter than any she'd ever seen before. Even brighter than the crown heir's. It felt like she was looking at strands of pure sunlight float-ing around – just as it did now.

Milúà closed her eyes, exhaled and slowly opened them again. She was trying to follow a star amongst a sea of them. She could see the brightest one – the one she knew had to be L'ọrẹ's. But like yarn when jumbled together, the core threads of everyone else around her crisscrossed over each other,

497

distorting her true sight. Milúà still wasn't sure why L'ọrẹ's core looked like everyone else's – albeit remarkably brighter and stronger. She'd seen the girl's evil magic. It wasn't anything like agbára oru so why did her core look like others'?

Tofa joined her and placed a hand on her shoulder. She glared at it, and he slid it off. 'We need to get into position on the roof if we want to see them coming this way,' he said, avoiding her gaze.

A soldier came running to the group nearly out of breath by the time he reached them.

He greeted the crown heir first by prostrating flat on the floor, shining the light of his agbára at Tofa's feet. Then he stood and saluted Captain Méjìlá and the Lord General. It was clear by the look on his face that he had no idea how to greet a maiden.

'Speak, boy,' the Lord General said. 'What is it?'

'Scouts from the outpost, sir; they said there's a sandstorm on the horizon. Coming in quick.'

The men's eyes widened.

'Tell the men on the last wall to get inside. I want no one on the battlements,' the Lord General said, then turned to captain Méjìlá. 'Let the squad know we're relocating to the inner gate keep.'

'No!' Milúà shouted. 'We have a plan. We just discussed this.'

'Damn your plans, girl,' the Lord General said. 'I know these storms don't break through the magic barrier for the inner rings so you have no idea what it means to have your home flung into the wind with you in it, but out here, we don't play silly games when the gods are angry.' He turned to the soldier who brought the news. 'Go now!'

'Will you not stop this?' Milúà said to Tofa.

'The crown heir has lived here among us for many blood moons,' the Lord General scowled. 'He knows what it

498

means to be caught in these storms. Look at my keep,' he said, pointing at the large building. 'See how it's chipped and broken in different sections. The storms did that. With every hit, I lose more and more of my men and my home. I'm not risking any more life for this. And there's no way anyone survives the storm coming. If they try to escape, the sands will strip them to their bones.'

Milúà could see his core stirring – she could tell from how their colours changed and blended exactly what the person was planning to do. She ignited her agbára.

'We are not stopping this hunt so your men can cower and hide in the sand,' she said, glaring at him. She didn't care how strong he was or what a terrible reputation he had. Thanks to her fight with Command, she had learned how to predict agbára attacks by using her true sight to watch the core's movement. So when the Lord General's core churned again, she took a step back, recognizing the attack. The bastard was loading up an energy blast.

'Enough of this,' Tofa said. 'I'm tired of this bickering. Lord General, you may clear the guards from the last wall; I don't expect Alawani and L'ọrẹ to make it to the graveyard anyway, and if they do, let the storm take them. You may move out of this keep but leave at least a squad of men at every checkpoint between here and the inner gate keep and have your men keep up the search there as well.'

'And where will you be?' the Lord General asked.

'I'm staying here with Milúà. In case they make it this far,' Tofa said.

Milúà frowned even as her chest tightened. She'd never been in a position where someone took her side before.

The Lord General looked at her with so much anger, she was sure he'd throw that blast he'd been brewing, but instead, he sighed, frustrated, and said to Captain Méjìlá, 'Do as the crown heir has ordered. Take the men. I'll stay here with two squads.'

'You don't have to,' Tofa said. 'We'll be fine.'

'I'm staying,' the Lord General growled. 'I won't be the coward who let the future king of Oru die out in the grave-yard. The Lord Regent will end my line.'

'I'd like to help too,' Rèmí said, his voice soft in the sea of brash voices that dominated the group. 'I'll stay with the crown heir.'

Captain Méjìlá glared at him, the vein on his forehead nearly popping under the strain of his frown.

'That's fine,' Tofa said. 'You can stay. Captain Méjìlá, take the squad. Protect your people.'

The captain looked at the Lord General, who nodded in agreement, and then he walked back into the keep and out of sight.

Milúà stood to face the graveyard, feeling the wind pick up. This was it. The end of the road. Here she would get her revenge and complete her mission.

The Prince Àlùfáà was hers.

*Among those present on the day of the First Sun
were some who did not receive agbára oru,
for out of their hands came darkness like the void.
One by one, they were exposed, separated from the
rest of the kingdom.
The Aláàfin and Holy Order studied
this strange phenomenon
waiting for the gods to reveal their plans.
But the longer they waited, the greater
this dark agbára grew.
Soon, the darkness known as agbára òtútù could
not be hidden or ignored.*

38

Ìlú-Òdì, Sixth Ring, Kingdom of Oru

L'ORẸ

The hourglass had just about a light bead's worth of sand left and L'orẹ held it close to her ears, listening to the grains drop and fighting the despair that clawed at her insides, knowing that they'd missed their chance at freedom.

Alawani and L'orẹ had fallen silent in the darkness, their terror and hunger growing with every minute. L'orẹ tried her best to not fall asleep, but she must have because next thing she knew, she was trapped in her mind. Àlùfáà-Àgbà had kept his promise and haunted her dreams with ravenous fury.

She woke up screaming and held on tight to Alawani, welcoming his embrace and allowing his voice to calm her mind.

'Was it him?' Alawani asked.

L'orẹ nodded, her face still glued to his chest.

'I'm so sorry,' he said and lifted her chin. He lit his agbára and a soft yellow glow fell upon their faces. His eyes sparked with flakes of gold and his soft smile warmed her heart.

'Do you want to talk about it?' Alawani asked.

L'orẹ shook her head.

'He's in my mind too,' Alawani said. 'He's getting desperate.'

L'orẹ jerked up, 'What's he saying? Are you okay?'

'I'm fine. His voice has been in my mind for long enough

that I know how to tune him out,' Alawani said. 'Nothing he says will stop us from getting out of this kingdom.'

'I'm so sorry,' she said.

Alawani shook his head, 'My grandfather's problems with me started long before you. Like you, I've considered going back and putting an end to all this, if only to save those we left behind, but as long as he keeps trying to hurt you, there's nothing I wouldn't do to keep you away from him.'

L'ọrẹ smiled at that.

'I love you,' he said, with his hand on his chest. 'I hope you know that. I hope you know that I've loved you from – well, I don't remember when I started loving you, but it doesn't matter because I don't remember not loving you.'

His hands roamed from her neck to her hair and she leaned into his touch, allowing him to distract her from her nightmares. She pressed her lips to his and kissed him. He put his hand around her waist and pulled her closer.

'I love you too,' she whispered between breaths.

Something loud crashed outside, sending echoes and vibrations through their cell, and they jumped, scrambling apart and then together in a tight embrace. The shakes quelled, and L'ọrẹ said, 'Do you think it's the storm?'

'Maybe,' Alawani said. 'We need to get out of here.'

'We already tried the door, there's just one exit,' L'ọrẹ said, and Alawani put his hands over his face and groaned. Earlier, he'd tried using his agbára to melt the metal door but his agbára had burned him. They figured the doors were spelled with old magic just like the cuffs had been. Luckily, Rèmí the guard had taken off their cuffs when he tossed them in, so Alawani was able to light up the cell occasionally.

'When that door opens next, we attack whoever comes through. We can't spend another day rotting in here. We'll miss our chance,' Alawani said.

L'ọrẹ didn't respond. She just rubbed his thighs to ease his nerves. If he got nervous then so would she. Again. And she was just about out of hope.

Alawani chuckled dryly. 'Imagine if they knew they'd locked up the Queen of Oru in a dungeon.'

'Don't call me that,' L'ọrẹ said, playfully punching him.

'I can hardly believe it,' he said. 'L'ọrẹ, Queen of Oru. And to think Baba-Ìtàn kept this a secret.'

'I think that's the craziest part to wrap my head around,' L'ọrẹ said.

'Do you want to be queen?'

'Of this land trying to kill me? No. Not even a little bit. What do I know about ruling a kingdom? What do I know about anything? I'm just trying to not die.' Then she added, 'If I could though, the first thing I'd do is end the Àlùfáà trials.'

'Then our agbára would disappear. Maybe not immediately, but over time, new generations would be born without it and it'll be the end of our connection to the gods.'

'Curse the gods,' L'ọrẹ said indignantly. 'I'm sure there are other ways.'

'After a thousand years, I doubt it,' Alawani said.

'I want nothing to do with this. The crown, the throne. None of it.'

'We didn't know it then but leaving at the time we did was the best decision we could have made. If you were anywhere near the capital when they figured out who you truly were, we may not have made it this far.'

'I can't believe my birth father is the Lord Regent. I can't believe he's trying to kill me,' L'ọrẹ said quietly.

'I think we've got my grandfather to blame for that. The Lord Regent doesn't seem like someone who wouldn't at least want to meet with you.'

'You can't expect me to believe that the Holy Order is doing all this on its own. The Lord Regent knows and rules everything. Milúà has been hunting us like dogs, and your grandfather has been tormenting our dreams. Who do you think sent them all?'

'I suppose you're right,' he said.

'I guess whatever he felt for my mother died with her,' L'orẹ said dryly.

Alawani sat upright and pulled her close. 'I am going to protect you, Tèmi, and if that means finding refuge in the north, then that's what you need to do. I'd be bound to you forever if I could.'

'What do you mean?' she said, staring into his eyes, trying to find meaning through the shadows cast by the flames.

'I don't know what the future holds, but I know I can't imagine a world where your heart doesn't beat next to mine,' he said, placing his palm on her chest.

She tried to form a smile, her lips curling slightly, but it faded just as quickly. Her heart rate quickened, and she could feel her pulse at her fingertips. It was as though she could no longer tell fear from anxiety or nerves from excitement. Everything felt heightened and raw, and the more she tried to hold on to something – a thought, an idea, or hope – it faded as quickly as it ignited in her.

'You can turn off your agbára. Save your strength,' L'orẹ said.

Alawani did as she asked and they sat in silence, holding each other as the darkness engulfed them again.

'I can't believe you grew up here before we met?' L'orẹ said, breaking the silence after a long moment.

'Thanks to Command, I only spent about two first suns here,' Alawani said. 'I owe her my life.'

'Was it that bad?' L'orẹ was glad he couldn't see her face, and the guilt written across it at the mention of Command.

'It was, but I had no choice. Even after Gbàgede, this place was still in my future. The Lord General assured me he'd have a place for me as captain whenever I returned. Whether I wanted it or not.'

L'ọrẹ shifted. 'Don't you get to choose? Isn't that what being a prince is all about? No responsibility and no orders?'

'Yeah, that's true, but most royal children end up here; I think everyone just expects it. Half of the soldiers here are descendants of kings and queens going back many generations. The Lord General and all those who lead or have led the military before know that anyone with even a drop of royal blood will have stronger agbára than the average person. So they believe it is our duty to use those powers to protect the kingdom and the crown. Even though anyone can join the army, royal descendants can become high-ranking officials – no matter how far removed from the ancestor who sat on the throne. I know for a fact my mother expected me to take over from the Lord General one day. She's ambitious like that.'

'Oh gods, your mother. Do you think she's okay in the capital? I mean since everything happened.'

'I'm sure she's fine. She is a queen. There isn't much the Lord Regent can do to her,' Alawani said. 'And trust me. She can take care of herself. I'd worry for anyone who crosses her path more than I would for her,' he said. 'But I wish I'd seen her before leaving or spoken to her. She'll be so confused about everything.'

L'ọrẹ squeezed his hand. 'We can find a way to get a message to her. I'm not sure how, but I promise to try.'

'Didn't think we'd ever be leaving our home,' Alawani said.

'This isn't my home. It's never really been.' She felt a surprising pang of loss as she said the words. 'This kingdom has taken everything from me.'

Alawani pulled L'ọrẹ back into his arms. 'You haven't lost everything,' he breathed. 'You have me.'

L'ọrẹ smiled, 'Yes, I do.' He was the last person she had left, the last pillar standing, the love she couldn't afford to lose.

He closed the gap between them, and she let him kiss her, slowly welcoming his lips to hers. She climbed over his legs and straddled him, allowing him to take her mind off misery, and with open arms, he welcomed her in.

L'ọrẹ jumped at a loud click in the door. They both froze. Another click and they were up. Alawani's agbára shone bright, L'ọrẹ pulled out short thin blades from her hair. The soldier who tossed them in had taken their bags and weapons and searched them but hadn't searched her hair. His mistake.

The door cracked open an inch and as soon as they moved, Rẹ̀mí said, 'If you attack me, I'll raise an alarm. Hold your fire, I'm here to make a deal.'

He waited for Alawani's light to dim before he walked in. L'ọrẹ was ready to pounce.

'Speak. Quickly,' she growled.

Rẹ̀mí tossed them their belongings. 'The storm is picking up. I'm guessing that was your plan?' When they didn't respond, he went on, 'Look, the winds picked up about a light bead ago. The storm and hail will be here soon. The crown heir and the maiden Milúà are in this keep together with the Lord General. The main keep has emptied of soldiers and the last wall, as usual, has gone underground to avoid being tossed off the battlements. I can get you out.'

'The crown heir is here?' L'ọrẹ said, her heart racing in her chest.

'I promise I can get you out,' Rẹ̀mí said again.

'You locked us in here for an entire day. Why would we trust you?' Alawani said, the light of his agbára slowly growing again.

'I want out. I want out of this wretched kingdom, but I can't do it alone. I'll help you if you help me. Whatever happens, I need to leave Oru today. Deal?'

'And how do we know this isn't a trap?' L'ọrẹ said.

'You just have to trust me,' Rẹ̀mí said. 'I could've taken you to the Lord General. The crown heir arrived yesterday. I know you're the prince Àlùfáà, I saw your tattoos as soon as you climbed the wall. I saved your life and now I'm asking you to save mine.' He tossed a bag at them. 'These are the keep's guard uniforms. Wear them, and no one will recognize you.'

Alawani walked up to Rẹ̀mí, his face close enough to the soldier's that L'ọrẹ thought he might head butt the man.

'If you do anything to put her in danger,' Alawani said, pointing to L'ọrẹ, 'I will kill you.'

L'ọrẹ stared into the soldier's eyes, looking for something to give her a reason to call his bluff or uncover whatever lies he was peddling.

'I'm not lying to you,' Rẹ̀mí said as if reading her mind.

L'ọrẹ leaned in closer to him, her full weight pressing against him and her knife at his throat.

His lips curved into a sly smile, 'You don't have to kiss me. I already said I'll help you.'

At that she shoved him off. 'I hope for your sake you're not lying.'

As they moved up the stairs, they crashed into a horde of servants who were running down them, rushing to hide from the incoming storm in the dungeons while the three of them fought their way through to the ground level.

'The crown heir and his group are on the roof, watching

for you,' Rèmí said. 'We should be able to sneak out if we stay under cover.'

The hallways and corridors were clear of soldiers with only the random servant occasionally passing by them without glancing in their direction. But the keep was a massive fortress and as confusing as a maze. They went through corridors that led into a myriad of rooms, and out into stairwells.

The last of these landed them in what looked like a ballroom with swinging chandeliers, broken windows through which the building storm was starting to howl, and the stench of food that had been left to rot after what looked like an incredibly raucous party. In the middle of the room, tables were pushed aside to create what looked like a makeshift fighting pen. The patches of dried blood sprayed across the floor showed a glimpse of the chaos.

'Across here,' said Rèmí. He pointed to a set of double doors on the opposite side of the room. 'Once we're through those doors, we're nearly out of the keep.'

An explosion blasted open the double doors and L'ọrẹ shielded her face from a sudden light. When she recovered, she recognized a figure running towards her, hands and eyes aglow with agbára. *Milúà*.

'Run!' L'ọrẹ shouted. She turned, heading back towards the stairwell.

Milúà's energy blast exploded against the entry to the stairwell and knocked the trio back against the tables. L'ọrẹ staggered towards the stairs again but another blast from Milúà hit the ceiling, raining sand and glass on them and blocking the stairwell.

Now, the only exit was the door Milúà had come in through. L'ọrẹ, Alawani and Rèmí ducked beneath the nearest table, crawling through puddles of spilled palm wine, rotten food and what L'ọrẹ could only imagine was vomit. Clouds of dust from the collapsed ceiling temporarily hid them from the maiden.

'How does she keep finding us?' L'ọrẹ whispered.

'It doesn't matter, we're trapped,' Alawani said. 'We're never going to make it past her to those doors.'

The storm outside bellowed and howled now, kicking against the ragged windows with everything it had picked up. A crash of hail broke through and the heavy winds sent Milúà flying against the side wall. This was their chance.

'Let's go!' Rẹ̀mí said, jumping onto the tables and racing for the windows. L'ọrẹ followed, using all her strength to fight against the wind. She didn't dare look back to see if Milúà had found her footing. One moment, Alawani was behind her, and the next, he'd slipped and went down quick, tumbling onto the floor.

'Alawani!' L'ọrẹ turned to help him but Milúà was already at his side. Rẹ̀mí grabbed her arm and pulled her towards the broken windows.

'You can't help him if you're dead!' he shouted over the wind.

L'ọrẹ glanced back and saw that Milúà had knocked Alawani unconscious with her spear. The maiden stood defiantly staring them down with a sly smile on her face. As L'ọrẹ moved back towards them, Milúà stretched forth her hands, and the sand rushing in swirled around her. Using her agbára, Milúà ignited the sand, turning it molten hot, and shoved a wall of glass shards at L'ọrẹ. Rẹ̀mí pulled L'ọrẹ by her collar and they jumped out the window just as the glass wall shattered behind them. They escaped the worst of it, but they both had to pluck out burning shards from their hands and legs. Outside, the wind was like a wild animal flinging itself against her body and the sand grated painfully against her skin. Rèmí pulled her around the side of the building and they hid behind a huge stone statue, providing barely enough shelter to talk.

'Curse the sun! They weren't supposed to be here. The keep was meant to be empty. We have to go back for him,' L'ọrẹ said to Rèmí. 'Do you know if they have any guards with them? How many?'

Rèmí looked in the direction of the last wall and shook his head. 'We're so close. We need to get out.'

'Not without Alawani,' L'ọrẹ said, frowning.

'No one is worth dying for,' Rèmí replied.

'You said you'd help us.'

'And I did!'

A barrage of stones rained against the pillar that shielded them, and Rèmí grabbed L'ọrẹ in an embrace and swung her against the wall, allowing some of the stones to crash into his back. He groaned and tensed in her grip until the worst of the hail passed, and only the wind blew against his hair. L'ọrẹ breathed, trying not to take in the scent of coconut oil that wafted from his locs. She looked at him, finding his eyes. 'Fight with me,' she said in a whisper. 'I know we don't know each other very well, but if you help me, I promise not to leave you behind.'

'You haven't been fighting. You've been running,' Rèmí said. 'Since I met you, you haven't put up a fight. Not when I captured you, not when the maiden came at you. You're asking me to die with you. Where I'm from, you marry the man first before you ask him for his life,' he said with a coy smile.

L'ọrẹ shoved him off, and he dusted the sand from his hair.

'How can you joke about this?' she said.

Rèmí glanced at the last wall again and when his eyes fell

back upon her, they were glassy. 'I've waited too long to miss this chance, I'm sorry.'

'Fine. I don't need you,' she cried out. She ran into the storm and made her way back to the keep. Part of her hoped Rèmí would follow, but even if he didn't, she was done running from the maiden – Rèmí was right about one thing: she'd been running for too long. It was time to stop and fight.

Two things broke the kingdom of Oru in two.
One day, the priests discovered a child born without
agbára – an abomination.
Agbára, as gifted by the gods, was hereditary,
passing from mother to child every single time.
So, who or what was this child?
Time revealed the truth that
the parents who sired the child
had agbára oru and agbára òtútù.
And this was, to say the very least, unacceptable.

39

Ìlú-Òdì, Sixth Ring, Kingdom of Oru

TOFA

The deserted foyer in the Lord General's keep was half as large as its ballroom. So when the doors burst open, Tofa had time to study the girl who raged towards them to save Alawani. The way her hair bobbed as she ran, the strength in her arms as she swung the blades by her side, the anger in her face as she drew nearer. The storm raged in with her, breaking the windows and swirling around her like a hurricane. She looked as wild as Àlùfáà-Àgbà had described.

Next to him, Milúà stood tall and unmoving, her armour glistering in the morning light. She gripped her dagger to Alawani's neck. She'd known the girl would be back for Alawani and had decided to wait for her here while the rest of the keep sheltered deeper inside, where the storm couldn't reach them. 'Stop. Walk slowly or watch his blood spill before your eyes!' she said, pulling the cuffed prince into view.

L'orẹ slowed instantly and started a slow prowl in Milúà's direction, her face like thunder.

Tofa no longer believed in the subtle strategy the palace had used previously. If it were up to him, L'orẹ and Alawani's portraits would have been pasted on every wall in the kingdom until he'd found them. Trying to keep the world from knowing that the temple had lost an Àlùfáà and there was a survivor of Òtútù living among them was the only reason L'ọrẹ and Alawani had got as far as the sixth ring without being caught. The one who sat upon the throne could not leave it to fight battles such as these, so this might very well be Tofa's last foray into battle. Tofa couldn't take his eyes off L'ọrẹ. He wasn't sure what he'd expected her to look like. But as she drew closer, he saw glimpses of Kẹni in her eyes. He saw his father's nose and cheekbones carved into her face and it terrified him.

L'ọrẹ stood defiantly, her eyes shifting to meet his gaze. Tofa wondered what she saw when she looked into the eyes of her brother. Her mouth opened, her hands now shaking so visibly the blades she held were nearly vibrating. Good. She knew to be afraid.

'It's over,' Tofa said quietly. 'Drop your weapons. You're done.'

'Let him go and I won't kill you,' L'ọrẹ growled.

Tofa smirked and walked closer to her. She took a step backwards. Tofa kept walking until he cornered her against the nearest pillar.

'Tell me the truth,' he said. 'Who are you?'

'Who do they say I am?'

'Who is they?'

'Whoever sent you here to kill me.'

'I haven't decided yet if I want to kill you.'

'You could've fooled me,' L'ọrẹ said, glancing at the storm outside the windows, bellowing and flinging streams of sand inside.

Tofa smiled slyly, 'I bet your plan was to escape while the keep hid from the storm.'

'Can't blame a girl for trying,' L'ọrẹ said.

'I can blame you for trying to steal my throne. I mean, it's only fair I fight for it,' Tofa said.

'I don't want your throne. I don't want anything to do with you or your kingdom or your gods. I just want to leave this cursed land – with Alawani!' L'ọrẹ shouted and glanced at Milúà.

Tofa watched all the emotions that flared up with her every word. He wanted to believe her but how could he? She had managed to deceive Alawani into blindly following her but he wouldn't be such easy prey. 'Tell me, L'ọrẹ of Òtútù, on this adventure of yours, has anyone in my kingdom bowed to you and sworn the sovereign oath?'

Her eyes widened and that was all the answer he needed.

'So you don't want my throne but you claim the servitude and lives of my subjects.'

'That's not what happened. I couldn't stop them.'

'I was born for this throne,' Tofa shouted despite himself, 'raised to sit upon it. The crown has been a burden since my first breath, but it has been my burden to bear. How dare you?'

L'ọrẹ pushed herself off the wall, her eyes furrowed in a deep frown. 'I've told you once. I won't say it again. I do not want your cursed crown.'

'Then why are you here!'

'I was born here!'

'You shouldn't have been,' Tofa said.

L'ọrẹ tilted her head, 'I shouldn't have been born?'

Tofa looked into her eyes for a long moment, not sure what he was looking for. Parts of him hoped he'd feel some sort of kinship with her. She was his sister after all. But he felt nothing but rage. He beckoned to the Lord General and half a dozen guards appeared. 'Tie them up. We're done here.'

'Tofa!' Alawani shouted. 'Tofa, please don't do this. Just let us go, and you'll never see either of us again. I promise.'

Tofa glared at him, 'You! I will deal with you later, *brother.*'

As the Lord General stepped towards L'ọrẹ, Àlùfáà-Àgbà's

words rang clear in his head. *L'ọrẹ of Òtútù is a threat to your throne and our kingdom.* Tofa slowly released the breath he'd been holding. And in a little whisper, his father's voice pleaded to bring his daughter home alive, promising him that the throne would always be his, as he'd done before Tofa left home. He stopped in his tracks and took another look at her. The familiarity of her features became clearer to him, and he realized one thing. Àlùfáà-Àgbà was right. L'ọrẹ of Òtútù, firstborn of the sun and heir to the throne of Oru, had to die, and she had to die by his hand.

L'ỌRẸ

L'ọrẹ hadn't imagined what her brother, the crown heir, would look like. A part of her thought she'd instantly recognize him. She'd never seen the Lord Regent or any of his children before so when she felt like she could see part of herself in him, it was all she could do not to turn on her heels and run and run and keep running. If Ìyá-Idán was right, Tofa wanted her dead more than anyone else in the kingdom. He was the crown heir to the kingdom of Oru. He was her brother and enemy. If she died today, she knew it'd be by his hand.

L'ọrẹ missed Command more in this moment than ever before. Her guiding voice was gone. And for the first time in many first suns, she felt like that little girl, alone in the desert night, surrounded by people stronger than she was. And the one who'd saved her then was now trapped and bound by his maiden. Fear filled Alawani's eyes as he watched the soldiers surround her, unable to move past the blade held to his neck. L'ọrẹ blinked, and the soldiers came into focus. She could do this.

For the first time in her life, she *shouted* the words that awakened her blades – she had nothing to gain by whispering them now; the Holy Order wanted her dead anyway. She called upon the old god of fire and thunder: 'Ṣàngó, Dìde. Fún mi ní agbára rẹ. Jà fún mi!' *Wake up. Give me your power. Fight for me.*

Her blades crackled to life, and she started swinging. The soldiers closest to her didn't get the chance to ignite their agbára before she cut them down, targeting the parts of their bodies uncovered by armour. She cut through flesh and bone, swinging wildly in her fury. Her mind was blank. Silent. Still, she knew when to duck low and slice through calves, when to rise in time to meet blows aimed at her head. The three soldiers left standing tried forming energy blasts; she had moved before they could form their attack.

She lunged for the soldier heating the air around her, drawing close enough for him to burn her skin. But she'd grown up tormented by the villagers in her home. The pain of burnt flesh was as familiar as biting her own tongue. She screamed through the pain and kicked him off, and the next swipe of her curved blade left a deadly line across the soldier's neck. Another soldier kicked her in the chest, throwing her back a few feet. She heard her chest crack on impact, and her vision blurred as she slumped to the ground. As soon as she caught her breath, she ran at him, climbed him like a wall, stepped on his torso, then kicked his chest before flipping back to the ground – the whole time, running her blade through him. He fell in a heap.

Something snapped in her, as the blood sprayed across her face. She turned on the others but a blast of energy sent her sprawling across the room. She crashed into the stone wall and crawled to her feet, spitting out blood and rising to meet the soldiers. Her head throbbed and the ringing in her ears nearly drowned out the sound of Alawani screaming for her. She heard him scream again in pain and guessed that he'd attempted to ignite his agbára, and the magic cuffs had burned him.

L'orẹ noticed that Tofa, Milúà and the Lord General didn't join the fight or interfere. It was almost like they were making her put on a show for them. She spat out another chunk of blood and wiped her mouth. If it was a show they wanted, she'd gladly oblige. She ran for the two remaining soldiers. As she got closer, she flashed the fire in her blades. The men blinked and shielded their eyes and L'orẹ slid across the floor, cutting at their legs, turning in a single move and sinking a blade into both their backs.

The chandeliers above them swung and crashed into each other, raining glass on all of them. The relentless wind picked up speed even as it hammered into the building.

'You can't think you'll make it out of this alive,' Tofa said, watching the fight from a distance like a master setting his hounds on a prey. L'orẹ glared at him, ignoring the aches in her body and the fear that gripped her heart with a firm unyielding hand.

'I do,' she said coldly, 'brother.'

Tofa slowly stalked towards her and Milúà followed. L'orẹ stood tall and brushed away the sweat that had gathered on her brows, the sound of her breathing the only thing she could hear. She was ready, blades out and fiery. Then suddenly, she felt an intense heat rising beneath her feet. Alawani let out a deep guttural growl and screamed at the top of his lungs. Hunched over, she couldn't see what had happened to him and her body grew cold, her fingers trembling, her agbára itching to burst as she waited for him to stand. When he did, his arms were scorched, and the magic cuffs fell from his wrists.

'Tèmi, run!' Alawani shouted.

L'ọrẹ jumped back, and the ground began to blacken and simmer. Soon it cracked open, bringing forth magma from its core. The hot orange liquid poured out, bursting into bubbles that splattered everywhere. Milúà was closest to them, and the deep animal growl that came out of her mouth let L'ọrẹ know that it hurt as she fell to the ground. She barked at her leg, holding it as the skin sizzled. Even from a distance, L'ọrẹ could see the piece of scorched flesh across her leg.

'No!' Tofa shouted but he was too far from the maiden.

He rushed towards Milúà, attempting to cross the magma divide but the Lord General grabbed Tofa and pulled him away. 'You are our future king!' he shouted. 'I cannot let you put your life in danger.' As the Lord General turned to run too from the expanding firepit, a bubble of magma burst under his feet. He fell to his knees – the crash of his weight against the cracked floor sunk his leg deeper. He fell on his side in agony, the magma crawling up his body. Tofa rushed to his side, but by the time he was pulling the man out and cooling the heat, L'ọrẹ knew from the melting flesh and fading screams that the man wouldn't make it.

'You've killed him!' Tofa shouted at Alawani, his voice hoarse from the smoke.

But Alawani had used the distraction to run to L'ọrẹ's side of the foyer, near the main entrance – now, the lava field protected them from the crown heir's group, which was pushed towards the inner stairs. Alawani collapsed into L'ọrẹ's arms when he reached her, visibly shaking from overextending his waning agbára. He'd made a deal with the gods, and they were taking what was owed.

'We have to go!' L'ọrẹ said – but Alawani was too weak to walk and L'ọrẹ didn't have the strength to carry him.

The magma spread across the broken floor, and the air around them grew so hot that L'ọrẹ felt the sweat soak into her clothes. Looking across the boiling pond of burning earth and stone, she noticed Tofa's agbára shining brightly through the smoke. He was cooling the magma and sending it back down. But Alawani's strength was recovering – he lifted himself a little from her arms. 'Okay. Let's go,' he said, shakily.

'Lean on me,' she urged.

Mercifully, the wind spread the smoke and steam from the cooling magma all over the room, obscuring them from view, and L'ọrẹ and Alawani were out of the keep before anyone could cross the floor.

L'ọrẹ bore Alawani's weight against her side and helped him as fast as she could towards the graveyard; all that stood between them and the wall. Sand blurred her vision and each step against the wind took so much effort that L'ọrẹ wondered if they were moving at all. Without looking back, she could still feel the maiden's presence hovering over her like the grains of sand that stuck to her neck. For the first time since Rèmí left her, L'ọrẹ wished he had chosen to fight with her. If they wanted a chance at escaping in the storm, L'ọrẹ knew she had to make sure the maiden couldn't follow. The fighting wasn't over yet.

The clouds started to turn dark and in the distance, L'ọrẹ heard the rumble of thunder.

They were halfway across the graveyard, a mile-stretch piece of land full of the bones of those who'd tried and failed to cross without permission. Sparse rocks and loose stones littered the scorched, exposed land that led to freedom. A sudden explosion flung them in the air and knocked them to the ground, proving that L'ọrẹ had been right. Milúà marched out of the storm, her maiden's spear glowing beneath the darkening sky. L'ọrẹ activated her blades with the old magic spell and ran towards the maiden, cutting her off mid-stride. Milúà plunged the sharp end of her agbára-fuelled spear at L'ọrẹ. She dodged – but not fast enough. The spear sliced her mid-rib. L'ọrẹ yelled as the cut sent a jarring pain all through her body. It wasn't just the cut, but the burn. The burn of flesh, and the smell of it, made her want to vomit.

She raised her blades in anger.

L'ọrẹ and the maiden were locked in a deadly dance, their weapons clashing in a blur of steel. Milúà laughed as she caught each strike, knocking one of L'ọrẹ's blades out of her hands. She spun around, delivering a swift kick to L'ọrẹ's chest. L'ọrẹ kept an eye on Alawani, still sprawled on the dirt.

Milúà cackled and the sound of her voice made L'ọrẹ's blood boil. L'ọrẹ launched herself at Milúà. She was nothing if not relentless. L'ọrẹ gritted her teeth and redoubled her efforts, unleashing a series of rapid strikes that forced Milúà to step back. When she saw a clear path, she used the back of her hand to slap the maiden across her cheek. The shock on Milúà's face was all the satisfaction L'ọrẹ needed. She didn't pause long enough to enjoy it. She kept going. A sharp kick to the stomach and Milúà heaved over in pain. L'ọrẹ drew nearer and struck her face with her knee. Finally, she threw her blade to the ground and went in for a blow to end it all, but Milúà dodged it and formed an air cannon in her hands. L'ọrẹ didn't see the air around the maiden's glowing hand simmer and boil until Milúà sent it towards her, and it exploded near her face, sending her straight to the sand.

L'ọrẹ lay in the sand for a few moments. Next to her, she could hear Alawani's voice calling to her as he crawled over. Her breaths came in even shorter bursts. Without Command's voice in her head, every move felt unsure, weaker and with much less vigour. She felt like she was fighting blind, unable to predict her opponent's next move. Unable to hear her commander's words. She was losing. They were losing, and it'd all be for nothing. Nothing.

L'ọrẹ lay on the floor gasping for air, trying to breathe as the heat engulfed her. Every part of her body stung from the blast. Her ears rang, and her eyes watered. Before she could stand, Milúà rushed to her, driving the sharp end of her spear down towards her. L'ọrẹ caught the scorching-hot staff in her hand and stilled herself, preparing for the burn. No. She couldn't die here. This couldn't be the end of her story.

As she groaned beneath the weight of Milúà's strength, she realized there was no burn. Her palms were glowing. *Curse the sun.* Her agbára had forced itself out. Water formed where her palms held on to the spear, and her hands slipped. The blade's edge was now just a few inches from her face.

Suddenly Alawani got to his feet and shoved Milúà off her. She lost her spear in the fall, just a few feet away, but Alawani reached it first and threw it further away.

L'ọrẹ got off the ground and flexed her hands, trying to send her agbára back beneath her skin. Its constant buzzing was a reminder of what she'd done to Command and with Alawani right next to her, she couldn't risk unleashing the darkness within her.

'Why are you protecting a murderer?' Milúà shouted at Alawani.

L'ọrẹ gasped. She wouldn't. Somehow, the thought that Milúà might expose her made her panic more than when the sharp edge of her spear was mere inches from drilling a hole into her skull.

'You need to stop this, Milúà!' Alawani shouted back at her.

Milúà rose to her feet, her face bruised. She spat out something crimson and wet. 'You don't know, do you?'

L'ọrẹ tried to avoid her gaze, but that was what gave her away.

'You did not tell him,' Milúà scoffed.

'Tell me what?' Alawani said.

'That she's a murderer!' Milúà said, pointing at L'ọrẹ. 'I thought there were no secrets between lovers?'

Alawani turned to L'ọrẹ. 'What's she talking about?' In the middle of the storm every word spoken was shouted above the howling wind.

'Not here,' L'ọrẹ said. 'I'll tell you everything, but not now.'

'I can tell you now, this girl isn't worth saving,' Milúà seethed.

'Who –' He couldn't finish the sentence, or he did not want to.

'Tell him, or I will,' Milúà shouted.

'It was an accident,' L'ọrẹ said, her voice choked with tears.

Alawani moved closer to her, and she stepped back. The silence grew between them, and when Alawani tried to move closer to her again, she blurted out, 'Command. I killed Command.'

The words were a weight lifted off her, easing her heart for a moment before letting in the flood of grief and guilt. L'ọrẹ held her eyes shut and when she opened them, the tears fell.

'It was an accident. I promise. I tried to save her.' She turned on Milúà. 'She was supposed to save her!'

'You knew she was beyond saving the minute you filled her with that curse in your veins,' Milúà spat back.

Alawani looked down at her hands, and she could see that confusion turned to dread and then something she could not recognize. Finally, he said, 'You killed Command?'

'It was an accident,' L'ọrẹ said, taking a step closer to him. 'She loved you.'

'It was an accident,' L'ọrẹ said again, taking another step closer, her voice pleading with him.

'She was like our mother.' Alawani moved out of her reach, tears brimming in his bloodshot eyes.

'I'm sorry,' L'ǫrẹ begged, shaking her hands, desperately trying to turn off the light in her palms. 'I swear to you, Alawani, I'd never – you know me – it was an accident.'

'You can't control these powers,' Alawani said, his voice firm yet full of pain.

From the corner of her eye, L'ǫrẹ saw Milúà smiling.

Alawani waited for her to say something, but there was nothing more to say. It *was* an accident. He should understand that, and the fact that he didn't get that made her angry even as guilt and shame threatened to bury her alive.

'How?' he asked.

'Does it matter?' Milúà scowled. 'Command is dead. A frozen body lost to the mud of Ìlú-Idán.'

Alawani swung his head in L'ǫrẹ's direction. 'Since then? Since Ìlú-Idán? You've had every opportunity to tell me.' He moved in closer to her, close enough that she could feel his breath. 'Last night, in the dungeons. We spent nearly a day in silence. You –' His voice broke. 'Why do we keep doing this to each other? Why is there always a secret, something you can't trust me with? And now this. In the name of all that burns, L'ǫrẹ, what have you done?'

'Command was trying to take me back,' L'ǫrẹ said, tears streaming down her face. 'I just wanted to get away.'

'Then why would you kill the only woman who ever treated you like a daughter and leave her body in the streets?'

'I don't know how many times I have to tell you. It was an accident!'

'Her story didn't add up to me either,' Milúà added.

L'ǫrẹ sneered at her, but the maiden glared right back at her.

'I'm guessing she didn't tell you the woman's last words either. The àṣírí she refused to leave this world with.'

'You hold her dying secrets?' Alawani asked L'ǫrẹ.

'I'll tell you what she said,' Milúà started.

525

'Curse the sun! This has nothing to do with you!' L'ọrẹ shouted at her.

'Command said that your father, the king, was murdered,' Milúà blurted out.

Alawani froze, and then – to L'ọrẹ's surprise – he threw a blast at Milúà, flinging her away from them. He faced L'ọrẹ, still as a statue, as though he was trying and failing to understand the words that had shaken his world. She wanted nothing more than to run into his arms and hug him. This wasn't how she wanted him to find out. She wanted to tell him when all this was over, when they were safe and alone and could mourn their losses together, but she'd ruined it all. The fragile thread they'd hung on to since their oath snapped; the pillar in her mind cracked in half and slipped into the sinking sand. To her horror, she realized that the gods hadn't been the ones to force him out of her life – she'd done that all by herself.

A royal decree was passed.
Anyone who took to bed a person with
agbára different from theirs
would meet their end on the executioner's block.
For a while, it worked, but as fate would have it,
that was the least of their problems.
The discovery that those with agbára òtútù
could take the energy of another,
freezing out their core and stripping
them of their agbára,
was a reality the Aláàfin and Holy
Order simply could not accept.

40

Ìlú-Òdì, Sixth Ring, Kingdom of Oru

L'ọRẹ

Of all the stories Baba-Ìtàn told the children under the tree, the story of Queen Aníwúrà – whose agbára filled not just her hands or arms but her entire body – was the most unbelievable of them all. And L'ọrẹ had always expected that he exaggerated for the sake of the children, who got excited at the prospect of one day being like the great queen.

So L'ọrẹ was stunned at the human flame approaching her. Tofa no longer looked like the person she'd met just a few moments ago. His body glowed like the sun, every inch overcome with agbára oru. It was spectacular and terrifying, lighting up the whipping sand until the storm haloed him in gold. A blaze of fire ignited around him, leaving a trail in his path. Nothing or no one could stand next to him. His brown skin was no longer visible, completely transformed by a yellow light so bright that L'ọrẹ had to avert her eyes. He was still a few yards from them, but the heat that filled the air around them made her feel like the sun had left the sky and was standing before her. *How was that possible?* She looked at Alawani, who was wide-eyed with shock. They weren't getting out of this fight alive. That much was sure.

Tofa formed an orb in his hands, his energy radiating through its unstable form. He threw it at them. Alawani jumped in front of L'ọrẹ and redirected it, his stolen guard's uniform rippling in the wind. He sent the orb spinning a few feet away, where it exploded. Tofa looked at him and smiled as if accepting the challenge.

L'ọrẹ noticed Milúà out of the corner of her eye but the maiden kept her distance from Tofa, trying not to get burnt alive in the crown heir's flaming fury. Soon, the storm blocked her from sight and L'ọrẹ felt her heart race in her chest. She was glad for the cover the storm provided but Milúà had proven that she could always find them. Somehow.

'Get back, L'ọrẹ!' Alawani shouted at her above the noise, sweat pouring from his forehead, dripping into his eyes.

'No, I can help. I can –'

'Get back,' he said in such a distant tone that it was clear he wasn't just trying to keep her safe. 'Your agbára!' he shouted, pointing at her hands.

She glanced down, noticed how white light continued to glow from her palms. Holding back her powers felt like rubbing scotch bonnet on a raw wound. It burned like the sun.

'We only need to disarm him,' Alawani said. 'Whatever trouble we're in will pale compared to what will happen to us if you kill the crown heir!'

So this was about her powers, after all. L'ọrẹ stepped back, her body stiffening at the harshness of his voice, but she respected his wishes . . . for now. She found a sheltered spot far enough for Alawani and Tofa to have the floor all to themselves. She combed the storm for Milúà, spotting forms and shapes shifting in and out of view as the sand whipped around the graveyard – but she couldn't be sure of who or what she was seeing.

Tofa was laser-focused on Alawani, accepting the prince's challenge as Alawani's agbára lit up his skin.

'Don't do this, Tofa, I don't want to hurt you,' Alawani said.

Tofa scoffed, 'If you couldn't beat me when we were boys, what makes you think you can now?'

'I'm begging you. If our friendship ever meant anything to you, let us go.'

'We were brothers once, Alawani,' Tofa said, his eyes lighting up with agbára. 'Now you're just in my way.'

L'ọrẹ stepped aside as the ground beneath Tofa blackened under his feet. He sent another energy blast at Alawani – the prince dodged it, sliding across the sand and picking up his sword, filled with his agbára. The winds made it hard for Tofa to aim and Alawani took advantage of that, dodging and redirecting – perhaps hoping to tire the heir rather than overpowering him. After all, his blade wasn't going to do much against the god-like figure he fought against, L'ọrẹ thought.

Try as she might, her agbára refused to dull, its white light glowing stubbornly from her hands. She couldn't fight Tofa without agbára, but Alawani was right; without control over her powers, she was scared of what she might be capable of. Command's face, cold and dead, flashed in her mind.

Tofa sped up his attacks, barely giving Alawani chance to breathe between blasts. When he ducked, the next one met him on the ground, and when he jumped, he came falling with rock debris in the aftermath of Tofa's attacks. L'ọrẹ had seen this trick before, but energy balls generally took a while to form, and even then, not all were skilled or powerful enough to create them. But as she watched the fight, Tofa seemed to create his in the blink of an eye, and as much as Alawani tried distracting him, it was just a waiting game, and Tofa was clearly in control. Taunting. Soon, he would be tired of playing with his prey and launch an actual attack.

L'ọrẹ flinched as Alawani redirected less and less, catching more than he missed and being tossed to the ground, into walls, against burning rocks. The sky grew darker, and the thunder rumbled nearer; lightning tore a silver line across the sky and L'ọrẹ felt panic flood her mind. This was it, this was how they'd die.

Tofa suddenly stopped shooting. L'ọrẹ knew instantly that it was a bad sign. He looked at his hands, and she could see the slightest shimmer grow in his palms. She saw the air boil and knew something terrible was brewing. Alawani raised an arm, trying to create a shield with his agbára, but the simmering glow sparked out of existence. He was too weak.

Her heart stopped. The world slowed. Even the howling wind went silent, and she watched in slow motion as Tofa's energy boiled the air and the sands, turning them from grains into shards of glass. A sea of glass raged around him just as the winds did and L'ọrẹ felt her agbára fight for survival with her. Whatever part of her wanted to keep it down, the guilt of Command's death, the fear of the unknown, the panic of losing herself to this curse – all of that was nothing in the face of certain death.

She tapped into the heat in the sandstorm around her. The hot desert sands filled her core and when she breathed out, she exhaled white mist. Summoning her agbára didn't feel like ice freezing her insides. A fiery heat burned within her, and her arms flooded with silver light.

The first time her agbára had broken free, it had been something like an out-of-body experience, watching herself do something she couldn't understand. But at this moment, she knew exactly what she wanted to do, she only hoped to not die in the process.

She unleashed a beam of light and frost towards Tofa. As her light passed through the glass storm coming down on her, they froze and burst into soft flakes of ice. L'ọrẹ channelled her agbára at Tofa again, engulfing him in a dome of ice so thick she couldn't see his figure within. Alawani picked up a slow pace, limping towards her. Within moments, Tofa blasted through the dome, sending ice shards flying in all directions.

The loud crash made her jump, and Tofa was panting heavily when she turned to him. The dome was completely gone. Around her were sharp ice splinters littered across the ground. Behind her, Alawani was on the floor, groaning in pain. A shard of ice stuck to his side. She gasped, and then bolted to him, her feet flying across the floor.

Angry, L'ọrẹ growled at Tofa, and sparks kindled at her fingertips. Her screams were drowned out by the cracks of lightning and the roaring of thunder. All she could think about was that if she could take energy from the sands around her, she could also channel the energy from the lightning that sparked nearer with each explosion. Until this moment, L'ọrẹ hadn't considered that if the stories Ìyá-Idán had told her were true, and she really was born before Tofa, then she would be not just as powerful as he was but more so.

She raised her hands and shone her light into the sky. She reached for the energy in the storm, and when the next bolt of lightning struck, she felt an explosion inside her core. It rippled through her in an incredible wave that made the hairs on her body stand. The energy raged inside her, and when she pointed her hands at Tofa, the shock in his eyes showed that he knew what was coming. Sparks flew, thunder roared around them, and the crown heir was blasted out of her sight. Even in her anger, L'ọrẹ felt the urge to check and make sure she hadn't killed him but instead she rushed towards Alawani.

'No, no, no!' She fell next to Alawani and lifted him to sit up against her body. He groaned with every move. L'ọrẹ reached for her blades and awoke the heat energy in them by speaking the old tongue. She placed it over the shard and melted it off. Blood and water oozed from the wound.

She winced as she pressed the blade over the wound to cauterize it, and Alawani let out an animal-like growl that made her shudder. The haze got thicker with smoke and ash and a dark overcast cloud formed all around them. L'ọrẹ tried to breathe through it but every breath burned. Tears streamed down her face as she struggled to stop a fit of coughing.

'We need to go – now!'

L'ọrẹ turned towards the voice. 'Rèmí!' She had never been happier to see someone in her life. Rèmí pulled up beside her and dismounted the mighty war horse he'd ridden into the graveyard. 'Alawani is hurt. We need to carry him,' she said.

Together, they placed him across the horse, then L'ọrẹ jumped on, and Rèmí climbed behind her, firmly gripping the reins. L'ọrẹ felt his body tense around her as he struggled to stay saddled on the horse.

'Hold on,' Rèmí said into her ear and kicked the horse, sending them racing towards the final wall out of the kingdom of Oru.

The graveyard had stony terrain and large red rocks, which only got bigger as they rode the half-mile between them and the wall. The wind picked up, and much of the sand got into L'ọrẹ's eyes as the horse raced on, but she didn't care. She was determined to reach that wall. Her best friend wouldn't die, not on her watch. One way or the other, they were leaving the kingdom.

They reached the base of the wall by some miracle and as soon as they jumped off the horse, it ran away in a frenzy, frightened by the lightning that struck the wall.

'You came back for us?' L'ọrẹ said as she put Alawani to rest against the stone wall. The north wind blew from the other side of the wall so the closer they stayed to the base on this side, the less sandy it was. Just enough to keep their eyes open.

Rèmí shuddered as another bolt of lightning struck the wall. He looked up and closed his fist in the air as if catching the wind. He opened it to gaze at the sand in his palm. 'You were losing. Quite terribly too,' he said plainly. 'What's the plan to get to the other side of this wall?'

L'orẹ gazed at the heavy stones that formed the wall all the way up to the sky. 'He was supposed to blast through,' she said, looking at Alawani, leaving the rest unspoken.

'What happened to him?' Rèmí asked.

L'orẹ exhaled a deep, heavy sigh. 'He was impaled,' she breathed, holding back the sobs that burned in her throat.

'Why did you take it out? You could have killed him,' Rèmí said, walking towards Alawani, who now lay flat on the ground.

'There's nothing you can do. He needs a healer . . .' L'orẹ hadn't finished speaking when a thought crossed her mind. She did know a healer.

'What is it?' Rèmí asked.

'I just remembered something.' She quickly loosened her braid and reached deep into her sand-filled hair until she found it. The vial Ìyá-Idán had given her.

Alawani groaned as she emptied the contents of the vial into his mouth. Holding his head up, she forced him to swallow every last drop, ignoring the pain that hummed in her own body.

His wound began to close, and her eyes widened at the sight. The blood stopped flowing. And in a few moments, his breathing was already less laboured. A scar remained, but soon the wound was fully healed.

Rèmí didn't seem surprised in the slightest. Perhaps he had seen the effects of such a potion before. 'We still need a way out,' he said, squinting into the storm. 'I can't get caught again. Could he do it, now his wound is healed?'

'I doubt it – he's been fighting for ages; I don't think he has much power left. Can you do it? Blast a hole in the wall? It's literally the only thing between us and freedom at this point.'

Rèmí shook his head. 'No. I have no agbára oru.'

L'ọrẹ froze. 'What? What do you mean?'

His words sent a pang deep into her chest. She felt a tightness and seemed to hold on tighter with every breath. Until that moment, she believed she was the only one in the entire kingdom without agbára oru. And here, this boy was claiming the same. She looked back at Alawani, who had regained consciousness and now sat upright against the wall.

'I'm not from this kingdom,' Rèmí said slowly, as if cautious.

'Are you from the north?' she said, her words pouring out quickly.

'From the ice mountains? Òtútù?' he scoffed. 'Definitely not.'

'Then who gives you life? The old gods?'

'My gods are not of the sands and storms, nor are they your old ones. They are the ones you've long forgotten,' he said as he swung his bow across his chest. 'Why can't you?'

L'ọrẹ placed a trembling hand on the stone wall. Every time she used her agbára there was a risk that she'd hurt herself or someone else. Even while she tried protecting him, Alawani's wound had still been from her agbára. 'I don't know,' she said finally, unwilling to discuss her powers.

Rèmí's shoulders dropped in disappointment as he let out

a sigh. 'So we are dying today, then. I really didn't think the storm would be the thing to take me out.'

Alawani slowly rose from the ground, leaning against the wall, but he still didn't look at her. He pointed in the direction they had come from, 'They're coming!'

*And so started the first and only civil
war in the history of Oru.
All children born without agbára were killed,
dragged from their mothers' breasts
and tossed into the fire.
All who had what could only be described
as the cursed agbára met their end.
Fathers slayed sons, and daughters slayed mothers,
all in pursuit of a land glowing with
the pure light of agbára oru
as was intended by the gods of the sun and sands.*

41

Ìlú-Òdì, Sixth Ring, Kingdom of Oru

L'ORẸ

Fear had always been L'ọrẹ's greatest enemy. Fear of being beaten up as a child because of who her father was. Fear of living up to the name coward. As she grew older, she had more to lose and more to be afraid of. She couldn't tell when it formed around her like a shadow following her every step, but fear led her to where she was today. Fear of losing her best friend to the gods. Fear of living in a land that would never accept her. Fear of losing the people she loved so much.

Fear. It was what made her lose fights she'd been trained to win. It was what activated her agbára òtútù. Fear killed Command. It made her lose control of what should come as easily to her as breathing. L'ọrẹ's chest tightened as she heard Tofa and Milúà draw nearer, their energy blasts radiating an ominous hum in the air. Curse or not, this agbára was all she had left, and she wasn't going down without a fight.

L'ọrẹ saw the shadows in the distance, and the choice was made for her. She could either die in the storm or die at the hands of her brother. She walked away from the wall, allowing the winds to push her, and when she stopped, she reached into her core, feeling the energy all around her. Her agbára crackled to life inside her. She forced Command's dying face out of her mind. If this was to be a fair fight, she had to match their energy. She focused on Ìyá-Idán's lessons. Then stepped forward, took a deep breath, and allowed the heat inside her to boil over as she turned the air around her to ice. It didn't matter if she made mistakes as long as she wasn't directing any of them towards her friends. She formed an ice wall, shielding them from the attacks, exactly like she had done in the temple – but bigger, stronger. Immediately, it shook and groaned, pummelled with attacks from the other side.

'I don't know how long this will hold for,' she said, turning to Alawani and Rèmí, whose mouth was hanging open as he glanced between the ice wall and L'orẹ. 'We need to figure out how to get out of here.'

Rèmí's expression quickly settled into one of acceptance and L'orẹ knew this wasn't the face of someone seeing agbára òtútù for the first time.

'Maybe we just let them keep shooting at the wall. Eventually, they might create that hole we desperately need,' he said.

'That's if we don't die first,' Alawani said. 'That's a terrible plan.'

'I don't see you coming up with much else,' Rèmí spat back.

'Stop arguing! What are we going to do?' L'orẹ shouted.

Just as she asked, the next attack completely shattered her shield, sending them all hurtling against the wall.

Pain shot through her back, right into her head. L'orẹ got up despite it. Her agbára buzzed as sparks flew around her fingertips.

'I've got this,' L'orẹ said, quickly finding her footing against the wind. This was her fight, after all. She closed her eyes and tried to imagine exactly what she wanted to do. Her hands felt heavy, and this time the agbára felt more like a sting in her veins, flowing with thorns. When she opened her eyes, she knew they were blue. She could feel the burn. She raised her hands behind her head.

Rèmí and Alawani looked on in awe as the ice formed from nothing and raged against the sandstorm.

Screaming as she threw her hands down, the ice shards shot towards Tofa and Milúà.

The crown prince and the maiden stood together, hands interlocked, one hand each left free. They held their free hands forward against the approaching ice-storm. It looked like they were forming energy blasts, but they didn't form fully; instead, they kept the air around them hot and simmering. L'ọrẹ watched as her shards reached Tofa and Milúà and melted away in front of them, overwhelmed by the heat shield. Another use of agbára oru that L'ọrẹ had never seen before. It was a good trick. But they couldn't keep that up without boiling themselves alive.

It only became clear what the two planned to do when she saw them push their hands out forcefully in her direction. It was too late to do anything to stop the energy blast. She felt the heat before she felt the impact. Then she felt the sharp pain going through her body as it hit something solid, and she fell to the ground in a slump.

She felt someone pull her hands, and she thought it was Alawani until she heard Milúà's voice. L'ọrẹ took in deep breaths as pain surged through her body. She sat up and wiped the blood that streamed out of her nostrils, then rose to her feet.

'Come with us now,' Milúà said, her braids flying in the wind like tendrils. 'Or die here and let the vultures use your bones for their nests.'

L'ọrẹ looked at her captors. Milúà no longer looked like the pristine maiden. Her white robes were stained with blood and sand and torn in several places, although her gold armour still shone brightly. Tofa, on the other hand, looked like he had just had a good day at training. Not a single cut or tear marred his bare chest or trousers. L'ọrẹ sighed, her breath ragged and trembling as she exhaled. It was over.

Tofa's voice cut through her thoughts. 'Take the prince and the captain's ward back to the city. That's an order, maiden,' he added in a steel voice.

Alawani glared at him and moved closer to L'ọrẹ. Her eyes grew wide with terror. She knew exactly what her brother meant and felt a chill crawling up her spine. 'No. Why are you separating us? Wherever they go, I go.'

'As the words have left my mouth, maiden,' Tofa said, ignoring the looks on their faces.

'So let it be done, Crown Heir.' Milúà nodded and pulled Alawani closer to her.

L'ọrẹ was still lost in a cascade of emotions, her mind spinning in circles. He was going to kill her. Why else would he separate them? It was just like Ìyá-Idán had told her. Of all the people in the kingdom, he most desperately needed her to die. At that thought she allowed her agbára to hover just beneath the surface, and in her mind, she calculated how many steps she would need to take to touch him.

She was still stunned, unsure of her next move, when she saw Alawani move in the corner of her eye. When she turned, he pulled out Milúà's dagger from her sheath and braced it against his own neck. With each step, he moved further away from their reach.

'Let her go,' Alawani said, pressing the blade to deepen as they all turned to look at him.

'Stop that!' L'ọrẹ shouted above the storm, and she could taste sand in her mouth. 'What are you doing?'

Alawani drew blood.

Milúà shouted, 'Stop!' The maiden's eyes were filled with

terror, and her outstretched arms trembled in his direction. 'Don't you dare!'

L'ọrẹ looked at her and realized at that moment that Alawani and Command were right after all. The maiden wanted him alive, and by the look on her face, it was more than that. She needed him alive. L'ọrẹ couldn't help but wonder what the Holy Order would do to a maiden who lost her Àlùfáà – let alone the Prince Àlùfáà.

On this, they could agree. Alawani couldn't die.

Rèmí stood back from the four of them, putting enough distance between himself and Tofa.

'I don't care what you do to yourself, Alawani. Join your father if you must, but this girl isn't going anywhere,' Tofa growled and pointed at L'ọrẹ.

The blade moved, and more blood spilt.

'No!' Milúà screamed, mad with fury. She turned on Tofa. 'Let her go, Tofa!'

'How can you ask me that? Don't you know who she is?' Tofa said.

'I don't care who she is. I don't care what she is. Let her go now!' She turned on Alawani. 'Stop this madness! Stop it!'

Crimson wet the prince's hand, and he pressed deeper.

Milúà pulled out a gold rod from her thigh strap, and with a single tap, it grew, bringing out the sharp end of a spear from within it. She looked to L'ọrẹ and said, 'Go.' Then pointed it at Tofa, 'Let her go.'

L'ọrẹ moved back to where Rèmí stood by the wall. There was no way to reach Alawani with Tofa and Milúà standing between her and him.

She shouted over them, 'Alawani, don't do this, please!'

'You have your orders, maiden. Don't make me repeat it,' Tofa growled at Milúà.

Milúà's frown deepened. She ignited her spear, pointed it

at the crown heir, and said in a low, defiant tone, 'Let the girl go. I can't let him die. He's Àlùfáà. *My* Àlùfáà.'

Tofa brandished his dagger in response. What good would that do against the maiden's blazing spear? In the next heartbeat, Tofa had poured his agbára into it, turning the black blade furnace red. It melted in his hands. He pressed and pulled until it turned into a thin, razor-sharp sword. Even Milúà stepped back in surprise at the transformation, but it didn't change her mind. She moved towards him and struck. Where the gold staff and the black sword met, sparks flew. She withdrew and went in again, this time trying to cut the blade off his hands, but he caught it to strike. The sparks must have gotten into her eyes because she screamed and held her arm up to shield them. Clearly, Tofa was not trying to hurt her because he had the chance to end the fight immediately but he held off, allowing her to recover.

L'ọrẹ tried to meet Alawani's gaze but he stood in place on the other side of the fight, avoiding her eyes. This wasn't the time for this. If he could just find the energy to blast a hole in the wall . . .

Behind her, Rèmí looked like he was ready to run as well. She knew if he left this time, she'd never see him again.

Milúà's shout pulled L'ọrẹ back to the fight. The maiden snapped her spear over her knee, breaking it in two. Then she went in again, this time striking from both sides. Tofa turned his sword into a shield, hiding from each blow and using its weight to knock the maiden off balance. *How was he doing that?* It had to be old magic. But he clearly used his agbára. L'ọrẹ didn't understand it.

She kept her eyes on Alawani. There was no way through to him without going through the fight that played out before her. Her agbára burned at her fingertips, waiting to be unleashed. The maiden landed on her back more often than the crown heir did. It wasn't a fair fight, but L'ọrẹ noticed that Milúà was still standing where many would have fallen and retreated. She kept going. Nothing was keeping her from saving her Prince Àlùfáà. And for that, L'ọrẹ was grateful.

The thing in Tofa's hand went from dagger to sword to shield to axe, and now, a sword which he swung at Milúà with full strength. Milúà grunted every time she struck it, clearly exhausted but keeping up with his moves.

Finally, Tofa said, 'Enough of this, Milúà. I don't want to hurt you.'

'Let the girl go,' was all Milúà said through heavy pants.

'He's not worth this,' Tofa said, looking at Alawani, who hadn't moved from his position or tried to stop the blood that soaked his shirt.

The pillar in L'ọrẹ's mind bled as Alawani did. Blood pooled over his hands and the sight of it made her sick with panic. Had he sliced an artery? Was he dying? *No. No. No.* She felt her mind fraying, coming apart, and she couldn't find the words. Her mouth couldn't speak. She didn't care if it was a trick or a ploy to distract Milúà. She wanted the bleeding to stop. She wanted him to stop. She just wanted it all to stop. Freedom shouldn't come at such a cost, but if this was how her brother wanted it to be, she'd gladly oblige. Her hands glowed bright, and she felt the energy in the storm billowing around her. L'ọrẹ forced her racing heart to slow and poured all her focus on the crown heir before her. As she stared at him, she reached deeper, finding his core, and then she pulled from it. L'ọrẹ moved closer, drawing energy from him. She could feel her own energy rage through her like the lightning striking the wall. Sparks fell off her body like rain, and Tofa fell to his knees and crawled into a foetal position.

'What are you doing to me?' he cried out in pain.

'What you would have done to me,' L'ọrẹ said, her out-stretched hands trembling as she drew his agbára from him, fuelling her own agbára with his core. The light in her hands crawled up her skin, covering her entire arms. She could feel his energy boosting hers and she felt as though her heart would burst.

'Stop!' Alawani shouted.

Hearing his voice, she recoiled and quickly quelled her agbára.

'Curse you!' Tofa shouted and flung his hand at her.

He'd clearly expected something to happen. Something with agbára oru. But she'd taken it from him, and his eyes widened in horror as he fell back. 'What did you do?' he shrieked, and slumped to the ground, trembling with cold.

'Gods of the sun and sands!' Milúà exclaimed.

L'ọrẹ shot her an icy glare, and the maiden stepped back.

Milúà rushed to the crown heir, pouring her agbára into him and heating his body. 'You are a curse! You've frozen his core!' she shouted at L'ọrẹ.

L'ọrẹ felt a sharp pang in her heart as the words hit her. She'd said as much to herself. She ran to Alawani and pulled the knife from his hands, placing her hand over his wound. She tore off a piece of her top with the knife and wrapped it around the wound.

'Were you going to kill him?' Alawani asked.

'No!' L'ọrẹ said. 'Even though he was definitely going to kill me.'

'What did you do?'

'I made it impossible for him to hurt me or you or anyone,' she said, glancing back at Tofa on the ground. She didn't know whether what she'd done was permanent or not. She didn't even fully understand what it was that she'd done, but she could still feel his energy inside her, pushing against her core with a violence to match the raging storm.

Alawani's head shook, his eyes fixed on her. 'Tèmi.' My own. That was all he said, and L'orẹ felt her heart fail within her. His eyes, his beautiful brown eyes. The ones she'd lost herself in many times looked at her now, and she felt like he was looking through her. 'I've gone as far as I can with you, Tèmi,' he said, and walked towards Milúà, who was still warming up Tofa's core to keep him from freezing to death.

Milúà rose to meet him, standing too close to him, her face almost buried in his neck. Alawani whispered something to her that L'orẹ couldn't hear over the howling wind.

'What's happening?' L'orẹ said.

Milúà looked at Alawani, and he nodded.

'Step back!' Milúà shouted at L'orẹ when she moved forward.

Rẹ̀mí took L'orẹ by the hand and pulled her away, putting distance between them and the maiden.

Milúà formed an energy ball and launched it at the wall. Then another, and another. She took a break, exhausted and choking from the dust that ensued and the sand that blew. The storm was closer, and had layered the ground with about half an inch of sand.

'Keep going,' Alawani said, encouraging her.

L'orẹ didn't understand what was happening. Was Milúà helping them escape? Why? What did Alawani say? What in the damned names of the gods was going on?

Milúà resumed, and one by one, more pieces of the wall came loose until, finally, there was light at the end of the tunnel. The hole was just big enough to crawl through.

'Let's go,' L'orẹ said to Alawani once the dust settled.

'He's not coming with you,' Milúà said, a knowing look on her face.

'Yes, he is!' L'orẹ replied.

'No, I'm not,' Alawani said from behind the maiden.

'You see, L'orẹ,' said the maiden, 'a deal is a deal. I help you out of the kingdom, and he returns to his true calling, the Holy Order, and his oath to the gods.'

'Never!' L'orẹ shouted.

Alawani took a few steps closer, and she could see the concern in his eyes. He held her face in his palms, and she shoved them away. 'You made a deal with her? When?'

'We have our ways,' Milúà said, enjoying the look on L'orẹ's face as the realization hit.

'After Ìyá-Idán's house. When Command took me. That's why you let them go.' L'orẹ turned to Alawani. 'Were you going to leave this kingdom with me?'

'I can't, Tèmi. I swore an oath.'

'To me! You swore an oath to me, Alawani!'

'I swore an oath to my father, my grandfather. To the gods of our land. I survived the Red Stone. I am Àlùfáà,' he said, holding L'orẹ's hand. 'I wish we could have left this place before the call. I wish so much for you to be free, and when I saw you in that temple, I knew you wouldn't leave without me. My love, I cannot exist in a world where you are not. It breaks my heart to lose you this way, but at least you'll be safe. My place is in the temple with the chosen. My destiny is here in Oru, and yours is not. I wish the gods hadn't called me, and my father hadn't . . . but fate has decided, and I am Àlùfáà.'

She slapped him across the face. 'No, you are not! You are not called or chosen. You are nothing!' Tears stung her eyes as she screamed the words at him.

He held his face in his palm but did nothing. Then he said, 'I want you to be safe. I want you to find your people, wherever they might be, and be happy with them.'

'If you say another lie to me, I will slap you again! All of this, all of this was for nothing! I loved you. I love you!

I risked my life for you. My father rots in the dungeons because of you!'

'I never asked you for any of those things! It was you who went looking for trouble. I told you from the start I have to do this. You just wouldn't listen. You never listen. And look what's happened, Tèmi. Everything is a mess. Kòyà is in the dungeons with your father. We don't know what happened to Ìyá-Idán. Everyone who's helped us in this self-imposed exile has suffered for it. Command is gone.'

L'orẹ's agbára flared in her veins as his words crashed into her.

'You would have killed him!' Alawani pointed at the crown heir, shivering on the ground.

'He tried to kill us. He tried to kill you!'

Alawani's hands remained at his side, but he could've sunk his dagger into her heart, and the pain would be more manageable than what she felt at that moment.

'If you felt this way all along, why did you come this far?'

'I chose for you the same way you chose for me. You decided all on your own that I needed saving. You put my life and yours at risk. But I realized that it was you who needed saving; they'll never stop coming for you and I was going to make sure you got out of this kingdom alive. I'd never have let you cross all the rings alone. But I am going back.'

'Curse you, Alawani!' she spat at him.

'We don't have time for this,' Milúà said, breaking the glare between L'orẹ and the prince.

The world was a blur behind the tears that fell from her face and the sandstorm that swirled around. 'I could kill you,' L'orẹ said, every word filled with bitterness.

Milúà sneered, 'The oath-breaker's son and the coward's daughter. Even I could see how this would end.'

The look L'ọrẹ gave Milúà could've burned the whole earth to ash.

'Tèmi, there is no place for you here,' Alawani said. 'Not in this kingdom. No one wants you here. I don't want you here!' His words seemed to hit him as hard as they hit her. He sighed and wiped the sand from his eyes. 'I don't want to spend the rest of my days thinking you're somewhere here in Oru waiting to be caught and killed.'

'Alawani, look at me,' L'ọrẹ said, holding his face firmly in her hands, her voice breaking. Tears streamed down her face as the storm raged on around them. 'I love you. I love you, and I choose you. I'm choosing you, and I'm asking you to choose me. I will fight with you, and I will fight for you. I will fight gods and men alike. I will not let them take you. Alawani, the gods cannot have you because you are mine. Mine,' she said, and planted a firm kiss on his lips.

He held her face and kissed her so passionately that the sour tang of blood blossomed in her mouth, and she pulled him even closer, welcoming the taste of him, holding on to him like he would vanish before her eyes. Desperate for that moment to last forever.

'I love you, Tèmi,' he said, panting and wiping at his sand-filled tears. 'I love you, and I *am* fighting for you; I am putting myself between the gods and those who want you dead.' His voice broke, and he put his head to hers, 'But I am Àlùfáà.'

'You self-righteous bastard! You swore loyalty to me. To me! I am your queen! I am the firstborn of the sun!' L'ọrẹ shouted. She wasn't sure if she even accepted it herself – she just didn't know what else to say. Every word was a desperate act to bring him back to her.

As she looked at the boy she'd built her life around, the uncanny resemblance to his grandfather flickered across his face again and she recoiled. He was lost to her. She screamed and launched herself at him, but Rèmí caught her, holding on to her waist and pulling her towards the tunnel. She fought him off; her elbow crashed into his nose and she heard the crack but kept fighting. His grip on her didn't loosen. In her rage, her eyes turned blue, and she grabbed his hands. Ice seeped into his skin, and he screamed. He dropped her, and she fell in a slump. It lasted only a moment, but her fingers still left a brand on his hands. L'ọrẹ felt her chest tense up. Horrified and desperate, her thoughts swirled like the storm around her. She couldn't take her eyes off Alawani. She couldn't understand who she saw standing next to the maiden.

At that moment, she heard her father's voice: *Remember the daughter of whom you are.* Even though he was miles away, Baba-Ìtàn always found a way to say the right thing at the right time. Her shoulders slumped as she released a deep, sorrowful sigh. She went to Alawani, close enough to feel his breath if it weren't for the wind, and she shifted his shirt to reveal his tattoo. Their bond.

'I'm sorry,' he whispered. 'I release you from your blood oath.'

L'ọrẹ placed her hand on it, weeping and sobbing. 'I don't.' She summoned her agbára in a flash and burned it off. Alawani screamed at the pain and shoved her hand away.

'I never want to see you again. Let your heart burn to dust, oath-breaker,' she spat in the sand.

When blood-oaths are broken, both parties eventually go mad as penance to the gods. She tried to remember the exact wording of the oath. *Us against the world. Till the sun falls from the sky. Hand to flame, we burn the same.* L'ọrẹ could already feel her mind fraying but in this moment, her fury was greater than her fear of losing her mind. *Let him see if the temple won't spit him out when his mind crumbles.*

'Let's go,' Rẹ̀mí shouted, 'the storm is getting worse.'

L'ọrẹ ignored him and kept her eyes fixed on Alawani. Her best friend. Her lover. Her everything. In her mind, her fortress and prison – the platform she'd stood on her entire life, protected by the pillars of her father and best friend – shattered in a single explosive burst, throwing her into the storm that raged within her. It was nothing compared to the storm that raged around now, which started to graze away layers of her skin. She felt her world break open, and she sank deep into the darkness of the sand, consumed by everything she'd ever been afraid of.

Tears streamed down her face as her sobs wracked her body, making it difficult to breathe. How was this what her life had become? She'd started with so little. Desperate to keep her family together, she'd lost it all; lost her father, her friends, and her – Alawani. She hadn't realized how much she had to lose. Maybe if she had, she wouldn't have stormed that temple. She'd have had a better plan. She'd have avoided all the pain and death that followed her like an evil spirit. And all that for what? For Alawani. Alawani, who had broken his oath to her. Alawani, to whom she'd given her life and body. Alawani, whom she'd held on to like the breath in her lungs, fighting to keep him in. Still, she had lost him. Still, he was leaving. *I am not enough.*

She turned towards the tunnel, the pitifully small opening Milúà had created. If she was to leave, she would leave standing, not crawling. With trembling hands, a broken heart and an anguished howl, she raised her hands to the sky and pulled on the energy around her. She channelled the core of everyone around her. As the energy rushed into her, she could see and feel every inch of her body light up as bright and brilliant as moonlight. Ignoring their screams, she reached for the lightning that flashed in the sky and with a loud cry she blasted her agbára at the hole Milúà had created. The great wall shook and groaned as nearly half the stonework came crashing down and blasted out, creating a huge tunnel, large enough for a building to pass through. Without looking back, L'ọrẹ walked through. Rẹ̀mí followed closely behind her, and together they left the kingdom of Oru.

Convinced that agbára òtútù was the prophesied
darkness come to wipe out the continent
the Aláàfin of Oru ordered a swift and
merciless massacre of his people.
What he had not known was that his daughter,
the princess,
had concealed her agbára òtútù.
In the dark of night, the princess of
Oru gathered all her people,
those with powers of the darkness and
void, and they fled their home.
They ran deep into the mountains, never
to be seen or heard from again.
Until now.

42

Ìlú-Òdì, Sixth Ring, Kingdom of Oru

ALAWANI

Alawani and Milúà rode back into the city with Tofa nearly passed out in between them as they raced to the Lord General's keep. The battle rhino thundered through the graveyard, its heavy steps slowed by gusts of strong wind. The sandstorm had worsened and it blocked their vision, and grated against their skin, filling every part of their clothes with sand.

Curse you, oath-breaker. The wind carried L'ọrẹ's last words as Alawani raced away from the wall. Tears stung his sand-filled eyes, and he wanted to go back and hold her, and tell her he loved her. Had he really done the right thing? His heart broke as he remembered his grandfather's words: *Remember the son of whom you are.* He knew he was bound never to forget the destiny he was born for.

Àlùfáà-Àgbà. The man who changed his life. The Elder Priest who called him Àlùfáà. His father's father. The one with a plan to change the world. Alawani wished more than anything that his grandfather had devised a plan that didn't include him. But fate was never so kind.

He'd only seen four first suns when he met his grandfather for the first time. It was shortly after his father's death. He'd been in the king's chambers crying at the foot of his father's bed when a tall man dressed in white linen came and sat beside him. Alawani recalled those words he'd put out of his head: 'Wipe your tears, my child. The king is gone, but you will be greater than he ever was.'

He had done his best to block those words, mostly because as he grew to understand his true insignificance as a prince in the kingdom of Oru, it felt like a cruel thing to say to a grieving child. So, while he had been unaware of the true nature of his grandfather's plans, the moment he had seen L'ọrẹ in the temple of the gods, he had determined to rescue her. He knew that if he did not go with her, if he didn't keep her safe from the wrath she'd unleashed for such an unthinkable crime, she would not see the following dawn. For the Àlùfáà-Àgbà of the Order of the Sun Temple was not a kind or forgiving man.

So it was not a surprise when the Elder Priest plagued his dreams every time he lay to sleep. Àlùfáà-Àgbà invaded his mind in a storm of rage, instructing him to return, revealing the plans he and his father had made. Alawani had considered telling L'ọrẹ some of the things his grandfather said to him as they raced towards the edge of the kingdom. But how would she have trusted him to lead her to safety, if he did?

On the first night after their escape, Àlùfáà-Àgbà had come to him at the farm inn with a story Alawani could not have imagined in his wildest dreams. 'A long time ago,' the old man had begun, 'there was a young boy from Ìlú-Oníṣọ̀nà – home to the weak and poor, the fifth ring of servitude – who thought his entire world would begin and end in the thatched mud pile he called home.' Àlùfáà-Àgbà had smiled down at Alawani as his image cleared to show his true form. Alawani knew he was dreaming, but it felt so real – his grandfather's face and voice were as clear as if Alawani truly stood in the old man's presence. Terror kept him frozen, listening, and unable to escape whatever magic the Elder Priest used to tether him to the realm. 'The gods called that boy Àlùfáà. *I* was that boy,' his grandfather said proudly.

'The greatest day of my life was when your father, my son and your king, was born. The kingdom rejoiced. We threw a party like never before. The people did not sleep for seven days, and the talking drums didn't stop beating. A new king, a new era, a new kingdom. I had great plans for this kingdom and for my people, and as Lord Regent, I wanted to fulfil them all. But like every regent, I had to yield the throne to my son.' He sighed. 'Your father started well, but he had his demons. Then the gods gave me a vision. He wasn't the son to bring glory to our kingdom. That son would be you and every subsequent son born to our family.'

Alawani hadn't understood what his grandfather was talking about. That wasn't the way the throne of Oru worked – the crown did not pass from father to son, as it once had before the day of the First Sun. It always went to the firstborn child of the next High Priest. A new child born of a gods-chosen Àlùfáà. He wanted to ask, but he could not – when he tried to speak, pain jolted through him, as if the priest was holding him down, keeping him silent.

'Allow me to explain,' Àlùfáà-Àgbà had said. 'Our family line must continue. Our seed must always be on the throne of Oru. The gods have declared it. Only then will our kingdom be safe from the hands of our enemies in the north. Our family will wage war on this continent, and bring under the command of the gods of the sun and sands all who have scorned their names. Your father understood this.' He nodded. 'Yes, yes, he did. So we did what had to be done. My child, we had to make it so that the call for Àlùfáà would be within the same sun cycle as the ascension to the throne.' He choked on his words, and Alawani thought he saw tears form in his eyes.

Everything stilled around them, and Alawani could hear the loud drumming of his own racing heart. He had thought the timing meant that he could never be selected as High Priest.

Àlùfáà-Àgbà's gruff voice broke through his thoughts. 'Using the temple records and going back as far as the day of the First Sun, we worked out the timelines for the next few cycles of stripping ceremonies. Our calculations led us here. Where you, a prince of Oru, can become part of the Holy Order. It had to be the gods' will to give us such a wondrous moment as this. The Order allowed your entry because of how young the crown heir is and how many more first suns and stripping ceremonies they expect him to see. But they did not consider that kings die all the time. Most of all, they did not consider the real threat of their decision and expected you to die long before your final stripping. But this moment is one we created knowing they would want to test you with the Red Stone first, and once you passed, our plans could begin.' He laughed. 'I suppose I cannot blame them for underestimating you, but in doing so they underestimated me and my ability to keep you from the brink of death. I may have yielded my position of High Priest to Babátúndé, but the gods have taken their power from me.'

Alawani found the voice that had been stuck in his throat. Despite the throbbing pain, the need to get his words out was stronger. 'How?'

'The Àgbo that Milúà gave to you. What did you think it was for? Did you not feel its effects as it pulled your soul back into your body?'

The realization struck Alawani like thunder, and he remembered. He had felt it. He knew that with every sip,

557

his breaths came easier, and the pain dulled, but he never would have imagined that he was cheating death. That he had cheated. With this thought came another. L'ọrẹ did all she did for nothing. His life was never in danger.

'How could you?' Alawani's strained voice croaked with fury.

'Your self-righteousness serves no one. The Red Stone will not claim you. Not after all we have sacrificed for you. Not when my son sacrificed his life for you. If he had not left the throne when he did, you would never have had the chance to be a part of this cycle of chosen ones. As your fate had decided before I intervened, you would have been nothing.'

'What do you mean leave the throne?' Alawani's anger fuelled his core. 'Did you kill my father?'

'No! Never. The king took his own life. I only provided the means.'

'The means?'

'The king chose poison. May his soul find the city of light.'

Alawani's voice was raw, 'You killed him!'

'Your father knew and understood our family's purpose. His sacrifice made it so that you could be the right age to join the Order, just as Tofa approaches his coronation. Another ten first suns on the throne, and you'd have been too old to be called. But this way, you are where you need to be – young enough to be called to the stripping ceremony that is close enough to a king's coronation to make our plans work. Moments like these are not coincidences; the gods placed this plan in my heart many first suns before even your father was old enough to walk. My son sacrificed his life because he understood that we cannot continue this system of kings, regents, priests and heirs. We need a stable throne, a true line blessed and chosen by the gods. The crown must return to our bloodline. We are the true heirs of Oru, and we must occupy the throne until the day the sun falls from the sky.'

Alawani's heart had raced as he tried to absorb the shock of the news. His tears poured as he remembered his father's words, the ones he made him repeatedly chant, even on his deathbed. *Death may come for us, but our line will never end.* So this was what he truly meant. This was what he'd agreed to.

As if his grandfather could hear his thoughts, he said those exact words himself.

'Your plan can't work. The order can't choose a High Priest until the death of a king. Tofa is young and will ascend the throne in a few blood moons. He won't die. Your plan depends on the death of a healthy boy you trained yourself and you can't kill him.'

'I am not a murderer, boy! I won't kill him. In fact, your sole purpose until the boy takes the crown is to keep him alive. If he dies before taking the throne, the crown will go to his sisters, and more people will have to die. No, he will stay alive until he is crowned king. But as is the way of the world, young kings always die in battle, and it is time for us to conquer the north. There, the boy will meet his fate. I tell you, my child, before the following first sun comes, you will wear your father's crown.'

'How did the Lord Regent not see through this plan? You manipulated them all. You did all this to kill his only son.'

'I have loved Tofa from the moment I held him in my arms. No one in this kingdom will ever think that I would kill the boy who I have so openly cherished. His sacrifice will hurt me just as my son's death did.'

Alawani listened in horror as his grandfather's voice thundered through him and he wondered how he could ever weave himself out of this fate.

*

He was pulled out of his dream memories now as the battle rhino stopped at the entrance to the Lord General's keep. Regardless of his grandfather's proclamations, he always assumed the old man would find another way to rid Tofa of his crown. But when he had found out his L'orẹ was the true firstborn, it had broken him. For if L'orẹ died and Tofa's claim was revoked, Àlùfáà-Àgbà would have his plan work without having to kill the boy he'd raised like a son. She was an easy target and one Àlùfáà-Àgbà would never let out of his grasp. So Alawani had been even more determined to get her to freedom. Even if it cost everything he held dear.

And it had.

Once the soldiers helped them off the rhino and attended to Tofa, who was now awake but barely conscious, he walked into the keep and made his way to the dungeon where he'd spent the night with L'orẹ. The air was filled with her scent. He sat on the bench, folded his knees up to his chest and wept.

He cried because he knew he'd never see her again. Sometimes Alawani felt that he was doomed to lose everyone who was dear to him. For a long time, he'd wanted desperately to explain to her that his father had requested more than a promise from him. He'd drawn an oath from his lips. An oath to fulfil another which had been made on his behalf. He wasn't free to make vows. Not in the way she'd wanted. He'd hoped the Red Stone would take him and free him from all oaths and the consequences of the decisions he wasn't brave enough to make but it hadn't. Instead, he'd survived and it had proved to his grandfather that he was the chosen one. Every time he'd tried to tell her, his fear of his grandfather had kept his lips sealed. L'orẹ would never be safe in Oru. His grandfather would never allow it. Just like her brother, their days were counted.

Alawani lay across the bench in a foetal position. He didn't know when he drifted to sleep and found himself back in the Sun Temple, lying on the Red Stone. Once again, he found himself looking up into the eyes of his grandfather. He screamed and shuffled off the stone, holding his torso to fight the pain until he realized there was no pain.

'Where am I? What's happening?' Alawani asked as he spun to face his grandfather.

'Where is the girl?' Àlùfáà-Àgbà said in an even tone.

'She's gone.'

The black of his grandfather's eyes ran over the whites and Alawani found himself staring into what felt like a pit of darkness.

Terrified, he took several steps back. The further he moved, the closer his grandfather seemed to be to him. 'My son died so you could claim that throne and you risk it all for a girl? A spawn of your enemy. How dare you?' The old man's voice boomed in his mind so loudly, he felt his ears bleed.

'I'm here, aren't I?' Alawani said, finding courage within his fear. 'I'm here, and she's gone.'

'You could have killed her and ended this!'

'I have done everything you've asked of me. I accepted your call, I broke my vows to L'orẹ, I have chosen your gods and your Order. I have nothing more to give you,' Alawani said, his voice breaking. 'I could have died on this stone. I've given you my life.'

Àlùfáà-Àgbà's voice softened, 'My dear child, I would never have let that happen.'

As he spoke, Alawani felt the shame of knowing that death by stripping was never a risk. His life was never in danger. His soul would never have been forfeited to the Red Stone. L'orẹ had done all she did for nothing.

'The gods have declared that you, my boy, are special beyond words. You will no longer be prince in name alone, without power or authority. You are to be our king,' Àlùfáà-Àgbà said, holding his face.

'Once you become High Priest and Lord Regent of this land, you will perform your duties in the marriage ceremonies and have your heirs, but you will not yield until your death, and your firstborn will rule until his death, and every firstborn will rule, and our kingdom will reign forever. Don't you see the glorious plan the gods have for us, my boy?' Àlùfáà-Àgbà said, urging his words to convince him.

In the light of all he knew now, even through all the fighting, he felt pity for Tofa, the boy who'd soon meet his end. Now that the crown heir was without agbára oru, that end might come even sooner. Despite everything, Alawani couldn't deny the appeal of the throne. A chance to redeem his father's legacy. To keep the oaths his father broke.

He missed L'orẹ. He loved her. His Tèmi was his sun. His guiding star. The one who held his heart in a gentle embrace and loved him in ways he'd not thought possible. And without her, he could feel a darkness shroud over him. She'd kept him from sinking into himself more times than he could count, and he needed her. He desperately needed her, and he would love her until his dying breath. In his way, he'd upheld their oath: he had chosen her, chosen life for her, and in his heart, it would always be them against the world for he would always protect her. So as much as it hurt, he knew he'd made the right call. L'orẹ could never claim the throne to the kingdom of Oru, not if she wanted to live. Because the throne was already his.

A knock on the door made him jolt up. It took a moment to reorientate himself in the darkness of the cell. He shone his agbára against the door and his heart ached at the dull orange light that came from his core. 'Leave me alone, Milúà,' he shouted at the door.

'It is me, Márùn,' the voice called from the other side.

'Márùn?' he asked. 'What are you doing here? Come in!'

The girl walked into the dark cell, and he stood to meet her.

'How did you get here? Are you okay?' he said, worried. 'Did you get Baba-Ìtàn and Kòyà? Where are they?'

'I'm fine,' Márùn said in a low voice.

She seemed to stand taller. Her clothes were different. If he had met her on the street, he might have thought she was a soldier in her brown leather outfit, nearly matching the tawny colour of her skin.

'I've got a message for you,' Márùn said as she cupped her hands in front of him and whispered old magic spells. A tongue of flame blossomed inside her palms.

Alawani looked from her to the fire and back. 'What's this?'

She stood still, not making a sound. A heartbeat later, a voice boomed from the flame, 'Come home.'

Àlùfáà-Àgbà. His grandfather's voice still echoed from his dreams.

He opened his mouth to speak, but all that came out was a confused silence as he looked at Márùn. 'I don't understand.'

Márùn let out an exasperated sigh. The flame disappeared as she let her hands fall to her side. 'Àlùfáà-Àgbà sent me to keep an eye on you since you left the temple,' she said. 'Perhaps he didn't trust you to return, and I was to make sure that you did.'

'Your life debt,' Alawani gasped. 'You're not bound to my mother, you're bound to him.'

Márùn nodded, a frown formed across her face. 'I had no choice. Just like you.'

'You made us trust you. Were you ever going to free Baba-Ìtàn and Kòyà?'

'No,' Márùn said plainly. 'Were you ever going to leave the kingdom with her?'

Alawani glared at her, then said, 'No,' his voice raw with shame and guilt.

'Why did you swear the sovereign oath to L'orẹ?' Alawani asked after a moment's silence.

'The same reason you did. Everyone bowed, and so I had to.'

'So you don't believe her claim?'

'It doesn't matter what I believe, she's never going to be queen. I pushed her to leave the kingdom because if she didn't, I'd have had to kill her. And I'd grown quite fond of her,' Márùn said.

'Why did you let us get so far? You could have taken us back to the temple since the third ring when we met you.'

'My orders weren't to bring you back. They were to watch, follow and report. I believe your grandfather had other plans,' Márùn said, eyeing him knowingly.

'But what about the Order of the Twelve and everything you told her?'

'It wasn't for her sake I revealed that secret, it was for you.'

'Won't Ìyá-Idán encourage the others to fight for L'orẹ's claim to the throne? She has influence and she will use it,' Alawani said.

'The Twelve are split in loyalty. Some will support Tofa until their last breath, and others like Ìyá-Idán will choose L'orẹ. We just need to have more people on our side.'

'And where do your loyalties lie?' Alawani asked.

'Your grandfather said we are returning to the days when the crown was passed from father to son.'

Márùn knelt to the ground before him and shone the light

of her agbára on his feet. 'I am Márùn, Five of Twelve. On this day before the sun in the sky and the sands beneath our feet, I swear loyalty to you, Aláàfin Alawani Àkanní Adédìran, King of Oru. May your heart burn like the sun, bright, hot, and undying!'

À ń sọ̀rọ̀ olè jíjà, aboyún náà ń dá sí i;
Ṣíọ̀! odidi èèyàn ló gbé pamọ́ o.
*We were condemning theft and the pregnant woman
had the effrontry to join in; Isn't she herself
concealing a whole human?*

Epilogue

Ìlú-Idán, Fourth Ring,
Kingdom of Oru

1314 FS

MÓREMÍ

Nine blood moons and a night.

That was how long Móremí hung in the balance between life and death.

As she watched the dark spots grow and the light faded from her vision, she heard the voice of everyone she'd ever loved. She heard Ẹniìtàn's voice echoing through her mind, beckoning her. She heard her sister's soft voice singing to her. She heard her baby's cry. There were no words when L'ọrẹ called to her, just the hiccupping sound of a child that knows its mother will never return.

In those final moments, as the voices of the soldiers faded, and she could no longer feel the pain in her body as it was dragged from the streets, she heard a thunderous voice filled with bitterness and pain. Even at the point of death, she recognized her dear mother's voice. She could not pick out the words that boomed in her mind, but she knew that her mother would raze this kingdom to the ground for taking her daughter from her. *Nothing will survive the destruction that the kingdom of Òtútù will bring. Nothing will survive the death that comes — not even her mother who brings it.*

A war was coming, the north was awakening, and try as she might, Mọ́remí had not brought salvation to Oru. She remained as she was called at home — *the one who brings death.*

That's enough for now.
Take a break and come back soon,
I'll still be here.
Remember the laws of the land:
Don't keep this àṣírí to yourself.
Tell all who have ears.

Family Tree: Royal Family of Oru

Can you fill in the blanks of this family tree with the heirs of each Ìlú?

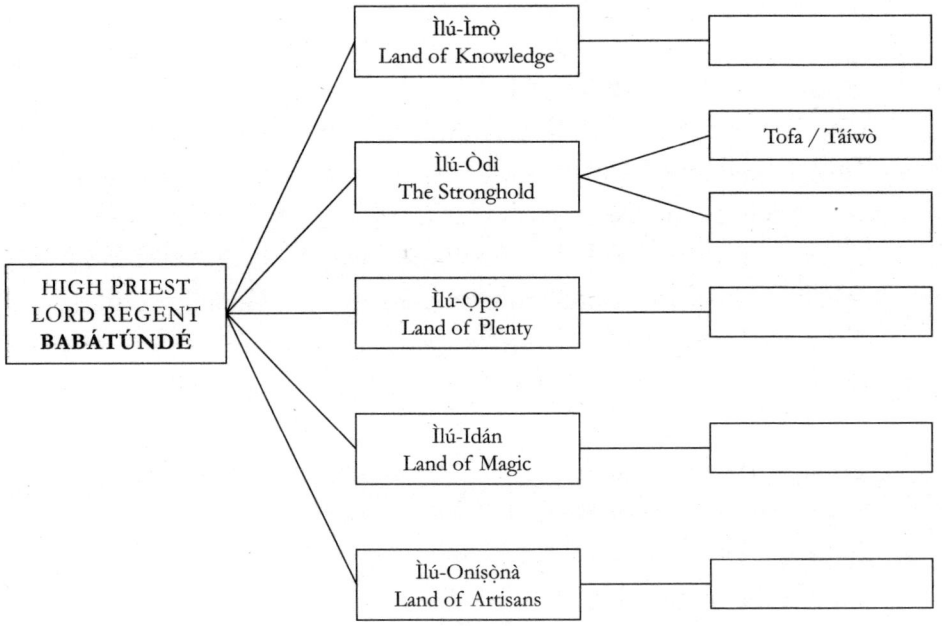

HIGH PRIEST
LORD REGENT
BABÁTÚNDÉ

Ìlú-Ìmò
Land of Knowledge

Ìlú-Òdì
The Stronghold

Tofa / Táíwò

Ìlú-Ọpọ
Land of Plenty

Ìlú-Idán
Land of Magic

Ìlú-Oníṣọ̀nà
Land of Artisans

Acknowledgements

Olúwa ẹ ṣeun.

It takes a village to build anything worth bringing to life. I have never had to walk the writer's road alone, and for that I am ever so grateful. To my grandma, who held my hands and taught me how to write, and then taught me to string words together, and through her stories, opened my eyes to the multiverse of worlds that she created through the stories she told. To my mother, who saw the writer I could be long before I did and did not let the spark die out. To my dad, who made me believe that no dream was ever out of reach. To my husband (editor, designer, best friend), David, who is absolutely as obsessed with this book and the world of Oru as I am. I love you. I don't have the words to describe how much your support means to me. Thank you for all the midnight debates on the complexities of the world woven into the delicate fabric of these characters' lives.

To every storyteller and folklorist who has kept the Yoruba tradition alive with their words and songs that we might know our roots today – thank you.

When I started writing *Firstborn of the Sun*, I hoped to write something magical and fantastical, and the true magic has been everyone I've met along the road to publication who has loved this story as much as I do. To the agent who plucked me out of the slush pile, Kesia Lupo, thank you for seeing the magic in my story long before the world could. I went looking for an agent and found a friend. To my incredible editor, Rebecca Hilsdon, your passion and excitement for this book is so contagious, I leave every encounter with you so grateful that we found each other. All of this is possible because of you. To my agents, Ciara Finan and Flo Sandelson at Curtis Brown, thank you so much for being absolute superstars. Our meeting feels like one written in the stars, such that our paths will always have collided in the best of ways.

I want to thank the entire team at Penguin Michael Joseph who have worked on this book. To Ruth Atkins and Clare Bowron for editorial support, Hayley Shepherd for copyedits, Annie Moore and Yasmin Anshoor for marketing, Frankie Banks for publicity, and Riana Dixon for production. To the fantastic design team, thank you so much for your vision. To my incredible cover artist, Juliet Nneka, you are so brilliant, I am forever in awe of your talent. Huge thanks to Timothy Gonzales for a map worthy of the kingdom of Oru.

Thank you to the team at Jericho Writers, with special thanks to Debi Alper, an absolute powerhouse and incredible tutor. Debi, your support has meant the world to me. Thank you to Lola Shoneyin, your passion for literature is inspiring, and your support makes me believe in my work as a story-teller. Thank you to Emma O'Connell and Ellie Owen, with special thanks to Ellie, whose early edits helped build a firmer foundation for this story. Thank you to the Future Worlds crew, Sarah, Andi, Ben and Adjoa for creating a launch pad that is desperately needed for authors of colour. Thank you for all you do. Thanks to the FWP 2022 cohort: Calah, Ali, Ama, Anne, Arianne, Mahmud and Mel.

Thank you, Mindy, you are my favourite person to write with. Here's to many more years writing together. Thank you to Temidayo Shittu-Alamu for checking all the Yoruba in this book – I could not have done it without you. Thank you to my earliest readers and the founding members of our little Writers Connect – Blanka, Amel, Erin, Steve, Jenny and Stuart.

To my bestie, Dr Nafisa Yusuf, I love you. To my NCMD girls, Davina Oriakhi-Idris and Patricia Olufemi, you're all a girl could ever ask for and more. To my Les Femmes group chat, Ade, Ayo, Chioma, Eno, Monoyo, Nnenna and Neche, here's to killing it since '11!

To my brothers, Emmanuel and Eriayo, I love you.

Thank you to Katie Cummins, Lola Babalola, Sere Oluwayemi, Tope Owolabi, Andrea Stewart, El Lam, Natalie Simmonds, Jacqueline Silvester, Malak Saleh, Ehi Okosun, Alice Chao and the Fatilewas. To those whose names I remember and those I forget because it's the middle of the night, thank you for being a part of my story.

To my family, whose unwavering support reminds me that I am never alone, thank you.

To the narrators whose voice will bring the songs of Oru to life, thank you for lending your voice to the sands of time.

To you, dearest reader, thank you. Hope you stick around.